"This bittersweet novel captures the struggle to honor one's ancestors and fulfill one's promises while recognizing the power, beauty, and burden of history as it shapes our lives and our choices about love."

—MARCIA ANN GILLESPIE,
former editor in chief of *Ms.* and *Essence*

"Pogrebin masterfully explores issues of race, gender, ethnicity, and religion through her characters who struggle with conflicting moral imperatives in a sea of clashing cultures. Her exceptional intelligence shines on every page."

—HELEN FREMONT,
author of *After Long Silence*

"This novel confronts unflinchingly the issue of Jewish continuity in a diverse and changing America. Most of all, though, it is a love story, delicious and sweet, and a book to be read with pleasure and savored long after the last page has been read."

—ANNE ROIPHE, author and journalist

"Pogrebin is a writer of great depth and soulfulness, and with this book she catapults herself into the ranks of novelistic royalty. Her lovely prose gets to the very heart of what the heart wants, while also mining the legacies and commitments that define the rich history of African Americans and American Jews."

—THANE ROSENBAUM, author of
Second Hand Smoke and *How Sweet It Is!*

Also by
LETTY COTTIN POGREBIN

How to Make It In A Man's World

Getting Yours

Growing Up Free

Family Politics

Among Friends

Deborah, Golda, and Me

Getting Over Getting Older

Three Daughters

How to Be a Friend To a Friend Who's Sick

Stories for Free Children
(editor)

Free to Be, You and Me
(editorial consultant)

Single Jewish Male Seeking Soul Mate

Single Jewish Male Seeking Soul Mate

LETTY COTTIN POGREBIN

Published in 2015 by the Feminist Press
at the City University of New York
The Graduate Center
365 Fifth Avenue, Suite 5406
New York, NY 10016

feministpress.org

First printing May 2015

Cover and text design by Drew Stevens

Library of Congress Cataloging-in-Publication Data
Pogrebin, Letty Cottin.
Single Jewish male seeking soul mate : a novel / by Letty Cottin Pogrebin.
pages ; cm
ISBN 978-1-55861-887-9 (pbk.) — ISBN 978-1-55861-886-2 (hardback)
— ISBN 978-1-55861-893-0 (ebook)
I. Title.
PS3616.O35S56 2015
813'.6,—dc23

2015002123

For

Bert
Abigail, Robin, David
Ethan, Benjamin, Maya, Molly, Zev, Arlo

Learning to love differently is hard,
love with the hands wide open, love
with the doors banging on their hinges,
the cupboard unlocked, the wind
roaring and whimpering in the rooms
rustling the sheets and snapping the blinds
that thwack like rubber bands
in an open palm.

—Marge Piercy,
"To have without holding"

Single Jewish Male Seeking Soul Mate

CHAPTER 1
SECRETS AND SCARS

ZACHARIAH ISAAC LEVY GREW UP IN A FAMILY OF SECRETS, of conversations cut short by his entrance into a room, of thick-tongued speech and guttural names and the whisper of weeping. His parents spoke in short, stubby sentences, as if words could be used up, and often in a language they refused to translate. From the grammar of their sighs, he came to understand that Yiddish was reserved for matters unspeakable in English and memories too grim for a child's ears.

Zach's father had a remarkably light tread for a man of six feet with broad shoulders and rope-thick muscles; however, once you knew that he'd spent the war years disappearing himself in the forests of Poland, his bearing, and everything else about Nathan Levy, made sense. Like most Jews, Nathan revered education and intellect, but he put even more stock in strength, speed, and stealth, the attributes responsible for his multiple escapes from the SS. After he and Zach's mother immigrated to the

Bronx, Nathan steadfastly maintained a fitness regimen of extreme rigor so he would be ready to defend himself and his family if—or rather, *when*—Jews once again became prey. On weekdays, Nathan hiked from their apartment at the corner of University Avenue and Kingsbridge Road, to the hat factory in the Manhattan garment district where he labored over a cauldron of scalding steam, shaping felt into fedoras. When inclement weather impeded his outdoor journey, he whipped through thirty minutes of calisthenics before taking the subway to work. Walking the city, playing schoolyard handball, and spending time at the schvitz—the Russian baths—were Nathan's preferred physical activities. For quiet pleasure, he read the *Forverts*, the Yiddish *Daily Forward*, with a glass of warm milk at his side, or listened to broadcasts of the Metropolitan Opera on the radio, always with the volume turned down low, in deference to his wife.

Zach's mother, Rivka Levy, was a piano teacher who hated music. Though the piano enabled her to contribute to the family income, she treated her Baldwin upright like a threat, as if its potential for sound was itself a kind of clamor. The instrument stood against one wall in the vestibule, locked most of the time, and draped in a peach shawl with long silky fringe, an incongruous luxury accent in an apartment whose palette ran from beige to brown. Only when one of her young pupils arrived for a lesson did Rivka retrieve the key from the pocket of her housedress and unlock the keyboard. Before she opened it, Zach noticed, his mother had a ritual: she hugged her rib cage, gazed upward, and murmured something he couldn't hear. Then she placed her straight chair slightly back from the piano bench and instructed the pupil on the proper rendition of "Moonlight Sonata" or "Für Elise," without ever touching the keys. For as long as he lived at home, Zach never heard his mother play the piano.

The world beyond his hushed apartment unspooled against an ordinary sound track—blaring phonographs, crying babies, women calling children in for supper. Kids roller-skated in the building's cavernous marble lobby, couples bickered in the elevator, American-born adolescents argued with their immigrant parents. Zach could hear them through the walls begging for more allowance or pushing their curfews. He associated other people's families with sound, his with silence. All it took to make his mother flinch was the scrape of a drawer or the ring of the phone. Zach's whistling brought a finger to her lips. When he wanted to listen to *The Lone Ranger* on the radio, he would press his ear to the mesh-covered speaker; still, his mother would insist that he wait until she went down to the laundry room or left to go grocery shopping to avoid "the noise."

From the time he was a small child, he knew his mother was not like others. Other mothers wore red lipstick, dangling earrings, flowered blouses. They got dressed up in netted hats, soft kid gloves, and high-heeled shoes, painted their fingernails, gave themselves Toni home permanents. And their hair was any color but white. For as long as Zach could remember, Rivka's hair had been yellowish white, like the strands that clung to cobs of corn. In his friends' apartments, the women talked and laughed as loudly as the men. They listened to soap operas on the radio, or sang along with Kate Smith or watched quiz shows and yelled out the answers while they did their housework. In Zach's apartment, his mother was a voiceless wraith adrift in a sea of half-done chores. Dust motes swirled on bars of sunlight while her feather duster rested on her lap like a sleeping hen. Smudges of jam evaded her sponge and strange ingredients turned up in her stew—a rubber band, a scrap of butcher paper, the stringy tip of a turnip. Once, her Hoover swallowed Zach's socks.

He was six years old that day in 1956 when the accident happened. His mother was ironing his father's shirts while Zach, having pestered her for a grown-up assignment, was folding towels. With considerable effort, he had produced a neat stack and carried it intact to the linen closet, but when he tried to push the pile into one of the shelves, something hard was in the way—a flowered pillowcase with an album inside, its cover scarred. He set the towels on the floor and sat on top of them with the album on his lap, turned its black pages and studied the faded snapshots, each held in place by four corner brackets. Finding no one he recognized, he was about to put the album back in the linen closet when his eye was snagged by a picture of a beautiful woman standing in front of an enormous castle, her light hair arranged in a crown of braids, a flower tucked behind one ear. Her fingers rested on the handle of a great tub of a carriage in which sat a baby with a mop of blond ringlets. Years later, when Zach Levy thought about what made him try to decipher the caption handwritten on the border of the photo, he wasn't sure if it was the castle, the woman's radiant smile, or the baby's riotous curls.

Zach had learned to read in kindergarten and now he was in first grade, but he'd never seen such strange words—"Zamek Wawelski, Czerwiec"—so he carried the album back to the kitchen, propped it against the ironing board, and asked his mother what they meant. Before her brain could register what her eyes had seen, Rivka translated, "Wawel Castle. June."

"Can we go there, Mama? Will you take me to the castle?" His eyes riveted to the picture, Zach didn't see the color drain from his mother's already wan cheeks or notice her grip tighten on the iron's handle and her thin shoulders pitch forward. "Where is it? Where is Wawel?"

Finally, she whispered, "Kraków."

Zach had heard of that place; it was a city in Poland, which was in Europe, which was where his parents used to live before the "Notsies" murdered all his relatives.

"Who's that?" he asked, pointing to the woman. He thought she might be one of his dead aunts or cousins. When his mother didn't answer, he looked up and saw that her face had collapsed like one of his father's wrinkled shirts and her full weight was bearing down on the handle of the steam iron. As if in protest, the appliance hissed and snorted while the shirt beneath exuded the acrid stench of scorched starch.

Rivka breathed out, "*Me*."

Impossible. The woman in the picture was smiling. She was beautiful. She had a flower in her hair. "Then who's the baby?" Zach asked.

Rivka threw back her head and rasped, "Yitzhak. Mayn kleine yingele. Mayn zisseh tataleh."

Summer nights, when the windows were open and he could hear stray mutts howling in the alley below, Zach had a hard time falling asleep because the animals' mournful calls sounded human. Today, his mother sounded like the dogs. Rivka cried frequently but not like this and she usually confined her breakdowns to his parents' bedroom where her sobs were muffled by a pillow or muted by the reassuring thrum of his father's voice. This time he was inches away and her cries were feral wails and his father wasn't home to comfort her and make them stop. Scarier still, she was oblivious to both Zach and the smoldering triangle that had spread beyond the rim of the iron and produced glittering orange embers that seemed to be eating up the fibers of his father's shirt.

Mayn kleine yingele. That much Yiddish Zach understood: the baby in the picture was her little boy. But how could that possibly be? Zach was an only child. How could his mother have a son who wasn't him?

It took a tongue of flame licking up from the ironing board to shock Rivka back to the room. Raising the iron and wielding it like a cudgel, she smashed it against the board until every spark was extinguished then slammed it onto its metal cradle. When, in her panic, she grabbed the cord to yank it out of the wall socket, the board overturned and sent the iron hurtling toward Zach, its pointed snout splitting his right eyebrow before it struck bone; the gash, which took eight stitches to close, would later heal into a thin white scar that bisected his brow as neatly as if it had been the purposeful result of a rite of passage. He waited months for the missing hairs to grow back but they never did. What remained was a scar that marked him as the imperfect second son, a poor substitute for his parents' blond angel, and whenever he saw himself in the mirror, the split in his brow reminded him of the dividing line between before and after, between knowing and not knowing why his mother cried so much and spoke so little, and why she could not love him.

After the accident, from age six until his bar mitzvah day, he was obsessed with his brother and wanted to know everything about him, when he learned to walk and talk, his cute sayings, and what traits, if any, they had in common. In order to compensate his parents for their loss, Zach was determined to achieve twice as much as any other boy he knew. Yet when he brought home an A or a trophy, his mother's sorrow seemed to deepen, as if his triumphs reminded her of all the schooling and sports that Yitzhak had missed and everything he might have accomplished had he lived. Sometimes Zach felt guilty for growing up.

He revisited the album a few times a week from then on, retrieved it from the linen closet, took it to his room or stretched out on the living room floor, and pored over every photograph. There were only six of his brother—two taken in infancy, a snapshot of Yitzhak on a pony, another in a bubble bath with a young Rivka shampooing his hair, a studio pose of him wearing a sailor suit, and the mesmerizing picture taken at Wawel Castle. Zach had dozens of questions about each picture but the mere mention of his brother's name started Rivka weeping.

"Quit upsetting your mama! You'll give her a stroke," Nathan scolded.

At six, Zach took words literally, so he stopped directing his questions to his mother but continued to pester his father. After dinner, or after finishing his homework, he would carefully remove the album from the flowered pillowcase and ask about various photographs. He wasn't curious just about Yitzhak but about other people in the pictures, their relationship to his parents, who they were, what they did, where the shot was taken, what happened to them, each query a step in his self-assigned journey to learn all about his parents' lives in Kraków, each a preamble to the question he was afraid to ask but most wanted answered: "How did Yitzhak die?"

Zach's nightmares, however, all seemed triggered by the first photograph he'd seen: He is pushing his brother's carriage around the castle grounds when, as if grabbed by an invisible hand, the carriage pulls away from him and starts rolling down the hill, picking up speed, and he can't catch it. No matter how hard he runs, it's always just beyond his reach until, at the bottom of the hill, it tumbles into the river and instead of diving in to rescue the baby,

Zach, in his dream, skids to a stop on the bank and stands there horrified as Yitzhak's soft yellow curls sink below the surface of the water.

Hoping to short-circuit the nightmare, which had recurred several times the first year after he learned Yitzhak existed, Zach decided to avoid looking at the Wawel Castle picture and, to ensure that he didn't turn to it accidentally, he paper-clipped that page to the preceding one. Nonetheless, a few weeks later the nightmare returned, his helplessness more vivid and terrifying than before. He awoke trembling and ran to find his father.

"You have to teach me to swim, Papa!" he exclaimed to Nathan, who was in the bathroom shaving.

"Swim? What are you talking about? It's February."

"The Talmud says every father must teach his son to swim. It's a commandment. Rabbi says so." Because he knew the strictures of Jewish law did not carry much weight with his father, Zach had cited the authority of the family's long-time rabbi, Eleazer Goldfarb, who, having traded a thriving law practice for a life of service to the Eames Place Shul and its congregation of refugees and Holocaust survivors, was so revered in the Levy household that Nathan simply referred to Goldfarb as "Rabbi."

"Okay, okay!" Nathan said, gliding the razor over the ledge of his jaw and up the slope of his cheek. "Next summer, at the beach."

"I can't *wait* until next summer, Papa." Zach kneeled on the lid of the toilet seat and planted his elbows on the sink. "I have to learn *immediately*!"

"So when we're at the schvitz, I'll teach you."

"Not in *that* pool!" The boy shivered in his pajamas. "I'll freeze to death."

Nathan gazed into the mirror. "It's good training, cold water. Once, in the High Tatras, winter like now, two Krauts on my tail, I'm racing through the woods, way out in front of them, thinking, 'Nazi bastards'll never get me.' Then—oy, gevalt! Up ahead I see a big stream with rocks sticking out. The rocks are shiny with ice, so I know the water's cold. What are my choices, Boychik?"

"Jump in or get shot," Zach replied eagerly.

"Right. So what do I do?"

"Jump in."

"Right again. But what do I do first?"

Zach said he didn't know.

"Take off my jacket and roll it up like ball. Then I jump in and hold the ball up out of the stream while I paddle across." Nathan set down his razor, folded a towel, held it above his head and made swimming motions with his other hand. "Always remember to keep your clothes dry if you can," he said. "So I'm paddling across, my legs are going numb, but I make it to the other side. Guess how."

"How?"

"By taking my mind off the cold. I said to myself my grandpa's favorite prayer, six words, one for each stroke: *Sh'ma. Yisroel. Adonai. Eloheinu. Adonai. Echad.* Three times I repeated it—swam across in eighteen strokes, put on my jacket and hid behind some bushes, quiet like a cat. Nazi bastards came crashing through the woods, one took a look at the stream and shook his head. 'No Yid would ever dive into this ice bath,' he says. 'They're all cowards.' The other bastard agrees with him. Germans can't imagine a Jew taking a swim in February. So one of them runs north, the other runs south. And biff, boom! the Yid gets away."

"Wow, Papa. I never heard that story before. That's *amazing*! Rabbi's going to love that story!"

"Why that story?"

"Because the Sh'ma got you across the stream! In Hebrew school, Rabbi taught us it's the most important prayer in Judaism. It's our declaration of faith in God. "

"To tell the truth, Boychik, I'm not that interested in God."

"What? You make the brachas on Friday night, you go to shul . . ."

"I don't go to shul to pray. I go to hear Rabbi's talks. He's really smart, that man. You've got yourself a helluva teacher."

"But if you don't believe in God, why did you say a prayer in the stream?

Nathan shrugged as he wiped off the last patch of shaving cream. "Because my zaide said the Sh'ma when he was worried. I figured if it helped him, it might help me. He was the last of the believers in my family. By the 1930s, everyone else was a communist. Me, I never trusted God *or* Stalin."

Zach stared at his father in disbelief. "But the Sh'ma worked, Papa. You escaped."

"I escaped because I know how to swim with one arm in freezing cold water. A Jew can't always choose his conditions. Prayers are nice but when you're in trouble, power and strength are better. You'll see." Nathan removed the blade from the razor, slid it into the safety receptacle, and handed the empty razor to Zach. "Forget the swimming, Boychik. This papa is going to teach his son to shave."

ABOUT HIS HARROWING escapes, Nathan was willing to talk endlessly. Other experiences he refused to discuss at all. Certain questions infuriated him or shut him down entirely; to most questions about the past, he'd reply by reiterating basic biographical facts that Zach already knew from his previous interrogations. For instance, the fact that his parents met in medical school and married after graduation; that they bought a townhouse in Kraków and set up their practices side by side on the ground floor; that Yitzhak was born on June 21, 1939; that the "Nazi bastards" invaded Poland three months later and murdered Yitzhak three years after that. Nathan would never say how, only that on that awful day, he had escaped to the forest and from then on, lived in hiding and fought with the partisans while Rivka was shipped to Auschwitz, a concentration camp where Jews got worked to death or exterminated. After the war, Nathan said he tracked down Rivka in a displaced persons camp and persuaded her to move to America for a better life. "Period. The end."

That's what Nathan always said when he was tired of talking or fed up with his son's questions. "Period. The end." Though Nathan controlled the narrative, Zach kept trying, month after month, year after year, to extract from his father bits and pieces of the Levy family history the way his mother had once plucked broken glass from his knees with her tweezers, one sliver at a time.

ELECTION DAY, 1960. Nathan came home from one of his long walks with a box of sparklers he had bought in the Irish neighborhood. "Quick, Boychik! Put on your jacket. We'll go up on the roof and help the Catholics celebrate."

They took the elevator to the top floor and climbed a steep iron ladder to the open air. The sky was almost as black as the asphalt tar and gravel roof and there was no moon to outshine their fireworks display, no one to tell them that sparklers were illegal in New York. All around them were six- and seven-story apartment buildings, dozens of windows flickering with the blue glare of TV screens, some sashes raised to the autumn air so snippets of the election night coverage reached Zach's ears.

"You think we'll ever have a Jewish president?" he asked.

Nathan tore open the box of sparklers. "We just got a Catholic, so why not a Jew? In America, anybody can be anything."

Zach, always alert to a natural opportunity to pursue new information, followed with, "Then how come you and Mama can't be doctors here?" His father had been dodging that question for months.

Nathan acted as if he hadn't heard. Fishing out one of the sparklers, he handed it to Zach. "Just hold the stick like a lollipop and keep it away from your face," he cautioned, then flipped open his Zippo and ignited the stick.

A fountain of white-hot sparks spewed forth. Thrilled, the ten-year-old squealed with delight and raced around the roof shouting, "Yay, President Kennedy! Yay, JFK!" as the sparkler, trailing glitter, lit up the night.

"All yours, Boychik," Nathan said, offering his son the full box. "Happy Election Day!"

Zach ran around with one sparkler after another until the last stick sputtered into ash and only stars illuminated the sky.

"I never saw you so excited," Nathan said, as they climbed down the iron ladder. "Maybe you're part Irish!"

While they waited for the elevator, Zach tried again. "Before, you said anyone can be anything here. So why can't you and Mama be doctors? I really want to know."

Nathan pursed his lips and punched the down button several times, though they both knew it wouldn't bring the elevator any sooner. "Genug!" he said.

Genug, Yiddish for enough, was another of Nathan's cutoff lines.

Zach's next interrogative opportunity came one winter day after a bully yanked his arm out of its socket and the school nurse called Rivka to pick him up and take him to the hospital emergency room. As soon as she arrived, his mother diagnosed his injury as a dislocated shoulder and with a quick, sure-handed jerk, popped the ball of his humerus back into its socket. The pain, which had been excruciating, vanished as if by magic, and Zach was sent back to class.

That night at the supper table, he told his father what she had done.

"I'm not surprised," Nathan said. "Your mama was a fine doctor!"

"Then why does she give piano lessons now?" Zach felt weird speaking of his mother in the third person when she was sitting right there but he'd been warned not to ask her questions. "And how come you work in a hat factory? I mean if you're both doctors, why *aren't* you doctors?"

It was never clear what made his father answer this time. Maybe because Rivka was listening and her husband wanted to give her the recognition she deserved.

"We had a tough time when we first came here," Nathan began, putting down his fork and knife. "Foreign physicians were not allowed to practice in the United States unless they got training to bring them up to American standards. Then they had to take a test to be reaccredited. Your mama and me, we couldn't afford the training course, not even for one of us to sign up. We were lucky to get a cash advance from the Hebrew Immigrant Aid Society to cover the first six months' rent on the apartment and a stipend for food while I looked for a job. I was ready to do any work at all, but the GIs were home from the war, flooding the labor market and employers were in no hurry to hire a Polish Jew ahead of an American war hero. Who could blame them?

"When the HIAS stipend was about to run out and our social worker was reviewing our file, she happened to notice that your mama once performed with a famous amateur chamber music ensemble in Kraków. She told us she could get someone to donate a used piano if Rivka would agree to give lessons to children in the neighborhood. It would provide a service to the community and, since the minimum wage was forty cents an hour and piano teachers charged three dollars a lesson, Rivka could make some real money."

"That sounds great," Zach said, rapt.

"Yes, except your mama hadn't touched a piano since . . ." his father glanced at his mother across the table. She was burying her peas in her mashed potatoes, ". . . since before the war. Still, we needed the money, so even though she didn't want to, she said yes and HIAS delivered the Baldwin like they promised. I ran all over the neighborhood putting up signs in lobbies, laundry rooms, synagogues, barber shops, and the pupils came in droves. Thanks to your mama, we made ends meet until I got hired at the factory, first seasonal, then permanent. She got us through." Nathan reached for Rivka's hand. She pulled it away and started stacking the dirty dinner plates.

Zach asked, "Once you got the job in the hat factory, why did she keep teaching piano? Anyone can see she doesn't enjoy it. Do you still need the money?"

Rivka cleared the dishes and carried them into the kitchen. Nathan leaned closer to the boy. "I pay our expenses, her earnings go in her knippel," he said softly so his wife wouldn't hear him over the running water. "That's the little pouch she keeps in her underwear drawer. What she makes from the lessons, she's saving for your college . . ." Nathan glanced toward the sink where Rivka's back was visible through the kitchen door. "She does it because she wants to be sure we can give you an education—and because she loves you."

Zach wondered why his father was always trying to build his mother up in his eyes. "But, if she hates teaching . . ."

"Period!" Nathan said.

For Zach, it was a comma. The next day he took down the album, slid off the paper clips—because he hadn't had the nightmare in months—letting the pages fall open to the snapshot of his mother and brother in front of Wawel Castle, and for the first time, noticed the splendor of Yitzhak's carriage, especially compared to the baby buggies on the sidewalks of the Bronx. It had shiny wheels and the contours of a princely coach, its outer surface enameled to a high gloss, the brass hardware scrolled and polished, its lining tufted and cushioned.

"Did you have a lot of money in Kraków?" Zach asked, studying the picture.

Nathan, deep in his Yiddish newspaper, murmured, "Hmm?"

"Yitzhak's carriage looks really fancy. Were you and Mama rich?"

"We did okay," Nathan said, still looking down.

Zach studied the picture through his magnifying glass. "Yitzhak's ears stuck out, right?"

Pause. Beat. "A little."

"As much as mine?"

"Yeah." Nathan crossed his legs but kept his eyes on the paper. "You couldn't see them, though. His hair always covered his ears."

"Like mine!" Zach said, thrilled when any of his traits matched his brother's. "What happened to him, Papa?"

Nathan slapped the newspaper on his knee and glared at his son. "How many times do I have to tell you? The Nazi bastards killed him."

"I know. But how?"

"Never mind *how*. Dead is dead. Period. The end!" Nathan stalked out with his paper, leaving Zach alone with the photographs.

THEN THERE WAS the time the two of them were waiting for chairs in Sam Kranzberg's barbershop and Zach noticed on the floor mounds of platinum hair that had been harvested from a previous customer.

"Was Yitzhak's hair that color?" he asked his father.

"I know his was much curlier but was it as light as that?"

After a quick downward squint, Nathan became visibly agitated and without a word, charged out of the shop.

"Don't be mad, Papa," Zach said, trotting to keep pace with his father's long strides. "You can't blame me for wondering what he looked like, can you? I was just curious."

Not until they passed between the marble lions flanking the entrance to their building did Nathan reply, "*Too* curious."

That was their last visit to the barber. From now on, Nathan announced, Rivka would cut their hair. Her shears were as sharp as Sam Kranzberg's and her haircuts would save money. The new policy suited Zach fine. He had never been fond of Sam's buzz cuts anyway. He preferred his mother's snip-and-trim barbering; Rivka always let his hair grow long enough to cover his ears.

The first Saturday of every month was haircut day. Nathan usually went first and left the kitchen once his cut was done, but occasionally he would linger afterward, pour himself a glass of seltzer, and watch Rivka barber their son's hair. Zach worshiped his father but resented the intrusion. His half-hour haircut was his most intimate time with his mother, her hands touching his head the only physical contact she seemed able to tolerate.

NATHAN'S LOVE ALMOST made up for Rivka's inattention and distance. Sunday mornings, Zach and his father would walk to Daitch Dairy, the appetizer store on Kingsbridge Road, and buy lox, bagels, and all the trimmings. On Sunday afternoons, the city's streets were their hiking trails or, because he wanted his son to be a schtarke—a strong man able to survive in all terrain—Nathan would lead Zach through the wilds of Pelham Bay Park that spread out beyond the sooty barbeque grills and beer-can-littered basketball courts. While they wended their way past placid salt marshes, through acres of mugwort and bayberry, brambles, bushes, and vines, and under canopies of oak, pine, and spruce, Nathan would identify edible plants, and branches that, were Zach ever forced to spend the night outdoors, would make the best shelter. Almost invariably, they would end up at the hoary post oak that Nathan claimed was the oldest tree in New York City. Its bark was scarred by fire, its limbs chipped, bleached, and whacked by storms and salty winds but Zach grew to venerate the old oak for standing bold and tall in the stingy earth, a survivor in the woods of the Bronx, as his father had been in the Polish forests.

WHEN ZACH TURNED twelve, his father started taking him along to the schvitz, the Russian baths where Jews from Eastern Europe, whose flags changed with every war, paid a couple of bucks to stew together in a steam room.

Why Nathan would spend his free time sweating after he'd sweltered all week over boiling water and hot rollers at the hat factory, Zach could not fathom, but he was overjoyed to be included in the grown-up masculine camaraderie of the schvitz. The fragrance of Eucalyptus oil perfumed the air a half block from the baths and inside, the slap of rubber flip-flops on the tiled floors sounded like applause. When the burly clerk at the front desk gave Zach his own towel and locker key, he felt as if he'd been initiated into an exclusive club.

Spending time with Nathan and his lontzmen from the Old Country—Herman the butcher, Sol the druggist, and Izzy the furrier—was as much fun for Zach as hanging out with his own friends. He loved watching their pinochle games and breathing the smoke from their cigars. He marveled that they didn't cry out when big burly men who couldn't speak a word of English gave them pletzers—rubdowns with soap suds and oak leaves that could peel off a layer of skin. He adored listening to the stories they told each other during a nosh in the cafeteria—maybe herring and black bread, or steak and onions with a shot of vodka, neat—and afterward, when they took naps on rickety, white iron cots in a dormitory that looked like a hospital ward, Zach was flattered when they trusted him to wake them after twenty minutes. Cocooned in their thick white robes and contrapuntal snores, they reminded him of babies in bassinets, except that the lontzmen had paunches and more hair growing out of their ears than on their heads. Zach took guilty pleasure in the fact that, unlike Izzy, Sol, and Herman, his father's physique matched that of Charles Atlas, the bodybuilder in Marvel Comics ads who promised to transform a ninety-seven-pound weakling into a He-man. Only after witnessing a shocking event did Zach understand that Nathan and his lontzmen didn't go to the schvitz just for their health. They went to test themselves and each other. They went for forgiveness and love.

The steam room was thirty feet square with three levels of wooden benches along which large wooden buckets were stationed at several points, each fed by its own spigot. There was an airtight door to the locker room on one wall, and directly across, a revolving glass door that gave way to a pool. The first time Nathan brought Zach to the steam room, he instructed his son on proper conduct.

"Remember, Boychik: the higher the bench, the hotter the air. As soon as you feel the heat close in on you, you have to cool down—right away. Don't wait to faint. Go out and take a plunge in the pool or else splash yourself with a bucket of water. If you use the pail, don't dump the whole thing on your head like Niagara Falls. Do it right—like this." Nathan picked up the nearest pail of water, brought it close to his chest and slowly tipped about a third of its contents onto his torso, another third onto his face, and the rest onto the top of his head. Then he returned the empty pail to the spigot. "Don't forget to put the bucket back under its spigot so it fills up for the next guy," he said.

One day, as they undressed in the locker room, Nathan

told Zach the lontzmen were going to be having a competition to see who could hold out the longest in the steam without cooling down.

"Don't ask to join the contest," Nathan said. "It's not healthy. You'll get dehydrated."

"If it's not healthy why are *you* doing it?"

"Men do dumb things."

Zach wanted to do dumb things with them.

Sol, Izzy, and Herman were already lined up on the top bench like three sweaty Buddhas, their wrinkled balls dangling between their legs.

"You're getting to be such a big boychik," Herman said, pinching Zach's cheek. "In two shakes of a lamb's tail, you'll be taller than me."

"Everyone's taller than you," said Sol.

Izzy let loose with a torrent of mamaloshen, the mother tongue.

"English, please," said Nathan.

After ten minutes, Zach, sweltering and light-headed, left to take a plunge in the pool. While circling back through the revolving door, he noticed a flurry of naked limbs on the top bench—Izzy throwing a punch at Nathan and hitting him *in the face*! Even more incredibly, Nathan, who towered over the little furrier, did not return the blow, just stood there, rubbing his jaw and shaking his head. By the time Zach scrambled up to the top bench, Sol and Herman had Izzy in a hammerlock, his feet off the floor. Zach went for him anyway, fists cocked.

"Don't touch him, Zachariah!" Nathan shouted.

Zach stopped in his tracks. Never before had his father called him by his full name. "He *hit* you, Papa! I saw it!"

"I said back off."

Back off? Was this the same man who was always lecturing Zach on the importance of self-defense? The boy turned to the lontzmen. "Please! Will someone tell me what's going on?"

"A minute ago, your papa told us he didn't feel right," Herman replied. "He said he was dropping out of the contest."

"He went for a bucket," Sol added, "but he slipped on a puddle and the pail tipped."

"Izzy got splashed," said Herman.

"Danks Gott he didn't hurt himself," said Sol, as the two men dragged the little furrier to the exit.

Zach sank down on the bench. "I don't get it."

Nathan sat beside him. "It's simple. Izzy was doing great—no pails, no pool, his best time ever—until I tripped and splashed him."

"So he got wet! Big deal!"

"To him it was. I spoiled his record."

"It was an accident, Papa, a stupid contest! Why would you take a punch from your so-called friend over a stupid contest?"

"Izzy lost a wife and three little girls in the camps," said Nathan, as if that explained everything.

In the world of Zach Levy's childhood, it did.

CHAPTER 2

PROMISES TO KEEP

EARLY IN 1963, THE YEAR LEADING UP TO ZACH'S BAR mitzvah, Rabbi Goldfarb assigned his students a paper on "any issue related to tzedakah," the Hebrew word that means both charity and justice. Because the James Meredith case was in the headlines and Nathan's union had marched in civil rights demonstrations, Zach chose to write about race and justice. He began with the Supreme Court ruling that ordered Meredith's admission to the University of Mississippi, then described the riots that erupted in response, and Mississippi Governor Ross Barnett's decision to send state troopers to bar Meredith from the campus. Zach ended his paper with President Kennedy dispatching US Marshals to protect Meredith, the first African American ever admitted to Ole Miss.

"For justice to be served," Zach wrote in conclusion, "each of us must take a strong stand against bigotry and speak out like the Hebrew Prophets of old."

Rabbi gave him a B+ with the notation, "Fine writing,

solid research, good understanding of American law (I predict a legal career). But, given that this was a *Hebrew school* assignment, could use more Judaic references and parallels to Jewish law and ethics."

The Meredith case was still on Zach's mind when, while paging through the photo album a few days later, he was captivated by the picture of his father and a friend, rackets crossed, posing in their tennis whites on a court in a glass conservatory with potted palms and French doors opening onto a garden.

"Were black people allowed to play tennis in Kraków?" Zach asked.

Nathan, watering the plants on the windowsill, muttered, "I don't remember any black people in Kraków."

"Who's the guy you're with at the indoor court, the man with the pointy beard?"

"A friend."

"Jewish friend?"

Nathan snapped off the brown stalks on the geranium plant. "Yes. Leo Henschel."

"Could Jews play tennis with regular Poles or only with other Jews? Were you allowed to join gentiles' clubs? When the Nazis came, did they . . ."

The watering can came flying across the room, his father after it. "Stop with the pictures already, goddammit!" Nathan grabbed the album and slammed it on Zach's head. "I'm sick and tired of your fucking questions!"

The shock was worse than the pain. Zach had been yelled at before, sent to his room without dessert, but he'd never heard his father swear and neither of his parents had ever hit him. His head was throbbing. Even his hair hurt. "I just wanted to know about life in Kraków . . ."

"Forget Kraków! Kraków's a piece of shit. It's a dead place!"

Noise being no small event in the Levy household, Rivka, who was in their bedroom, could not have missed her husband's railing, the thud of the album, nor the crash when he slammed the door, yet she never emerged. Perhaps she was afraid Zach would ask *her* the obvious next question: If Kraków was such a terrible place, why did Nathan look so pleased on the tennis court, and why was she smiling so brilliantly in front of Wawel Castle?

ZACH USED TO think only Catholics believed babies were born guilty until Rabbi Goldfarb pointed to Exodus 20:5, which said the sins of the father are visited on their children unto the third or fourth generation. If God was going to punish Zach for something his parents did in Poland before he was born, he felt he should know what it was. And if they hadn't committed any crimes, he wanted to know that, too, so he could enter manhood on his bar mitzvah day with a clean slate. Nathan's outburst was the first of many, a new development in his personality and a source of great distress for his son. The Eames Place Synagogue was riddled with nonbelievers, Jews whose gods were labor leaders like David Dubinsky and Harry Bridges. Though Nathan attended services regularly, prayer was just prologue to the Oneg Shabbat reception where he loved to schmooze with his friends and enjoy a shot of schnapps and a slice of honey cake. His seat in the sanctuary could as easily have been a rocking chair on the porch of a general store.

Rivka's spiritual life puzzled Zach even more than Nathan's did. She seemed to believe in God only to blame him. After the war, she held firm to the principle that divine intervention was a pipe dream and Jews must be responsible for themselves. What kept us alive as a people was our loyalty to our traditions, she would say, and therefore every Jew—Democrat, Republican, Communist, Socialist, or Atheist—must maintain the rituals and customs of our ancestors. It was Rivka who had insisted that Nathan, believer or not, play the traditional male role at the Sabbath meal and attend services; that a mohel, not a doctor, circumcise their son; that Zach be Jewishly educated so he would qualify to marry a woman from any denomination, even the Orthodox.

But despite all her efforts to ensure his bona fides, Zach felt like a Jewish impostor. Ashamed of his mother's disdain for the Almighty and his father's sacrilege, he faulted himself for collaborating in his parents' charade of a Shabbos. On Friday nights, Rivka would prepare traditional dishes (chicken soup, brisket, tzimmes, and kugel) and say the blessing over the candles, and Nathan would bless the challah and wine (always Manischewitz Concord Grape). But once they finished dessert (usually apple strudel), Nathan would repair a chair or write a letter and Rivka would pick up her mending or turn on a lamp. On Saturday, she would give her husband and son their haircuts, all of which was forbidden on the Sabbath because Jewish law considered such activities to be "work." The closer his bar mitzvah day loomed, the more troubled Zach was by his parents' infractions, until one Friday night, he looked up from his chicken soup and accused them of hypocrisy.

"I can't understand why the two of you keep blessing a God you don't believe in."

Nathan smiled. "We believe in him. We just don't trust him."

"Papa, I mean it. Why say all these brachas if you don't think God exists?"

"We say them for the frummers," Rivka murmured.

"She means the Orthodox Jews who died in the camps," explained Nathan. "She saw women save up crumbs so they could say the motzi. She saw them risk their lives to light a thimbleful of oil when they couldn't get a candle for Shabbos. One of her friends got caught with a schmatta on her head bentching—saying the blessing over the light—and a Nazi bastard cut out her tongue to make a lesson of her. Your mama watched people go to their deaths with God's name on their lips. It's for them, she wants us to say the brachas."

ON THE FRIDAY night before his bar mitzvah, Zachariah Levy came to the Sabbath table expecting nothing out of the ordinary—it wasn't his parents' habit to mark big days with fanfare—so he was astonished when, at the end of the meal, his mother brought out a cake. More surprising still, after he blew out the candles, his father came over to his chair, planted a dry kiss on his head, and delivered a speech.

"Your mama and I are very proud of you, Boychik. You're a good student and a good boy, and tomorrow you are going to be a man, so tonight we want to talk to you about the kind of man we hope you will be. We decided I'll talk first," Nathan said, and raised his kiddush cup. "I want you to be a mensch. Treat people right. Respect everyone no matter who they are or where they come from. Remember they're doing the best they can, even if they're not always nice or polite. Try to be sympathetic to the parts of their life you'll never know."

Zach didn't understand how he was supposed to sympathize with things he didn't know about but Nathan made more sense as he went along. "You told us you want to be a lawyer. If that happens, you should represent the workers, not the bosses. Argue for the poor people who are trying to make a better life for themselves, not the powerful people who already have more than enough."

Nathan took a sip of wine then lifted the cup even higher. "One last thing: if the world goes crazy again, promise me you'll fight back and not be afraid. You get what I'm saying? You'll fight. You'll be a mensch, okay?"

Zach said he would.

His mother's pre–bar mitzvah entreaty would prove to be far more challenging. "I want you to promise to marry a Jewish girl," she said, when his father sat down. She pulled her chair a little closer to Zach's but stayed seated.

"Tomorrow you're going to become a man and too many Jewish men are marrying out. I'm worried about what's going to happen to us. Suddenly, the goyim like us—too much for our own good, if you ask me. Gentile girls, they want Jewish husbands. It's nice to be accepted for a change, but intermarriage isn't good for the Jews. For us, it's the beginning of the end. If we keep watering ourselves down, we'll evaporate and it won't be the anti-Semites who got rid of us. It'll be us who did it to ourselves."

His mother wasn't asking Zach to be religious. He could have faith or not, she said, as long as he had babies to replenish the Six Million. Every Jewish child was "a nail in Hitler's coffin." So, for that matter, was every loaf of challah, potato latke, square of matzah, or triangle of hamantashen that appeared on a Jewish supper table. Each proved to the world that we're still here, eating what Jews eat and doing what Jews do. When a member of the tribe won, as Rivka called it, the "Noble Prize," it reminded the world that Jews are not just sad survivors, we're smart, we excel. Albert Einstein and Jonas Salk were as much nails as they were "nobles." Helena Rubinstein and Estee Lauder, Jack Benny and Fanny Brice, Leonard Bernstein and Arthur Rubinstein, all testimony to Jewish endurance and excellence. Also nails. But the only sure way to deny Hitler a posthumous victory was for Jews to marry Jews and give birth to more Jews and teach them their heritage. Pride may be a sin but Jewish pride was a survival skill.

"Promise me you'll marry a Jew," she repeated. "And raise Jewish children."

Zach promised.

AT SERVICES ON the morning of Zach's bar mitzvah, Rabbi Goldfarb gave a sermon about Hillel, the first century Talmudic sage. A gentile once came to Hillel and said, "I will accept Judaism if you can teach me the entire Torah while I'm standing on one leg." Hillel replied immediately, "What is hateful to you, do not do to others. That is the whole Torah. All the rest is commentary; now go and study it."

Rabbi said the gentile's request reminded him of Americans' tendency to demand quick and easy answers. "I often hear people say things like, 'Cut to the chase,' or, 'What's the bottom line?' or, 'Just give me the bullet points.' They want their information pre-chewed and spoon-fed. They're busy; they only have time to read the digest, not the full report, the Cliffs Notes, not the play. But life is too complicated to be reduced to a few sentences. Even Hillel's distillation concludes with, 'go and study it,' a direct order to go deeper.

"That's my message to Zach Levy, our bar mitzvah boy, but also to all of you," Goldfarb thundered. "*Study it*, whatever your 'it' happens to be. Ponder it deeply. Live life at a deeper level. Give it the time it deserves. Don't make major decisions while standing on one leg. Ask yourself the big questions: 'Why am I here?' 'What really matters?' 'What kind of Jew do I want to be?'"

On their walk home from synagogue, Nathan seemed pensive most of the way, then put an arm around Zach's shoulders. "It's called the Golden Rule, that message Hillel told the gentile. What you hate, don't do to no one else. Remember that, Boychik."

Zach hated to contradict his father but—"I think you have it backward, Papa," he said, gently. "The Golden Rule says, '*Do* unto others as you would have them do unto you.' Hillel says, '*Don't* do.'"

"It's the goyim who got it backward," Nathan said. "Their Golden Rule could lead a person to do terrible things to someone else. What if I don't *want* a Christian to do to me what they want done to them—get baptized, for instance? You follow me? *Don't* do protects the weak from the strong. Our rule is more . . . nuanced."

Whenever a new word popped up in his father's vocabulary, Zach knew Nathan was back at night school secretly taking English lessons. But Zach, having just been declared a man, wasn't thinking in nuances, he was grappling with his rabbi's questions: Who did he want to be? What really matters? He had made a vow about the kind of mensch he would strive to be, the kind of woman he would marry, the kind of children he would raise. Shouldn't he also commit to being a certain kind of Jew? Clearly, he could never fulfill the 618 commandments that the Torah demanded of Jewish men. Nor could he promise to be a believer. Then again, if he didn't believe in God, who would he beg? Who would he blame?

Simply by being born in New York City in 1950, he was a different kind of Jew than his parents. By 1963, they had been living in America for seventeen years yet still acted like guests in their own country. Especially Rivka, who was always on her best behavior for fear of committing "a shande fir de goyim"—a gaffe that might humiliate her, cast shame on the Jewish people, or provoke the anti-Semites. Her advice to Zach, the few times she gave it, ran to simple axioms: "Keep a low profile." "Don't attract attention." "Always be vigilant." On the one hand, she thought America was the best country on earth for a Jew. On the other hand—wasn't there always another hand?—tomorrow morning Uncle Sam could turn on his adopted nieces and nephews and start a pogrom—reason enough to support the Jewish State.

When Zach was thirteen, Israel was only two years older yet already a solid bulwark against his parents' lingering fears—a sovereign Jewish nation with a government, army, navy, and air force powerful enough to fight future Cossacks, fascists, or Nazis wherever they might rise up. Rivka said they would move their family to Tel Aviv if things ever got scary in the Bronx. And this time they would get out before it was too late. America was their country but Israel was their homeland and if the going got tough, it would be their refuge.

Having never seen a ghetto or a Gestapo roundup, the idea of Israel as a haven had no resonance for Zach. His relationship to the slice of land between the Jordan and the Mediterranean was as muddled as his relationship to God, and his parents were no help in sorting it out. Rivka's views on Israel ranged from unconditional love to knee-jerk paranoia. She said it was smart for Jews to have a state of their own but stupid to call it the Jewish state, and suicidal to advertise its mission as "the ingathering of the exiles." As if America wasn't good enough for us. Besides, if every Jew in the world "made *aliyah*"—moved to Israel permanently—it would no longer be a sanctuary, it would be a target. Rivka wanted American Jewish organizations to quit bragging about supporting Hadassah Hospital or Hebrew University or the Israeli Defense Forces. She said Zach should love Israel from a distance and not make a fuss about it.

"The goyim already accuse us of divided loyalty," she told him. "If they knew we were sending so much money to help build the Jewish state, they might put us in camps like they did with Japanese Americans during the war."

Still, she always deposited her grocery change in the blue-and-white tin box emblazoned with a map of Israel, and when the box felt full, she would open it with a tiny key, tally its contents, and send a check for that amount to the Jewish National Fund with instructions to plant trees in the Negev in memory of her slaughtered relatives. Zach couldn't help noticing, however, that she kept her little tzedakah box behind the big box of kosher salt, and not out in the open where their Czech plumber or Hungarian building superintendent might see it.

Zach also couldn't help noticing how many of those JNF certificates his friends received: "A Tree Has Been Planted by the Rubin Family in Celebration of Simon Persky Becoming A Bar Mitzvah." Zach got the fewest certificates of any boy in his Hebrew school class, a reminder, as if he needed one, that his parents were his only living relatives, his friends his only family. (He felt less aggrieved after his classmate, Mitchell Saperstein, went to Israel for spring vacation and reported back that he couldn't find his trees because there were no plaques. Apparently, in keeping with the collectivist ideology of its founders, Israel's forests belonged to the whole Jewish people.)

Israel also elicited contradictory views from Zach's father who, in one breath, would declare Zionism "the national liberation movement of the Jewish people" and trumpet Israel's Labor Party government as the standard setter for all Socialist states while in the next breath, would call for a world without nationalities, flags, and borders. Zach knew for sure that his father was back in night school when Nathan paraphrased Robert Frost: "Israel is the place where, when we have to go there, they have to let us in."

By the time he went to bed that Friday night before his bar mitzvah day, Zach Levy had made four promises to his parents: that he would grow up to be a mensch, marry a Jew, raise Jewish children, and tithe ten percent of his earnings to help keep Israel safe so it would always be there if a Jew needed it.

CHAPTER 3
DETAILS

THE FROSTY, STEEL-GRAY DECEMBER MORNING SNAPPED with the promise of snow as he and his father made their way home from their weekly outing to Daitch Dairy. The warmth of a dozen bagels, purchased straight from the baker's oven, radiated from the paper sack that Zach cradled against his woolen jacket. Nathan carried the butter, eggs, onions, tomatoes, farmer cheese, scallion cream cheese, and a half pound each of whitefish and lox—an abundance guaranteed to yield a surfeit. That, too, was part of their ritual: Nathan always bought much too much food for the three of them, which meant that Zach inevitably would be sent across the street to give their untouched leftovers to the staff at the Jewish Home for the Aged. Even as a boy, he understood that the impulse to stuff the larder and overload the table was beyond Nathan's control, a need born of wartime privations, a hedge against an old hunger.

That Sunday morning after his bar mitzvah, Zach

decided to appeal to his father man-to-man and this time refuse to take no for an answer. Like the lawyer he would become, he began to build his case.

"Rabbi Goldfarb said I'm a man now, right?"

"Right."

"Do *you* think I'm a man?"

"If Rabbi says you're a man, that's good enough for me."

A yeasty aroma wafted up from the paper bag—onion, sesame, poppy—but Zach resisted reaching for a bagel, knowing it would set his father off on a tear about how instant gratification was a sign of weakness. Swallowing hard, he scrunched down the edges of the bag to trap the mouthwatering aroma.

"If you really thought I was a man, you would quit treating me like a child. You'd tell me what happened in the war."

"Don't they teach the war in school?"

"Not the whole truth." (A line he'd picked up from Perry Mason.) "Not what happened to my brother."

"Such details, nobody needs," Nathan said.

Zach, having anticipated his father's obstinacy, had an argument at the ready. "People *do* need details when something matters to them. Take you and President Kennedy. He was assassinated more than two weeks ago but you're still glued to the TV. The whole reason you bought a television was to watch the funeral. You've seen the motorcade replayed twenty times. You get upset every time you see Oswald or Jack Ruby. Mama asks you to turn off the set but you keep watching the replays. Why? Because you want more details."

"Oswald wasn't Hitler, Boychik. Ruby's not Himmler." Without breaking stride, Nathan transferred the shopping bag to his other hand.

"I'm not saying *they're* the same, I'm saying *we're* the same. You and me. We want the whole truth. I think I deserve to know my family's history. And that includes what happened to Yitzhak." The whoosh of Zach's corduroyed legs sounded like waves on a beach. "I never knew my brother, but I love him."

Nathan's jaw clenched. His eyes seemed to drill through the stolid brick buildings to a distant place. A cutting wind sliced through the seams of Zach's jacket and snaked up his sleeves. Shivering, he grasped his father's hand—the mitt of a hat blocker, palm stiff as sisal, fingers calloused, their surgical finesse long gone—and pulled him into the recessed entryway of Herman's butcher shop.

"Let's stop here for a minute, Papa."

A handwritten message with no punctuation hung on the door of the lontzman's shop: CLOSED NOW PLEASE TO COME BACK. They propped their parcels against the brick wall of the entry area and sat on the concrete step. Zach, who often gagged watching his mother pluck a chicken, found himself eye level with the butcher's refrigerated window display—a goose and two ducks suspended by their necks from iron hooks, a side of beef, a cow's tongue, a slab of liver, bloody in its white metal tray. Nauseated, he had to turn away.

Despite the cold weather, Nathan's face glistened with sweat. "Okay, Boychik. When you're right, you're right. I'll give you details but you have to promise not to tell your mama I told you."

For what felt like the tenth time in two days, Zach said, "I promise."

NATHAN AND RIVKA lived and worked in a four-story townhouse on Florianska Street, a few blocks off Kraków's Grand Market Square. The ground floor was split into two medical offices, each with a separate entrance for their separate practices. Rivka, a pediatrician specializing in premature and low birth weight infants, was also known as a gifted diagnostician with remarkable success treating the gravest childhood illnesses. Nathan, a pulmonary surgeon, had a slew of grateful patients—gentiles and Jews—who credited him with their very breath. Life was good for the two young professionals. They were well settled in a cosmopolitan European city with a thriving Jewish population and, thanks to the esteem in which they were held, their relations with their gentile neighbors and colleagues were cordial, even warm. Yet when the hate was uncorked, everything they were, and everything they had done, counted for nothing.

On November 9, 1938, the Nazis attacked and over two days burned more than four hundred synagogues and Jewish-owned shops in Germany and Austria. By the end of Kristallnacht, the Night of Broken Glass, thirty thousand

Jews had been arrested, nearly a hundred killed. When Rivka and Nathan learned the extent of the carnage, they considered leaving Poland for Palestine or the United States but were impeded by the fact that she had just discovered she was pregnant and he had just been inducted into the Polish Army.

After less than a month in combat, his unit was captured and sent to a POW camp. Nathan was still confined there when Yitzhak was born the following June. The Nazis invaded Poland that September, rounded up all the artists and writers, and the professors at Jagiellonian University, and shipped them to the Sachsenhausen concentration camp. Rivka was certain that the doctors and lawyers would be next but with Nathan imprisoned in Germany and an infant to care for, she felt immobilized.

On Yom Kippur 1939, Nazi storm troopers charged into the Kraków synagogue and ordered the men and boys outside at gunpoint to fill in the trenches that, only days before, the Jews had been forced by the Polish Army to dig to defend the city against the Germans. Jewish shops were looted, Jewish businesses shuttered or seized, Jewish homes commandeered for German officers. The Nazi Governor General and his family took up residence in Wawel Castle. Rivka Levy was given forty-eight hours to shut down her practice, pack all of their belongings, and vacate the house on Florianska Street.

A wealthy medical school classmate offered temporary shelter for her and her parents, three younger sisters, unmarried brother, and two grandparents in a large manor house in the South of France. Without Nathan's signature, Rivka could not access their personal bank account but she withdrew the last penny from her medical office account and bribed the stationmaster to secure a couple of first-class compartments that would accommodate her entire family. Early the following morning, without incident, all of them had settled in their seats in the first passenger car when it became obvious that Yitzhak's diaper needed changing. Eager to get the job done before the train started moving, Rivka carried him to the ladies room several cars back and was just pulling up his rubber pants when she heard a plane overhead. Seconds later, a deafening blast cracked the ladies room mirror. She scooped up the baby, ripped off her yellow armband, raced out onto the platform, and ran toward the front of the train, only to find the first car a tangled mass of twisted, flaming metal, and flung here and there, a blackened seat, a shard of china, a charred human leg. The Luftwaffe had scored a direct hit. No human body could survive such a fiery inferno, one needn't be a doctor to see that. The freakish silence, the absence of cries or screams, confirmed the futility of a search for a living person to treat or rescue. A part of her wanted to stay and grieve over the remains of her beloved family, but, were she to have any hope of saving herself and the baby, she realized she must avoid being associated with any of the Jewish victims, that staying would serve no purpose except to ensnare her and Yitzhak in the unfolding horror and sear on their brains the image of her parents' corpses.

With these thoughts swirling through her head, Rivka steeled herself against any show of emotion that might reveal her to be a Jew. She walked past the stone-faced German soldiers on guard around the conflagration and calmly turned away from the platform as if she had been a disinterested passerby, a Polish mother who'd been attracted by the explosion and had stopped to do some rubbernecking. Outside the station, her feet raced as fast as her mind. But where to go? Most of her and Nathan's friends had already left Kraków. Who was left? Whom could she trust? The word conjured her father's law partner, Kadish Freifeld, whom her father once said he would "trust with his life." Kadish had bought out her father's share of the practice and given him a farewell party that Rivka and Nathan had attended at the Freifeld's home. Where was it? In the Jewish section, for sure, but what street? Jozefa. *Yes*. She couldn't recall the number of the house but she remembered its front door was painted red and affixed with a huge brass knocker.

Hasia and Kadish Freifeld, who had heard about the airstrike on the radio while they were having breakfast, insisted Rivka stay with them until Nathan was freed. Their son's room was empty; he was at university in England and under the circumstances, would not be returning anytime soon. Kadish called his office and instructed two of his non-Jewish law clerks to hurry to the station to claim Rivka's luggage, assuming it was still in the rear baggage car—which she'd seen was undamaged by the blast—and, if necessary, to bribe the Germans to release it. Hasia went up the street to borrow a portable crib from a neighbor whose grandchild lived in the States. Within hours, Rivka was in possession of her belongings, including her medical equipment and infant supplies, and in utter despair of her future.

Three weeks later, Nathan showed up at the red door, twenty pounds thinner, with long hair, an Old Testament beard, and a harrowing tale of escape. He had been assigned to the laundry detail, which required him to collect the German officers' dirty linen from their living quarters and dining rooms and deposit it in a large canvas bin that, when filled to capacity, would be loaded into a van and trucked off the premises to an industrial laundry. One afternoon, while the guards were looking the other way, Nathan had leaned over the bin with his last pickup of the day and let his body fall in with the laundry. Then he'd burrowed under the smelly heap and waited. No one had noticed that the bin was heavier than usual when, sometime later, he felt it being tilted and rolled up a ramp. Hearing the van's doors slam shut, the hum of the engine, the clank of the gates closing behind the vehicle, he knew the van had left the camp; all he had to do now was get out of the van to safety.

Because of the traffic sounds and the frequent stops and starts, Nathan surmised that the van was being driven through a city, and when the stops became more intermittent and he heard fewer cars whishing by from the opposite direction, he figured they were riding through an outlying district, a sparsely populated area, and he had better make his move before the driver reached his destination and came around to open the doors. Scrambling out of the stinking laundry bin, he crept over to the van's porthole window and, seeing no traffic coming up behind, threw open the doors and rocketed his body to the side of the road.

It took Nathan six days to make his way to Kraków where one glimpse of the Gestapo patrol outside the house on Florianska Street told him to keep his distance and head for the Jewish Quarter. A few discreet inquiries brought him to the Freifelds' house and a blissful reunion with his wife and son; however, their safe harbor on Jozefa Street was short-lived. On March 20, 1940, a new order came down from the occupying forces: all Jews remaining in Kraków must either relocate to the Podgórze Ghetto on the other side of the Vistula River or evacuate the city altogether.

The ghetto was sealed. The municipal trolleys continued to run through the area but passengers were not allowed to get on or off within its walls. Yet Polish people rode the trams as if nothing had changed. Gentiles who had been Rivka's and Nathan's friends, neighbors, and patients, had only to look out the window as the tram chugged through Podgórze to see desperate Jews suffering and starving. The Poles looked but wouldn't see. They didn't want to know. Or they knew but didn't care.

Hasia and Kadish elected to relocate to the ghetto. Nathan and Rivka took refuge with his cousin, Chaim, who had a small chicken farm in a village near Niepolomice, twenty kilometers southeast of the city. Chaim was a bachelor with a bad case of asthma so the prospect of having two physicians under his roof, one of them a pulmonary specialist, was more agreeable to him than it might have been otherwise. In return for access to his eggs and pullets, Nathan treated Chaim's asthma and Rivka cooked their meals. Chaim looked after Yitzhak when both doctors were out on calls. At that point, of course, no physician had the luxury of a specialty so the Levys provided whatever medical care the local families needed, from vaccinations to skin grafts, obstetrics to amputations. They ministered to malnourished babies, old folks, people crushed by tractors or riddled with worms, anyone in pain. As circumstances grew more dire and medication scarce, they bartered their services for goods and produce, a few bruised tomatoes for a tetanus shot, some goat's milk for a plaster cast. Like all Polish Jews, they wore the yellow star and stepped off the curb at the approach of a German, or a Pole for that matter, and watched helplessly when the Nazis amused themselves by scissoring off the beards of old Jewish men or forcing old women to dance in their underwear until they dropped.

Still, nothing prepared the Levys or anyone else for the liquidation of 1942. As usual, the German orders were precise. On August 25 at 8:00 a.m., every Jew within a six-kilometer radius of Niepolomice was to assemble at the stone church with a maximum of ten kilos of baggage, a weight limit that forced the Levys to choose between their medical supplies and a stockpot, an extra pair of shoes and Yitzhak's stuffed dog, Bubbee. In Rivka's practice, under circumstances far less traumatic than those her son had endured in his first three years of life, she had frequently observed the fierce attachment between children and their comfort objects. This next dislocation would be difficult enough for Yitzhak without trying to wean him off of Bubbee, so she crammed the stuffed dog into the valise and when the scale tipped a hair past ten kilos, she removed the heavily fringed piano shawl.

Aware that the homes of deported Jews were routinely pillaged by German troops (unless the locals got there first), Nathan's cousin Chaim decided that they should fill a metal footlocker with things they wanted to save, and bury it under one of the chicken coops until the war was over. Once he had packed his favored belongings, there was barely enough room in the trunk for Rivka's Shabbos candlesticks (a wedding gift from Nathan's parents), a few items of clothing, the piano shawl, Yitzhak's bronzed baby shoes, and the photo album she had wrapped in a flowered pillowcase to protect it from mold.

The air was still and sultry on August 25 when a long line of Jews began their arduous march from the stone church to a soccer stadium about five kilometers away. A group of disheveled people in night clothes were already there, some in bedroom slippers, others with bare, bloody feet. They looked like victims of a natural disaster or fugitives from an insane asylum, but turned out to be Jews who'd been evicted from another nearby village. A man wearing a bathrobe said the Germans had roused the town at 2:00 a.m., their trucks rumbling through the streets, bullhorns blaring, their mobile execution squads breaking down doors and barging into homes. Anyone who resisted the roundup had been summarily shot. He said he'd seen a crying baby thrown against a brick wall and a frail old woman dispatched at the point of a bayonet.

Inside the stadium, Nazi guards ordered women and children under twelve, to one end of the field, men and boys over twelve, to the other. When a mother clung to her terrified young teen and refused to be separated, one of the guards shot her in the back, killing both of them with a single bullet. In that instant, Rivka immediately released Nathan's hand and, clutching Yitzhak to her chest, folded herself into the mass of women. A bullheaded Nazi handed out chalk, shouting for the women to write their names on their handbags and luggage and place everything in the roped-off section to be claimed later. After she printed R. LEVY on her valise and purse, Rivka thought she would memorize the objects nearby to facilitate locating them later. She noted the straw satchel, tan suitcase, large carton, muslin bag, then, looking beyond them, realized there was far more luggage in the roped-off area than could reasonably be accounted for by the ten kilos allotted to the people currently detained in the stadium. Clearly, others, many, many others, had been here before them and had left *without* their baggage. Requiring the Jews to label their belongings, she realized, was just a ruse to get them to surrender everything without a struggle and thereby spare the Germans the inconvenience, time, and effort to take the plunder by force.

The items Rivka had so carefully chosen to pack for the journey were gone for good. Her stethoscope would amplify Nazi heartbeats. An Aryan woman would inherit her ivory comb. The son of an SS officer would wake up to find a plush stuffed dog in his crib. As the new arrivals dutifully chalked their names on their luggage, Rivka understood that as of today, she and Nathan owned nothing but the clothes on their backs and the few items in the trunk buried under the chicken coop.

Though she had packed raisins, almonds, cheese, and chocolates in the purse she would never see again, she'd put nothing in her pockets. No wonder Yitzhak was growing cranky; he hadn't eaten since dawn. As he squirmed and fussed, she marveled at how, without consuming a morsel of food, a three-year-old could gain weight in his mother's arms. Shooting pains radiated along her spine but fear trumped the spasms; she would not lower her son to the ground. She shifted him to her other hip.

The selection process complete, one of the idle SS guards discovered a soccer ball under the stands and started kicking it around, and when other men joined him, enough for a game, the action on the field took Yitzhak's mind off his empty stomach. He watched for a while, then suddenly shouted, "I want to play!" and craned his little body toward the men. Rivka tightened her grip. "Mommy, let me go! I wanna play ball!" His shrieks grew more shrill, more piercing; it was obvious they were getting on the players' nerves.

A thick-necked guard with a gap between his front teeth glared at Rivka as he ran by. "If you don't shut that kid's mouth, I'll do it for you!"

When Yitzhak burst into tears, wailing and flailing his arms, his mother did everything she could to soothe and distract him.

"Stop that, Mommy. *Put me down. Put! Me! Down*!"

The ball came to the gap-toothed guard; he missed

it. His head had been turned toward the boy's incessant cries.

"I WANNA PLAY, I WANNA—"

Rivka clapped her hand over her son's mouth with so much force that his curls whiplashed. The blow shocked him into silence. Too late. The guard was running toward them.

"You wanna play, sonny? I'll play with you." He grabbed Yitzhak by his blond head and pulled until Rivka, afraid her son's neck would break, loosened her grip on him. Tossing the little boy up in the air like a ball, the guard drew his pistol and fired. Yitzhak fell to the grass. Rivka dropped to her knees, rounding her back over him like a tortoise shell. The man holstered his gun but got off a powerful kick to her ribcage before rejoining the game that had been so rudely interrupted by the demands of her noisy Jewish child.

Nathan, on the other side of the field, was oblivious to what had happened until a wheelbarrow was rolled through the men's section with Yitzhak's tiny body flung across the corpses of the mother and son who'd been shot because they would not let go of each another. To keep from screaming, he bit the flesh of his lower lip clear through, but he did not tear his garments or rush after the wheelbarrow, realizing with absolute clarity that he was powerless to avenge his son's murder, that every Jew in the stadium was not just powerless but doomed, that they would surely be transferred to a place with more guards and more guns, with high walls, barbed wire, and killer dogs, but while they were still out in the open, he could break free. Just as Rivka had turned her back on the train and opted for survival, Nathan turned his back on the wheelbarrow. Survival would be his revenge. He couldn't save his wife or kill his son's executioner but if he could escape from the stadium and connect with the partisans, he might be able to kill dozens of Nazi assassins. Eventually, he would find his wife. Now, he would save himself.

For the second time since the start of Hitler's war, Nathan Levy slipped away from his captors, not in a laundry van this time but on his belly. He wormed his way between the legs of his fellow prisoners, flattened himself under the bleachers, and sprinted for the woods. The dogs would have had no trouble tracking him—his lip was gushing blood—but the guards never realized he was gone. They were too busy playing soccer.

THE CONCRETE DOORSTEP of Herman's butcher shop had leached its dampness into Zach's corduroy pants and sent a bone-deep chill through his body. All his life, he'd been wondering why, before unlocking her keyboard, his mother always grabbed her torso and murmured to the heavens. Now he wished he could blot out the guard, the gunshot, the kick. For the past seven years, since he'd first discovered the album, he had been badgering his father to tell him what happened to Yitzhak. Now he knew and he wished he had let his brother rest in peace, without details, without a story; the sight of his father's anguish had cracked open Zach's heart. Not once in his thirteen years had he been forced to look at anything he didn't want to see. Until now, he could avert his eyes. But yesterday he had become a man and today he *made* himself look. Made himself *see*. To look and to see could be torment; it could also be a moral act. If his parents were able to endure all that savagery, he would match their courage with his own, stare life down and keep looking long after others had stopped. To test his resolve, Zach turned toward the butcher's window and eyed each raw, repugnant item in the refrigerated case, one by one.

"What happened after the guard kicked Mama?" he finally asked.

Nathan frowned and shook his head. "Only she can tell you that. It's not my place. Don't ask me that again."

Snow was drifting down in soft swirls as Nathan, weary as an old man, grasped the butcher's doorknob, pulled himself to his feet, and retrieved the shopping bag. "Let's go home, Boychik."

Zach picked up the paper sack. The bagels were cold stones in his arms.

ZACH WOULD ALWAYS feel that he entered manhood not on his bar mitzvah day, but that Sunday when, entrusted with his parent's story, he vowed to fulfill the promise that would keep him connected to them long after they were gone. In November of his senior year in college, Rivka was diagnosed with breast cancer. Over Thanksgiving break, he told his parents he wanted to drop out of school to help Nathan take care of her, that he would go back to his classes after she got better, after she finished the surgery, chemo, and radiation. But she refused to undergo the operation and would not agree to treatments. She insisted he return to school and complete his studies.

"I've had enough," she said. "Papa will call you when it's time."

Nathan summoned Zach home in April. "Come quickly," his father sniffled into the phone. "Your mama has something she wants to tell you."

Zach flew to New York that afternoon. Rivka looked like a gray rag doll bundled into a heap of white bedclothes, a rag doll who, the moment he entered her room, beckoned him to sit on the bed, closer than they'd been to one another since she'd last given him a haircut nearly four years ago. He was astounded when she took his hand. What she wanted to tell him was this: He was blameless, a good boy, always a good boy, but after what happened, she couldn't be anyone's mother. It was simply impossible for her to hold or hug him. He would have bruised her ribs. He would have crushed her heart.

Tears slicked her wrinkled cheeks as she told him the part of the story his father had refused to divulge. The Nazis killed her baby then made her take care of their babies. After the guard's kick broke four of her ribs and ruptured her spleen, they nursed her back to health then ordered her to minister to the officers' children, her reputation as a pediatric specialist having preceded her to the soccer stadium. Rivka said she wanted to murder a German child, to make a German mother suffer the agony she had, but she couldn't bring herself to harm the little boy who had cardiac fibrosis, or the one with bladder cancer; she couldn't hurt the boy who had braces on both legs, or the one with a hearing problem and sad brown eyes. She couldn't hurt any of them. All she could do was treat them, alleviate their pain, and try to heal them. She hated herself for it, she said, but that was all she could do. So while Nathan was disappearing himself into the Polish forests, Rivka was performing lung surgery on German preemies. While Nathan was smuggling weapons, Rivka was treating a Nazi's child for rheumatic fever. While Nathan was forging passports, digging secret tunnels, and blowing up supply depots, Rivka was saving the lives of the next generation of SS officers and Jew-haters.

She squeezed Zach's hand. "Remember what you promised me?" she asked, staring deep into his eyes. "You'll do it? You'll make up for the ones I . . ."

As he did the night before his bar mitzvah seven years before, Zach promised his mother that he would marry a Jew and raise Jewish children. Then, he asked her permission to kiss her goodbye, and when her soft smile told him yes, gently, without touching her ribs, he leaned over and pressed his lips to Rivka's papery cheek.

HIS NEXT THREE years were bracketed by loss: his mother died just before Zach started law school, his father, shortly before he graduated. Though Nathan remained fit and powerful to the end, dementia was the one enemy he could not dodge. Alzheimer's kidnapped the man, father, friend, worker, walker, and lontzman. Each time Zach came home on break, his father showed new signs of mental deterioration: in restaurants, Nathan tried to eat off other people's plates; shaving, he cut himself; showering, he scalded himself; cooking, he burned himself. Though no longer able to work, he walked to Manhattan several times a week, once barefoot in the snow. The night he was found wandering around inside Macy's after hours with no idea who he was or where he lived, Zach set the wheels in motion for his father's admittance to the Memory Disorders floor at the Jewish Home for the Aged.

"You know this place, Pop," he said, reassuringly, as a staff member led them to a dorm room with heavy locks on the windows and door. "You used to send me here every Sunday morning with our leftovers. They're going to take good care of you."

Nathan looked at him blankly, having long since forgotten Zach's name.

Months later, the director of the Jewish Home sounded almost as embarrassed as distressed when he phoned Zach to report that Nathan had gone missing; somehow, despite the security guards, barred windows, and locked doors, Mr. Levy had slipped out of the building. Never happened before. Can't imagine how he pulled it off. None of us can believe it. But Zach believed it; stealth was his father's default, escape his forte. After three interminable days, Nathan's body washed up on the shore of Orchard Beach, a denouement that allowed his son to imagine his final hours—the long hike to Pelham Bay Park along their familiar route, a stop at the venerable old oak tree, then on to the lagoon, where Nathan simply waded into the water and chose not to swim.

When Zach went to collect his father's belongings at the Jewish Home, the resident psychiatrist mentioned having looked in on Nathan the night before he disappeared.

"He was davening, rocking back and forth. I'm Jewish so I recognized that he was saying the Sh'ma. All three paragraphs by heart," the man commented, admiringly. "He didn't use a prayer book."

Zach demurred. "You must be confusing my father with someone else. He hasn't said a word in months, you know that. And I know he stopped praying years before he stopped talking. My dad quit doing anything Jewish three years ago when my mom died. He was a confirmed Atheist."

"It was definitely him," the doctor insisted, kindly. "Nathan Levy. And he davened like someone who's been doing it his whole life. Except he said the first line of the Sh'ma in a weird way—one word at a time, really slowly—and repeated it three times."

Zach flashed on Nathan's mantra crossing the icy stream.

"With our patients who were raised observant," the doctor continued, "this isn't unusual behavior. The constant repetition of prayers and blessings throughout a person's childhood can carve deep grooves in the developing brain. Even after they've forgotten everything else, these guys remember how to pray."

CHAPTER 4
NOT QUITE PERFECT

ONE BLAZING HOT DAY, THE SUMMER AFTER HIS FATHER died, Bonnie Bertelsman accosted Zach in front of his office building and thrust a clipboard at him.

"Got a minute for a kid?" she demanded.

He had graduated from law school in May, a twenty-three-year-old wunderkind, started his job at the ACLU even before he passed the bar exam, and found his cases so engrossing that sometimes, as happened on that steamy August day, he would forget to eat lunch. It was two-thirty in the afternoon before he finally left the office to grab a sandwich.

"Can't now, thanks." He tried to edge past her. He was ravenously hungry.

She glided sideways, obstructing his passage. "Ten seconds is all it takes." She yanked a ballpoint out of her elastic ponytail holder, dragging a few strands of her long brown hair with it. "Just sign here."

"I don't sign things without reading the small print."

"Come on! It's a petition, not a subpoena." She tucked the stray lock behind her ear and stood firm.

"Sorry, I'm in a hurry." He was getting annoyed.

"I'll speed-read it for you," she said, and ripped through the text like one of those radio announcers delivering a frenzied disclaimer about a drug with serious side effects. The petition demanded that the city council allocate more funds for after-school programs so that latchkey kids could have adult supervision, safe play equipment, and healthy snacks. Partly because Zach agreed with those demands and partly because he was captivated by her perseverance—as well as the flecks of gold in her deep-set brown eyes, her sexy collarbones, and the flyaway tendril that had snaked down her neck—he accepted the pen.

She glanced at his signature. "Zach-a-riah Lee-vee!" she read aloud. "Thank you, Zach." With a brisk swing of her ponytail, she pivoted toward the next passerby, held out her clipboard, and asked if he had a minute for a kid.

"One second!" Zach called out, his hunger pangs suddenly eclipsed by a schoolboy crush. "Before you go . . ." The ponytail swung back. Her dark brows arched above eyes that said, "Make it quick." I need a lot more signatures. Don't waste my time. Thinking, stalling, fidgeting with his tie, Zach finally said, "I have a suggestion that might help your campaign."

She looked at him. "Okay, talk to me."

"Last summer I interned at a public interest law firm in Detroit where I helped organize a poor people's protest against increased water rates."

She folded her arms below her breasts, framing them.

"We picketed the homes of city council members—not their offices, their homes. The idea was to publicly humiliate them for voting for the increase and shame them into retracting it. I don't think politicians should be allowed to hide behind phrases like 'fiscal responsibility,' or 'budget shortfalls,' do you?"

"What happened to the rate increase?"

"Retracted."

She pumped her fist. "You're saying I should find out where our council members live and picket out front?"

"Not just you." Zach replied. "Get a bunch of angry parents to march around with you carrying signs—handmade signs. One person should shout, 'It's three o'clock. Do *you* know where your children are?' And everyone else should respond, 'No! Because our kids have no place to go!'"

She smiled. "I like it."

"Call a press conference so people can say how much they worry about their kids after school and how unfair it is to penalize children with working parents who can't afford private nannies. There's nothing wrong with your petition. But politicians ignore petitions every day of the week. I'm suggesting you try humiliation."

By now, he had her full attention; she was twirling her ponytail, the gold flecks in her eyes glinting in the sun. "That's a pretty polished presentation for a man in a hurry."

"It's just basic media strategy—give them a photo op, they'll show up."

"For whom do you usually strategize, pray tell?"

"I'm a staff attorney for the ACLU but I also do pro bono legal work for a nonprofit called Families of Holocaust Survivors. I advise them on things like advocacy, fundraising, coalition-building, you know the drill."

The girl shook her head. "Actually, I don't. I absolutely loathe nonprofit speak."

"FHS represents survivors and children of survivors who are fighting for reparations or restitution of what the Nazis stole from them—property, bank accounts, houses, insurance money, fine art. In plain language, I try to get their stuff back."

She seemed to be looking at him differently now. "Well, thanks for the picketing idea. And forgive me for browbeating you before."

"I'm the one who should apologize. I'm weird when I'm hungry."

"Come to think of it, I could use some fuel myself." She stuck the pen back in her ponytail and tucked the clipboard under her arm. "How about we do some coalition-building over lunch?"

Ten months later, Zach Levy married Bonnie Bertelsman in the Crystal Room at the Tavern on the Green and felt like the luckiest man in the world—though he wondered why the universe had to take his father before giving him a wife, why his cosmic karma could not seem to tolerate two people loving him at the same time.

By then, he had become aware of other things Bonnie "absolutely loathed," among them, romantic platitudes and gratuitous references to female anatomy, which explained why, in his wedding toast, he avoided mentioning her sexy collarbones. Zach knew she considered beauty to be "an unearned attribute"—like inherited wealth and privilege—and therefore undeserving of approbation. So, he told their wedding guests that he had fallen in love with Bonnie's passion for justice, her moral probity, her candor, and her fighting spirit, all of which was true. But so was her beauty. He also told everyone that while his parents had not lived to see this day, there was no doubt in his mind that they would have been thrilled by his choice because his bride was perfect.

Bonnie's wedding toast, which she had insisted come after Zach's, was the verbal embodiment of the woman herself: quirky, idealistic, and endearing—also doctrinaire, sanctimonious, and slightly irritating. However, like all her friends, he took the smug with the sweet because her motives were clearly selfless. Standing beside her at the microphone, besotted, Zach hardly noticed that her remarks were less a declaration of love than an ideological proclamation.

"I'm sure you've all noticed I'm wearing a simple cotton dress," she began. "My dear parents wanted to buy me a gown with a train, tiara, and veil, but that's not me. And it's not Zach. Both of us felt kind of weird about having a big shindig at the Tavern on the Green while millions of our fellow citizens are hungry and homeless, but we wanted to celebrate with all our friends and my wonderful, enormous, extended family so we agreed to let Mom and Dad give us the wedding. Unfortunately, Zach's father died shortly before Zach and I met; he lost his mother when he was in college and he has no other living relatives, which is why every family member here is from my side. But my aunts, uncles, and cousins adopted him wholeheartedly and he loves them, too, so I know he joins me in thanking all of you for coming from near and far to share our happiness. And, I'm sure none of you give a fig what I'm wearing.

"Instead of spending a fortune on an outfit I would wear for one day, I asked my parents to donate the equivalent amount of money to Women Strike for Peace and a couple of other groups working to end the Vietnam War, and since Mom and Dad are great people with great politics and they love me hugely, that's exactly what they did. Then I went to Macy's and bought this lovely frock for $69.95—and my new husband just told me I look like a million bucks."

Affirmation came as a round of applause.

"We also decided not to spend money on fancy centerpieces. Instead, as you can see, there's a beautiful doll on each table that was handmade by a women's craft collective in Guatemala. You might think we did this to be politically correct—I'm often accused of that—[*laughter*] but wouldn't *you* prefer to support women's economic self-sufficiency than some Park Avenue florist? Now, listen up everyone: check the underside of your service plate. If there's a Band-Aid stuck to it, you're the lucky person at your table who gets to take the doll home. Please give it to your favorite little girl—*or boy*—with love from me and Zach."

After much clinking of china and table-by-table eruptions of "I got the Band-Aid!" Bonnie went on. "Speaking of giving, we don't need stemware, silver, ice crushers, or knife sharpeners. If you want to give us a gift, we'd prefer it be a contribution in honor of our marriage. Just send a check to a worthy cause like Planned Parenthood or the Sierra Club or . . ."

"The ACLU!" Zach interjected, leaning into the microphone. "Don't forget, they pay my salary!"

Bonnie grinned. "And boy, does he earn it!" She turned to her groom and raised her glass. "To the kindest, most principled man I've ever known. For everything you are, and everything you do, I love you, Zachariah Levy. Thank you for signing my petition."

THEY HONEYMOONED IN Costa Rica, five days hiking in the Monteverde Cloud Forest, five picking beans on a small fair-trade coffee plantation in Llano Bonito. Back in New York, they found a cheap rental on Spring Street—a floor-through loft with huge windows, wide-planked wooden floors, in a former warehouse with a cast-iron facade, gargoyles, and Doric columns—and furnished it with Bonnie's family hand-me-downs. They cooked dinner together every night and ate at a small table pulled close to the windows that overlooked other buildings with cast-iron facades. They drank cheap Chianti from jugs wrapped in straw and talked about what each of them did that day. They watched the news of the summer unfold on TV—Watergate, the Nixon tapes, the President's resignation—and made love, sometimes in bed and sometimes, when they couldn't wait, on the wide-planked floor.

Contentment was not something Zach Levy took for granted. He was grateful for his wife, for his marriage, and for his work, which, rewarding in itself, also had begun to earn plaudits from his peers. Bonnie opened a small store in the East Village and sold artifacts from the progressive political campaigns and social movements of the nineteenth and twentieth centuries—women's suffrage handbills, labor union leaflets, civil rights buttons, antiwar posters, antinuke bumper stickers, mimeographed position papers from a wide array of women's liberation groups. She named her shop, "Solidarity Forever." Zach called it, "The Little Shop of Lost Causes."

He admired his wife almost as much as he loved her, but, despite that line in his toast, he discovered she wasn't perfect. Her rigidity could be infuriating; once she took a position, there was no budging her, so unless he was prepared for a major argument, Zach thought twice before differing with her on anything that she cared about. As comfortable as he was confronting his legal adversaries, conflict on the home front made him anxious. He seemed to have inherited his mother's aversion to the raised voice and his father's commitment to keep the peace.

Sports was the only issue on which Zach pushed back. Growing up playing stickball in the streets of the Bronx, rooting for the Yanks or Knicks, and memorizing box scores and stats, he had felt like a normal all-American boy, rather than the heir to a European catastrophe. Sports had provided refuge from the oppressive atmosphere in his parents' apartment and the horrific images that sporadically flashed through his skull. Bonnie, however, "absolutely loathed" sports and expressed her antipathy not just in disinterest but disdain, shunning anything that required physical exertion, involved a ball, or required keeping score. Her passions were politics and history, fiction and poetry, theater and movies, activism and sex. Her views brooked no contradiction: Professional athletes were mercenaries who sold themselves to the highest bidder and endorsed sneakers most kids couldn't afford. Sports fans were fanatics who drank the Kool-Aid. Fandom was a capitalist conspiracy to dull the pain of poverty and distract workers from their grievances. She often said that were it not for home team hype and the "we won, they lost" mentality, millions of Americans would long ago have taken to the streets demanding higher wages, better working conditions, and universal health care.

Bonnie told him she'd been seduced into partisanship only once—when Billie Jean King played Bobby Riggs in the so-called "Battle of the Sexes." After the middle-aged Riggs taunted the country's top-ranked female tennis players, bragging that he could beat any of them—and Margaret Court, then the number one woman in the country, took Riggs on and suffered a humiliating loss, on Mother's Day, yet—the headlines were unavoidable, even for Bonnie. Riggs's arrogance having raised her hackles, she watched the telecast from the Houston Astrodome along with sixty million other people and felt euphoric when the feminist icon beat the male chauvinist pig in straight sets. As far as Bonnie was concerned, it wasn't a tennis match, it was gender warfare.

When Zach watched an occasional ball game on TV or attended a sports event, she raised no objection, so he was unprepared for her reaction when they were going over their monthly bills and she lit into him for wanting to re-up at the gym.

"A year's membership costs as much as some people's rent," she said. "I think it's obscene to spend that kind of money on your body."

"And I think it's important to stay fit." Zach opened the checkbook. "You're way too sedentary, Bonnie. A protest march doesn't qualify as a workout."

"If you need exercise so badly, go volunteer with Habitat for Humanity. Build a house. Paint a school. Clean up the waterfront."

"Don't be ridiculous. I work ten hours a day. I have a full-time job."

"If you have time to jump around on those machines, you have time to do something useful." Bonnie reached for the checkbook. Zach held it close and shook his head ruefully. His back was up now.

"I'm already doing something useful," he said. "I've got a huge workload. I'm under a lot of pressure. You want me to work out at the gym or have a heart attack like your Uncle Sid?"

Of her six well-loved uncles, Sid had been Bonnie's favorite. "Okay, forget it," she murmured, as graceful a retraction as Zach would get from his wife on any subject. In the end, he wrote the check to the gym for a two-year membership at a discount price. He also persuaded Bonnie to walk to her shop a couple of days a week, rather than take the bus. Then she got pregnant—without meaning to, and far earlier in the marriage than they'd intended, though they were thrilled nonetheless—and suddenly, she was as interested in health and fitness as he was.

"I think I'm going to stop by the gym," she announced, one morning. "I hear they have special classes for pregnant women."

In her fourth month, Bonnie came home with a book of baby names that had separate alphabetized sections for girls and boys, each name followed by its meaning and biblical, ethnic, or national origin.

"Aren't you jumping the gun?" Zach asked, remembering his mother's superstition. "I've heard it's bad luck to name a baby before it's born."

"That's just an old wives' tale—or an old husband's," she grinned. "Come on, let's pick out some names. It'll be fun."

He opened the refrigerator and took out a blueberry yogurt. "Want one?"

"No, thanks," she flipped the pages of the book. "You tell me your favorite girls' names and I'll tell you what they mean."

Zach pulled off the yogurt lid. "I've never thought about baby names," he replied, though, of course, he had. "All I know is Jewish people are supposed to name a baby after someone in the family who died."

Bonnie found a yellow highlighter in the pencil cup near the phone and made a few marks in the name book.

Zach stirred up the fruit. "You're lucky your parents are still alive . . ."

"Thank God! Poo-poo-poo!" she said, a poor imitation of the Eastern European Jews who, whenever someone said something positive about them, spit out a "thpu-thpu-thpu" sound to stop the evil eye from jinxing their good luck. "My Uncle Sid's been dead for a while, but I'm not ready to name a child after him. I don't think I could bear it. Now listen while I try out a few girls' names on you." She scanned the page. "How about . . ."

Zach interrupted, "Rebecca is a beautiful name. I really like Rebecca."

"I'm sure you do. I know Rebecca's English for Rivka, but I don't think it's a good idea for our daughter." Bonnie said, flipping through the pages and stopping now and then to use the highlighter. "How do you feel about Fiona?"

"Fiona's not a Jewish name," Zach barked, as if its Scottish-Irish origin was what bothered him. Stunned by her blunt rejection of Rebecca, he quickly spooned up the last of his yogurt and threw the container in the trash. "Why are you in the Fs anyway?"

"For my Aunt Frieda," Bonnie said, blandly.

"Are you saying we shouldn't name our girl after my *mother*, but we should name her after a Great Aunt you hardly ever saw? How many times did you visit your Aunt Frieda in the ten years before she died?"

Bonnie turned the name book face down on the counter and approached him. "My Aunt Frieda was a cheery, jolly woman. I don't know how to say this kindly, Zach, but from what you've told me, your mom was a tortured soul. She had every reason to be traumatized, still . . ."

Zach flinched. The expression on Bonnie's face was both compassionate and uncompromising. She stroked his hair. "I'm sorry but I really feel strongly about this, Zach. I just don't think it's fair to saddle our baby with such a tragic backstory; it's bad karma."

He pushed her hand away. "On that basis no one would ever name a child after someone killed in the camps."

"That's fine with me." Bonnie went back to the counter and snapped a banana off the bunch. "There are other ways to memorialize Holocaust victims. Besides, you're the last person in the world who needs another reminder of the dead." She peeled the banana in three smooth pulls. "Just yesterday you were wallowing in some old misery."

Yesterday, they'd been forced to evacuate the building because of a gas leak in the neighborhood and while they were out in the street waiting for Con Edison to check the source of the problem, Zach had made the mistake of telling Bonnie about Etty Moskowitz.

ZACH HAD BEEN doing his math homework when Rivka said she smelled gas and sent him to find the super. He decided to take the back stairs. Two floors below, the smell hit him full blast. He knocked loudly on the Moskowitz's kitchen door several times then turned the handle and let himself in. Etty was kneeling on the floor with her head inside the oven, her body limp, a towel tented over her head to trap the fumes.

At fifteen, he could not believe that a woman who had survived Treblinka, made it to America, married a kind man, and had four sweet kids would end her own life. Especially the way she did it. Gas was the terror of the camps. Both of Etty's parents had been exterminated in the gas chambers. Yet she chose gas. Or maybe that's why she chose it.

She was Zach's first "survivor suicide." There would be others—Primo Levi's being the most notable—but it was her death that brought home the power of survival guilt. It also gave Zach the idea that his mother might kill herself. After they came home from Etty's funeral, he asked his parents if either of them had ever considered ending their lives. Nathan said he wouldn't give Hitler the satisfaction. Rivka said she owed it to the Six Million to stay alive, but if not for the Torah's commandment to "choose life," she would have done herself in years ago.

"Your mama's upset about Etty," Nathan had put in, quickly. "She doesn't mean it."

Something in Zach changed after Etty Moskowitz died. He developed a morbid fascination with the Holocaust, the workings of the concentration camps, the Nazi killing machine, and specifically Zyklon B. He learned that twelve cans of the German gas—hydrogen cyanide crystals that released their toxins when heated to twenty-seven degrees Celsius—could only incinerate fifteen hundred prisoners per day and when the ovens couldn't keep up with the output of the gas chambers, bodies were dumped in a giant pit and set afire. There were times when Zach thought he smelled the stench of Auschwitz on University Avenue, times when the Bronx became Birkenau in his mind, times when, during a walk with his father in Pelham Bay Park, he saw a cop in high leather boots turn into a Nazi commandant. In the steam room at the schvitz, a skinny old man morphed into a cadaverous inmate. The shower fixtures in the locker room at DeWitt Clinton High School became gas jets. And on Saturday, when Zach and Gary Elkind were jammed up against one another in a packed subway car on their way to the theater district to see *Fiddler on the Roof*, the D train turned into a cattle car.

The first year that the Holocaust visions appeared, they freaked him out. But after enduring a dozen or more of them, he realized he could simply wait them out and they would dissipate, like a sudden dizzy spell. An occasional vision seemed a small price to pay for having escaped his brother's fate. He called them "flare-ups," not flashbacks, because how could a kid flash back to something he had never witnessed?

WHILE CON ED WAS checking the pipes under Spring Street and Zach and Bonnie were waiting to be allowed back in their building, he had told her about Etty's suicide but not that Holocaust hallucinations still visited him now and then. Why make a big deal about something he couldn't change?

"I wasn't wallowing in misery yesterday," he countered, watching her eat her banana and finding it erotic despite himself. "I was recalling a sad childhood memory. The gas leak triggered it."

"That's my point. You don't need any more triggers. You have enough sad memories as it is." Bonnie marked another baby name with the highlighter and folded down the corner of that page. "Hey! What about Emma? I *love* Emma, don't you?"

"Let me guess: Emma, as in Goldman? While you're in the E's, why not Eleanor, as in Roosevelt?" Zach meant it sarcastically.

"Great idea!" she raved.

"I'm holding out for Rebecca," Zach replied, annoyed. He plopped down in front of the TV and turned on the Mets game.

"And *I'm* holding firm against the intergenerational transmission of trauma," Bonnie said, before she put on her Walkman earphones and looked up Eleanor in the book.

They argued about baby names for the next four months. Bonnie refused to entertain anything beginning with a Y for Yitzhak but she did agree, if they had a boy, to name him Nathaniel. In return, Zach gave up on Rebecca. For a girl, they compromised on Anabelle, an amalgam of the names of one deceased relative from each of their families, neither of whom had died tragically: Bonnie's Great Aunt Anna, who petered out at ninety-two, and Zach's maternal grandmother, Belle, who expired of an ordinary heart attack before he was born. Bonnie declared unilaterally that Anabelle would also be named in memory of Anna Strunsky, the radical writer who was a Socialist, Quaker, war resister, and cofounder of the NAACP; and in honor of Bella Abzug, the crusading feminist Congresswoman, former union lawyer and indefatigable political activist, who had just introduced in the House the first federal gay rights bill in US history—and who was famous for wearing big-brimmed hats.

Anabelle Emma Eleanor Bertelsman Levy was born on November 24, 1975.

HER TAFFETA PARTY dress stained with cranberry sauce and pumpkin pie, Anabelle had fallen asleep in her car seat on the drive home from Bonnie's parents' house on Long Island. The smears of chocolate icing on the baby's cheeks were evidence of her birthday having fallen this year on Thanksgiving, and her grandmother having added a birthday cake to the feast. Zach had congratulated himself for successfully carrying her to her room, undressing her, washing off the icing, and putting her to bed without waking her. He was at the sink trying to floss out the shred of turkey that had wedged between his molars, when Bonnie appeared in the frame of the bathroom door wearing a flannel nightgown the color of smog.

"There's no right way to say this, Zach." His wife paused to tug at her sleeve. "I've met someone. I want a divorce."

Later he supposed he should have been grateful for her blunt delivery but just then all he could do was grab the sink to steady himself and try to keep her face in focus in the mirror. The spray of freckles on her nose had blurred since he'd last taken note of it, her cheeks paled, the roses on her nightgown faded, as if, in retreating from the marriage, she'd been blanched. There was a bow at the neck of her nightgown, a soft, girlish tie that suited the flannel if not the chiseled plane of his wife's jaw. He zeroed in on the knot of the bow for ballast.

"It's not your fault," she said. "It's nobody's fault. It just happened. Last summer, the night of the blackout when I got stranded at O'Hare. I went to Chicago that day, remember?"

Zach remembered. Her Uncle Howard, recently widowed, was selling his house in Skokie and moving to an assisted living residence, and had to get rid of everything in his attic, including his mementos from the Spanish Civil War. A proud veteran of the Abraham Lincoln Brigade—the cadre of idealistic American volunteers who fought against Franco in the late 1930s—Howard was a hero to his niece who feared that his collection would fall into unappreciative hands or, worse yet, get tossed on the junk heap by someone who didn't recognize its value. On Thursday, July 13, 1977, Bonnie had hopped a plane to Chicago to rescue it and that evening, had called Zach from O'Hare with good news and bad news. The good news was her uncle's cache was a bonanza, one of the pictures might even be a Robert Capa. The bad news: because of the lightning strike that had knocked out the electrical grid in New York, all flights to the region had been canceled. Zach remembered that night well; Manhattan was a zoo, plunged into darkness, people walking in the middle of the street, traffic lights snafued, phone circuits overloaded. He'd been amazed her call got through.

"Remember I told you the airline was giving out meal tickets and putting us up in a hotel overnight?" Bonnie stared at him in the bathroom mirror. "Please don't look so blank. I was in Chicago. You were here. Remember?"

Until he caught a glimpse of the dental floss dangling from his lips like drool, Zach thought he had absorbed her opening salvo and kept his dignity. Not quite, it seemed. He yanked out the floss and flicked it into the trash. "Chicago. Blackout," he repeated, sounding idiotic, even to himself.

"Right. Well." Bonnie looked away, as if the sight of him was too pitiful to behold. She pulled at the shower curtain, white sailboats silhouetted against a blue sea, her fingers pleating its folds. "Anyway, when I called you, I had no idea what was about to happen."

What happened, she said, was Gil Benedict, an Australian magistrate, who'd been attending an international judicial conference in Chicago and was similarly stranded. The two of them had met, meal vouchers in hand, at the coffee shop in the airport hotel. It was crowded. The hostess asked if they would mind sharing a table. Most innocent situation in the world, Bonnie said, except that by the end of dinner, a fever burned inside her, feelings she had never experienced before. "We talked until the restaurant closed." Bonnie was crimping the edge of the shower curtain like a piecrust. "The next morning, when the airport reopened, we flew back to LaGuardia together, postponed Gil's return flight to Melbourne, booked a room at the Hilton, and saw each other on the sly every day for a week. I truly regret deceiving you, Zach, I know it sounds crazy, but I'm in love."

Mundane phrases like "whirlwind courtship," "head over heels," and "once in a lifetime" spilled from her lips, and then a sentence that knocked the breath out of Zach. "Obviously, an Australian magistrate can't make a living in the United States but I can open a branch of my shop in Melbourne, broaden my inventory, expand the mail-order side of the operation, carry more international stuff—the Russian Revolution, the Greens, the ANC, the IRA . . ."

"Are you *crazy*, Bonnie? You're not moving to *Australia*!"

"Melbourne," she said, quietly. "We'll need several months to get organized but Gil should have everything settled in time for me to enroll Anabelle in nursery school. In Australia they take kids under three if they're toilet trained."

"Anabelle?" Zach said, weakly.

"She'll *have* to come with me," Bonnie said in her most declarative tone. "A little girl needs her mother. But you can visit whenever you like for as long as you like. I've already thought it through. Until she's old enough to travel on her own, I'll bring her to New York for Thanksgiving at my parents' place, as always, then I'll bring her here to the loft for the whole month of December and you'll have her all to yourself until New Year's. Promise I'll keep out of your way; I'll hang out on Long Island with my folks. You'll come to Melbourne every July and stay with us. Gil's building a new extension, I've seen the plans, a lovely guest suite that's separated from the rest of the house by a breezeway, so you and Anabelle will have complete privacy while you're there." Bonnie paused for a breath. "I wouldn't be surprised if you end up spending more time with her than you do now. People tell me that's a common by-product of divorce. It makes better fathers."

Wife. Leaving. Taking. Anabelle. Paralyzed, Zach watched Bonnie release the shower curtain and, as if preparing for bed on any ordinary night, squeeze a thin snake of Crest on the bristles of her toothbrush, and scrub her teeth methodically, front to back, gum to edge, then rinse her mouth and wipe her lips with the towel marked, YOURS. The monogrammed set—YOURS, MINE, OURS—had been his surprise gift for her, all three towels arrayed side by side on the rod when he brought her and Anabelle home from the hospital. He felt like ripping Yours to shreds.

"Fuck you, Bonnie."

"Come on, now." She capped the toothpaste. "I know it's a big shock and I'm sorry, but there's no going back, so let's be adults about it, okay?"

"Are you out of your mind? You meet some damn Aussie in a coffee shop, ditch your husband like a bad date, and *I'm* supposed to be the adult?" Zach slammed down the toilet seat so hard its lid cracked. "How can you *do* this, Bonnie?!"

Fear flickered in her eyes then quickly vanished. Calmly, she padded back across the tiled floor and, as if tucking a blue blouse into a white skirt, calmly arranged the shower curtain inside the rim of the tub. "I'm *really* sorry," she said and patted his arm. "I don't know what else to say."

More than the bedrock in her voice, it was her maternal pat that told Zach his marriage was over. He looked her up and down in her granny nightgown. "I bet you don't wear flannel with Gil. I bet you wear satin for him."

"Her," Bonnie corrected him. "Gil's short for Gillian."

CHAPTER 5

A FATHER IN WINTER

THE DIVORCE BECAME FINAL THE FOLLOWING JULY AND his ex-wife and daughter were gone before Labor Day. Zach anesthetized himself with alcohol, a too-heavy caseload, and obsessive workouts. Bonnie had been unfailingly accommodating throughout the separation process, agreeing to leave behind most of Anabelle's toys, books, and clothes so her room would look familiar when she arrived in December for her first visitation. That turned out to be a mixed blessing. More like a shrine, it was no longer a lived-in, played-in space, but at least her things were there to help him conjure his absent little girl.

A week after they had decamped for Melbourne, a large envelope arrived with a chatty letter from Bonnie describing their long flight, along with snapshots of Gil's house and a heart-searing photo of Anabelle at her new nursery school. It didn't take a picture of his daughter to bring Zach to tears; all it took was the discovery of her hair clip in his coat pocket, the sight of her yellow rain boots in the hall, or the line of tiny garments hanging in her closet. Some mornings before leaving for work, Zach would open her closet door, run his hand along the hangers, and mourn his loss—the miracle of the ordinary, the simple pleasure of helping her button her blouse or tie her shoes. At night, in lieu of tucking her in, he would hug the Big Bird shirt she'd worn on the last day he walked her to nursery school or the powder-blue snowsuit he'd bought for her at Gap Kids after she fell in the Central Park lake and got drenched.

That Saturday Bonnie had to be at her shop so she wasn't with them when Zach loaded his backpack with breadcrumbs and took Anabelle up to the park to feed the ducks. They had stationed themselves in the gazebo at the water's edge where the mallard ducks always swam close to the shore and gobbled up crumbs as fast as she could throw them. A pair of turtles with shells the size of dinner plates had suddenly surfaced about a yard away, and Anabelle, thrilled, had leaned forward, lost her balance, and toppled into the water. For a split second, Zach had flashed on the old dream, his brother's blond curls going under, but Anabelle's puffy pink parka kept her afloat long enough for him to scoop her out of the lake before her face got wet. Dripping but undaunted, she'd giggled as Zach clutched her to his chest and jogged over to Broadway, where he remembered having seen a Gap Kids. He'd bought her an entirely new outfit: underwear, long-sleeved shirt, sweater, tights, fleece-lined boots, and a hooded, powder-blue, one-piece snowsuit to replace the soggy pink parka, as well as a Snoopy towel to wipe her dry. The clerk at the cash register snipped the tags off his purchases and Zach hustled Anabelle into a fitting room where he removed her wet clothes and redressed her top to toe, then he had carried her back to the park and they'd gone directly to the carousel. At home, she had recounted their adventures to her mother while he threw her soggy clothes in the washer and, though the pink parka came out good as new, from then on she would only wear the blue snowsuit. Before they left for Australia, she insisted it remain in her New York closet so she could wear it to feed the ducks when she came home in December. *Home*. Zach had nearly wept.

Without his wife and daughter, colors dimmed, figures blurred, voices grated. He could not stop thinking about Bonnie, how he could have missed her deceit, why he hadn't sensed her betrayal. Could he ever again trust his perceptions? How was it possible for love to leak out of one partner's heart while the other's remained full? He hated himself for his weakness, for not fighting for his marriage, for letting Bonnie take his daughter away.

"A lawyer who represents himself has a fool for a client." Everyone knows that, yet somehow, he had signed on to a visitation schedule that consigned him to six weeks of frost-bound fatherhood—Anabelle would come to New York in December, the coldest, darkest month of the year, and Zach would spend two weeks in Melbourne in July, the start of the Down Under winter. No wonder he would come to associate his daughter with the flu.

At about three o'clock in the morning, a few months after they were gone, Zach was lying in bed revisiting his mistakes for the thousandth time when his sorrow weighed so heavily on his chest that he felt he would suffocate if he didn't get some air. Throwing off the covers, he grabbed the blue snowsuit and climbed out onto the fire escape. What killed him was not that his wife had left him for a woman—her abandonment would have been no less excruciating had she fallen for a man—it was the asymmetrical custody arrangement that gave him his daughter only twice a year, always in winter, only in winter.

Out on the fire escape, clad in nothing but a T-shirt and boxers, he bunched the blue snowsuit around his neck like a muffler, looked down at the yard, and wondered whether a flying leap six stories to the ground would put an end to his anguish or merely cripple him. There were no trees or bushes to cushion his fall, only hard packed dirt in the area between the rear of his building and the surrounding warehouses and tenements. While staring down, imagining his fatal splat, a sudden movement snagged his eye, the slanted doors to the basement pushed open, a figure in dark pants and a hooded sweatshirt emerging with a bundle in his arms wrapped in a blanket. Zach's breath froze in his lungs as the man carried his burden to the far corner of the yard, set it down, dashed back inside, and reappeared moments later with a long-handled shovel. The man gouged at the crusty earth and dug up clods of earth until a small rectangle took shape. From the dimensions of the cavity, Zach knew it was a child's grave.

Like the voyeur in *Rear Window*, he was riveted to the scene except that it wasn't a movie, it was happening in real time. He crept back inside, dialed 911 and described, quickly and coherently, what he had witnessed. Then, intending to restrain the man until the police arrived, he raced down the six flights of stairs and out the basement door into the yard.

"Jesus, Zach. Thank God it's you!"

"M. J.! What the fuck!"

The man gestured to the bundle on the ground. "It's Possum," he sobbed. "Poor girl was looking right at me when she passed, eyes blue as pilot lights. I think she was begging me to let her go."

"Why didn't you come get me, for Christ's sake?"

"Didn't want to wake you," M. J. said, his craggy cheeks glossed with sweat. "I've got to bury her quick and quiet or the city's gonna hit me with a summons."

As if on cue, two squad cars screeched to a stop on the street out front and four cops charged into the yard, brandishing pistols. "Hands up! Both of you!"

Zach raised his bare arms in the air.

The red-haired officer aimed his gun at M. J. "Drop the shovel, mister! Hands above your head!"

The man complied. An officer with a Zapata mustache snapped handcuffs on M. J. while a third cop, skinny, with a boyish face, manacled Zach's wrists. Aware of how ludicrous they must appear, one nearly naked with a child's snowsuit draped around his neck, one dressed for graveyard duty, Zach assumed the just-the-facts tone that years of courtroom exposure had taught him law enforcement officers preferred.

"I'm Zach Levy. I'm the one who called 911. I'm an

attorney. This is M. J. Randolph. We're friends and neighbors up on the sixth floor. I'm sorry I got you guys over here for nothing. I misperceived the situation."

"*Misperceived the situation*, did you?" mimicked the red-haired cop. He had an Irish accent and seemed to be in charge.

Zach was so cold his skin looked like elephant hide. "I couldn't sleep so I went out on the fire escape for some air. That's when I noticed someone carrying something down here in the yard. From six stories up, it looked like a child's body. It was dark so I didn't recognize my friend. And I didn't know Possum had died. I jumped to the wrong conclusion."

"Possum?"

Zach gestured toward the bundle. "I knew she had cancer, but M. J. didn't tell me she'd passed. He said he didn't want to wake me."

The skinny cop trained his revolver on Zach's neighbor while the cop with the mustache unwrapped the blanket.

"It's a goddamn dog!"

M. J. took a step forward and got a strong shove back. "I took good care of her, I made her home cooked meals," he moaned, and, as if his culinary claim required a credential, added, "I'm a chef."

The Irish cop shook his head. "I've never seen blue eyes on a dog."

"She's a Labrador," M. J. said.

The lead cop gestured to the other officers to unlock both sets of cuffs. "One of you might want to shut her eyes," he said to M. J. and Zach.

His hands trembling, his shoulders shuddering with grief, M. J. kneeled beside Possum's body and gently lowered her eyelids.

Zach had a feeling it wasn't every day that New York's Finest saw a grown man bawl over a dead dog.

"I need to say a few things about this, um, *situation*," said the lead officer. "City law permits the burial of a pet on its owner's property. Is this your building?"

"He rents," mumbled Zach. "We're all tenants."

"In that case, he has to bring her over to Animal Care Control on East 100th Street and give them fifty bucks to have her cremated. Otherwise, he has to put her in a heavy-duty garbage bag, label it 'dead animal,' and set it on the curb for the next sanitation pickup." With the jab of a thumb, the officer signaled his colleagues to leave the premises and when the basement door shut behind them, he laid a freckled hand on M. J.'s shoulder. "You didn't hear this from me, Mr. Randolph, but if I was you, I'd send your friend upstairs to put on some clothes and bring down another shovel."

M. J. WAS THE only one of Zach's friends who let him rant and cry and act as miserable as he felt. Others mouthed clichés like, "Time heals," or advice like, "Forget about the bitch." One tone-deaf pal assured Zach that Anabelle would do fine without him. ("Kids adjust faster than you think.") Months later, while he was still grieving, someone urged him to "reach closure" and move on with his life.

The rest of his buddies simply avoided mentioning his wife or daughter.

But ten minutes after Bonnie and Anabelle had moved out, M. J. had barged in with a bottle of Glenlivet Single Malt Whiskey in one hand, a platter of parmesan, prosciutto, and melon in the other, and a baguette stuck in the back pocket of his jeans like a flashlight. "I'm here to take the bull by the horns," M. J. announced. "You can buck and snort as much as you like but I'm sticking with you all night whether you like it or not. Now wrap a thin slice of prosciutto around a hunk of honeydew and dig in."

MILLARD JAMES RANDOLPH was a celebrity chef known for his humility, a Texan who'd never forgiven Lyndon Johnson for the Vietnam war, and the heir to an oil fortune who'd put half his inheritance into solar energy and the other half into starting Lovage, the first New York City restaurant with a farm-to-table menu.

"My granddaddy was rich before money became popular," he liked to say. "Couldn't find his ass with a flashlight but he struck black gold in his backyard."

The *Times* critic gave Lovage a two-star review that set it on firm footing from the start, but judging by his oven burns, knife scars, and sixteen-hour workdays, M. J. wasn't coasting on his inheritance, he was cooking for all he was worth. Yet he always found time for his friends, especially for Zach, who, after Bonnie and Anabelle left, spent more time in his neighbor's loft across the hall than in his own. M. J.'s red velvet sofa became Zach's therapy couch, a safe place to lament his life, and when his crying jags turned into eating binges, M. J. produced truffled mashed potatoes and fettuccine Alfredo no matter how loudly Zach protested from his prone position on the sofa.

"You just worked two shifts at the restaurant. I can order in."

"The hell you will," replied M. J. "If you want corn chips and Cheez Whiz, go eat with your jock friends. I specialize in comfort cuisine."

Six feet two and by his own description, "thinner than a stalk of celery," M. J. was the kind of guy who tells you the kind of guy he is, a habit made palatable by the accuracy of his self-assessments. "I'm an even-tempered fella, not neurotic like you East Coast types," he'd say. Or, "I got the energy of a rancher chasing a herd of runaway horses." "I'm a Fruit Loop in a box of Cheerios" was how he summed up his "happily homosexual" way of life. If you came to visit and found a small Texas flag stuck in his mail slot, you knew M. J. was in the midst of one of his "amorous endeavors." Otherwise, as he put it, "I'm an open door guy, so don't bother to knock 'cause I'm always going to be glad to see you, and if I'm not home, come on in and take what you need, 'cause if I *was* home, you know I'd give it to you."

M. J. offered compassion without pity and always had a positive spin on life. "Instead of complaining about how you're not gonna have enough time with Anabelle, you should plan a bunch of special outings so the time you *do* get to spend with her will be so much fun that she'll always look forward to comin' home." With M. J.'s persistent nudging, Zach spent hours researching diversions for his daughter—child-friendly restaurants, age-appropriate plays, movies, and museum exhibits. It was M. J.'s idea that Zach accumulate his sick leave and personal days so he could hang out with Anabelle on weekdays. And it was M. J. who suggested Zach make a big deal about Hanukkah. (Chef Randolph knew all the Jewish holidays because half of his restaurant clientele disappeared on those nights.)

That first year, Anabelle alighted like Tinker Bell, sprinkling pixie dust on her father's earthbound life and acting as if they'd been apart for days, not months. Everything they did together seemed to delight her—ice-skating in Rockefeller Plaza, outings to the Bronx Zoo, the aquarium, the puppet show in Central Park, the Staten Island Ferry. When weather was inclement, they stayed home and built castles out of blocks. He bought her wooden puzzles with pieces large enough for a toddler to handle, and boxes of cheap pipe cleaners that he helped her shape into eyeglasses, giraffes, and octopuses. When they played hide and seek, he pretended not to see her shoes sticking out from under the bed. On New Year's Day, when Bonnie picked her up to take her to the airport, Zach felt his heart split open. It broke twice a year from then on.

In July, he went to Melbourne. The flight was interminable but he would have commuted weekly just to be greeted by his ebullient little girl. As Bonnie had promised, Gil had built a wing with separate guest quarters and he was able to spend every waking hour with his daughter without interruption. The few times he interacted with his ex-wife and her lover—over coffee before Anabelle woke up or after she went to bed—he found them warm and welcoming.

In years two and three, the custody arrangement was less harrowing for being predictable. More than that, to her credit, Bonnie had routinized the communication between them and once Anabelle could read and write, he also received short letters from her that helped him feel less like a stranger. She seemed to have adapted well to the semiannual arrangement, but each time they parted, loneliness engulfed Zach like a cold winter fog.

As his daughter grew older, he adjusted their activities accordingly—added hikes in the Palisades or Bear Mountain State Park, bowling, ping pong, miniature golf, biking, and ball games, many ball games, because, to his utter astonishment, Anabelle had become an accomplished athlete and a spirited sports fan. The person Zach had to thank for this, he discovered, was Gil Benedict. Once ranked among Australia's elite women's tennis players, Gil had persuaded Bonnie that female athletes have more confidence than other girls. Though she always came to New York in winter, when their breath made gray steam in the cold air and their fingers froze, Zach coached Anabelle's pitching, honed her sliders, and felt as if he had something to offer her besides entertainment, devotion, and love.

The entire month of December and half of July were all Anabelle, all the time, but six weeks weren't enough for him. Nor was one child. He wanted more. "Be fruitful and multiply" was both a biblical obligation and his mother's last request. Of the two dictates, Rivka's was the more compelling and by failing to produce more fruit, Zach felt as if he were dishonoring her memory, squandering her sacrifices, and mocking the miracle of her survival. In the post-Holocaust world of his parents, an only child was anathema. Even two children didn't suffice. What's more, though much of his law practice was devoted to fighting gender discrimination, Zach wanted a boy, not for any specific boyness but to carry on the Levy name. If Anabelle had children, they would most likely bear her husband's name—still the custom, even for most feminists—and "Levy" would dead-end with Zach. For the sake of the father who had mothered him and the brother whose name had been snuffed out with his life, Zach had to produce a namesake.

The issue of Jewish continuity also weighed heavily on him. However rarely he showed up in synagogue, something in his DNA told him the tradition was worth preserving and transmitting. Since his parents' deaths, he had become a once-a-year Jew, not abstaining altogether, lest he tempt the evil eye, but always buying a High Holy Day ticket for the nearest shul, usually an overflow service presided over by a nervous rabbinic intern and a newly minted cantor. The rest of Zach's Jewish life was driven by random invitations—a rooftop sukkah party billed as a singles mixer; a Shabbos dinner at the home of a colleague; a "Matzoh Ball" party during passover; his friends' seders, where he realized that, given the choice, most hosts would rather have an eligible bachelor show up at their table than the prophet Elijah.

Meanwhile, Bonnie had joined a synagogue and enrolled their daughter in Melbourne's King David Academy, a Jewish day school and, by her account, she and Anabelle celebrated all the home-based Jewish holidays with the full support of Gillian Benedict. Gil had not only been scrupulously respectful of Judaism but had embraced Bonnie's lively hodgepodge of traditional practices and feminist inventions: women's seders, healing ceremonies, and life cycle rituals. Meanwhile, Zach's sole contribution to his daughter's Jewish life was Hanukkah.

Though the holiday isn't mentioned in the Torah and received lackluster attention in his childhood home, Hanukkah had become deeply meaningful to him because of Anabelle. Since her first visitation, he'd been determined to create enough Hanukkah hoopla to make Christmas pale in comparison. He took her shopping for a menorah at the Jewish Museum gift shop, where she chose one made of clay in the shape of a baseball team, eight players sitting on a bench, their caps serving as candle holders, the ninth player gripping a baseball bat that stood above the rest with a slot for the shamash. He bought her eight different dreidls—metal, wood, glass, and ceramic—and invented a different top-spinning game for each of the holiday's eight nights. He hid Hanukkah gelt all over the loft and she searched every corner to find the chocolate coins—all eighty of them. He gave her eight presents without worrying about spoiling her. Hanukkah was his excuse to show her that, despite their many months apart, he knew her taste and interests well enough to buy her eight things she really wanted.

They made Rivka's recipe for latkes. Anabelle peeled the Idahos, Zach grated them (and his knuckles). He cracked the eggs, she beat them. He measured the flour, she stirred the batter. She peeled the onions, he sliced and chopped them. When the onion fumes brought them to tears, Anabelle laughed at her daddy's bloodshot eyes.

The smell of pan-fried potato pancakes was what lured M. J. across the hall that first time. Zach had invited him to stay for candle lighting and latkes, and after pronouncing them "crispylicious," the chef had appropriated the recipe and his bite-size version of Rivka's latkes—topped with caviar and crème fraîche instead of sour cream or applesauce—became one of Lovage Restaurant's signature appetizers. Every December since, M. J. had joined them for at least one night of Hanukkah, adding his homemade sufganiyot, traditional Israeli jelly donuts, to the holiday meal. Anabelle taught her "Uncle M. J." to sing "I Have a Little Dreidl" and "Rock of Ages," (in Hebrew) and tried not to giggle at his Texas twang. Zach repeated the story of Hanukkah, how the tiny band of Maccabees rebelled against the Syrian Greeks who wouldn't permit them to practice their Judaism, how the Jews conquered the enemy, recaptured the temple that had been defiled, and hoped to rededicate the temple by lighting the holy lamp but only found enough oil to burn for one day.

"What happened next?" Zach asked Anabelle the year he'd let her light the candles for the first time.

"The oil burned for eight days," she replied proudly,

in her perky Aussie accent. "It lasted much longer than anyone expected; that's why we add one more candle each day until we have eight. We increase the light. My Hebrew teacher says Hanukkah is called The Festival of Lights because it's all about bringing light into the darkest days of winter." She picked up one of the dreidls and read out loud the Hebrew letters on the top's four sides. "Those initials stand for the words 'Nais gadol haya sham,' which means, 'A great miracle happened there.' But I think great miracles also happen *here*, and in Melbourne, or wherever a person brings light to a dark place."

M. J. whistled softly. "How'd you get so smart, little lady?"

Zach, shushing him, hugged his little girl. "Maybe that's why Hanukkah always reminds me of your grandma and grandpa. They weren't supposed to last either—but they did. They lived through a terrible time in a very dark place, but they didn't give up. They traveled across the ocean so I could be born in a country where the future was bright and no one could ever tell me, or you, that we can't be Jewish."

The glow of the candles, eight glittering points of light, glistened in Anabelle's dark eyes. "Grandma and Grandpa were like the oil," she said. "They lasted longer than anyone expected. They were miracles."

"We're all miracles," Zach said, swallowing hard. "Who wants another latke?"

CHAPTER 6
A NICE JEWISH GIRL

ONE YEAR AFTER THE DIVORCE, THANKS TO THERAPY, antidepressants, too much vodka, and meaningless sex—or maybe because he'd just turned thirty—Zach finally felt ready to move on. It was 1980, a new decade, time to turn a new leaf. He wanted help finding his bashert, the woman he was destined to marry.

"I'm looking to get married again, Herbie. Know any nice Jewish girls?"

After work one Friday, at the gym with Herb Black, director of the ACLU's Children's Rights Project, both of them pumping away on their adjacent Nautilus machines, Zach blurted through breathless gasps: "You need to set me up already."

"I don't know any more single women than you do," Herb panted.

"You have a million ex-girlfriends," Zach insisted.

Perspiration plastered Herb's "Reelect Carter" T-shirt to his chest. "I'm afraid most of the Jews I know are WASP wannabes."

"What's that—Jews who change their name from Schwartz to Black?"

Herb took the personal jab with grace. "I didn't change our family name, Doug did. And it's not like he stole it off the Yale Club roster. *Schwartz* is black in English—Doug just translated it from the German."

Yale, straight nose, blond hair, calling his parents by their first names—the whole package telegraphed Herb's tony origins. They'd been friends and ACLU colleagues for years yet Zach couldn't quite believe that Herb was in the tribe. And in a sense, he wasn't. Herb's "people" were German Jewish royalty, white-shoe Jews from the *Our Crowd* crowd. His father's ancestors emigrated from Baden in the 1850s, arriving with the family silver, cash to buy land, and trunks of salable merchandise. His mother's relatives were distant cousins of the Warburgs. Two of his great-grandfathers fought for Massachusetts in the Civil War, for God's sake, and all four of his grandparents, women included, were, at minimum, college graduates.

In Boston the Blacks were to shtetl Jews what the Kennedys were to shanty Irish: ethnic elites. (In fact, Doug and Miri had recently cohosted a fundraiser for Teddy's primary campaign against Jimmy Carter.) The Blacks had a big house in the Back Bay section, a box at the Boston Symphony, and seats over the dugout at Fenway. But they weren't Boston Brahmins; Miri (née Miriam), whose light verse had been published in *Granta* and the *Partisan Review*, helped the women's collective that wrote *Our Bodies, Ourselves*, served on the board of Planned Parenthood, and shopped at Filene's Basement, and Doug, a retired corporate lawyer who read James Joyce for fun, took death penalty appeals that no one else would touch.

Herb Black was proud of his parents for being traitors to their class and they, in turn, boasted about their son, not because he'd become a lawyer—the family had plenty of Esq. suffixes—but because he worked for the ACLU, which they'd been supporting since before he was born. What most impressed Zach about Herb's parents was their lack of angst. Where Rivka Levy had been taciturn and dour, Miri Black was chatty and cheerful. Where Nathan had been stolid, Doug was buoyant. If your relatives left Germany eighty years before Kristallnacht, Zach supposed, buoyant came easy.

He pressed the pulse in his neck and finding it insufficiently aerobic, upped the resistance on his Nautilus machine. "You and your parents could pass for WASPs in a heartbeat."

"Don't start," Herb cautioned. "I have no problem being Jewish."

"Not that you're a believer."

"Show me a Jew who believes in God."

They both laughed. "So," Zach asked, "what makes you Jewish?" Lately he'd been posing that question to every Jew who crossed his path, chalking it up to his identity search, which seemed to have been reignited by his search for his bashert.

"I don't dissect it, Zach. I'm *just* Jewish."

"Tell me one thing you do that's Jewish."

Herb thought for a moment. "Friendship. I have Jewish

friends. Causes. I write checks. Every five seconds, some Jewish organization is honoring Doug; I always buy a top price ticket to the gala." Herb wiped his face with the front of his shirt and slowed his machine to a crawl. "Did I mention I had a bar mitzvah? I'll never forget the strapless dress Laurel Plotkin wore to the reception and the ice swan with a raw bar on its back—clams, oysters, shrimp, crabs, lobster . . ."

"Shellfish at a bar mitzvah?" Zach clucked. He could see his teacher, Rabbi Goldfarb, spinning in his grave. "I hope someone had the wit to say, 'Mazel tov, Herbie! Today you are a clam.'"

"Enough with my Jewish bona fides," Herb said.

"Right. Let's get back to the wannabes. Define the species."

"A WASP wannabe is a Jewish girl who goes to France for the churches."

"That's called sightseeing, Herbie."

"Not when she genuflects at the stations of the cross, analyzes the symbolism in Annunciation murals, or 'ohs' and 'ahs' over statues of saints who slaughtered our ancestors during the Inquisition."

"Whoa!" Zach exhaled audibly. "For someone who's 'just Jewish,' you sound awfully ardent. Okay, don't fix me up with any wannabes."

"That complicates matters." Herb toweled off. "Let's go get some sushi. My treat."

THEY SETTLED INTO a booth at a minimalist Japanese restaurant and ordered a couple of Kirin beers. Warming to his matchmaker role, Herb asked, “Age limit?”

“Twenty-five to thirty-five,” Zach replied. Push it a year or two if she’s fertile.”

“How the hell do I gauge that?”

“If you know she’s had an abortion. Or she has kids. Or her sister has kids. Fertility runs in families.”

“Next you’ll want proof of virginity.”

“I don’t care if she slept with the Giants backfield. I just want some babies.”

“How pretty does she have to be?” Herb rubbed his chopsticks together like a Boy Scout trying to start a fire.

“Cute. Spunky.”

“I suggest you stop using those words if you’re going back on the dating market.”

“What’s wrong with ‘cute’ and ‘spunky’?”

“They’re so seventies.”

The waiter brought menus and squat gray cups of steaming tea. Zach burned the roof of his mouth on the first sip and cooled his palate with the icy beer.

“Blond, brunette, redhead?” Herb asked.

“No preference.”

“Shape?”

“Jesus, how can I answer that?”

“Don’t be coy. Every man has a type: supermodel, starlet, Playboy Bunny.”

“Lacrosse,” Zach replied. “Or crew.”

“Does she have to be an athlete?”

Zach flashed on his ex-wife. "She doesn't have to *play* a sport, just be willing to watch a game now and then. Is that too much to ask?"

"Ask whatever you want, pal. It's a wish list. Mine has two words on it: Cybill Shepherd."

"Cybill Shepherd's *Jewish*?"

"No, but she was in a Jewish movie."

"*The Heartbreak Kid* isn't a Jewish movie, Herbie. *The Sorrow and The Pity* is a Jewish movie." Zach tried to imagine what it was like for his friend, never having to worry about replenishing the Six Million. "You know I can't do a mixed marriage."

"Every couple is a mixed marriage—man, woman, mixed."

"She has to get what I come from."

Herb rolled his eyes. "Life is about where you're going, not what you're coming from." He showed the waiter the menu pictures of miso soup and sushi deluxe. "I'd like these." Zach ordered vegetable dumplings and shrimp tempura. "Let's agree to stipulate 'nice' and 'girl,'" Herb continued. "But please tell the court your criteria for 'Jewish.'"

"Long story short: I'm not looking for the female equivalent of you. You may have formidable genes, Herbie, but you lack yiddishkeit."

"What do you mean? I have candlesticks."

"I mean I want a woman who knows how to make a Jewish home."

"May I direct the witness's attention to the fact that it is Friday night and he just ordered shrimp?"

Zach cocked his chopsticks like a bow and arrow and mimed a shot across the table.

"How do you feel about converts?" Herb asked.

Zach closed his eyes for a moment. "I think we should probably rule them out." He was in awe of people who'd undertaken the Jewish conversion process, but he wanted a girl who knew what it was like to be called a kike in kindergarten. "I need someone who was raised with the same ghosts I was. If I were to marry a convert and she said something critical about a Jew—which born Jews do all the time—I might suspect she's a secret anti-Semite. And the next time a suicide bomber blows up a bus in Jerusalem, I might wonder if she feels the same kick in the gut as I do."

"You'd never stop spying on her soul," Herb said with mock melodrama.

"Maybe."

"Okay, no converts. How about an import? A Sephardi from Seville? A Jewess from Johannesburg? You could be between Iraq and a hard place."

"Very funny, but no. I once spent a weekend in Michigan with my Iranian Jewish roommate's family. It was unbelievable, so painfully awkward. His mom wasn't allowed to appear in male company unless his dad was in the room. She and the kids couldn't touch any food until the father had eaten as much as he wanted. At night, he dropped his shoes in her lap and told her to shine them and have them back in his closet by seven in the morning."

"Sounds like a nice deal," Herb teased.

"No American woman would stand for that."

"Neither would an Israeli. I have this friend, Aviva, early thirties, PhD from Hebrew University, policy wonk, works at a think tank. She's also an IDF sharpshooter and looks great in camouflage." Herb stared at the ceiling. "On second thought, you might not get along."

"Why? She sounds amazing."

"Hawk. Rabid Likudnik. She'll call you a self-hating Jew and accuse you of being too easy on the Palestinians. She'll tell you to either move to Israel or shut up and quit criticizing the government. You'd have to bury your back issues of the *Nation*."

"Not happening," Zach grinned. "Okay, never mind Aviva."

When the appetizers arrived, the two men instinctively shared; Zach plopped one of his dumplings on his friend's plate and got a spoonful of soup in return.

"I'm not sure I can scare up a fertile, liberal Zionist with lacrosse leg muscles by the time you get back from Melbourne."

"Take as long as you like," Zach replied between chews. "We're talking about my soul mate here."

"Prediction: the minute you fall in love, all your criteria will fly out the window."

Zach smiled but knew better. People who weren't children of survivors couldn't seem to grasp how it felt to be the last man standing. And have promises to keep.

When their main dishes came, Herb pinched a tentacle of octopus between his chopsticks and waved it at Zach. "Exhibit A: No fins or scales. Ergo unkosher. Suppose your bashert asks you to keep the dietary laws? The Duke of Windsor gave up the throne for the woman he loved. Are you willing to give up bacon?"

"The question's moot; you know I don't eat pork."

"You're eating shrimp. Shellfish is underwater pork."

"Shellfish is treif," Zach said. "Pork is anti-Semitic."

Herb hooted. "You're parsing, Levy. And badly. Face it: You're the same kind of Jew I am. You eat what I eat. You don't keep the Sabbath like I don't keep the Sabbath. You eat on Yom Kippur like I eat. The difference is *you* beat yourself up about it."

"Not true! I always fast on Yom Kippur." But he knew his Judaism was deficient, at best its definitions murky. Unlike Herb, Zach wasn't a haven't-been-to-shul-since-my-bar-mitzvah Jew, who felt it was enough to be "just Jewish" and not want to be anything else. Herb thought that doing the right thing—in his case, legal advocacy for children—made you as Jewishly legit as the black hats. He carried no freight from the Old Country, no Holocaust hangovers, no escape plan—it never having occurred to him that he could ever be in danger—and felt no compulsion to marry a Jew or produce Jewish progeny. Herb was at peace with his secular self.

Zach, meanwhile, was a pretzeled Jew who agonized over what he owed to his ancestors, a guilt-ridden Jew who went to shul on the High Holidays because he was afraid not to, a lefty Jew, a wannabe-a-better Jew, though to what end, he wasn't sure. There were so many stripes along the spectrum. He wasn't a Socialist, unionist Jew like his father, who equated economic exploitation with original sin, or a Survivalist Jew like his mother, for whom the purpose of ritual was to honor the dead. He wasn't a True Believer like Izzy the furrier, the lontzman who lost his entire family in the death camps yet never faulted God. Or a schnapps-and-honeycake Jew like the rest of the lontzmen, who were bonded to the Jewish people by steam, sweat, and stories. At the moment, sitting across from his friend, Zach Levy was a neurotic, guilty, utterly confused Jew.

"For argument's sake," Herb continued, "let's say you fall in love with a girl who has sexy calf muscles and a high fertility score but also happens to take Jewish law literally. Say her name is Hannah Horowitz and she doesn't want you to use electricity from sundown Friday to sundown Saturday. No TV. No breaking news. No championship games. I'm talking NIT, NCAA, Stanley Cup, World Series, *for the rest of your married life*!" Herb flashed his confident courtroom smile. "Would that not constitute a prima facie case of push comes to shove? Can you truthfully testify that you would skip even *one* American League playoff for Hannah Horowitz?"

This is how I talk, Zach thought; this must be how lawyers sound to normal people. "I'd get a Shabbos goy to turn on the set," he said. "Jewish law doesn't prohibit watching, only turning things on or off. "

"And what would the divine Hannah be doing in the meantime, reciting Psalms?"

Zach shook his head ruefully. He knew he would balk if anyone demanded he not turn on lights, answer the phone, watch TV, drive, ride, carry things, or handle money for twenty-five hours every week. He knew that some Orthodox Jews tear off squares of toilet paper in advance rather than perform that "work" on the Sabbath; no way would he do that. Nor would he give up a gold medal Olympic performance if Carl Lewis or Florence Griffith Joyner were running in a Friday night meet, or Greg Louganis was in a diving event on a Saturday afternoon. Zach finished the last of his shrimp and signaled the waiter for another round of beer.

"There's got to be a middle ground here, Herbie. I want to live in a Jewish home, not a Boro Park yeshiva."

"You keep saying Jewish *home*. What does that even mean?"

Zach studied his leftover shrimp tails, bright pink against the black enameled tray, one of many details that made the restaurant unmistakably Japanese. Others were the cool black slate under Herb's sushi, the fingerlings of fish on pillows of rice, the rosebud of pickled ginger nestled beside a pinch of green wasabi. Ditto for the translucent screens, the wait staff padding about in plain gray tunics and split-toe slippers, the bonsai trees and smooth stones artfully placed on a bed of combed white sand, the softly trickling fountain—each element contributing to the serene, Asian aesthetic.

The Jewish aesthetic, at least to Zach, included Shabbos candlesticks, a kiddush cup, a Hanukkah menorah, and maybe a spicebox on the sideboard, a pot of matzoh ball soup on the stove, a tallis folded into its velvet sleeve, a blue and white tzedakah box, exposed or concealed. Beyond those items, he couldn't quite capture how the ambience of a Jewish home registers on all five senses but he knew it added up to a sixth: the sense of belonging.

"It's hard to define," he said. "Kind of like what Justice Potter Stewart said about obscenity."

Herb produced the relevant quote: "'I know it when I see it.'"

"Right," Zach replied. "When I see a mezuzah on a doorpost, I know Jews live there and if I were on the run, they'd take me in. Except a Jewish home isn't a secret. We advertise it. We put our Hanukkah menorah in the window where everyone can see it. We build our sukkah in the front yard. We may as well shout, 'Over here! The house with the thingy on the doorpost!' The one where, for several days every autumn, the family eats outside sitting in a weird little booth with a roof that's open to the sky. It might as well have a ten-foot sign: 'Jews live here!'"

Herb laughed. "And inside the house?"

"Inside, we're sitting around a table, arguing. Not in my apartment, of course; I told you I lived in a quiet zone, but in everyone else's. On the table might be a bottle of seltzer, maybe a flickering yahrzeit memorial candle, a book with the place marked by an old zipper, a glass of hot tea with a spoonful of jam melting in it. The room would be rocking with laughter, Jews mocking their misery, telling jokes. In a Jewish home, when someone says, 'Stop me if you've heard this,' everyone pipes down and listens."

Zach was remembering the house on Long Island where Bonnie grew up, the long, leisurely dinners with her parents and relatives, who often would eat a big meal then stay at the table, cracking nuts, cracking wise, or venting about an editorial, sermon, or book they disagreed with. He remembered the night when Bonnie's Uncle Sid extolled Howard Fast, her Aunt Pearl decimated Ayn Rand, and her grandfather teed off against Judge Irving Kaufman who presided over Julius and Ethel Rosenberg's espionage trial and to everyone's horror imposed the death sentence on them. Bonnie's family table was where Zach learned to get a word in edgewise.

"In a Jewish home, a joke trumps everything," he said.

"Great! Tell me a good one," Herb commanded.

"Okay, stop me if you've heard this: Hymie meets his friend Moe walking down the street. 'How ya doin' Moe?' he asks. 'In a word? Fine,' says Moe. 'I'm in no rush,' says Hymie, 'Take two words.' 'In two words?' says Moe. 'Not fine.'"

The gag was older than Jack Benny but to Zach it embodied the condition of the Jewish people—fine and not fine, both. Fine was Bonnie's family accepting him as if he were a newly discovered cousin. Not fine was losing them when he lost her.

Herb said, "Okay. So far we've got mezuzah, family arguments, and jokes. That's your Jewish-home fantasy?"

"That and Jewish food—a little kasha varnishkes, a plateful of brisket or flanken, some gribenes crackling in a fry pan; to me Jewish food smells better than Chanel No. 5."

Herb shook his head. "Not in my house. In my house we knew the ham was done when the smoke alarm went off."

Zach suggested they order a carafe of hot sake. "Books!"

he said, still in definition mode. "In a Jewish home the shelves are groaning with books."

"Now *that* rings a bell," Herb said. "You've seen my folks' library."

"It's incredible. It looks like the French Bibliothèque. I remember a huge King James Bible on a beautiful wooden stand, right?"

"Right. That Bible contains handwritten records of all the births and deaths in our family over the last hundred and thirty years."

"You should have your DNA tested, Herbie; you could be a Cabott or a Lodge." Zach mimed a dandy with a monocle, then poured the hot sake. "I wasn't even allowed to *read* the New Testament. For us, the Bible is the Old and only."

They ordered green tea ice cream and marveled when the waiter delivered two tiny scoops.

"Small portions are definitely *not* Jewish," Zach commented.

The penurious dessert reminded Herb of home. "Thursday was the cook's day off so we made do with tuna or Spam. Doug and Miri aren't into food."

The restaurant served them complimentary plum wine in small metallic goblets that reminded Zach of the kiddush cup his parents gave him for his bar mitzvah. "It's sterling silver, with my name engraved in Hebrew and English," he recalled, as if in midthought. "They must have saved up for months to buy it. I haven't seen it since Bonnie left me."

Herb tried to lighten the moment. "For my bar mitzvah, my mother's mother gave me a silver seder plate that belonged to *her* grandparents, but I'll be damned if I know what goes into those little wells. Miri and Doug have a cabinet full of fancy Judaica they never use; it just gets handed down, from generation to generation."

Zach leaned back and stretched; the plum wine almost could pass for Passover wine. "At least you don't feel guilty about not knowing. I feel guilty about *everything*—things I don't know, things I don't do, the women I'm not dating, the kids I'm not having, the kiddush cup tarnishing in the cabinet."

"Don't worry, we'll find someone to shine it for you."

"I'm not looking for a maid, Herbie, I'm looking for a mate. A woman to love, honor, and . . ."

". . . impregnate. And I'm going to help you locate her!" Herb gave his friend's shoulder a light jab. "Only she won't hold a candle to Cybill Shepherd."

They went their separate ways, Zach Levy to his Soho loft where he had every intention of unearthing his kiddush cup, Herb Black to catch a late train to Boston to spend the weekend with his parents in the big house where he grew up, never doubting that he was the right kind of Jew.

CHAPTER 7

TAKING SIDES

SOME COUPLES MEET CUTE: HE FINDS HER WALLET, SHE picks up his mail by mistake, her beagle mounts his schnauzer. Zach Levy met Cleo Scott at the founding conference of the Black-Jewish Coalition of New York.

Zach was aware going into it that tensions between the two communities had reached a boiling point. Jesse Jackson had recently called New York City "Hymietown" and, in response, a group called "Jews Against Jackson" had run a full-page ad in the *Times* describing the black candidate for president as "a national disaster," and excoriating him for once saying he was "tired of hearing about the Holocaust," for hugging Arafat and Gaddafi, and for refusing to repudiate Louis Farrakhan. Alarmed by these provocations, two prominent New York clergymen, Rabbi Sheldon Kahn and Reverend Jeremiah Birmingham, convened fifty community leaders—half of them black, half of them Jewish—to "foster respectful dialogue and intergroup harmony."

The first meeting of the nascent coalition was held on Sunday afternoon, April 15, 1984, in a large lecture hall at the New School in Greenwich Village. The sign-up sheet contained so many boldface names from politics, law, business, and the arts—including "Bacall, Lauren" and "Belafonte, Harry"—that "Levy, Zach" felt like an interloper. Though his name tag, which said, "ACLU Attorney/Chair, Families of Holocaust Survivors," clearly entitled him to be there, Zach's reasons for accepting the clergymen's invitation were personal. A national poll that revealed a sharp increase in anti-Semitism among educated African Americans had aroused in him his mother's fears and his father's warning—"Once the intellectuals turn against you, the masses will follow." He'd been recently rattled by the vitriolic ravings spewed by callers to a black talk show that he'd tuned in to by accident. Unnerving on a daily basis were the Jew-hating lies barked by proselytes of the Nation of Islam on a street corner Zach passed on his way to work. A clean-shaven black man wearing a white shirt and dark suit ranted incessantly about "the Jewish conspiracy" while his bearded partner, in a kente cloth robe and white crocheted cap, hawked incense, fragrance oils, and pamphlets promulgating anti-Semitic canards. The lawyer in Zach would defend their right to speak freely but the child within him hyperventilated when he heard the incendiary screed, *The Protocols of the Elders of Zion*, described as if it were the Magna Carta.

Each participant who arrived at the New School received a packet of background materials including a timeline of key events in black-Jewish relations starting with the earliest days of the civil rights movement. "Ocean Hill Brownsville, 1968," was the first event labeled a "clash of interests." Zach remembered vividly what happened that year. He was a senior in DeWitt Clinton High School when the clash between black parents and white teachers over community control of the schools sparked a two-month teacher strike and riots in the streets throughout the city. Mostly, he remembered the Ocean Hill Brownsville brouhaha because his parents, who raised their voices about once a decade, had a big fight about it. Rivka believed that parents were entitled to take control of a school system that had failed their kids while Nathan insisted that the teachers, whom he called "the workers," had the right to defend their jobs. The quarrel ended when Nathan stormed out, slamming the front door so hard that a framed picture of David Ben-Gurion shaking hands with John F. Kennedy popped off the wall and crashed to the floor, shattering the glass. It was the loudest memory of Zach's childhood.

Another item on the timeline, "Andy Young Affair, 1979," reminded Zach of the heated arguments that erupted among his friends five years before. The African Americans had uniformly blamed Jewish pressure for the resignation of the young black US Ambassador to the UN, while most of the Jews had supported Carter's contention that, by talking to the Palestinian Liberation Organization, Andrew Young had violated American law and thus could no longer represent the nation.

About the recent "Hymietown incident, 1984," the timeline noted, "Jackson does not deny using word but calls it 'innocuous street slang.'"

Now, as Zach watched blacks and Jews file into the lecture hall, he was struck not by gradations of their skin color but by their wildly varied hairdos—there were buzz cuts, Beatle bangs, shaved pates, spikes, dreadlocks, Afros, and pony tails on the men; and on the women, straight hair, ironed hair, ballet buns, ringlets, corn-rows, and sprayed bouffants. People's clothing, too, ran the gamut, everything from church finery to tribal dress, business suits to sweat pants.

Something else fascinated him even more—the fact that nearly everyone who came into the hall hesitated before taking a seat. VIPs Zach would have expected to be decisive and sure-footed, eyed the room warily and ventured down the aisle with a tentative gait, suggesting that they were struggling with the same worry that had bedeviled him when he first arrived—the possibility that his choice of seat might betray a bias he didn't feel. Worrying about "how things look" being a habit Zach had learned at his mother's knee, he sympathized with the white man who was seemingly weighing whether to sit beside a black, a Jew, or neither. Zach smiled when the man chose a seat in an empty row, effectively shifting to the next person the decision of whether or not to sit near *him*.

Watching a stylish white woman—Chanel suit, silk blouse, pearls—come down the aisle, Zach couldn't help labeling her a JAP then immediately berated himself for even thinking the slur when the poor woman was simply well dressed and well coifed. Funny, how we internalize our own caricatures, he mused as the white woman effusively greeted a black woman in an orange tracksuit, smothering her with hugs and laughter. And how wrong we can be.

Soon afterward, a bearded Jew crossed the color line and sat beside a black man in horn-rimmed glasses. Then again, Zach realized, the black man could be an Ethiopian Jew and the bearded man could be a light-skinned African American. The permutations of race, religion, ethnicity, and peoplehood were complex and the intersection of competing interests and priorities was potentially as gnarled and fraught as the crossroads of four major thoroughfares on a day when its traffic light was broken. Zach wondered how a black Jew would self-identify at today's meeting. If intense conflicts arise, which side would she or he be on? Would such a person feel schizophrenic, change sides depending on the issue, struggle with split loyalties? Like most Caucasians, Zach took his race for granted, as if whiteness were normative, and thus enjoyed the daily luxury of not having to think about being white—which gave him more time to think about being Jewish.

Even the political luminaries stopped jabbering when the real star power showed up—Ossie Davis, Ruby Dee, Harry Belafonte, Lauren Bacall, Tony Randall, and Mandy Patinkin—followed closely by the two who had called the meeting: a tall, rangy black man in a clerical collar and a diminutive white man crowned by a royal blue yarmulke.

Zach turned to the back of the room to check the wall clock against his watch and saw the latecomer float in, a slender black woman wearing tan leather pants and a moss-green sweater set who wafted down the aisle like a sprig of spring. She sat two rows down and three seats over from Zach's, providing him with an unobstructed view of her arresting profile, her long, graceful neck, the hollow beneath her cheekbone, her dark, close-cropped hair. She rooted around in her brocade satchel and pulled out a pair of glasses with tortoise shell frames that had been wrapped in a pink square of fabric. Unfolding the temple pieces, she exhaled on the lenses and polished them with the microfiber cloth. Her movements were efficient, yet languorous, the actions of someone who, even in her most quotidian behaviors, feels at one with her body and at ease in the world.

Jeremiah Birmingham, senior pastor at the Good Shepherd Baptist Church towered over his coconvener, Sheldon Kahn, rabbi of the Manhattan Jewish Temple, who stood even with the minister's Adam's apple. Their stark physical contrast almost seemed calculated to symbolize their message: if *we* can get along, so can you.

"*Welcome* Sisters and Brothers!" Birmingham called out in a rich alto. "As we wrote in our letter of invitation, Shelly and I are deeply concerned about the growing rift between Jews and African Americans, but we're confident it can be bridged if community leaders such as yourselves lead the way. Each of you has been handpicked because of your prominence and because you command many troops. By the end of today's session, we hope you'll agree to be foot soldiers in an army of reconciliation."

The minister stepped back, the rabbi forward, as though they'd rehearsed the choreography. "Jerry and I have declared war on every racial and ethnic stereotype—

including the idea that Jews suck at basketball," Sheldon Kahn joked, in a voice that seemed far too big for his frame. "I may be vertically challenged, but I'm here to tell you this Jew can shoot a three-pointer. Right, Jerry?"

"Gospel truth!" Birmingham bellowed, squatting slightly to hip bump the little rabbi. "As God is my witness, Shelly went ten for ten in my church schoolyard."

"One stereotype down, hundreds to go!" rumbled the rabbi from a tunnel deep in his chest. "Working together, we can vanquish them all. In our many years of interfaith work, Jerry and I have seen Christians, Jews, and Muslims change from other to brother in just a few dialogue sessions."

"Which doesn't mean we've converted each other," Birmingham cut in, with a grin. "I already know my blessed savior. Shelly's still waiting for his. But that's okay because, like our Father in heaven, we celebrate difference. If God didn't love and respect difference, why would He have created man in his infinite variety?"

"Excuse me." The latecomer with the long neck and green sweater set was on her feet. "Sorry to interrupt, Reverend, but I feel like I'm drowning in Y chromosomes here. Are we women part of this effort? So far, we've heard brother, father, man, war, foot soldiers. Where are the sisters in this battle for hearts and minds?"

A few women called out, "You go, girl!" Others applauded.

"With all due respect, you guys have been on some kind of testosterone trip," continued the speaker, the mellifluousness of her voice at odds with its brusque claims. Zach recognized the voice, couldn't place it, but noticed that it had aroused in him a vague disquiet. After decades of representing women plaintiffs in sex discrimination cases, he could understand why the clergymen's boyish banter might raise a feminist's hackles. Still, this wasn't the time or place for Helen Reddy. The clergymen had convened this group to discuss black-Jewish relations—not sexism. Zach waited for Birmingham to cut the speaker off. Instead, the pastor tipped his brow and sent her a small salute.

"Point well taken, Sister, thank you. As it says in Proverbs, chastisements purify the sins of man—uh, woman, too—for whom the eternal loves, He chastens."

"He, him, his," the woman answered back, with a half smile. "You can't help yourself, can you?"

Zach had expected tensions between blacks and Jews but not between two blacks.

The Reverend defended himself. "You know full well that I don't think God is a 'he' any more than I think He's—" Birmingham caught himself, "than I think *God* is white, black, or green. Divinity transcends gender and color. Forgive me if I seem to be suggesting otherwise."

"Old language habits die hard, my dear," interjected Sheldon Kahn.

The black woman swirled slightly toward the rabbi. "If you don't mind, sir, I'd prefer not to be called *dear*. I'm not a little girl."

Kahn's cheeks flushed bright red around the borders of his snow-white beard. "Forgive me. I meant it as a term of affection."

"Even so. This is supposed to be a serious meeting about serious matters. Calling me *dear* is belittling. It's inappropriate. *Dear* is to woman as *boy* is to black man. *Dear* is what a man calls a wife who bores him. Allow me to introduce myself, Rabbi Kahn. I'm Cleo Scott."

Zach sat upright in his seat. That's why her voice had been unsettling. He'd been listening to her every Sunday night for the past few months, at first with dismay, more recently, with growing admiration.

"Sister Scott hosts a talk show on WEBD," Birmingham said, eliciting an audible hubbub. Though WEBD was a relatively small radio station whose programming was primarily targeted to a black audience, and though her face was not always recognized, in some circles, for instance among many in this lecture hall, Cleo Scott was a star.

Zach's initial dismay had been aroused when he happened on her program for the first time on the night it was deluged by a flood of anti-Semitic callers. But his negative feelings had been displaced by admiration after the following week's show in which she had presented a dramatic rebuttal to the extremists and since then, he had become a fan, increasingly impressed by her ability to straddle the line between passionate advocacy and fair-minded journalism. Without fear or favor, she marshaled a broad spectrum of opinion on the most controversial issues of the day, challenging the bloviators to back up their pronouncements with facts, changing her own views when faced with compelling opposing arguments, and confessing her disappointments and vulnerabilities without trading on pathos. Merely from listening to her on the radio over the past six or seven weeks, Zach had come to recognize in Cleo Scott a kindred spirit, someone who, like him, was trying to actualize a rich but complicated legacy by being a spokeswoman for her people while also serving as a principled interpreter of events in the wider community. And she knew her history.

"You and Jerry aren't the first black-Jewish pair to initiate a common enterprise," Cleo was saying to Rabbi Kahn. "W. E. B. Du Bois, whose initials happen to be the call letters of my radio station, cofounded the NAACP with the great muckraking black journalist, Ida B. Wells-Barnett, *and* the activist rabbi, Stephen Wise. I doubt that Rabbi Wise called Ida Wells-Barnett *dear*."

Sheldon Kahn bowed slightly at the waist. "I'm truly sorry. I beg your pardon."

Cleo raised her arms in the universal gesture of surrender. "My parents taught me to accept an apology with good grace so I'm going to sit down now. But I'm going to get up again if you and Jerry don't show the same respect toward the women in this room as you're asking blacks and Jews to show toward one another."

Zach was glad he came.

Cleo sat down and stayed down while the clergymen attempted to advance the day's agenda. "We're here to build on the alliances of times past—the struggle for voting rights, civil rights, economic justice," Birmingham said. "We need each and every one of you to commit to become founding members of the Black-Jewish Coalition and to join together in solidarity and strength."

Kahn jumped in. "With commitment, comes healing. We're stronger acting together than apart. We have the same pressing needs . . ."

"One question," interrupted Cleo Scott, on her feet again. Enough already, Zach thought, steeling himself for another digression. He was surprised when she hiked up the sleeves of her moss-green cardigan that the gesture struck him not as pugnacious but erotic. Getting turned on by naked arms was a first for him. "Please don't be offended, Rabbi, I'm not picking on you, I'm just trying to understand how what blacks do can benefit the pressing needs of Jews. From everything I read, the main threats to your community are assimilation and intermarriage. If that's true, I can't for the life of me figure out how twenty-five black folks can stop your kids from quitting Hebrew school after their bat or bar mitzvahs, or stop them from marrying goyim."

She must have known that line would bring down the house yet she didn't crack a smile, just stood there with her bare arms crossed, waiting for the ruckus to calm down. "I appreciate how much work has gone into organizing this meeting and I support the idea of collaboration in theory. But let's not kid ourselves. Our horses aren't starting from the same gate. Your forebears and mine have a radically different relationship to the American Dream. You came here to escape oppression; we came shackled. When blacks were a few centuries off of the slave ships and Jews first arrived in steerage, maybe our situations were more comparable. But we're not in the same boat now. These days, most of your relatives are lounging in deck chairs. Mine are still pulling oars and bailing water."

She looked around the room, left to right, and back. It was the unhurried pause of a speaker accustomed to being both listened to and heard. Her self-assurance was impressive. Not an um or a fidget. Shoulders relaxed. "I hope this doesn't sound hostile, Rabbi, but I think it's important to be honest with one another from the outset. Our two groups have vastly disparate needs and resources. Blacks need more of everything material and Jews, materially, have more to give. Obviously, then, the payoff for each side won't be equal. Before we can create a meaningful coalition, I think we blacks need to know if the Jews in this room are okay with that imbalance?"

A man with an argyle vest and Brillo-pad hair called out, "I'm okay with that imbalance. What I don't want to hear is that our suffering was equal."

"Your name, sir?" asked Rabbi Kahn.

"Jack Fingerhut, Professor of Jewish Studies. I've been in many so-called dialogues over the years, so I think I know what's coming next. Ms. Scott is going to equate American slavery with the Nazi genocide. She's going to say the Middle Passage was also a form of extermination. She's going to bring up white Europeans' exploitation, enslavement, and killing of Africans in Africa. I'm going to insist they're not the same, that the Holocaust was both quantitatively and qualitatively worse than any other crime against humanity. The Holocaust was about the total annihilation of a people. Ms. Scott is going to call me a racist. I'm not; I'm a historian. Slavery lasted for more than two centuries and the Holocaust for only a few years, but bondage is not the same as systematic, industrialized slaughter for the sole purpose of obliteration. Your people suffered unspeakable misery and dehumanization. But there was no grand design to wipe blacks off the face of the earth." He shot a cold look at Cleo. "Are you okay with *that*?"

Cleo bristled, "I hate when these discussions devolve into a competition of tears. First of all, Professor, you have no idea of what I'm going to say. Second, the salient point is not moral equivalency; the salient point is this: The Holocaust didn't happen here. *Slavery* happened here. Therefore, slavery is every American's responsibility."

Fingerhut demurred, "The Holocaust is every human being's responsibility, Ms. Scott . . . "

Birmingham slapped the podium. "Cleo! Jack! We have a lot of ground to cover this afternoon. Let's move the agenda and save the colloquy for later."

Zach had not intended to speak but because he sensed the vulnerability beneath Cleo's unflinching bluster, words came out of his mouth. "If we don't address Ms. Scott's question first, there may not *be* an agenda."

The little rabbi raised an eyebrow. "Name please?"

"Zach Levy. I'm a lawyer for the ACLU. Also the board chair of FHS, an organization that represents families of Holocaust survivors. I think this coalition has great potential but the lady over there—"

"Cleo," she interjected.

"—Cleo," Zach continued, "has asked us to confront something real: the fact is, our two groups don't have equal needs or resources. She's asking if we Jews are willing to accept that the rewards of whatever we do here may also be unequal."

"I don't need a translator, Counselor," Cleo snipped at him scornfully.

"I wasn't translating, I was affirming," Zach replied, torn between respect for her assertive panache and annoyance at her belligerence. He decided to engage. "Instead of upbraiding us, you might want to answer your own question. What's in this for you? If you stay in the group, what do you expect to get out of it?"

"Me? I'm just trawling for guests," she said. "I've got a show to do tonight."

"Please!" Again, Reverend Birmingham smacked the podium. "Sit down, both of you." As if shoved, Zach and Cleo obeyed in tandem. "Thank you. Now we're going to go around the room and introduce ourselves. Name, affiliation, and one sentence about your hopes or goals for this new coalition. Everyone gets a minute and I've got a stopwatch."

Fifty participants at one minute each, plus assorted reactions, counterreactions, and detours, took up an hour and a half. After listening to everyone's hopes and goals, Zach allowed himself to believe the enterprise might actually accomplish something. Harry Belafonte was the last to speak. The singer, who had once delivered the keynote speech at an ACLU benefit, classed up a room merely by being in it. Flashing his radiant smile, he introduced himself as "an activist, entertainer, actor, and idealist," and articulated his hopes and goals for the group as "mutual respect, collective action, and fomenting revolution."

Zach Levy raised his hand. "Will the chair entertain a motion?"

"I suppose so," said the rabbi.

"I move that we skip the rest of the preliminaries and just let people say what's on their minds."

Zach's motion passed and, despite its incendiary potential, yielded a polite, yet sinus-clearing, candor.

The director of the Synagogue Council of America wanted to know why black leaders didn't repudiate Minister Farrakhan when he called Judaism "a dirty religion."

The head of the Urban League countered, "How come Jews only care about what we say when they want us to condemn one of our own? I don't ask you to repudiate Meir Kahane. Why should I have to repudiate Louis Farrakhan?"

"Not comparable," said the woman in the Chanel suit and pearls. "Most of us treated Kahane like a lunatic. Most of you treat Farrakhan like a redeemer."

"He wears a clean shirt and bow tie," said the African American man in the horn-rimmed glasses. "My generation's heroes were Dr. King and Malcolm X; today's black kids worship millionaire athletes and foul-mouthed rappers. When my sons use proper English, their friends accuse them of acting white. They have few positive role models. Farrakhan, at least, tells black youth to stay in school. So what if he makes a few unfortunate comments about Jews; nobody pays attention to that."

"*Jews* pay attention," Zach protested. "We've seen

where 'a few unfortunate comments' can lead." He saw Cleo Scott take off her green cardigan and fold it in her lap, before she turned to face him.

"Correct me if I'm wrong, Mr. Levy, but didn't the ACLU defend the neo-Nazis' unfortunate comments in Skokie? If you were able to tolerate *their* hate speech, why can't you tolerate Farrakhan's? Or does the First Amendment only apply to white people?"

Zach said, "We defended the neo-Nazis' right to demonstrate. Not their ideology. We called their speech abominable. We didn't condone it."

Cleo turned away. A black assemblyman called out, "We're not here to talk about Farrakhan, we're here to talk about *real* problems, like substandard housing and racial profiling." A Hillel director objected to anti-Israel activities by black students on her campus; she wanted to know why anyone would side with suicide bombers. A black community leader from Crown Heights said Hasidic Jews were disrespectful to their Caribbean American neighbors and got special breaks from the police.

Zach felt embarrassed when a Jewish woman in harlequin glasses asked if she could solicit the group's help with a domestic problem, a personal black-Jewish problem: "My live-in nanny refuses to eat with our family. It just kills me to see her sitting at the kitchen table eating by herself. My kids think she's punishing them for something; they don't understand why she doesn't like them. What should I do?" Advice came flying at the woman from all directions. "Honor your nanny's wishes; she must have her reasons." "Maybe your kids can eat with her in the kitchen." "Ask her how you might make her feel more comfortable about eating with the family." "Ask if she'd prefer to take a tray to her room." Though Cleo kept her own counsel, Zach thought he saw her back stiffen.

Rabbi Kahn pointedly took back the reins. "Before ending the meeting, we want your thoughts on what our coalition might actually *do* together." The participants called out their suggestions and Reverend Birmingham wrote each one on the chalkboard:

"Attend both communities' cultural events to foster mutual understanding."

"Coauthor op-eds."

"Watch *Roots* and *Holocaust* together."

"Speak in pairs at churches, mosques, synagogues, and community centers."

"Create a school curriculum on the history of blacks and Jews in America."

Cleo's suggestion was to revisit the entire premise of the meeting. "I'm sorry, people, but I'm still not convinced we need this group at all. I mean why *blacks* and Jews? Why not Arabs and Jews? Aren't Arabs your most threatening adversary? For us, the question is, why not blacks and Dominicans? Or Puerto Ricans? Or Koreans? We share our neighborhoods with Latinos and Asians. We patronize Korean markets and nail salons even though they never hire black people in those places. Doesn't it make more sense for us to organize dialogues with those groups?"

Somehow Cleo didn't sound adversarial; she sounded as if she were thinking out loud and inviting everyone to reason along with her. "I see it as a syllogism," she said.

"Blacks have issues with whites. Most Jews are white. Therefore blacks have issues with Jews. It's not your religion we challenge, it's your white-skin privilege. When I walk into a room full of Caucasians, I'm not thinking, 'Which of these white folks is a Jew?' I'm thinking, 'Which of these white folks gives a damn that there's so little research on sickle-cell anemia, or how many of these people care that more black men are in prison than in college?'"

Affirmative murmurs encouraged her to go on.

"On your side, it's different," she continued. "Jews have issues with gentiles. Most blacks are gentiles. But when you walk into a room full of African Americans, you don't see us as Christian, you see us as black, and maybe you're thinking, 'Which of these schvartzas hates me enough to hurt me?'"

"I would never use that word for blacks," Zach said aloud, in response to some audience snickers. "And I certainly don't assume every black person wants to hurt me."

Cleo ignored him. "Any Jew unfortunate enough to be listening to my show a while back heard several African American callers say some truly hateful things about your people, things that made me cringe. But you can't tell me that black anti-Semites constitute a greater threat to Jews than *white* anti-Semites. Lord knows, there are more of *them* than of us, and white folks have a helluva lot more power to do you damage. So why don't you start a dialogue group with French anti-Semites or Irish anti-Semites? Likewise, why don't we blacks start a dialogue group with white *Christian* racists. Lots more of them per capita than of racist Jews. I'll tell you why we don't. Because our real enemies are too scary. The people who burn crosses on lawns and paint swastikas on synagogues—now *there's* something the two of us have in common. Both blacks and Jews are too afraid to confront the *real* monsters."

Zach protested, "We have more in common than common enemies. We have a connection that goes way back. All of us gave up a beautiful Sunday afternoon to come here today because we occupy a special place in one another's heart."

Cleo Scott had a half smile on her face when she looked at him. "Isn't it amazing how some Jewish men know everything? Professor Fingerhut told me he knows what I'm going to say, now you're telling me you know what's in my heart—"

Reverend Birmingham cut her off. "I'd like a show of hands: How many of us are ready to sign on right now as official founding members of the Black-Jewish Coalition of New York?"

Rabbi Kahn counted thirty-nine yes votes, Zach's among them. Not Cleo's.

"This question is for the eleven people who did not raise their hands," said the reverend. "How many of you are willing to attend the next meeting and *then* make up your mind about joining?"

Everyone else was in, including Cleo.

"Hallelujah!" Birmingham crowed. "The next meeting will either be at my church or Shelly's temple. You'll get a notice in the mail. Until then, peace!"

Zach was almost out the door when he felt a tap on his back. “You free tonight?”

“Excuse me?”

Cleo had tied the sleeves of her green cardigan around her neck like a scarf. “I’m done trawling. You’re the one I’d like to interview. Would you come on my show and continue our discussion?”

“Was that what you call a *discussion*?”

She grinned. “The program’s called, ‘Cleopatra’s Needle.’ Tagline, ‘We prick your conscience, we puncture inflated egos, we stick it to the power brokers.’ In other words, you can say whatever you want. I’m not afraid of controversy.”

“I know. I’ve heard your show.” Zach didn’t say *which* show.

“Great. So you’ll be my guest?”

“You mean your house Jew?” he asked. “Sure. Why not?”

CHAPTER 8
CLEOPATRA'S NEEDLE

ZACH HEARD HER RADIO PROGRAM FOR THE FIRST TIME months before he met her. It was a Sunday night, he was at the Laundromat, zoning out on the suds sloshing against the window of his washing machine while surfing his Walkman when a smooth voice oozed through his headphones.

"Good evening everyone and welcome to Cleopatra's Needle. Tonight, we're going to be talking about blacks and Jews."

Zach turned up the volume.

"Many of you saw the 'Jews Against Jackson' ad in today's *New York Times*. Its criticism of Jesse was pretty harsh. We want to know how you felt about it. Supposedly, the ad was a reaction to Jesse using the word 'Hymietown.' What does that word mean to you? Did the Jewish reaction to it surprise you? And let's go macro: What's your overall impression of black-Jewish relations in this town? Or in America in general? The phones are open. Our number is . . . "

While the soapsuds drained from his machine and the rinse water rose in the porthole, Zach's headphones were awash in callers' anti-Semitic accusations: "The Jews control everything." "Jesse threatens Jewish power so the Jews are trying to destroy him." "The Jews turned the country against affirmative action by calling it a quota system." "Jewish landlords gouge us. Jewish storekeepers cheat us. Jewish developers redline neighborhoods." "The Hasidim's Grand Rebbe gets a police escort to visit his wife's grave. My priest gets a ticket for parking in front of his own church."

The talk show host dodged and weaved, pleading for reason, but her callers wouldn't let up, their odious claims mounted, each more outrageous than the last.

"Jewish drug lords hook black kids on crack."

"Jewish doctors infect black babies with AIDS."

"That's *enough*, people!" The host barked, her voice no longer supple but scorched. "The *Times* ad obviously hit a nerve but this is ridiculous. Now I want everyone to chill out during the break and when we return, I'll expect to hear more reasoned voices."

The spin cycle shuddered to a stop. Zach closed his eyes during the commercials—Salem Slims, Heineken, the *Amsterdam News*, an auto repair shop, a braiding parlor. Then—

"Welcome back to Cleopatra's Needle. This is your host, Cleo Scott, and we've been talking about blacks and Jews—much too nastily for my taste, so we're going to switch gears now and focus on what our two groups have in common, which is plenty. Both Jews and blacks have experienced bondage, the Israelites as slaves in ancient Egypt and us, well, you know our story. In the fifties and sixties, blacks and Jews marched shoulder to shoulder—think King and Heschel, Goodman, Schwerner, and Chaney. Your turn, listeners. What you can add?"

"Forget the shoulder-to-shoulder thing," declared the first caller. "The Jews were only in the civil rights movement to showcase themselves. They never treated us like equals. It was all about Jewish paternalism and black deference. The minute Stokely preached black power, the Jews jumped ship. They were never real allies."

"Tell that to Andrew Goodman and Michael Schwerner," Cleo replied, testily.

The caller punched back. "Just 'cause a couple of Jew boys got killed in a Mississippi swamp don't mean every Jew is our friend. They're not!"

"You're tarring a lot of good people with that broad brush. I'm moving on to politics now. New caller, you're on the air. Is Jesse your candidate?"

"Thanks for taking my call, Cleo, but before we talk about Jesse, your listeners have to realize that the original Israelites were black. The Jews are impostors. The Exodus is an *African* story. The Jews say they were slaves, but they *owned* slaves . . ."

Cleo interrupted. "Give me another call, Marcus."

Zach sprang from his chair, bounded to the pay phone on the back wall of the Laundromat and dialed the station. She'd been urging listeners with opposing views to call in but he couldn't get through, kept getting a busy signal until finally a recording: "Your call will be answered in the order in which it was received."

"*Who belongs to this*?" A black woman with a booming voice was standing in front of Zach's machine with her laundry basket balanced on her hip.

"Me," he replied from the back of the room. "I'm on the phone right now. Could you use another machine?" After all that time on hold, he wasn't going to surrender his place in the phone queue.

"The other machines are full."

"I'll unload it in a minute."

"You'll unload it *now*, Mister! Your wash is done. We all have lives."

Zach shook the receiver at her. "I'm on the phone!"

The woman hauled out Zach's wash and dumped everything on top of the machine. "Be glad I didn't throw the whole selfish load on the floor."

Embarrassed, Zach hung up and hurried over to transfer his wash to a dryer, after which he approached the woman, who was sitting in the plastic chair in front of the machine working on a find-a-word puzzle with a ballpoint pen.

"Excuse me, ma'am."

She fixed him with a cold stare.

"I really want to apologize. I had just heard something that upset me and I had to make a call. It had nothing to do with you. I was rude. I'm sorry."

He must have looked pathetic because her eyes went soft. "That's okay, baby." She waved him away. "I've been there."

The following Sunday night, Zach stayed home to listen to the radio. This time, he would operate strategically, call the station before her show began and immediately hang up so all he had to do when the host opened the phone lines was to hit the redial button. She started talking as her theme music faded out.

"Good evening and welcome to Cleopatra's Needle. After last week's program, I got to thinking about a fourteen-year-old boy named Isaiah who lived in Memphis, Tennessee during the Great Depression. Isaiah was the eldest of seven. Times were tough back then. Black folks, especially, were struggling to stay afloat. When his daddy got laid off and there wasn't enough money to feed his family, Isaiah went looking for an after-school job to help make ends meet. He applied to every store and filling station in town, tried the mill, the package store, and the moving company. But there was no work to be had. He was just about to give up when he noticed a Help Wanted sign in the window of a synagogue. They needed someone to help out around the place, collect the prayer books and prayer shawls that got left in the pews, straighten up the sanctuary after services, sweep, wash the blackboards, mop the floors in the Hebrew school, and turn the lights on and off on the Sabbath when the Jews are not allowed to use electricity. It was a menial job but Isaiah was grateful for it since black businesses had nothing to offer and other white folks weren't rushing to hire a six-foot-two-inch black boy, much less in a religious school where he might cross paths with little white girls.

"After Isaiah worked at the synagogue for a year or so,

the rabbi, a man named Jonah Solomon, was so impressed with the boy's intelligence, reliability, and good manners that he encouraged Isaiah to apply to college and wrote a letter of recommendation that helped him win a four-year scholarship. The summer between Isaiah's junior and senior year, the rabbi got him a job driving a truck for a friend of his who owned a lumberyard. One day, a white kid on roller skates hitched onto the truck's rear bumper and somehow got himself killed. The kid's father sued for damages and when the yard owner had trouble with his insurance claim, he tried to make the accident sound like it was the black driver's fault. Rabbi Solomon testified on Isaiah's behalf—mind you this was in Tennessee, in the 1930s—said he'd known him for six years, talked about how responsible and industrious he was, how honest and kind, said Isaiah was planning to train for the ministry and his life shouldn't be ruined because some daredevil kid he never even glimpsed in his rearview mirror decided to take a joyride.

"In those years, most white Southerners didn't think much more of Jews than of blacks, but a rabbi had some stature in their eyes, so Jonah Solomon's testimony won the day. Instead of being indicted for manslaughter, Isaiah returned to college that fall, graduated with honors, went on to divinity school, eventually took a pulpit, and became shepherd to a thousand souls. He also married his high school sweetheart and had two daughters. I'm one of them."

The silence went on for so long after "them" that Zach thought he had lost the broadcast signal. Finally, Cleo said,

"Isaiah Farnsworth Scott was my daddy. He died when I was ten but he's been on my mind these past few days, came down from heaven to scold me. Jonah Solomon is long gone, too, but I know he's ashamed of me for what I let happen on this show last week. I'd like to believe most of my listeners were appalled as well and I'm sure some of you tried to call to tell me so but couldn't get through because the lines were glutted by the nut jobs. Truth is, it wasn't your responsibility to stop them from hijacking my airtime. I should have stopped their ravings the way I'd want any radio host—any *person*—to stop a racist in his tracks. Jonah Solomon spoke up for my father when no one else did. But when the Jews were attacked on this program last week, I failed to speak up for them. For that, I owe them and every person in my audience my most sincere apology.

"Tonight, the phone lines belong to our Jewish listeners and anyone else who felt offended, hurt, or defamed by what was heard on this show last Sunday night. Any other crazies out there won't be put through. Everyone else: please call in. We want to hear from you."

Zach never had to dial the station that night. Not only did other callers express everything he felt, but the host's closing remarks made whatever he might have said redundant: "Aspirin, blue jeans, the combustion engine, the polio vaccine, the fax machine, oral contraceptives, the pacemaker, streptomycin, the Heimlich maneuver, sign language, the sonogram; every one of those things was invented by a Jew. So let me put it to you straight, people: if you have any complaints against, quote, 'the Jews,' why don't you just *give it all back*! Until next week, this is Cleo Scott. Good night."

From then on, whenever he was home, her show became part of Zach's Sunday night ritual. What made her monologues so provocative were the same qualities that had captivated him at the New School before he knew who she was—an intellect both hot and cool, dynamism packaged in an invincible calm. Now that he'd seen her in action, he thought she'd make a great litigator. She was entrancing. Smart. Intriguing. Sexy.

CHAPTER 9
THE ONE I FEED

CLEO'S FATHER, ISAIAH FARNSWORTH SCOTT, ALWAYS wore two silver items on a chain around his neck: a large cross and an oval pendant, a gift from Rabbi Jonah Solomon on the occasion of Isaiah's graduation from divinity school. One side of the pendant was engraved with a verse from his namesake prophet: They shall beat their swords into plowshares, and their spears into pruning hooks. The other side simply said IFS, Isaiah's initials. Whether the monogram had given rise to his nickname or vice versa, Cleo never knew, but by the time she came along, her father was called "Ifs," and many of his parishioners thought he'd been baptized with it.

Pastor Ifs Scott was a man of God who refused to speak in certainties, a preacher for whom "If" seemed the most sensible way to begin a sentence because, after all, everything was contingent on everything else, and in a world this complex and subject to change, it was hard to know anything for sure. Except Ifs always knew the difference between power and powerlessness, knew who needed him most, and how to reach them.

Once when asked the secret of his magnetic appeal to children, Ifs replied, "I guess they know I love them." Cleo thought it was because he *listened* to them with unwavering eyes and a heedful stillness that she would later find absent in others. He would draw on his pipe or cup its bowl in his palm and listen to children as if they were prophets. "I've learned more from babies than from bishops, more from kids than cardinals," he used to say, though he wasn't a Catholic, he was a black Baptist minister in the Church of God in Christ in Memphis, Tennessee. The truth is, children's questions and comments often inspired Ifs's homilies. When Cleo was eight, she started transcribing sections of his sermons into a blue leatherette journal with gilt-edged pages so she would always have them nearby for easy reference. She titled it "The Wisdom of Ifs Scott" and her first entry was an excerpt from his sermon about God's mistakes:

> Since the Lord created us in His image and *we* make mistakes, I have to assume that God does, too, and one of them, obviously, was slavery. A person who takes every word of Scripture literally might think slavery's okay because it's in the Bible. But if you're a decent human being, especially if your grandparents knew the lash, you likely condemn "the peculiar institution" of human bondage. So why did slavery make it into our sacred text? I can't prove it but I'm pretty sure God kept His mistakes in there to test us. I think He's challenging us to see the wrong and correct it. He can't do everything Himself. Some stuff God wants *us* to fix. It might

> even be the main reason He put us on this earth. So here's the question I want to leave you with today: Which wrong is God waiting for *you* to make right? It took folks too long to fix slavery. What else needs fixing right *now*?

That talk—and the very idea that God could be wrong about anything—caused a stir among Ifs's conservative parishioners but that reaction was nothing compared to the impact of his sermon about Saint Paul's letter to the Ephesians:

> I've always had trouble with what Paul says about wives—the part about how they have to submit to their husbands. It makes no sense to me. I know—we *all* know—hundreds of wives in this very church who are smart and strong and who work hard to make a better life for their families and communities. Doesn't seem right that these fine women should have to bend to the will of some dang fool husband just so he can feel big in his britches.
>
> I hope this doesn't embarrass you, Althea, but since tomorrow's our twenty-fifth anniversary, I want to say something about you, about my wife in particular. Althea Scott is an extraordinary woman—a devoted wife, a wonderful mother, and an invaluable partner in my ministry. I have never believed the good Lord wanted me to rule over her; I believe He sent me Althea to love, honor, cherish, and respect. For a quarter century, I've done just that—and she's done the same to me. I will always be grateful to the Almighty for bringing us together, and to you, Althea, for agreeing to become my wife.
>
> Finally, I want to address myself to the men in our con-

gregation. Please take time during the silent devotion to think about the most important woman in *your* life. If you love her, ask yourself if it's better for her to feel strong or servile. Because a person can't be both. If Saint Paul knew my wife, or your wife, or any of the great ladies of our church, I'm sure he would change his mind about that submission thing. He might even send them a special blessing for their good works and unfailing grace.

Amen.

The reverend sent a soft smile to the first pew where his wife and daughters sat beaming. "Praise Gods," and "A-mens" hummed through the chapel, and when Cleo turned around, the paper fans fluttering in affirmation looked like butterflies. She later heard that a few men found fault with her father's message; two of them, calling it heresy, left the church over it, taking their wives with them. But most parishioners felt God must have approved of Ifs's sermon because women walked taller afterward, and some of the most troubled marriages in town seemed visibly improved. Cleo asked her father for his manuscript so she could transcribe every word of the sermon into her journal. She did not yet understand how remarkable her daddy was but even as a child, she knew that what he said in the pulpit was worth putting in a book.

She was ten when Ifs Scott died. A cerebral aneurysm, the doctor called it, a weak spot in a brain artery—bursts like an inner tube. These things just happen.

That afternoon, Cleo and her sister Clementine, twelve years older and recently divorced, had gone to church to help their mother setup for a cake sale. Ifs was at his desk writing a sermon and keeping one eye on Josie, Clem's baby, who was napping in the portable crib by the window. The women returned two hours later to find a note scribbled on Ifs's desk pad: "Took J. to Dairy Dream. Yes, I changed her."

Witnesses at Dairy Dream reported that before he collapsed, Reverend Scott's last words were: "After much discussion, the young lady and I have decided we'd like strawberry ice cream cones with rainbow sprinkles."

ALTHEA HAD A short time to find a new home for herself and her grieving family before the new pastor was due to take over the parsonage. Money was tight. The cash proceeds of Ifs's life insurance and small savings account weren't enough to cover rent and living expenses for the four of them. Clementine had been deserted years before by Josie's father, so there was no support from that quarter. Clem had a job at the plant nursery that paid minimum wage, and at ten, Cleo was in no position to contribute to the family income. It was up to their mother to find a way to keep them afloat.

Swallowing her pride, Althea Scott put an ad in the weekly *Pennysaver*: "Pastor's widow seeks live-in domestic work: cooking, cleaning, minding children. Reliable. Industrious. Trustworthy. Lodging required for widow, two daughters, one toddler. Salary negotiable."

Sophie Bergman saw the ad the day after her unmarried sister, who'd been caring for the house and the Bergman's twin boys, ran off with the Electrolux man. The Bergmans, who owned a dry goods store, had an old icehouse in the yard behind their home that could easily be converted into living quarters. Althea Scott brought a loaf of her homemade cinnamon bread to her first interview. When that went well, she suggested that Mrs. Bergman come to the parsonage the next day to meet Clem, Cleo, and Josie because they were part of the package and a potential employer had a right to approve of them, too. Althea also wanted Sophie to come to the parsonage before the Scotts had to vacate so she could see for herself that Althea kept a neat, tasteful, and orderly house.

Indeed her cinnamon bread, spotless kitchen and parlor, and cheerful girls had all contributed to Althea's being offered the position at the close of the second interview. Sophie Bergman hadn't even felt the need to consult her husband, Morris; she knew a fine family when she saw one. For her part, Althea accepted the job without asking to see the old "icehouse," whatever *that* was, because she couldn't imagine anyone else in Memphis taking her in along with Clem, Cleo, and Josie. As Sophie described it, the icehouse had "three rooms with cute windows," which caused Althea to conjure a dingy shack with windows the size of slits and leftover hand trucks and ice tongs strewn about. In any event, it would have to do, she told her daughters; they needed a roof over their heads.

Two weeks later, Althea and her girls moved into a spanking clean, simply furnished cottage, with an open kitchen, a small bedroom for Althea, and one for Cleo and Clem with just enough space for Josie's crib. It wasn't their home, but it was a house. An hour or so after they'd unpacked their clothes, dishes, linens, and other personal effects, both Bergmans stopped by to make sure they were settling in well.

"If the curtains aren't your taste, Mrs. Scott, just go down to our store and exchange them for some you like better," Sophie said, tweaking the tiebacks. "I promise I won't be insulted." Her husband Morris, a chunky man with a bushy mustache, noticed Clem and Cleo laboring to assemble Josie's crib and insisted on finishing the job for them.

Althea started work that Monday. The front door of the icehouse led to the Bergmans' back door by way of a brick path that meandered through their garden. Over the next seven years, until Cleo left for Wellesley College, the path seemed to shorten between the two homes as the tender, bustling woman with the flyaway hair became her second mother, her Jewish mother, not at all meddlesome but rather the sort of woman who is happiest when making others happy. Whether working beside Morris waiting on customers in the dry goods store, taking care of their twin toddlers, Jeff and Alan, ferrying a friend to the hospital for cancer treatments, or soliciting donations for one of her Jewish charities, Sophie was always trying, as she put it, "to be of use."

The relationship between Sophie and Althea evolved with a natural ease unusual for two women whose circumstances were intrinsically unequal, a delicate dance of the domestically intimate and economically transactional. Sophie didn't treat Althea "like a member of the family," a claim some household employers proudly assert, albeit with one-sided evidence. Rather, she treated Althea with underlying awareness of the venerable social role of which the widow had been summarily stripped by her husband's sudden death. For her part, Althea marveled at the alternate reality in which she found herself since Ifs's death. On the one hand, she was being paid for things she used to do for love—cooking, cleaning, and being nice to visitors. On the other hand, she used to be the mistress of her own home and now she was a servant in someone else's.

Sophie dropped in on the Scotts regularly, careful not to cross the permeable membrane of their privacy without a reasonable excuse: either she had just finished this month's *Redbook* and thought Althea might like to have it, or the garden had produced a surfeit of zucchini and she hoped Althea would take the extra bushel. Once Cleo turned thirteen, Sophie hired her a couple of times a month to babysit for the twins and paid her fifty cents an hour, seventy-five after midnight, the top rates at the time. During one of her visits to the icehouse, Sophie noticed Cleo poring over a map of Europe in her textbook. "May I help you find something?"

Cleo explained she had to write a history paper on how the boundaries of Europe changed between 1939 and 1945 but the maps were so small, she could hardly make out the countries' names. Peering over her shoulder, Sophie said, "You're right. Me neither."

Shortly after Sophie left, Cleo answered a knock on the door. A delivery boy from the store handed her a package. "Mrs. B. said I should give you this."

Inside was an oversized atlas with an inscription: "To Cleo, who deserves the world. With love from the Bergmans."

Such generosities continued through the years. When Cleo's permanent teeth came in crooked, Mr. and Mrs. B. paid for her braces. When Althea was sick and couldn't work, Sophie brought her chicken soup and fruit salad. On the fifth anniversary of Althea's employment, the Bergmans gave her a big raise and a dishwasher for the icehouse kitchen.

Althea told her employers, "To know you and Mr. B. is to understand why the Jews are the chosen people."

"Yeah," Sophie responded. "Chosen to suffer."

Cleo, who'd been listening to their exchange, winced. When Sophie left, Cleo turned to Althea. "You don't have to be so obsequious, Mom. You work hard. You deserve everything they give you. Stop being so grateful that you get to clean their toilets!"

"You are fifteen, Cleo," said Althea, "and you have a lot to learn."

Althea went into her room and closed the door. That was the first of many conversations in which Cleo Scott took up the mantle of her activist father and challenged the accommodations she saw being made by her mother's generation. Ever practical, Althea modeled her belief that all work has dignity when the worker is treated with respect—but a piece of her was proud to see her husband's fire and courage alive in their daughter.

Not every Jew who crossed Cleo's path in those years was like Mr. or Mrs. B. Even the Bergman family had a clinker. She would always remember when Sophie's northern relatives came down to spend Passover with them and Althea recruited Cleo to help prepare and serve the seder meal. That was the year Cleo learned to make chicken soup, matzoh balls, and haroses, the mixture of apples, nuts, and sweet wine that Mrs. B. explained was meant to symbolize the mortar the Hebrew slaves used to build the pyramids. After the family had finished reciting the Passover story from their haggadah booklets, they sang a round of Hebrew songs and shouted, "Next year in Jerusalem!" and then most of them proceeded into the living room where they would be served dessert, coffee, and tea. Sophie was arranging a platter of macaroons when she noticed her Great Uncle Max still at the table. Stooped, with age-mottled hands, a straggly beard, and rimless glasses, the old man was methodically pouring the leftover wine from everyone's glasses into an empty Manischewitz bottle.

"What are you doing, Max?" Sophie asked.

"Wine shouldn't go to waste. I'm collecting it for the girl," he said, pointing to Althea, who was setting cups and saucers on a silver tray.

"No, you're not! She is not drinking our dregs! And she's not a *girl*." With a pained glance at Althea, Sophie retrieved the bottle from her uncle and gave it to Cleo to pour down the kitchen drain. "Please forgive him, Mrs. Scott. He saves everything. He meant well."

Althea said, "Don't worry, it's okay." But it wasn't; it stung.

"It most certainly is not okay." Sophie smiled with her

mouth, but her eyes revealed a distressed shame. She ran to the sideboard, grabbed an unopened box of Barton's chocolate creams and an untouched honey cake (kosher for Passover), and gave them to Althea to take back to the icehouse.

"Happy Easter," Sophie said. "Enjoy."

WHILE LISTENING TO half the people in the New School lecture hall respond to the woman who wanted to know what to do about her nanny, Cleo had been hurled back to that long-ago Passover. Mrs. B. never needed advice; she treated everyone with dignity. But not everyone treated her or Mr. B. with comparable respect. Long before the Black-Jewish Coalition was a glint in its founders' eyes, Cleo had witnessed the challenges faced by a Jewish family living as a distinct minority in a Southern city. On top of that, her work as a radio journalist had given her a front-row seat on the eruptions between blacks and Jews over the years. She had observed their Rashomon-like perceptions of identical events. She had moderated contentious panels on affirmative action, the Israeli-Palestinian conflict, and other flashpoint issues between blacks and Jews. She had seen their battles up close, and sometimes been caught in the crossfire. But she'd never experienced anything as vitriolic or venomous as the on-air fiasco she came to think of as the Shameful Show.

Marcus Charlton, her producer, had facilitated the ordeal; he may even have orchestrated it, Cleo thought, recalling his recent association with Farrakhan's Nation of Islam. She should have anticipated his mischief. A producer's job was to research a topic, book guests in advance, and, on the night of the show, screen calls and run interference for the host *before* putting people through to her earphones. That night, though, rather than filter out the loony birds, Marcus had released a flock of them into her live air. And where were the Jewish callers or other outraged listeners? She'd seen the station's market research report; she knew her audience was diverse and included a large percentage of Jews.

During a commercial break the night of the Shameful Show, she had demanded that Marcus do a better job of screening. He'd shot back that it wasn't his fault that Jews weren't calling. At any rate, blaming one's producer was a cop-out, Cleo knew that. Marcus worked for *her*. The red button was on *her* console. With the flick of a finger, she could have cut off the bigots, deep-sixed the crazies. Instead, she had let the hatemongers derail her. Replaying the audiotape, she registered a dozen missed opportunities when she could have gone on the attack. She could have reminded the caller who screamed "Zionism is racism" that Dr. King once responded to a hostile question, "When people criticize Zionists, they mean Jews. You are talking anti-Semitism." She could have noted how often Dr. King was likened to Theodor Herzl, the founder of Zionism. She *knew* those facts; why didn't she use them?

The Shameful Show was the nadir of Cleo's broadcasting career. Until then, she'd seen herself as a tough interlocutor and a voice for the voiceless. Whenever she guest lectured in journalism classes, she pointedly disavowed the label "objective journalist" because, in her opinion, no one with a brain, heart, and rudimentary grasp of history should pretend to approach certain stories with a blank slate. She faulted broadcasters for giving equal time to saints and scumbags; back in the sixties, for instance, a racist like Bull Connor—the Alabama police chief who used attack dogs and cattle prods against peaceful black demonstrators—should not have been allowed on the air. Yet when the anti-Semitic pit bulls were chewing up her phone lines the other night, she had failed to shut them down.

A simple apology would not suffice. Cleo decided to make reparations and respond immediately to the protests flooding the station by affording her Jewish listeners the chance to even the score on the following week's program. She had seen the power of reconciliation first hand. Besides being the daughter of two civil rights activists, at age eleven, the day before Martin Luther King Jr.'s assassination, Cleo had gone with Althea to the Mason Temple to hear his "I've Been to the Mountaintop" sermon (and Dr. King had given her a hug afterward). She had stood vigil with her mother and sister outside the Lorraine Motel after Dr. King was killed. She'd worked for the panthers' children's breakfast programs when she was in high school. And through all the phases of the movement—nonviolent resistance and black power—she had retained a soft spot for the Jewish people, mirroring Ifs's gratitude to his mentor and Althea's affection for Sophie and Morris Bergman.

Cleo's reparations show made headlines far beyond

the New York market. Pundits dubbed her "courageous," and applauded her prompt effort to publicly rectify an offense. Talking heads debated whether hate speech should be muzzled or have First Amendment protection. Jewish organizations sent thank you notes. Prominent African Americans said they wished more white people would respond to racism the way Cleo had responded to anti-Semitic bigotry. (She ignored the letters and phone calls from blacks who accused her of being an "Aunt Tom," and she threw out the funereal lilies that arrived in a long box with a death threat on the gift card.) Jeremiah Birmingham, who happened to be listening both weeks, later claimed that the two shows, obviously for different reasons, had inspired him to approach Rabbi Kahn with the idea of cofounding the Black-Jewish Coalition.

Weeks had passed since Cleo had made amends on the air but when her invitation to the New School meeting arrived in the mail, her first response was, no thanks, I already gave blood at the office. What changed her mind was the impressive list of confirmed participants; if all those honchos were willing to give up a spring Sunday afternoon to repair the black-Jewish relationship, there was definitely a new development to the old story. She decided to go to the meeting, though not without trepidation. Her apology to the Jews had ruffled some feathers in the black community. What if, in the course of the meeting, she found herself disagreeing with something a black person said? Would she be afraid to break ranks a second time? Would other blacks see her as an incorrigible turncoat? By the same token, if she disagreed with something a Jewish participant said, would she unconsciously censor herself to appease those Jews who had not forgiven her for the Shameful Show?

Now, thinking back on her behavior at the meeting, she asked herself a different round of questions: Had she hassled Rabbi Kahn and Professor Fingerhut because she was genuinely annoyed at their condescension—or was she trying to prove to her own cohort that she could still be tough on the Jews? Had she been honest when she challenged the premise of the group or was she preemptively discrediting it to avoid joining in a dialogue that might expose her complicated childhood loyalties? More than anything, Cleo hoped her prickliness hadn't offended Jeremiah Birmingham, on whom she had once bestowed her highest praise: Honorary Woman. Jerry didn't just talk the talk about supporting women and girls, he walked the walk day in and day out, ran a child care center in the basement of his Harlem church, and sponsored a rape crisis hotline and a project that trained men and boys to manage their anger and quit equating manhood with dominance. Besides Jerry's good works, what most endeared him to Cleo, she realized, was his uncanny resemblance to her father.

From the Adam's apple that bobbled above his clerical collar to his ministerial flourishes, Pastor Jeremiah Birmingham was a taller, darker, more urbane version of Pastor Isaiah Scott. At the beginning of the meeting, as the minister welcomed the attendees, spread his arms, pausing for a moment in the cruciform position, then swept his long, bony fingers forward as if to gather the entire group in his embrace, Cleo remembered her father performing similar sorcery in his pulpit. Jerry's singsong cadences, too, were hauntingly familiar: "If you're fed up with black-Jewish enmity but haven't given up hope, then you've come to the right place. If you've had it with the petulance and howling but you haven't given up on the possibility of healing, then you've come to the right place. If you feel angry and frustrated but you still believe the pursuit of peace is as sanctified as the fight for justice, then you've come to the right place."

Her daddy used to talk like that, sprinkling "ifs" the way a Catholic priest sprinkles holy water. After Ifs's funeral, Cleo had found the draft of his last sermon on his desk—the one he'd been writing before he took Josie for ice cream—and slipped it between the pages of her journal, whose entries stopped the day he died. Christ had no female disciples and the church had yet to see a woman ordained, yet at ten years old Cleo wanted to be a preacher like her daddy. And she became one, in her fashion.

When Jeremiah Birmingham told the group at the New School that they had the power to end the strife between blacks and Jews, Cleo almost expected him to prove his point by quoting Ifs's last sermon. She didn't have to read it to remember it:

> A Native American wisewoman became distraught over the growing animosity between her people and a neighboring tribe. One day, she was sitting before her tent, struggling with her thoughts, when her grandson came by.

"What's the matter, Grandmother?" he asked, noticing her distress.

"A terrible fight is going on inside me," replied the wise-woman. "A fight between two wolves. One wolf is full of anger and hatred, vindictiveness and violence. The other is full of joy and forgiveness, understanding and love."

The boy looked very frightened. "Which wolf will win?" he asked his grandmother.

"The one I feed," she said.

CHAPTER 10

THE DIFFERENCE THAT MAKES ALL THE DIFFERENCE

WHEN HE CAME TO HER STUDIO AND TOOK THE GUEST'S chair, Zach expected Cleo to badger him on the air. But the combativeness he'd seen that afternoon was gone; she was a gracious host and he was more than delighted when she suggested that they continue their conversation over dinner at a restaurant a few blocks from the station. Black-Jewish relations and similarly weighty topics were shelved in favor of martinis and conversation about their pet peeves, childhood fears, and most embarrassing moments.

It was nearly midnight when he walked Cleo to her apartment building on Central Park West at the corner of 103rd Street. She didn't ask him up but casually let drop the fact that the NBA press office had sent her a couple of courtside comps for the first game of the Knicks vs. Pistons playoffs the following night. "Any interest?"

"Are you kidding, Cleo? Absolutely."

They met in front of the box office at Madison Square Garden. After the game, they went to a bar across the street and had Irish coffee and again, they talked for two hours without mentioning politics or the Black-Jewish Coalition, this time bonding over their mutual disdain for cooked carrots, Strom Thurmond, and Pink Floyd, and their shared enthusiasm for fried artichokes, Thelonius Monk, and walking the city's streets at any hour of the day or night.

How could he not want to kiss her after that? How could he not want to see her again? Nothing serious, of course, just a lark, a short detour before he continued the search for his bashert. Since her religion ruled her out, a dalliance with Cleo felt safe to him. Within a week after they met, he was seeing her every night, convinced all the while that his feelings for her, though intense, would peter out like a teen crush. Instead, the relationship deepened. She complemented him in so many ways that he had to keep reminding himself of the difference that made all the difference.

Religion wasn't the only hurdle. The first time she invited him up to her apartment and he saw the display in her living room, her tchotchkes freaked him out and it occurred to him that Cleo might be as crazy as some of her callers. There, under track lights, arranged on shelves like rare archaeological finds, stood black figurines in various poses of humiliation—manic-looking pickaninies, slack-jawed Stepin Fetchits, mammies with pendulous breasts—as well as tobacco tins, calendars, ashtrays, chamber pots, and toothpick holders decorated with similarly denigrating black caricatures. A banjo man clock with a coal-black face and protruding white-orbed eyes hung on the wall, the eyes clicking from side to side like a metronome, making him look like a shifty-eyed thief. There was a shoe box marked "Postcards: Pickaninies, Cannibals, Lynchings, Etc." Three Aunt Jemima cookie jars. A menu from a place called "Coon Inn," a sign that said "Colored Drinking Fountain." A mechanized "Jolly Nigger Bank."

"Who's your interior decorator, Jim Crow?" Zach asked, unsure of how else to react. It embarrassed him just to be looking at the racist relics.

Cleo took a nickel from the dish of coins beside a cast-iron black head and placed it on the "Jolly Nigger's" outstretched tongue, which retracted into the head and instantly emerged empty, as if the coin had been a minnow swallowed by a shark.

"Local banks used to give these out as bonus gifts when you signed up for a savings account," she said. "And not because black people were signifiers of thriftiness or financial prudence. On the contrary; this guy is meant to evoke a beggar with his hand out or a thief stealing your nickel. He symbolizes negro shiftlessness."

Zach mumbled, "I've never seen anything like this."

She seemed to take that as a compliment. "These days the stuff is hard to find but it was as common as Coke when I was growing up in Tennessee. People hid such things in their attics after the sixties, but now they're collector's items, mostly for blacks; whites would rather be caught buying porn."

"Unbelievable," he said, still trying to parse what he was seeing.

Cleo picked up a ceramic figurine with big lips, a codpiece, and a nose ring. “Behold the cannibal. Iconic. Comedic yet fierce. Reminds white folks that under our go-to-meetin’ clothes, blacks are savages who can’t be trusted with freedom—or white women.”

“I don’t want to see any more,” Zach said.

“One more thing,” she insisted. “I got this at a garage sale in a nice suburb.” She held out a cartoon postcard. Under the headline “Happy Thanksgiving” was the drawing of a turkey devouring a black baby.

Zach shook his head, speechless.

Cleo looked amused and annoyed at the same time. “White people forget that blacks didn’t just survive slavery, we survived *this*. For more than a century *after* emancipation, day after day, year after year, on gas stations, phone booths, tourist shops, billboards, grocery stores—we were forced to look at these images of ourselves.”

“I get it. It’s terrible. But I didn’t need the lecture and I think it’s super weird to display this noxious crap in your living room. I thought you invited me up because you felt romantic.”

“I *do* feel romantic,” Cleo protested, stroking his cheek. “And I want you to spend the night. But first you have to feel comfortable here.”

“Are these knickknacks supposed to put me at ease?” Zach laughed. “Not happening.”

“That’s why we need to talk first. I told you I had an unusual collection. What’d you expect? Black Barbie dolls?”

"I would have welcomed Black Barbie dolls."

Cleo sat on the couch facing her display. "This is part of who I am, Zach."

"This isn't you." He sat down and put his arm around her though, at this point, he was pretty sure the evening was over.

"This is what I came from," she said. "It's my genesis."

"Showcasing these knickknacks in your home is bizarre, Cleo. You have to admit it."

She shook her head. "To me, they're not knickknacks, they're evidence. Don't forget, I'm the great-great-granddaughter of slaves. Nine-tenths of power is possession. What we own can't hurt us."

In time, Zach would recognize her shift into lecture mode and just roll with it. On this night—his first in her apartment—he pushed back. "Oh, really? Who's '*we*'?"

"Black lawyers, doctors, college presidents, intellectuals—that's who collects racist memorabilia."

"You've *got* to be kidding!"

Cleo shrugged off his arm, walked over to her tiny kitchen and emerged with a bottle of wine, a corkscrew, and two glasses. Suddenly, she was in hostess mode.

He was confused. "Living with this crap has to be toxic."

"Ownership is redemptive. Listen, you promised your parents and yourself that you would never look away from the horror of the Holocaust—your interests are hardly anodyne. Your refusal to forget . . . I respect that about you," she said, her gray eyes boring into his. "Now hush your mouth and drink with me." She set the tray on her small dining table. "The wine's white, in your honor."

Zach grinned. "I'll only open it if you give me the last word on the subject."

"Which is?"

"Yes, dear." He pulled the cork.

"That's more like it," Cleo said. "Now, I'm sure you'd prefer to study my collection in greater detail, but I think it's time to change the view. Follow me, and bring the wine." She led him to a softly lit bedroom as serene as the living room had been jarring; nothing on its walls but a painting of a wheat field, no shelves of grim bric-a-brac, no "evidence." The drapes were creamy white, the carpeting beige, the bed made up with satin sheets and a fluffy white comforter. She directed him to set the tray on one of the polished slabs of blond wood that extended from both sides of a platform bed built so high off the ground it required two steps to mount it. But once they were up there, glasses in hand, they had a clear view of Central Park, its velvety nightscape ribboned with serpentine paths lit by old-fashioned streetlamps.

AS THE WEEKS turned into months and he grew more enamored of Cleo, Zach marveled at the dynamics of difference—how otherness disappears with intimacy, and dissimilarity gets recast as wondrously unique.

One night, when he caught her slathering shea butter on her smooth caramel skin, Cleo said, "Black is beautiful, but it needs a helluva lot of help."

"I think you're perfect as is," Zach replied, barely able

to keep his hands off her. In truth he'd never had more intimate or exciting sex. She was open, affectionate, and comfortable telling him what was working. After years of wandering without a map, it felt euphoric to be with someone who could communicate her desires so freely, verbally and otherwise.

THE NEXT MORNING, after they made love again, Zach dismounted the platform and said he was going to bring her coffee in bed. Passing the living room exhibit on his way to the kitchen, it struck him suddenly that he'd been drawn to two women who collected things. The coincidence ended there, however; Bonnie's leftist tchotchkes were an homage to idealism, Cleo's racist doodads a perverse ode to bigotry. Bonnie's collection was for sale in a shop, Cleo's, a permanent display where she (and now he) ate and slept. Only a Faustian bargain would explain her choice. He filled the coffeemaker with water, inserted the paper filter, measured out the grounds. She must have made some internal deal that enabled her to leave her family behind and flourish in the New North *only* if she lived up close and personal with the ignominies of the Old South. While he waited for the coffee to drip into the pot, a quiet epiphany pushed through his morning haze. Hadn't he negotiated a similar bargain with his psyche? (You get to live without survival guilt only if you tolerate an occasional vision of the NYPD transmuting into the SS.) And wasn't there a parallel between her need to own symbols of black dehumanization and his penchant for collecting stories of Jewish suffering and working on Holocaust reparations? As much as he and Cleo had in common, there was this big difference: she was the child of another people's trauma.

Zach carried the mugs of coffee back to the bed. She held both of them while he climbed up on the platform, then she gave him his mug and they sat back against the headboard, their legs entwined with the tangled sheets, and gazed out at another beautiful morning in Central Park.

BORN A PREACHER'S KID—a PK in Southern parlance—Cleo Scott had seen God's hand at work when, on her first day of apartment hunting, she landed a plum rental on 103rd Street with all three rooms overlooking Central Park, which instantly became her personal country club and nature preserve, the venue where she hiked or biked its trails most weekends, played tennis in summer, went skating in winter. Cleo's athleticism was a welcome antidote to the sports-averse women in Zach's past—his ex-wife as well as the women he'd dated since the divorce. Babette, a poet with a map of blue veins under her papery skin and a life-threatening sun allergy; Trudy, a type A real estate executive whose outdoor leisure clothes (jog bras, running shoes, warm-up suits) belied the fact that she spent her weekends working the phones or hosting open houses for prospective clients; and the accident-prone Natalia, who twisted her ankle on the beginners' ski slope. Not a jock in the bunch.

Not only did Cleo match Zach nearly sport for sport but, because she was a volunteer guide for the Central Park Conservancy, she knew every inch of the park's 843 acres, which of its seventeen public restrooms stayed open in winter, the names of the guys who ran the carousel, and how many bird species flew in or over the park (275).

Her favorite destination in the park was the Shakespeare Garden, where many of the plants mentioned in the Bard's plays and sonnets were beautifully showcased. Zach had never known the garden was there until she led him up the rocky hill between Belvedere Castle and the Swedish Cottage and introduced him to its peaceful confines. That first April, when the two of them took turns reading aloud from the Shakespearean text on the plaques at the base of each tree and bush, the garden was bursting with hellebores and columbines, grape hyacinths and Virginia bluebells. In May, while holding hands before a budding rosebush, Cleo had recited a couplet from *Romeo and Juliet*.

> This bud of love, by summer's ripening breath, may prove a beauteous flow'r when next we meet.

Zach pulled her close and kissed her, though he knew she wasn't—couldn't be—his fated one and, with "summer's ripening breath," he'd be gone.

But they were still together when the roses bloomed, together when the marsh mallows swayed in the summer breeze, when the autumn asters withered and the broom sedges shriveled, together when the warblers flew south for the winter. Each time they strolled through the Shakespeare Garden, Zach kissed Cleo to stop himself from saying the words he could not admit he felt. The one difference between them was like a craggy pothole in an otherwise smooth and scenic road, a pothole one noticed only to steer around it.

Religion and race surfaced rarely when they were first getting acquainted; Cleo told Zach about her father's radical ministry and the role of the black church in her upbringing and Zach told Cleo how it felt to be raised by parents whose quirky amalgam of socialism and Judaism had consigned him to live in the long shadow cast by the Holocaust. One night, he confided to her the promise he had made to his mother; Cleo listened and nodded. She didn't say much but he felt that she got him, especially the fact that, though formally irreligious, he was nevertheless utterly Jewish. It was Zach who struggled with the paradox: why he remained so committed to a faith he didn't always feel, why he was willing to sacrifice Cleo for the sake of Jewish continuity, yet wasn't sure what in Judaism was worth continuing. Was he really obligated to choose guilt over love?

When deep snow blanketed the Shakespeare Garden, they were still together, still strolling its paths, clowning around, and reciting quotations in British accents. The following spring, Zach forced himself to face the truth: he was not leaving his beloved Baptist anytime soon. His lark had become his life; he was happier with Cleo than he'd ever been with anyone. A weight had shifted, his promise paled. And, because he'd made clear to her from the start that he could never marry someone who wasn't Jewish, and Cleo had registered no demands of her own, Zach allowed himself to surrender to the feeling he refused to call love.

Anabelle arrived in December without homework—her visitation always coincident with her summer vacation—and ready to dive into whatever activities her father had planned. When Zach asked her if his girlfriend could join them on their Saturday adventure in Chinatown, the plucky nine year old said, "Sure!" At Nom Wah Tea Parlor, he let Anabelle skipper the dim sum selections for all of them, and Cleo loved every one of her twelve chosen dishes. Anabelle read out her own fortune cookie, "You need not worry about your future." Cleo's said, "You will have good luck and overcome many hardships." When Zach refused to break open his cookie, Anabelle did it for him and read the message aloud, "Your love life will be happy and harmonious."

Zach laughed, "So much for Chinese wisdom." Cleo shot him a look that was hard to decode, but she didn't say a word.

After lunch, they walked to Columbus Park on Mulberry Street, observed a tai chi session and then a chess match between two men who each looked a hundred years old. They browsed the street stalls on their way to the Chinatown Ice Cream Factory, where they ordered the craziest flavors on the menu—stinky fruit, zen butter, and black sesame—tasting them, dumping them, and going back for strawberry, chocolate, and mint chip instead. In a store window on Mott Street a pair of lime-green Chinese mesh slippers that cost $1.98 caught Anabelle's eye and Zach bought them for her.

"Oh, Daddy, thank you, but it won't be fair unless we can get a matching pair for my new chum. May we please?" Anabelle and Cleo wore the green shoes home on the subway.

The following weekend, since the weather was unseasonably warm, Zach reserved an Avis car to drive to Hershey Park in Pennsylvania, the only nearby amusement park that was open in December and this time it was Anabelle who suggested they invite Cleo along.

"It's about a four-hour trip each way," Zach said. "We'll have to stay over at a hotel."

"Cool!" Anabelle enthused brightly. "I heard all the Hershey hotels have chocolate fountains."

"Where do you think Cleo should sleep?" Zach asked, gingerly.

"In my room, of course. Just get us two beds."

Zach smiled, called the travel agent, and booked two rooms at the Cocoa Motel.

Hershey Park was jammed when they arrived and somehow, in the crush, they became separated, or rather Zach lost sight of his daughter and girlfriend, who had been walking behind him hand in hand.

Once they realized Zach wasn't with them, Anabelle said, "Let's have a go on the Ferris wheel. We can keep an eye out for Daddy from above and yell down when we spot him."

Cleo was as excited as Anabelle when they buckled

themselves into their seats and the little car swung back and forth as the huge wheel carried them toward the sky. At the top of its arc, they surveyed the crowd below and screamed down to every man with tousled sandy brown hair, giggling hysterically as it became evident, on the way down, that none of the men were Zach. Afterward, they found the person in charge of the public address system and to Zach's consternation he soon heard, "Mr. Levy, *Mr. Zach Levy*! Please report to the Lost Child desk to claim your daughter and her babysitter." Rather than be offended, Cleo was amused.

Back in Manhattan, the night before Cleo left for Memphis to spend Christmas vacation with her family, the threesome made lasagna together at the loft. Zach had to restrain himself from asking his daughter if his girlfriend could sleep over. Anabelle was a sophisticated kid, she understood cohabitation, she'd seen Bonnie and Gil in the same bed for years, but at the Cocoa Motel, she'd claimed Cleo for herself; she hadn't suggested that he and Cleo sleep together in the same room in the same bed, so Zach didn't suggest it now.

On Thursday, January 1, after Bonnie picked up Anabelle to bring her to the airport, Zach resolved to start the new year with a new plan; he had to break up with Cleo when she returned from Memphis on Sunday or else another year would slip by before he knew it. Though nearly deranged by longing, he had tried to rehearse what he would say to her. He couldn't even make it past the first line.

On Friday night, he passed a synagogue with open windows and heard the congregation singing a familiar melody, L'cha Dodi, the song that welcomes the Sabbath bride, and thought to himself that his future bride, the woman he should be dating, the bashert he was destined to marry, was more likely to be in that sanctuary than at whatever party he was supposed to be heading for, so he changed course. Zach detoured to the bar at Lovage, M. J.'s restaurant, and waited for the chef to join him once dinner service was under control. Minutes later, M. J., spiffy in his toque, white jacket, and checkered pants, plopped down on the next stool, summoned Brian, his bartender, and ordered a Virgin Mary for himself and a high-test Bloody Mary for Zach.

"Polish vodka in mine, please," Zach told Brian, then turned to M. J. "I've decided to break up with Cleo as soon as she gets back on Sunday night, and I need you to put some starch in my spine. I'm afraid I can't do it, but I have to."

"Hold your horses, man. You're too fast for me."

Zach rubbed circles on his temples. "I'm going nuts, man. It can never work between me and Cleo. I've got to leave her and settle down once and for all."

"Honey, if you and Cleo aren't settled, I don't know who is."

"I mean get married. Have a family."

"You got Anabelle. Ain't she family enough? What's missing?"

The question shamed Zach. His daughter was all he could possibly want in a child. The point is, she was his only child—and *he* was an only child. "She's perfect," he said. "But I have to do more than replace myself. I have to have more kids."

The chef scowled. "Something's wrong with this picture, Zachy. You got it all and you want more." M. J. hopped off the stool. "I'm going back to the kitchen where the grateful people are—the ones who are just glad if they wake up every morning on the right side of the grass." He crooked a finger at his bartender. "Brian! Throw an extra shot of vodka in this guy's Mary and let him drink himself into the ground."

When Zach finally dragged himself home, he did as he always did when he felt depressed, made himself scrambled eggs. Then he watched *An Affair to Remember* and fell asleep before Deborah Kerr got hit by the car.

Sunday afternoon, Cleo called him from the airport. "I missed you," she said.

"I missed you too," Zach bit his lip.

She said she was going directly to the station to pretape an interview. "Marcus booked me three politicos tonight. But we could meet up afterward if you're not too tired. My place at ten?"

That was when Zach should have said they needed to talk about their relationship, and maybe do it on the phone, the new year was a good time for fresh starts, and he had to . . . Instead, his heart beating like the wings of a trapped bird, he said, "I'll be there."

At nine thirty, he practically sprinted to the subway and once they were nestled in each other's arms under her beige satin sheets, the idea of leaving her seemed insane.

The next day, he unloaded to Herb Black in the office

kitchen. Herb had made himself a peanut butter and Marshmallow Fluff sandwich on white bread, no crusts. Zach cadged an apple from the ACLU's community fruit bowl and bit into the waxy fruit.

"I need your advice, Herbie," Zach said. "You've left a few good women in your time. What should I say? How should I do this?"

"My advice? Don't."

Zach dipped a plastic knife into Herb's Skippy jar and spread a thick coat of peanut butter on the white flesh of his apple. "I have to. The longer I'm with her, the harder it'll be to end it."

"Who says you have to end it?"

"Come on. We've been through this a hundred times."

A thin strand of marshmallow goo stretched like a shiny silk thread between Herb's sandwich and his front teeth. He wound the strand around one finger and licked it off. "Tell me again why it's so important for you to marry a Jew even though it's not important for you to live like a Jew?"

The question stopped Zach cold. He slid into a long silence. "Why do you think we're still here?" he asked finally.

Herb rolled his eyes. "Is this about all the people who tried to kill us?"

"Babylonians. Romans. Spaniards. Germans. Arabs. How did we survive? Why are we still here?"

"Because Jews married Jews? Really, Zach?"

"I have to leave her, Herbie."

"No, you don't. But since you're clearly planning to,

I'm preaching to the coffee machine here. You asked my advice. I'm saying, let yourself off the hook. Marry Cleo. Let the next guy solder his link to the Jewish chain."

"What if we all said that?" Zach was eating the peanut butter straight from the jar now, licking it off his plastic knife, whose serrated edge scraped his tongue in a weirdly satisfying way, as if self-inflicted pain was an appropriate response to the situation at hand. "We're an endangered species."

"We're a paranoid species," Herb said, as he screwed the cap back on the Marshmallow Fluff. "I don't see us as fragile. We've got Oscars. Pulitzers. CEOs in the Fortune 500. We're fine. The Jews will survive without you leaving Cleo."

Zach shook his head. "Maybe you haven't heard, but we're actually *shrinking*. We haven't even recouped our numbers since the war. We have the lowest birthrate on the planet. It's not the anti-Semites who are killing us. We're destroying ourselves. You want Jews to vanish from the face of the earth?"

Herb licked the last of the sticky Fluff off his fingers. "Not Jews. But maybe Judaism, Christianity, Islam, and all the rest. Think about how many wars have been fought over God. Maybe we'd be better off without religion."

"I take your point. But do the Jews have to go first?" Zach tossed his apple core in the trash and went back to his desk.

CHAPTER 11

PLAYING FOR TIME

COHABITATION AGREED WITH THEM. THE MORE TIME they spent together the more Cleo relaxed into herself and the less inclined Zach was to fight his feelings. As for her racist relics, he trained himself to avert his eyes, recasting the living room as a hallway between the kitchen and bedroom, not a destination or a place to linger. Though he came to understand the power of the tchotchkes to buttress her commitment to remembering a painful history, it took one horrific old postcard to finally convince him to let up on her and stop complaining about the collection.

He was doing sit ups when she came home from one of her Saturday flea market outings, excited by her new find. "These postcards almost never show up north of the Mason-Dixon Line," she said, squatting so he could read the postmark: Asheville, N.C., September 2, 1942. She flipped the card to the picture side.

"Jesus, Cleo!" Zach flinched at the photograph. "That's sickening."

"Maybe you need a stronger stomach," she said, jabbing his gut. "More sit ups. More crunches."

The postcard showed a photograph of a black man with a noose around his neck hanging from a tree; white men brandishing shotguns, women pointing, children laughing, people picnicking.

"I can't believe they took *pictures*," Zach said. "They didn't even try to hide what they'd done."

"The opposite," she said. "Lynch cards were for sale at the corner drug store, two for a nickel. This one cost me a dollar."

"It's obscene!"

"Lynchings happened; better to face it than deny it. These cards were a terrorist ploy meant to intimidate blacks and scare us into submission. White folks only had to tack one of these up near the cash register and we got the message."

"Don't look at me like that." Zach shook out the towel he'd been using as a neck roll and wiped his face. "My folks weren't in Asheville in 1942; my mom was in Auschwitz."

"Well, my people were lynched in the US of A," Cleo said. "Asheville was *my* Auschwitz."

"I don't display yellow armbands in my living room, Cleo."

"You don't have to, Zach. They're building you a Holocaust Museum—on the Washington Mall, no less. I'm not saying Jews didn't suffer . . . "

"Thank you for that."

". . . but the Holocaust didn't happen here. My people were enslaved *here*. Where's our slavery museum?"

"Maybe you'd have one if you spent your time lobbying Congress instead of buying this repulsive junk."

"*Memorabilia.*" She corrected. "The word means 'worthy to be remembered.' Your 'Never Again' is my 'Never Forget.'"

"If it's worth remembering, donate it to a museum. Don't keep it on your wall. Send your collection to the Smithsonian."

"Someday," Cleo said. "When I'm done with it."

Zach gave up the fight. It was her heritage. And her home. Eventually, he would be gone. In the meantime, he would hang out in the kitchen and bedroom and concentrate on her other astonishments.

A COUPLE OF weeks after Zach's thirty-fifth birthday, he and Cleo were sunning near the Bethesda Fountain in Central Park when some kids whizzed by on skateboards, skimming the pavement like pond flies and click-clacking down the stairways, their boards, though unmoored, flying with them as if hooked to a toe, and solid as a landing strip when they slammed to earth. Since Zach was at home on skis, he thought he'd give skateboarding a try and was about to ask if he could borrow a board for a test run when he remembered he was thirty-five. Middle-aged. For his learning curve to pay off in the pleasure of mastery, he would need years of practice. Would he have enough time? Would there be limits to what his body could do? Were a few new thrills worth the risk of an injury?

He decided not to ask the kid for the board.

"You're frowning," Cleo said.

"I feel old."

She followed his gaze. "Don't be ridiculous. You could do that if you wanted to, but why would you want to?"

That wasn't the point. The point was, if he didn't have enough time left to learn to skateboard, he might not have enough time to find his bashert. Each day he spent cleaving to Cleo was another day stolen from his future. For all he knew, she might feel the same way about him. She was coming up on thirty, an earthquake age for everyone, and, given her biological clock, even more seismic. He had been honest with Cleo all along; she knew he was just passing through en route to the life he was supposed to be living. So why was she treading water with him? How long would she stay? What if she left him first?

The following Sunday night, he turned on the radio to listen to her show while preparing his shoes for a long-overdue polishing. He spread newspapers on the kitchen table, pulled the laces out of his cordovans, and opened a fresh can of brown shoe cream. Usually Cleo bounced her monologue off him in advance but she'd mentioned nothing about tonight's subject.

"Good evening and welcome to Cleopatra's Needle. The other day, I met with a group of well-educated black women to talk about men and marriage, or rather listen to the women complain about the paucity of educated black men. No surprise there, since fewer than half of black American boys finish high school and more black men are in prison than in college, which leaves a very small pool of appropriate black guys for middle-class, cultured, intellectual black women to choose from. This, in turn, explains why, when one of the classy brothers pairs up with a white woman, some black sisters get mad. My informants also commented on how much more common it is for black men to date white women than vice versa. So the first question I want to put to tonight's listeners is this: What's the story with black men and white women?"

Zach jammed his left fist into one of the cordovans to hold the shoe firm, then swished the sponge across the cake of polish and rubbed the cream into the leather. He looked over at the radio, waiting for Cleo's answer.

"My theory is that racism and sexism meet on the doorstep of romance," she began. "As long as whites are more valued than people of color and as long as males still hold most of the social prerogatives, the black man will want to, quote, 'trade up,' in the belief that having a white woman on his arm proves, or improves, his value. It doesn't seem to be the same for black women. When we date white men, we don't do it to trade up, we do it because the pickings are so slim among black males. As for white men—who hold *both* race and gender prerogatives—they're two-thirds less likely to date a black woman. Studies show that black husband–white wife couples are two-thirds more common than white husband–black wife couples. White men have no reason to 'trade down.'"

Zach put down the shoe. Where was she going with this?

"Instead of black men challenging these racist hierarchies, they project their own sense of inferiority onto black women so when they reject us, they can feel like they're discarding the inferior part of themselves. Everyone is always focusing on the plight of the black male. Tonight I'm interested in the plight of the black female, specifically her marriage prospects in today's society. W. E. B. Du Bois famously wrote about the 'Talented Tenth.' Where are those top-notch black men? Why are so many of them hanging with white women instead of with us? You know who you are, brother. Later you can tell us what your problem is and Cleopatra's Needle will puncture your balloons. But first we're going to take calls from the sisters and hear some truthful testimony.

"Girlfriend, if this problem rings true for you—if you can't find a man, or you settled for some bad-news black dude because that's all that was left in your neighborhood, or you took a fallback position with a white guy who might be perfectly nice but not quite in synch with your soul—give us a call. We'll be back right after these messages."

Zach whisked the shoe brush back and forth, watching the leather became a richer, darker, more gleaming version of its former self. So thoroughly did the polish cover the old scuff marks that he imagined slathering some of it on his face so when she came home, he could give Cleo the black man she wanted. It had never occurred to him that he was just her fallback, a placeholder for her bashert.

ON THE FIRST night of Passover—after he'd mentioned that he had no invitations to anyone's seder that year—

Cleo surprised Zach with chicken soup, matzoh balls, and haroses, the recipes she'd learned from Sophie Bergman.

"I'm really touched," he said.

Cleo smiled. "Don't get excited. I'm not converting."

If only, Zach thought. It wasn't such a far-fetched idea. She was a preacher's kid but not a Bible-thumping salvationist, and while she could quote scripture with the Holy Rollers who came on her program to proselytize, her religion had never presented any awkward moments in their relationship. Except once, when he asked her if she considered Jesus to be her personal savior.

"Just curious," he'd added, quickly.

Cleo had replied unemotionally, "The Son of God walks with me."

Zach wasn't sure if she was kidding but he didn't ask because, if she wasn't, he didn't want to know.

Other than that brief exchange, her Christianity looked to Zach like the mirror image of his Judaism. Culture without ritual. Connection without community. Yet, having been raised in the black church played a major role in Cleo's black identity while Zach's years in synagogue or Hebrew school seemed irrelevant to his whiteness. Race came up between them with an overlay of humor when Cleo once told him she'd booked a diverse panel for an upcoming show, "a white, a black, and a Jew," and Zach had protested. "We're not a separate race, Cleo. Jews are a religion and a people, but we come in many colors. I, for instance, consider myself *off*-white." By which he'd meant to say, "You could be Jewish, too."

But she couldn't. The sermons, traditions, and spirit of the black church were the strands with which she had rewoven her self-esteem after her father died. Knowing that she was African American, the daughter of a charismatic pastor and a powerful mother, was intrinsic to everything she felt about herself. Besides, she knew far more about her heritage than Zach did about his and she was eager to share it with him. Occasionally, a novel by Zora Neale Hurston or Toni Morrison would appear on his side of the platform bed. She'd introduced him to lectures at the Schomburg Center, plays by the Negro Ensemble Company, Harlem jazz clubs, the Alvin Ailey Dance Company. She'd told him all about the chitlin circuit—black vaudeville's borsht belt—and exposed him to music he'd known little or nothing about: ragtime, spirituals, gospel, African work songs, rap. She'd decoded the black oral traditions of "call and response," "talkin' and testifyin'," and "lyin' and signifyin'," and helped him appreciate the subversive comedy of Moms Mabley.

Conjuring Jewish parallels to black culture wasn't easy for Zach. Of course, he could have plied her with books by Marx, Freud, Arendt, Bellow, Roth, Malamud, Cynthia Ozick, or Grace Paley, but Cleo had already read most of these authors and, beyond the big names, what Zach knew about the Jewish canon, Israeli novelists, or Hebrew poets wouldn't fill a term paper. Kabbalah was a mystery. His Talmud study had been cursory. His exposure to Israeli dance and filmmaking began and ended with the special events calendar at the Eames Place Synagogue where Wednesday night was hora night and the film series might feature a documentary about Israel's hydroponic cultivation of tomatoes.

That Zach could convey to Cleo so little of the Jewish heritage he had vowed to perpetuate was both ironic and disquieting. Without mastery of his tradition or a substantive grasp of his people's history, all he could offer her were boyhood memories, a fondness for bagels and lox, a superficial sense of his parents' past, a reasonable familiarity with the Sabbath prayer book, and a recording of cantor Richard Tucker singing Kol Nidre. The essence of his Jewish identity, he realized, was his obsession with Jewish identity.

IT WAS A SCOTT family tradition to buy their Christmas tree on the Friday after Thanksgiving and spend the rest of the long weekend decorating it. Cleo usually traveled to Memphis for the holiday but this year the radio station assigned her to broadcast from Macy's Thanksgiving Day Parade, so she and Zach ate their turkey dinner with friends. At breakfast the following morning, she told him she was going out to buy a bunch of Christmas decorations—this being the first year she'd be setting up her own tree—and later in the afternoon, if he felt like it, he could go with her to pick one.

His English muffin was stuck in the toaster. "I can't get the damn thing out," he bleated. Since the year Bonnie chose Thanksgiving night to announce the death of their marriage, it had not been an easy holiday for him. Now Cleo was irritating him with early Christmas preparations.

"Don't use a fork or you'll electrocute yourself," she said, and came over to pull out the plug. "You don't have to go with me. I can manage the tree by myself."

"Let me think about it," Zach replied, buttering his mangled muffin. He had never bought a Christmas tree, much less lived with one, and given what happened when he was in the fifth grade, he wasn't sure he wanted to.

AT PS 76 IN 1960, every student was expected to help decorate the school for Christmas. Some wove red and green ribbons through the stair rails, others festooned the tree, baked Christmas cookies, rehearsed Christmas carols, or took on roles in the nativity play. That year, Zach Levy boycotted Christmas. It was unfair, he decided at age ten, for Jewish students to be pressed into service for someone else's holiday, indefensible to force Jews to sing about someone else's savior. "Dear Miss Shawn," he wrote in his note to the principal:

> Every Christmas, I feel like an alien in my own school because I am Jewish and all the holiday activities are Christian. This year, I would like to be excused. I do not think I should be expected to celebrate the religion of the people who killed all my relatives during the Second World War.
>
> You may think Christmas trees are just winter decorations but a Catholic friend of mine told me they are Christ symbols. The tree stands for the wooden cross, and the red

berries and shiny red balls symbolize drops of Jesus's blood, and the star on the top is supposed to be the star in the East. I believe these things should not be displayed in school because they remind people of the crucifixion, which Jews keep getting blamed for, even though the Romans did it. I don't think Jewish students should be forced to celebrate Christmas.

My father agrees, so he is signing this letter, too. Thank you.

Sincerely,

Zachariah Levy ______________________

Nathan Levy ________________________

Zach's penmanship was perfect and he'd purposely used a ruler to make the signature lines but when he presented the letter to his father, Nathan wouldn't sign it; he was afraid it would mark Zach as a troublemaker, get him ostracized, maybe even expelled. "Years from now," Nathan warned, "your name might turn up on some blacklist of subversive Jews and no one will hire you." Stunned by his father's timidity, Zach insisted it was more *un*-American for an American to have to celebrate a religious holiday he didn't believe in. Nathan held firm until Zach flatly refused to go to school at all without the signed letter. That did the trick. But getting his father's signature and Miss Shawn's permission were easy compared to what he went through with his peers: the Irish kids called him a "kike," the Italian kids stuffed dirt balls down his pants, the Polish kids stole his notebook and returned it with a great big swastika on the cover. Worse yet, none of the Jewish kids joined his resistance. While he sat out the Christmas pageant in the library, everyone else proceeded to the auditorium with their frankincense and myrrh and took their places in the straw-strewn manger where the baby Jesus was a rubber doll donated by Sarah Mandelstam, the daughter of two Holocaust survivors.

ZACH'S CHRISTMAS BOYCOTT was his first act of civil disobedience, the first pebble whose ripples actually altered the current in a majoritarian stream. Later, he would go on to defend the Rastafarian cop who sued for the right to wear dreadlocks on the job, the Muslim student who sued to be allowed to keep her head scarf on in school, the son of atheists who declined to pledge allegiance "under God," the incarcerated Jew who wanted kosher food in prison, the imam accused of noise pollution for broadcasting the Muslim call to prayer five times a day (though the church across the street rang its bells every hour with impunity). Miss Shawn's permission slip excusing him from Christmas hung in a frame on Zach's office wall alongside his Harvard Law School diploma and his certificate of admission to the Supreme Court of the United States.

By the time Cleo invited him to shop with her for a Christmas tree, his fifth-grade protest had long since been vindicated. In New York City, at least, wherever a school, store, bank, doctor's office, apartment, or office building displayed a Christmas tree it displayed a menorah, usually an electric candelabra with orange bulbs. And the sound of people wishing one another "Happy Holidays" instead of the exclusionary "Merry Christmas" made him feel less like an outlier in his home town.

Zach finished his English muffin with his second cup of coffee. He read the paper, worked on a brief. For lunch, he made himself scrambled eggs. When Cleo came home, dragging shopping bags full of red and green Christmas decorations and announced that she was going right back out to buy a tree, Zach said he would come with her.

Every November, even before the first turkey carcass was turned into soup, instant pine forests, as transient as Brigadoon, materialized on the sidewalks of New York, thanks to the many intrepid tree farmers who drove down from New England with truckloads of fir and spruce and sold them, day and night, braving the frigid outdoor temperatures until, on December 26, they just as magically vanished. At the corner of Columbus Avenue and Ninety-Sixth Street, a row of trees trussed up like fat women in girdles stood tilted against a wire that had been strung between two streetlamps. A Vermonter as massive as Paul Bunyan unsheathed six or eight fragrant specimens before Cleo decided on a white pine with a nicely tapered top. Zach carried it back to the apartment on his shoulder and they spent the rest of the day hanging shiny balls, stringing tiny lights, draping tinsel, making cranberry garlands, and choosing the right branch on which to hook each miniature Santa, reindeer, snowman, angel, icicle, and candy cane.

"Almost done!" Cleo said. "I'll spread the snowflakes around the base, you stick the star on top." By then, night had fallen, so when she flicked the switch, the tree, decorated to within an inch of its life, twinkled like a sequined gown, and Cleo, bathed in its shimmering lights, looked as luminous as every little girl Zach had ever seen in a Christmas movie. Her excitement was contagious.

They celebrated with eggnog and fruitcake (her family recipe), followed by a few puffs of Acapulco gold, a rather ceremonial removal of one another's clothes, item by item, and a stoned delight in the patterns the tree lights splashed across their naked skin. Zach turned on his side to cradle Cleo's head on his arm and found himself eye to eye with the Holy Family, three Magi, four camels, and a sheep. Zonked on pot and rum, he realized there was no getting away from it: Christmas wasn't about Santa Claus and candy canes, it was about the Nativity scene, and Cleo's need to display and celebrate the babe in the manger and the creation story of her faith. Another difference that made all the difference.

CHAPTER 12

THE LAST PICNIC

ZACH SURVIVED CHRISTMAS AND SMOOTHLY NAVIGATED through the first ten and a half months of 1986, none of which presented him with any religious challenges. That March, when Althea, Clem, and Josie visited New York, Cleo took them to some Harlem church on Easter morning. Zach joined them in the afternoon for the Easter Parade, schlepping down Fifth Avenue amid women in huge flower-decked hats and crazy costumes, dogs in straw boaters, men dressed as everything from Ronald Reagan to flamingos, small children lugging baskets of pastel-colored eggs. The evening of April 15, after he and Cleo mailed their tax returns, they had dinner at the Rainbow Room to celebrate the second anniversary of the day they met, steering clear of the conflicts which threatened to derail the Black-Jewish Coalition that had brought them together in the first place.

Just before Passover, they attended Rabbi Kahn's "Freedom Seder," which was jointly sponsored by Reverend

Birmingham's church—everything cozy and ecumenical. In July, Zach and Cleo rented a beach house for weekend getaways in a remote Fire Island community that had no churches or synagogues. Yom Kippur fell on Columbus Day, which made it perfectly natural for Zach, at Herb's invitation, to spend the three-day weekend in Boston and for Cleo to fly south to be with her family.

Throughout the fall, picnicking by the lake in Central Park became a Sunday ritual. Today, however, they got a late start because Cleo had heaved up last night's dinner and slept past noon. Though she claimed to feel fine when she woke up, she called Marcus and told him she wasn't going to do a live show that night; he should replay an old tape. By the time she was finally ready to face food, it was nearly two in the afternoon. They packed the picnic supplies and set off for the park, the handles of the wicker basket stretched between them.

The weather was unseasonably mild for mid-November, the trees aflame in fiery reds and speckled yellows, the sky a blue dome overhead. Rowboats dotted the lake and the stolid apartment buildings along Fifth Avenue and Central Park South stood like coastal rock formations lending the tableau its only sharp silhouette. At the grassy slope abutting the lake, their favorite picnic spot, Zach felt a deep serenity he could only call bliss.

Cleo shook out the checkered cloth, billowed it to the grass, and unpacked the Tupperware containers while Zach uncorked the wine. When he leaned toward her to fill her glass, she covered its rim with her palm.

"Stomach acting up again?" he asked.

"Nope." Cleo tucked her denim skirt under her thighs. "I'm pregnant."

"Oh, sweetheart!" Zach, stunned, grabbed both her hands. In the future, when he revisited that moment, he would see the white swan gliding along the shore and farther out, two boats rowed by teenaged boys, colliding on purpose, as if they were Coney Island bumper cars. The metallic glare of the autumn sun would come back to him, too, how it sparkled on the surface of the water, transforming the lake into a field of shattered glass.

"Cleo," he began, dry mouthed. He glanced at the waistband of her denim skirt. Her belly was as flat as a girl's.

She anchored her gaze to the far shore. "I'm having the baby."

Zach's voice stuck in his throat.

"Don't ask me not to," she added. "You know how I feel about that."

Actually, how she felt was a matter of public record. A recent guest of hers, a militant fundamentalist, had bullied Cleo into admitting—on the air—that, despite being ardently pro-choice, she would never have an abortion herself.

A sudden downdraft showered them with autumn's confetti. Zach raised her hands to his lips, kissed them, and spoke into the cage of her fingers. "Please, Cleo. I can't do this. You know that."

She took back her hands. "I'm not asking you to do anything."

"*Telling* is as good as asking." Zach picked at the crabgrass at the border of the picnic cloth, hesitated, looked up, and shook his head. "I thought you said you were on the pill." He yanked out another clump of weeds.

"I *was* on the pill. Obviously, it's not foolproof."

Zach's jaw tightened. "Shouldn't I have a say in this?"

"You just *had* your say." She twisted her napkin. "You said you don't want it."

"It's not that simple, Cleo." He gouged out another line of crabgrass. Half-moons of dirt frowned from his fingernails. "How am I supposed to go through life knowing there's a kid of mine out there?"

Her smile vanished before he was sure he'd seen it. "Millions of men do it every day."

"You're not thinking this through, Cleo. It's tough to be a single parent. You have no idea how hard it is to go it alone."

"Actually, I know exactly how hard it is," she replied, coolly.

Of course she did. After Ifs died, her mother raised two daughters alone. Her sister Clem raised Josie on her own ever since her no-good husband walked out on them years ago claiming he had to "find" himself.

Zach, desperate now, grasped at the only straw he had left. "Why would you bring an unwanted child into the world?"

"It won't be unwanted," Cleo said. "*I* want it."

She opened the container of chicken and without asking, put a leg and thigh on his plate, then served herself the breast. After two and a half years together, each of them knew the other's preferences on practically everything—his penchant for dark meat, hers for white, his for charred steak, hers for pink, his to sleep in a dark room, hers to awaken with the morning light streaming through the windows. By now, they also knew every detail of one another's family histories. Zach remembered that Cleo's mother, Althea, was an only child because *her* mother couldn't hold a pregnancy; that Althea had three miscarriages between the birth of Clem and Cleo, accounting for the sisters' twelve-year age difference; and that Clem needed in-vitro fertilization to conceive Josie. For the Scott women, there was no such thing as an unwanted child.

The sun dipped behind the twin battlements of the San Remo but the lake tenaciously held its glow. Zach yanked out more weeds as he watched a rowboat glide by, dad and daughter side by side, each working an oar, mom nursing an infant in the bow.

"Let's go," she said finally. Neither of them had touched the food.

"Sorry, sweetheart, I didn't mean to shout."

"Forget it. It's done." Cleo got up on her knees, returned both untouched pieces of chicken to the container, put away the food, cups, dishes, and cutlery.

It *was* done. Finished. Zach corked the wine, secured the bottle to the inside lid of the basket, and buckled the straps. Then, in that mindless way people have of repeating grooved behaviors even after their relationship has self-destructed, they each took hold of one handle of the basket and started walking back uptown, leaving behind a frame of scarred earth and mounds of weeds piled up like cairns in the wilderness.

Not a word passed between them until they shut the door of her apartment, emptied the basket, and gravitated to the kitchen table. As had been his habit, Zach sat facing the view. In the deepening dusk, the boulders just inside the park loomed as immense and immovable as the lovers' impasse. It needn't be spelled out: Cleo would tolerate no infant conversion, no bris; Zach would tolerate no baptism, no baby Jesus under the tree. She was the child of a Christian preacher; he couldn't be the father of a Christian child. His training in alternative dispute resolution was useless; there was nothing to negotiate.

"Want a beer?" he asked. The kitchen was so narrow he could open the refrigerator from his chair.

She tapped her stomach. "Not allowed." Her embryo, the size of a lentil, was the elephant in the room.

Zach tore one can from a six-pack. Cleo edged past him to go to the bathroom. It surprised him that she'd held out so long. Bonnie used to have to pee every twenty minutes when she was pregnant. This time, he wouldn't get to be around to witness the habits of the mother of his child, wouldn't get to see her belly swell, palm it like a basketball, feel the first kick. There would be no couple's Lamaze classes for him and Cleo. No arguments over names. Someone else would time her contractions and coach her breathing. After tonight, Zach would have to make himself forget this pregnancy ever existed.

Through two sets of walls, he heard the water run in the bathroom sink for quite some time after the toilet was flushed and he knew she was not just washing her hands but her face. "Clean face, clean slate" she always said after finishing something difficult. His heart ached when she returned to the kitchen with a wet hairline; how well he knew her. As she squeezed past him to her chair, the patch pocket on her denim skirt caught on a cabinet knob and ripped along its seam. Cleo sat down holding the torn pocket against her hip.

Zach fidgeted with the salt and pepper shakers. "You know I can't break my promise," he blurted out. "A million Jewish children were . . . I just can't . . ."

"Can we please leave the Third Reich out of this?" Cleo burped. "I think I might have to throw up again." Zach grabbed the trash pail. "No," she said, pushing it away. He raised the window. She leaned on the sill and stuck her head out. The air smelled of mulch but smacked of winter. "Speaking of murdered children, I hope you noticed which of us wants to kill this baby."

Zach flinched. "No fair, Cleo. I just can't see another way out."

"I get it, but spare me your lecture on family loyalty, okay? I'll match mine against yours any day of the week."

They were back to the day they met: black versus Jew all over again. Zach tried to imagine what was going through her head. Did she hate him for wasting two and a half years of her life? How did she expect him to respond? Did she think he would renege on his promise to Rivka, after all that his parents had lost? Thinking of his mother conjured his younger self, neglected, confused, and desperate for the slightest sign that she loved or wanted him. The pain of that ostensibly abandoned child provoked his usual protective response and by the time he turned back to Cleo, he was no longer her lover but her lawyer. He couldn't be there as a husband and father, but he could provide the contract that would protect Cleo and her baby. He knew the child would have a loving mother. Even absent, he thought he could ensure the rest.

The only sounds in the little kitchen were the hum of the refrigerator and the tick of the oven clock. Finally, Zach said, "If you're sure you want to have it, we should put certain things in writing."

"What *things*?" she mimicked, acidly.

The nearest paper was the pink phone message pad, each sheet imprinted WHILE YOU WERE OUT. The sentence completed itself in Zach's fevered brain: WHILE YOU WERE OUT . . . of touch with your roots, you went out of control. WHILE YOU WERE OUT . . . of your mind in love, you forgot who you are and what you come from. On the blank side of the pink sheets, he wrote the terms of his proposed agreement: that all future contact between him and Cleo would be conducted through a third party (the sight or sound of her, he knew, would make him want her back); that the third party would notify Zach of the baby's birth but not inform him of its name or gender; that he would pay all obstetric or pediatric bills not covered by the radio station's health insurance policy; that he would pay monthly child support, acknowledge paternity should it ever be required for health or legal reasons; that the infant's surname would be Scott.

He read Cleo his draft and asked if it met with her approval. She said the last clause was unnecessary. "Why would I ever name my child after you?"

Zach could see that she was both seething and fighting tears. It took all his will power to resist lifting her out of her chair and wrapping her in his arms. Her sorrow was his fault. Everything was.

"I love you so much," he said, his eyes welling up. "It's killing me to leave you. You must know that."

She walked to the front door.

He hadn't touched his beer. Now he took a few gulps. "Tomorrow, I'll have this typed and hand delivered for your signature."

"You do that, Counselor." She stood in the doorway waiting for him to go, the torn pocket dangling from her skirt like a shutter on a broken hinge.

OUTSIDE IT WAS already dark. His legs felt leaden but somehow carried him around the corner and down the steps of the 103rd Street Station to the deserted subway platform. How impossible that he would never see her again, never fall asleep with her breasts pressed against his back, never awaken to her alarm clock blasting "Oh, What a Beautiful Morning," her voice singing in the shower, the smell of her chicory coffee. *Never again.* A Jewish lament for his Christian lover.

Two teens, the only passengers in his subway car, were making out under a dermatologist's ad, their fondling reminding him of the early days when he and Cleo couldn't keep their hands off each other. The boy's whiskers had reddened the girl's cheeks, her smudged mascara made her eyes look like a panda's. The advertising placard above the teenagers' heads read like a comment on their skin: *Acne. Eczema. Psoriasis. Guaranteed relief! Moles removed! Scars corrected!*

Soon after they met, Zach had told Cleo about the accident that left him with the scar on his eyebrow and she had made him promise never to have plastic surgery to repair it. "I'm glad you're not perfect," she'd said. "Nobody is."

Neither are relationships, he told himself as the train sped through the tunnel. His and Cleo's had been close to perfect but doomed from the start. A man doesn't break a vow to his mother, especially if she's dead and can't protest. Pressing his forehead to the cool subway window, he resolved to draw up the agreement and have Herb take it up to Cleo's apartment for her to sign, and for the rest of his life, he would try not to think about the woman he would always love but could never, ever see again.

At Forty-Second Street, he took the shuttle to the downtown Lexington Avenue line, caught the 6 train, and got off at Spring Street. Rather than face the musty gloom of his loft, he went straight across the hall. Mercifully, M. J. was home, Lovage being shuttered on Sunday nights. Zach, who had entered without knocking, had caught his neighbor singing "I Feel Pretty" along with the cast album of *West Side Story* while arranging a fan of crackers around a wedge of brie and some green grapes. Even when snacking alone, Chef Randolph was a class act.

"Ah! The prodigal returns. How are things on the Upper Best Side, my man?" M. J. offered Zach the cheese board, butler-style, upper body tilted slightly forward, one arm behind his back. "Voulez-vous de fromage?" Zach shook his head, collapsed into the red velvet couch, and stuck his feet up on the kidney-shaped coffee table. Instantly, M. J. slid a *Gentleman's Quarterly* under Zach's shoes with the resigned sigh of a long-suffering valet. "Man, teachin' you manners is harder 'n strikin' a match on a wet mule." Usually, the Texan's colloquialisms got a laugh out of Zach. Tonight, nothing. "Okay, what's wrong?" M. J. asked. "You look like you been chewed up, spit out, and stepped on."

Zach let his head fall back on the couch. "Cleo's pregnant."

"Fuck!"

"That was basically my reaction."

"What do you want to drink? I have an amusing claret, a nice tawny port."

"Stronger. Harder. Cleaner. I plan to drink a lot of it."

M. J. went to the freezer and came back with a frosty bottle of aquavit and two cone-shaped flutes. "Begin at the beginning," he said.

"Long version costs extra." Zach held out his glass for an immediate refill and drank his way through his report on the day's events. The bottle of Swedish firewater was empty by the time he pulled out the notes he'd scribbled on the backs of the WHILE YOU WERE OUT sheets.

M. J. fluffed up one of the red velvet cushions and wedged it behind his friend's neck. "Between you, me, and the lamp post, I'm kinda surprised she made the ending so easy for you."

"Believe me, it was the furthest thing from easy." Zach snatched the pillow and punched it. "Christ! What have I done?"

"Mind the velvet!" M. J. checked the cushion for damage, then, as if to say friendship trumps upholstery, handed it back. "I know it hurts. That woman's got more on her plate than a man can say grace over, straight or gay. But you had to leave her."

Zach wiped his wet eyes with a cocktail napkin.

"You *had* to," M. J. repeated. "You been chewing on this bone since the day you met her. She's always known you can't marry her 'cause your brother died and you're the only one left. It's not like you took advantage of her. You were always on the up-and-up about it."

Zach hugged the cushion even tighter.

"You want my advice?" M. J. asked.

"That's why I'm here."

"It's only a couple of weeks 'til Anabelle gets here. I think you should suck up your misery for now, then focus on your daughter for the next month. Annie always takes your mind off your troubles. When she leaves, if you still miss Cleo, that'll tell you something."

"What?"

"That maybe you need to say the hell with it. You can't bring your brother back from the dead. You can't carry your mama's burden. You can't save the Jews by yourself."

Zach crossed his legs with a jerk that shook his glass and splashed aquavit on the red velvet couch. "I'm hopeless, M. J." He grabbed a sheaf of cocktail napkins and dabbed at the wet stain. "You should throw me out."

"I'm about to. Forget the spill, I'll deal with it, but you need to close for renovation." M. J. helped Zach to his feet and walked him across the hall and put him to bed in his clothes, but made him take off his shoes. Like a sentry, M. J. didn't return to his own place until he heard Zach snoring.

CHAPTER 13
NEW YEAR'S RESOLUTIONS

THE GRIND OF A SANITATION TRUCK SAWED THROUGH Zach's brain at dawn. His lips were parched, his eyelids stuck to his eyeballs. After a cold shower and two Tums with a V8 chaser, and despite the Tibetan gongs ringing in his head, he threw on some shorts and went to the gym. It would take forty minutes on the treadmill to shape him up for his 9:00 a.m. meeting with Jamar Abiya, who Zach hoped would distract him from his misery. Instead, Abiya reminded him of Cleo because she had shown so much interest in his case. Just last week, when they were jogging around the reservoir, she had asked after Abiya, the New York City cop fighting for the right to wear dreadlocks on the job while the NYPD insisted the force had to maintain uniformity of appearance in the interest of esprit de corps and public safety. Zach had been explaining the constitutional ramifications—religious freedom versus security—but Cleo had seemed to take the case personally. She'd kept asking questions about what Abiya looked like and how he behaved toward his superiors.

Dialing up the treadmill's incline, it occurred to Zach that Cleo must have already known she was pregnant and was imagining her baby growing up to be a rebel like Jamar Abiya. Many guests on her show had talked about how African American males seldom reach manhood without getting arrested, imprisoned, or shot. How much more unlikely for a black boy to survive unscathed if he grew up to be the type who makes waves. Cleo probably wanted Jamar Abiya to be allowed to wear dreads on the job so that when her son grew up he, too, could be a rebel.

Zach amped up the speed of the treadmill until he was running full out.

AS THE YEAR spooled by, his longing for her intensified on certain dates—their respective birthdays, the anniversary of the day they met at the New School, even Christmas. When June rolled around, there was a new date to dread: the child's birthday.

In keeping with their agreement, Cleo's lawyer (the official "third party") called as soon as she gave birth, not to tell Zach her baby's height, weight, gender, or name, just to inform him that "Scott's issue" had arrived and child support payments should commence immediately.

He chalked up a victory each time he resisted the temptation to run up to Central Park West to catch a glimpse of the baby and its mother. While his memories of his parents were fading fast—Rivka, a spectral figure, Nathan's vigor eclipsed by his dementia—Zach's image of Cleo crystallized with time. He studiously avoided listening to her show but could still hear her voice in his head. Whenever he saw a brown-skinned baby, he thought about her child and conjured the bliss of an imagined reunion. What he could not picture was the day after, or the week after that, or any way to bridge their divide.

Without frequent refresher sessions on M. J.'s red velvet couch—where he grew dependent on Texas-size empathy, pep talks, and aquavit—Zach could not have stuck it out. But with his neighbor's help, he hadn't called Cleo, snuck up to the radio station to catch her leaving work, crouched in the bushes to watch her jog around the reservoir, or followed fifty feet behind when she wheeled the carriage in the park. He did, however, send an anonymous bunch of balloons on the baby's first birthday, which was five months before Anabelle's thirteenth.

That November, for the fourth time since she was born, his daughter's birthday fell on Thanksgiving Day. Because her bat mitzvah was the following Saturday, she wasn't coming to New York this year. Zach was flying to Melbourne for the celebration and staying through most of December. He had already given Gil Benedict full credit for persuading Bonnie that sports were good for girls; now he had Gil to thank for talking Anabelle into having a bat mitzvah at all. Both her parents had tried to convince her, albeit for different reasons: Bonnie thought it important for Anabelle to know how it feels to succeed at a difficult challenge "before society has a chance to squelch her spirit." Zach wanted his daughter to solder her link to the chain of Jewish continuity. Despite their entreaties, Anabelle—citing the fact that none of her friends were doing it and most Australian Jews considered the ceremony to be a silly American import—had initially refused. Yet, somehow, Gil had changed her mind.

Zach's bat mitzvah gift was a purposeful echo of his chain metaphor. He'd bought her a bracelet made of fourteen-karat gold links, with charms attached that symbolized his and Anabelle's relationship: the tiny gold telephone for their main means of communication over the last decade; the tiny gold book for all the stories they had read together; the fork and spoon for their many meals; the bear, basketball, and ice skates reminders of their outings to the zoo, Madison Square Garden, and Wollman Rink.

A few nights before leaving for Melbourne, Zach brought the bracelet over to M. J.'s to show it off.

"I'm absolutely charmed. It's charming!" said M. J. preening at his own wit. He spent a fair amount of time studying each miniature object before zeroing in on the tiny gold dreidel and menorah. "How great that you found Hanukkah charms."

Zach said, "I couldn't choose between them so I got both."

M. J. held the bracelet up to the light. "The only thing missing is a golden latke. I hope you're not planning to wrap this gorgeous bijou in some corny Happy Birthday paper! Let *me* decorate it!" He opened a drawer and pulled out a sheet of handmade rice paper, a roll of raffia, and a sprig of lavender silk lilacs.

"What actually happens at a bat mitzvah?" M. J. asked, as he considered additional elements for his creation.

"Come to Melbourne with me and you'll see," Zach said. "Anabelle is desperate for you to be there."

"Don'tcha think I want to, but if I left Lovage for a week, there'd be a double murder. I'm the only one standing between my head cook and my pastry chef. Just tell me what I'll be missing." He cut a square from the rice paper that turned out to be exactly the right size to cover the box, secured the wrapping with drips of sealing wax, and pressed his ring against the splotches, imprinting his seal, a steer wearing a crown.

Zach applauded. "Basically, she'll be the star of the Sabbath service at her synagogue. She'll lead the congregation in some of the prayers, chant a portion from the Torah, give a little speech. Then, we'll all go to a big party and people will give her presents. And checks."

"That's the payoff for all the prep, right?" M. J. cut a length of the raffia and shaped it into a multilooped bow.

"Yeah, but I think she also gets how meaningful it is. It's like she's saying publicly, 'Okay, I'm in!' Or put my mother's way, a bat mitzvah hammers another nail into Hitler's coffin and tells the anti-Semites we've spawned another Jew whether they like it or not."

"Well, that sounds joyful." M. J. looked up from his handiwork. "Is this a rite of passage or revenge?"

Zach didn't answer, just smiled and picked up the beautifully wrapped package. "If the restaurant fails, you definitely have a future at Bloomingdale's."

HE RETURNED FROM Australia the day before Christmas, spent the rest of the week recovering from jet lag, then took off for a long weekend at Herb's Vermont ski house. On Saturday night, he put on a ridiculous party hat and shared his New Year's resolution along with the other guests. Out loud, he said he planned to learn Russian but in his mind, he made the same resolution he'd been making on December 31 for the last two years: "I will stop thinking about Cleo. I will stop thinking about Cleo."

The trip home on Sunday took five hours. By the time he reached Soho, he was so hungry he went straight to the pizza parlor and ordered a pepperoni to go. The counterman switched on a transistor radio. Cleo's voice filled the restaurant. Zach froze. He couldn't *not* listen, couldn't run out the door without his pie, couldn't ask the man to change the station.

She was asking her listeners to call in their predictions for 1989, but she may as well have been whispering in Zach's ear. He paid, dashed home with the pie, and picked up the phone.

As usual, Marcus Charlton was screening her calls. "First name and question, puh-leeze?" The producer always reminded Zach of a put-upon diplomat who had requested a post in Bermuda but got Haiti instead. Cleo used to call him an "in-group snob," because he was born in Minnesota and, though dark skinned himself, looked down on every black who came from a Caribbean island or the American South. Charlton also had little use for white people, especially the Jewish variety, and most especially, for Zach Levy. The whole time Zach was seeing Cleo, he could feel Marcus disapproved.

"First name and question! You're hogging a line here, brother."

Hoping to ingratiate himself, Zach affected the patrician accent of the ACLU's receptionist, who was from Barbados. "Uh . . . My name is Joseph, sir, and if you'd be so kind, I'd like to ask Ms. Scott her opinion of . . . " Zach glanced at the pizza box, "the relationship between Italian Americans and African Americans."

"Well now, Joseph, that's a fascinating topic," said Charlton sarcastically, "but if you had been listening, you'd know we're taking predictions for the coming year."

"Let me think about that for a minute—"

"I have others on the line who already know what they think," he interrupted. "I'm placing you in the queue."

Here's a prediction, Zach thought, as the line went to Muzak. Marcus Charlton will never put me through.

Caller's remorse set in as soon as Zach hung up. Pizza box in hand, he charged across the hall where he found M. J. wearing his "Kiss Me, I'm Texan" apron and bright red oven mitts, a cookie sheet in each hand. Every surface of his loft was sheathed in aluminum foil and dotted with cookies, tarts, eclairs, and pastries Zach didn't recognize.

"Baking in this space is harder than putting socks on a rooster," M. J. said, sounding frazzled.

"What's all this for?" Zach asked.

"Private equity firm. I agreed to do their dessert party in some partner's fancy apartment on the Upper East Side. They scheduled it for nine to midnight on New Year's Day.

That's tonight, if you haven't noticed. We had a grease fire at Lovage this morning. Perfect timing. The Ansul system went off and the fire department flooded the place with goop. Pastry chef called in sick, probably had a hangover, so I've been working solo all day, trying to make magic with this puny little Magic Chef. Two of my waiters are coming by with a van in half an hour to take the pastries uptown." M. J. found a place on the floor for the two cookie sheets he'd been holding. "Man, if ever I needed your kitchen, it was today! Of course you weren't home and your damn door was *locked*—and the *key*? Where'd that go to? What was wrong with the service door lintel?"

"Sorry. Forgot I moved it."

"Better grab a piece of couch before I cover it with cookies. And gimme a slice of that pizza. I haven't had a gram of protein all day."

Zach didn't sit, he paced. "I'm such a fucking jerk!"

"*Excuse* me?" The chef pointed a pastry bag at him as if to threaten death by icing. "Whatever this is about, it simply cannot be about you right now. Did you just hear what I'm facing here?"

"I fucking called her show!" Zach slapped the counter, causing the cookie tins to clatter.

"Crack my meringues and you're a dead man!" M. J. shouted. "What were you thinking, Zachariah? I've spent more than two years weaning you off that girl! I thought we agreed you wouldn't listen."

"I couldn't help it. The kid at the pizza place had it on the radio." Zach folded a slice of pie and handed it to M. J. who devoured it.

"What'd you say to her?"

"I never got through the Maginot Line."

"Fucking Marcus. You must have sounded a few clowns short of a circus." M. J. returned to his pastry bag and squeezed a tiny rosette of pink frosting on each petit four. "What *would* you have said if he'd put you through?"

Zach shrugged. "I hadn't planned that far ahead."

The chef sifted confectioner's sugar over a flourless chocolate cake and some of the chalky powder wafted toward Zach. "It's just fairy dust," M. J. trilled, brushing the white stuff off Zach's sweater. "Finish your pizza and you can choose your dessert—*after* you help me pack up everything." M. J. set a large plastic box across two bar stools. "Just be sure the tarts are completely cool before you put on the lid or they'll get soggy."

Zach pitched in willingly, grateful for the busywork. When his friend offered him a black-and-white cookie, he said, "I think I'll take a madeleine. Black-and-whites remind me of me and Cleo."

That night, while it was still January 1, Zach made a new New Year's resolution: "Find bashert by this time next year."

◉

HIS MISSION TURNED into a full-scale matchmaking project, enlisting not just M. J. and Herb but every friend, colleague, fellow tenant, or gym rat willing to help Zach find his Jewish soul mate, and in no time at all, he was awash in drink dates, which sounds better than it was. A flurry of one-night stands left him feeling depressed and depleted. Another martini, forced banter, hearing yet another woman's, "So tell me about you . . ." until he dreaded hearing himself tell his own tedious life story. The last straw, an interminable Harvard Club winetasting, persuaded him to take matters into his own hands.

Zach pilfered an issue of *New York* magazine from the dentist's waiting room and answered every ad in the "Women Seeking Men" columns that included the words "Single Jewish Female," "SJF," or just "Jewish." Many women were seeking men who were "smart, funny, and financially secure." Several described themselves as "clever and curvaceous" or "slim and spunky." A few of the seekers he met through those listings were all those things; others deserved to be sued for false advertising. When they showed up at the appointed wine bar or cafe, Zach knew almost immediately that they were wrong for him—the brunette who came to brunch in blue eye shadow and chandelier earrings; the alarmingly skinny woman who ordered a Cobb salad and picked out the cheese; the sophisticate who said she loved jazz but looked blank when he mentioned Thelonius Monk.

After six or seven duds, Zach decided to reverse the process and write his own ad. Unsure how to describe himself and still be likable, he sought inspiration in the magazine's "Men Seeking Women" columns:

"Venture capitalist with global interests, youthful fifty-six, seeks slender, cerebral vixen who can make me laugh, loves dogs, is mysterious, complex, and can karaoke!"

"Scott Fitzgerald searching for his Zelda. You should be witty and wear pearls to bed. Neuroses forgiven if you read *Gatsby* at least twice."

"I'm easy; all you have to be is over five foot eight, under 120 lbs., down-to-earth, and rich. Divorced okay, but no kids, please. "

"You: intelligent but not pompous, attractive but not vain, affectionate but not needy. Me: brainy but not overbearing, secure but not arrogant, sexually adventurous but not kinky."

Zach wondered how a woman must feel reading these absurdly exacting demands, but the nervy specificity of the men's ads emboldened him. Two hours and four heavily edited, handwritten, legal-size pages later, he called the magazine's classified department and dictated the following copy:

> SJM, 38, lawyer, 6'1", seeking SJF, 28–35, for permanent relationship. Me: left wing, athlete, dad of one (want more), nonobservant Jew but committed to Jewish survival. You: intelligent, sporty, family minded, comfortably Jewish. Nonsmokers only. Include letter and photo.

Listening to the ad clerk read his copy back to him, Zach had a Groucho Marx moment: he could not imagine being interested in the sort of woman who'd be interested in anyone who could write such an ad. It had no edge, nothing witty or artful, no spicy innuendos. Yet he recognized the man it described. To hell with edge, he decided. His ad was accurate. Better an empty mailbox than a fake pitch.

CHAPTER 14
GETTING AHEAD OF HIMSELF

AS ANY WOMAN IN THE WESTERN WORLD COULD HAVE predicted, his mailbox was swamped. Professors, doctors, lawyers, a fitness instructor, a museum director, an architect, a travel consultant, even a Jewish airline pilot; they all wanted to meet Zach and have his children. He pored over every letter and photo but the packet that kept landing at the top of the pile came from a young woman with the comical name of Babka Tanenbaum, who described herself as a "performance artist." She had enclosed a photo of herself dressed as a Hasidic man, above the caption "Babka Channels Yentl the Yeshiva Boy." Her costume—black coat, black hat, ear curls, tallis—couldn't disguise the fact that she was disarmingly lovely.

Cross-dressing was the least of Babka Tanenbaum's religious transgressions. Instead of a regulation tallis with fringes, hers ended in red ostrich feathers. She carried what looked like an etrog and lulav, ritual objects associated with the harvest holiday of Sukkot, but rather than the unblemished citron prescribed by Jewish law, her "etrog" was a misshapen grapefruit encircled by a crown of thorns. And instead of the regulation lulav, which is supposed to be composed of palm, myrtle, and willow stalks gathered into a simple sheaf, her stalks were bound in the shape of a cross. Rabbi Goldfarb would be apoplectic but Zach could not resist Babka's introductory note:

Hi SJM,

I'm a Barnard graduate, a thirty-four-year-old recovering investment banker turned performance artist and, as you can see in the enclosed photograph, Jewish themes are central to my work. Though some consider me heretical, my quarrel is not with Judaism, only with its sanctimony and sexism.

My "Yentl" piece was inspired by the first woman ever to run for a seat on a religious council in Israel (see tallis). The way the Orthodox machers treated her (see payess), you'd have thought she was a transvestite applying for the job of Chief Rabbi. The black hats nearly crucified her (see thorns and lulav) but she won (see ostrich feathers).

I went to a yeshiva and grew up Conservadox so I know a lot about Judaism, but I prefer to express my spirituality through my art. Feel free to check out my latest performance piece this Saturday night at the Broome Street Theater at 10 p.m. No admission fee. If you like what you see, come up and introduce yourself after the show. Otherwise, you can slink out and I'll never know I was rejected.

PS I want four kids.

Clever. Intriguing. Best of all, risk free, she was offering Zach the chance to judge without being judged. At worst, he'd blow two hours of his so-called life and skip out before the lights came up. At best, the woman with the coffee-cake name could be his bashert.

Babka's letter had promised free admission yet when he arrived, a girl with green hair was stationed at the theater entrance with a cigar box and a tented sign set up on a metal table, "Suggested Donation: $10." Zach's wallet contained nothing but four singles and the hundred-dollar bill a friend had given him to repay a poker debt. The deli had refused to break anything larger than a twenty and he'd had no time to stop at the bank. Ahead of him in the theater line were raggedy beatniks and bohemians, yet everyone tossed a ten into the cigar box. Zach wasn't sure if he should plunk down the four singles and feel like a cheapskate or hand over his hundred and stand there while she held it up to the light.

"I'm afraid I forgot my wallet," he mumbled when his time came, shambling past without donating anything. "I'll make up for it next time." The green-haired girl didn't sneer at his face, she sneered at his blazer.

The theater, a dingy former warehouse, was retrofitted exactly as he had imagined—brick walls, folding chairs, a platform stage the size of a freight elevator. What he could not have imagined was the breathtaking impact of the young woman who bounded into the spotlight. At first, Zach thought she was naked, but what looked like skin was a flesh-toned leotard that clung to her sculpted torso and long legs like a wet suit. Her auburn hair was pulled back in a bun and as she stood there, arms folded, legs planted wide apart, accepting the applause of the audience, she exuded the confidence of a woman whose body had never known anything but praise.

From the large steamer trunk at stage left, the performer pulled out a red kimono and a white Noh mask, transforming herself from a sinewy Martha Graham into a prim Madame Butterfly. However, instead of a carnation or camellia, she fastened to her hair a red satin yarmulke. Then, rocking back and forth, she chanted from behind the mask, "*Baruch atah adonai, elohaynu melech ha'olam, shehechiyanu, v'parmegiano, v'reggiano, la'zman ha'zeh.*"

Zach nearly cracked up. It was the Jewish gratitude blessing with two of its words replaced by the names of Italian cheeses. Other audience members echoed his laughter of recognition to which Zach added his private delight at her flawless Hebrew and pitch-perfect tonality. Babka Tanenbaum wasn't just a Jew but an educated one.

She bowed deeply and burrowed each hand into the opposite sleeve of her kimono. "Scene one," she announced from behind the white mask. "Two Tokyo businessmen soak in a bath house. The first man says, 'Hirokosan, I have unpleasant news. Your wife is dishonoring you with a foreigner of the Jewish faith.' Hirokosan immediately scurries home to confront his wife. 'I am told that you are dishonoring me with a foreigner of the Jewish faith.' 'That's a lie,' she says. 'What putz told you such drek?'"

When the laughter subsided, Babka bowed again. "Scene two: Haikus for Jews," she proclaimed, twirling around to show off her outfit:

The same kimono
the top geishas are wearing,
Mine comes from Loehmann's.

No fins, no flippers,
The gefilte fish swims,
With some difficulty.

Love your nose ring, son,
Don't mind me while I go and
Jump out the window.

The laughter built as the audience picked up on her parody of the seventeen-syllable Japanese poetic form.

Beyond Valium,
the peace of knowing one's child
Is an internist.

Sorry we're not home
to take your call. At the tone,
please leave your complaints.

Zach felt himself observing his pleasure from a distance, as if it were a dimly recalled emotion or a childhood playmate whom he hadn't seen in years. He leaned back and stretched out his legs beneath the chair in front of him. Babka, meanwhile, had tossed the Noh mask, yarmulke, and kimono in her prop trunk and put on a long, gray military topcoat garnished with three rows of medals and a fur hat worthy of a Moscow winter. Looking every inch the Russian commissar, she hauled a full bottle of Smirnoff out of the trunk and announced, "Scene Three: The World According to the Czar."

She dropped down on her haunches and danced a creditable Russian kazatzka while singing *The Internationale* in a Slavic accent with an occasional pause for a swig of the vodka. After finishing the song, she quoted various scholarly sounding opinions on whether Konstantin Levin in *Anna Karenina* was or wasn't a Jew. Zach was trying to unpack the meaning of this peculiar mélange of Russian references when a caustic growl arose from a man seated in the front row. Zach thought his interruption was part of the performance—the arrival of a Cossack? Stalin? the KGB?—until Babka jumped off the stage, fell to her knees before the groaning man, and, dropping her Slavic accent, shouted at him, "Show me where it hurts. Describe the pain."

The man clutched his chest. "Sharp. Crushing. Tight."

"Angie! Call 911!" Babka yelled to the green-haired girl, who had left the cigar box to operate the light board. "Tell them we've got an infarct."

Amplified by the theater's acoustics, the man's cries were raw and chilling.

Babka shrugged off the heavy coat and flung the fur hat toward the back wall of the stage. "Is there a doctor in the house?" she called out urgently. In a Marx Brothers movie, that line would cue Harpo to enter, honking. At the Metropolitan Opera, it would summon a brigade of cardiologists in black tie. In the Broome Street Theater on the Lower East Side, it drew one unqualified volunteer in a Brooks Brothers blazer.

"What can I do?" Zach asked, rushing forward. "I'm not a doctor but . . ."

"Help me get him down on the floor. Careful he doesn't hit his head."

Zach gripped the man's shoulders and the two of them lowered him into a prone position. Poor guy was scary looking: splotched bald head, ashen skin, lips bleached white with agony.

"Could be angina," Babka said. "Or an AMI."

"AMI?"

"Acute myocardial infarction. Heart attack." She unbuttoned the man's collar.

Angie flew in from backstage to announce that an ambulance was on the way; the show was canceled.

To his shame, Zach's first reaction was, "There goes my night." His second reaction, "Why do bad thoughts happen to good people?" was only slightly redemptive. He was a good person, he told himself, had simply been overexcited by the evening's prospects. Now, he shifted his full attention to the victim, felt for him, worried about his survival.

Babka had one hand on the man's chest, the other pressed against the side of his neck. "No pulse! We have to start CPR."

"I don't know how," Zach replied, embarrassed. Every January, his gym offered members a free course in cardiopulmonary resuscitation. He'd never taken advantage of it.

"It's not hard, watch me," she commanded. Her knees straddling the man's hips, she leaned over, pinched close his nostrils, forced open his mouth, covered it with her own, and blew two quick breaths into his lungs. "That's your part," she said, rising slightly. "I'll compress his chest fifteen times and when I say 'Blow,' you'll do what I just did."

Zach nodded, impressed by her self-assurance, humiliated by his inadequacy. He locked his lips around the victim's mouth like a gasket, felt the sandpaper stubble of a two-day beard against his chin, tasted aftershave lotion, then garlic and cheap wine and marveled that he had come to be exchanging body fluids with one stranger while taking orders from another who could be his fated one, or simply nuts. The moment felt surreal, yet profound. Falling into the rhythm of Babka's pumping, he lost count of his exhales, of all sensation in his jaw, of time and space and everything but her strong, steady count and the power in his lungs, until, suddenly, his mouth was pulled off the man's face like a suction cup off a tile wall.

"We'll take it from here, buddy." It was an EMS worker in green scrubs.

"Domino's could've made it here faster," Babka snapped, sweat staining the underarms of her leotard, loose strands of hair dangling from her bun. She fired off the facts as she accompanied the patient into the ambulance. "He showed Levine's sign about eight minutes ago. Typical ischemic cardiac pain. Passed out before I could get his name, age, or history."

Before the back doors slammed shut, Zach saw the paramedics hook the man up to an armada of blinking machines. Babka had a smile on her face when she came out. "EKG looks good!" She high-fived Angie while Zach, slumped in one of the folding chairs, could barely summon the energy to brush her palm.

After the ambulance raced off, sirens wailing, Angie set the work light on the stage and cast a disapproving eye on Zach as she headed for the door. Only then did he realize that he was still wearing his blazer.

"You're my SJM, aren't you?" asked Babka, her handshake firm.

"Is it that obvious?"

"No, but I'm psychic."

"I'm Zach Levy. You're incredible! What do you do for an encore, tracheotomies?"

"I thought you were in the market for an M-R-S, not an E-M-T."

"Why not both?" Zach massaged his numb jaw with both hands as Babka pulled a chair up beside him. He liked the way she smelled, a blend of makeup, sweat, and mint. "I mean it—that was one helluva finale. When you first jumped off the stage, I thought you were either gunning for a heckler or losing it."

She grinned. "Courage in women is often mistaken for madness."

"Where'd you learn CPR?"

"My last job. One of our senior VPs had a heart attack and died at his desk. Management made the course mandatory after that." (Zach had forgotten the "recovering investment banker" line in her letter.) "I once saved a guy in accounting. It was April 15, tax day. Put two and two together, it spelled heart attack, even without Levine's sign."

"You said that word to the medic. Levine's sign?"

"It's what the bald guy did when he was in pain," Babka replied. "If someone clenches his fist to his chest and uses words like 'crushing,' you know it's not a fish bone or stroke. It's cardiac."

Zach moaned. "Oy, a heart pain named for a Jew. That's perfect."

"Not the pain. The diagnosis. Levine did us a favor."

"You certainly did that man a favor. You saved his life."

Babka shrugged. "Save one life, you save the world."

That line had been woven on a tapestry in Rabbi Goldfarb's study, along with its source, Tractate Sanhedrin 37a, but Zach never expected to hear it from a woman he met through a personal ad. He studied her face; it was blank as paper. "Last I checked," he said, "most people don't quote Talmud on a first date."

"Oh, is this a date?" Babka said, with a mischievous smirk. "I thought it was an audition." She retrieved the commissar's coat and hat and dumped them in the prop trunk. "I just love the idea that the air we breathe contains 21 percent oxygen and the air we exhale contains only 10 percent oxygen, and yet it's enough to keep someone alive. We're the only species that can breathe life into one another." She hopped on the platform stage and picked up the Smirnoff bottle, sucking a dram or two before passing it to Zach.

The liquid scorched his throat. "Hey! I thought actors drank fake booze."

"I'm not an actor, I'm an artist," she frowned. "Wait here while I change into street clothes?"

Ten minutes later, she returned wearing an Indian-style chamois dress the color of butterscotch, a silver necklace studded with turquoise stones, beaded moccasins, her hair plaited in two thick braids, hardly the average person's idea of street clothes.

Zach gave her a thumbs up. "Your Pocahontas is even better than your Yentl."

For the better part of an hour the two of them sat in the vacant theater passing the vodka bottle between them while Babka peppered Zach with questions that none of his countless blind dates had ever asked. Did he ever experience anti-Semitism? Cheat on an exam? Consider suicide? Zach answered each query honestly, no slick fibs or exaggerations. If she turned out to be his bashert, he wanted her to see him for the person he was.

"Cheated, once, on an algebra test," he said. "I'd been out with the mumps when the unit was taught and never made up the class."

"Shoplift?"

Thinking back to the stores on Kingsbridge Road, he shook his head, "Most of the shopkeepers in my neighborhood were refugees like my parents. How could I stiff them?"

"Anti-Semitism?" she prodded.

"A kid called Brendan Riley once threw a handful of pennies at me and shouted 'Go fetch.' I'd never heard the stereotype about Jews and money. Every Jew I knew was poor."

Babka smiled, tippled the vodka bottle, was quiet for a minute, then bit her lip. "Ever want to kill yourself?"

He looked at her. "Never," he said firmly, then, as if his reply needed a rational justification, added, "My parents were survivors."

Babka's eyes widened. "No way! Mine, *too*. Mom, Dachau. Dad, Theresienstadt. Yours?"

Zach sighed. "Mom, Auschwitz. Dad, Polish Resistance."

"The way I look at it," Babka said, "being a survivor's kid is a reason *to* kill yourself. Didn't you hate being defined by your parents' tragedies?"

"I still define myself that way," he admitted.

She took his hand. "What do you say we move the party to my place?"

Though Babka's one-room studio on the Bowery, a fifth-floor walk-up, had a double-height ceiling, its ambience was that of a crowded, chaotic Middle Eastern souk. Kilim rugs were thrown helter-skelter across the floors and every piece of furniture—sofa, tables, chairs, hassocks, everything but the radiator—was topped by some color-saturated cloth. Yellow fabric studded with tiny mirrors draped the three windows on one wall. A huge skylight composed of long glass panels filled the slanted portion of the roof looming above a queen-size bed that was flanked by two end tables swathed in madras material. The bed was covered by a furry throw that, in a former life, could have been a llama, and scattered along its headboard was a row of throw pillows clad in jewel-toned silks.

Though dazzling, her place was more like a gypsy tent, not a Jewish home. A person couldn't light Hanukkah candles here without singeing some schmatta, and there was no room for a toy box, much less a crib or a changing table.

Just then a door swung open and a stocky black man bounded out of the bathroom wearing only a towel.

"Yo, Babs," he said, jauntily. "I thought I heard voices."

"Charles, meet Zach. Old friend, new friend. Zach, Charles." Babka toggled her thumbs at each man. She couldn't have been more nonchalant about the encounter. The half-naked man, equally sanguine, whipped a wave in Zach's direction before crossing the room to retrieve a large-toothed comb from the pocket of the Knicks jacket hanging over the back of a chair, then whistled his way back to the bathroom. "Charles lives in the bowels of Brooklyn and plays sax in a club down the street," Babka explained, "so when he needs a shower between sets, he comes here. Always calls first, but if I'm not home, I've always told him he can use his key."

Zach consciously decided not to be judgmental and to simply admire Babka for her generosity. Still, when she opened the louvered doors on the far wall exposing a kitchen alcove, he was relieved. He wanted her to be normal. She might have a naked man in her bathroom, but she had a sink, stove, and refrigerator like other people. She was literate enough to send up haiku poetry and

Jewish enough to quote the Talmud. They had survivor parents in common. She knew CPR. She could save their children's lives. Wait, he told his galloping thoughts, stop getting ahead of yourself.

Charles emerged from the bathroom wearing black pants and a chartreuse shirt with the tails out. He slipped his arms into the Knicks jacket, tossed off another wave, then mimed a jazzman cradling a saxophone and played himself out the door. Zach couldn't help but wonder how many other men had Babka Tanenbaum's key.

"Drink?" she asked.

"Beer would be great."

"For future reference, what's your brand?"

Future reference. She was getting ahead of *her*self, too. "Heineken, thanks." He lowered himself into one of her overstuffed armchairs.

"Favorite time of day?" she asked.

"Sunset. You ask a lot of questions for a nonlawyer."

"Questions save time." She went to the alcove and brought back two bottles of Corona, probably the last guy's brand.

"When do I get to ask *you* questions?" Zach leaned back in the chair.

"Now." A small, round ottoman that looked like a pincushion on steroids was suddenly wedged between his legs with Babka on it, her knees a few inches from his crotch. She smiled. "What do you want to know?"

Zach wanted to know everything about her, but her close proximity threw him. "What's your greatest regret?"

"That I'm not good at sports. Same question to you, greatest regret?"

Where to begin? Zach thought. Making a huge vow when he was too young to know what he'd agreed to. Losing his marriage. Letting Anabelle go. Leaving Cleo. Having to find "the right kind of woman" rather than to simply fall in love.

"Not meeting you five years ago," he replied, his one glib line of the night.

"Trust me," Babka said. "Five years ago I wasn't worth meeting."

Zach set his Corona on the side table, took hold of Babka's braids and gently pulled her face toward him. Her lips weren't Cleo's. Maybe it was too soon. He let go of her hair. "What's with your funny name?"

"It means fir tree." She shot him a teasing glance.

"I didn't mean Tanenbaum."

"Ohhh! Babka?" She laughed, exaggerating her delayed comprehension. "It's a coffee cake."

"I *know* it's a coffee cake. My folks came from Kraków, the birthplace of babka."

"Wrong. It originated in Russia. As an Easter cake. It took Polish Jews to add the good stuff—nuts, raisins, rum. Which reminds me: how about a rum and Coke?"

Zach said he would stick with beer. She withdrew her knees from between his legs, went to the refrigerator, pulled out a Coke, and carried it over to the bed, which puzzled him until she shoved aside the multicolored pillows and opened a sliding panel in the headboard to reveal a hidden compartment containing about a dozen different liquors and whiskeys. Zach's father used to keep one squat bottle of Manischewitz on the kitchen counter for Friday night kiddush and one round bottle of plum brandy, called slivovitz, on a top shelf in the coat closet, to be tapped only for a toast on Rosh Hashana. A fifth of slivovitz could last the Levys a decade.

If her copious supply was a shock to Zach, Babka's intake was stunning. She'd guzzled vodka at the theater and polished off her beer while he still had half of his left in the bottle. Now, he almost made Levine's sign when he noted how much rum she poured in her glass of Coke. Maybe she was drinking to compensate for a secret shyness or performance anxiety. Maybe she was under pressure to pass muster with Zach whose ad, despite his efforts to the contrary, may have sounded too exacting. Or perhaps the last guy, the one who drank Corona, had recently dumped her and the booze was dulling the pain.

She sat on the edge of the mattress with her glass. "My birth certificate says Barbara but I'm told my father used to say I was sweet as babka and the nickname stuck with me. Which is more than I can say for my dad."

Zach joined her on the llama spread and draped his arm over her shoulder. "You look sad."

"I was remembering Wharton's quote: 'Life is either a tightrope or a featherbed.'"

"Which is it for you?" he asked.

"Tightrope. You?"

Tightrope was Zach's answer too, but he said featherbed as a prelude to tipping her backward onto the many-colored pillows. He unbuttoned her chamois dress and thrilled when his fingers met no straps or hooks, just warm, bare skin. He glanced down at her chest. The flattering amber light from the bedside lamp did nothing to soften the impact of the tattoo inked in blue above her left nipple—a six-pointed Jewish star with the name "Tom" at its center.

Zach yanked back his hand as if it had been scalded. The biblical prohibition against defacing the body had been tattooed on his brain by Rabbi Goldfarb's repeated invocation of Leviticus 19:28. *You must not cut your body for a dead person nor imprint any marks on you.* Once, at the schvitz, Zach had seen a man with "Never Again" tattooed on one arm and a Lion of Judah on the other, and the next day, he'd asked the rabbi if tattoos were okay as long as they were of Jewish subjects.

"I don't care if the guy had the Ten Commandments tattooed on his pupik!" Goldfarb had railed. "God created human beings in His image, so when we deface ourselves, we deface God. It's like telling Him His creation wasn't good enough. It's asur! Forbidden!"

Zach explained why he'd recoiled.

"I'm a yeshiva girl; you don't have to quote Leviticus. Actually there's a lot of debate in the Jewish world about tattoos."

"There's a lot of debate in the Jewish world about *everything*," he snapped. "But I'm sure the Torah you read in Queens says the same thing as mine did in the Bronx." He heard himself sounding like a Hebrew school hall monitor. Why did he care? He'd met the woman a few hours ago; she owed him nothing. And since when was he a guardian of other people's piety?

"Are you telling me you've never broken a commandment?" Babka asked.

"Not this one."

"Well this one's ridiculous. Every time we cut our hair or have our teeth fixed we improve on God's creation. A tattoo isn't a desecration of the body, it's an art form." She gripped Zach's finger and guided it around the border of the six-pointed star.

Moments ago, Zach was aching to touch her; now he shook her off. "Was it art when the Nazis tattooed us?"

"I've got a Star of David on my chest, Zach. Not a number."

"The Nazis put Jewish stars on our chests too," he said.

"Theirs was a mark of inferiority. Mine's a proud declaration of my identity."

"*Your* identity? Who's Tom?"

"My late husband." She gathered up the chamois dress and covered her bare breasts. "Tom was killed two years ago. Hit and run."

Zach felt sick to his stomach. "I'm so sorry, Babka." He looked up beyond the skylight as if God had the next line. Hexagons of chicken wire were embedded in the glass, safety mesh to protect those below should the panes ever break. Suddenly, the mesh became barbed wire, the moon a searchlight.

As soon as his flare-up subsided, Zach apologized for overreacting. "My mother had numbers tattooed on her arm. She kept trying to scratch them off. There was dried blood on the left sleeve of every blouse she owned. The wound would grow a scab but when it healed, the numbers were always there."

"I'm sorry, too," Babka whispered. She let the dress drop and reached for his hand.

He laced his fingers through hers. "Let's give it a minute, okay?" He didn't want their lovemaking to begin with apologies.

Both of them leaned back on the pillows and waited for the pall to pass—his outburst, her husband, his mother, Rabbi Goldfarb, the past that never lets the present rest in peace.

The next morning, Zach awoke to Georgia O'Keeffe clouds floating on a deep blue field. Babka asked if he wanted to go out for pancakes; there was a great diner a few blocks away. Nothing would have pleased him more but he had a brief due the next day, Monday. She made coffee while he showered. He dressed quickly and was already down on the Bowery hailing a cab when he remembered the paltry contents of his wallet. For a second, he considered hiking back up the five flights to borrow some cash from Babka, then decided the four bucks would cover his fare to the office and, given the usual turnout of weekend workaholics, someone would lend him money for lunch, maybe dinner, too, if the brief took him that long to finish. From now on, though, he was going to insist that all poker debts be remitted in small denominations.

The taxi meter said $3.10 when they reached his building. Zach was careful to pull out the four singles, not the hundred—except there was no hundred, not in his bill compartment nor any other slot in his wallet. He paid the driver, rode the elevator up to his office, and emptied his wallet on his desk. Credit cards, business cards, social security card, gym ID, restaurant receipts, shoemaker's ticket, dry cleaners bill, snapshot of Anabelle—everything was there but the C-note. His pockets, turned inside out, yielded two gum wrappers and a paper clip. He'd been distracted lately but not so inept or flush that he would misplace a hundred dollar bill. Sorting through his mental calendar, he tried to recall the last time he'd seen it, the last person who'd been anywhere near his wallet.

Babka. She had pulled off his pants. His wallet was in his pants. The pants spent the night on the floor beside her bed. She had awakened before he did. While he was in the shower, she'd been alone with his pants, and his wallet. All true, but the idea of Babka Tanenbaum stealing from him was absurd on its face. She might live in a funky studio and drink a little too much, but she was a Jewish girl from Queens. A Barnard girl. The child of survivors. A recovering investment banker. A yeshiva girl, for God's sake.

CHAPTER 15

PERFORMANCE ART

THE NEXT TIME HE CLIMBED THE FIVE FLIGHTS TO Babka's studio, Zach was greeted by what appeared to be a Navajo sandpainting on the floor at her threshold. She said it was made of rice flour and she had dyed, sifted, and designed it herself, and based it on the ritual art done by Tamil women who make new patterns at their doorways every morning.

"It's called a kolam," she said. "It represents two things: the boundary between public and private space and the wonder of new beginnings."

Zach took great pains to cross the threshold carefully but his mere passage whipped up a dust storm. "God, I've ruined it!"

"Not ruined, altered." Babka smiled beatifically. "The kolam is meant to be transitory. It reminds us that life must be created anew each day."

Zach's kook detector was emitting a low whine. Holly Golightly popped into his head, crystals, the Age of Aquarius. He didn't need sand art to remind him of life's impermanence. He had only to think of his dead relatives. Touched as he was by Babka's effort, he also knew how appalled his mother would have been to see all that good flour go to waste. But he praised the kolam maker for her industriousness and offered to sweep up the flour so she could reuse it.

"There are no second chances in art," she said, "only in life."

About a month into their spirited, distinctly non-domestic relationship, Babka invited Zach for a home-cooked meal. Imagining her in an apron was a stretch but he needn't have tried; she met him at the door wearing a long black dress turned inside out and back to front.

"It's backward night," she announced, fingering the string of beads that hung backward from her neck down her spine. She walked backward to the table, offered Zach a backward-turned chair, and served him dinner in reverse order: coffee, after-dinner mints, baklava, veggie burgers, lentil soup, avocado, dip, chips, and a scotch on the rocks.

"It's a performance piece, right? You're bored with the normal order of things?"

"I'm never bored," Babka replied, stretching languidly on the llama spread.

"You feel we're going backward? We shouldn't move forward?"

"Don't be so literal, Zach."

"Then I give up."

"It's an exercise in mindfulness."

"Walking backward doesn't make me mindful, Babka, it makes me dizzy."

"Dizzy beats entropy, at least it's dynamic," she said. "It forces us to pay attention to things we usually take for granted. It's what happens when we make love. We're conscious of every movement, every sensation."

"Now you're talking," Zach laughed, walking backward to the bed, where they resisted entropy in the normal sequence, foreplay to climax.

Though she'd claimed the dinner was homemade, leaving the building the next morning, Zach caught sight of the store-bought containers spilling out of one of the garbage cans lined up on the sidewalk. He didn't think she could cook in the first place—her kitchen barely had enough flatware, much less a whisk or blender—so he wasn't entirely surprised to discover evidence of her culinary deception. However, he chose to take it as proof of something more flattering—her desire, as with the kolam, to please him.

"I'M READY TO share my space," Babka Tanenbaum announced one night as he walked her home from a movie. "Want to move in?"

They'd been seeing one another for scarcely three months. Zach waited for her to say, "April fool!" He knew what day it was. That morning in the office, he'd found an ice cream cone melting on his desk that turned out to be a trick rubber sculpture. But Babka wasn't kidding. She had cleared out two drawers and a third of her closet so he could move some of his stuff in.

No thanks. Been there, done that. Then again, bashert or not bashert, that was the question, and living together might be the answer. What greater test of compatibility could there be than to share a one-room studio 24/7?

Which is how it came to pass that eighteen months after Zach Levy left Cleo Scott's calm, beige, three-room apartment overlooking Central Park, he was lugging a suitcase five flights up to Babka's excessively swagged bower, having convinced himself that he was living with her "on spec."

Just because he never bothered to kiss the mezuzah nailed to his Spring Street doorpost—and didn't miss its absence when he lived at Cleo's—didn't mean he wanted to occupy a Jewish home without one. So he suggested that they put up a mezuzah on her doorpost and was pleased when Babka not only agreed but remembered to have the Judaica shop insert the proper handwritten prayer scroll inside.

A few weeks after he'd moved in, Babka went one step further; she suggested they make a traditional Friday night meal just to see if they remembered how. Foraging in one of her kitchen cabinets, she came up with a kiddush cup even more tarnished than Zach's and a dusty pair of candlesticks. He went to the Lower East Side and bought Shabbos candles, kosher wine, a braided challah, a quart of chicken soup, a pound of cooked brisket, a few side dishes, and a bunch of white daisies. They set the table with more fabric—white linen over the multicolored madras. Babka lit the candles and recited the blessing. Zach said the motzi over the bread and the kiddush over the wine, the one-line version that most Jews memorize in childhood, then sat down and was delighted when she picked up after the word "hagefen" and continued saying the rest of the blessing, the whole kiddush by heart.

In the full flush of his gladness, the words of the doctor at the Jewish Home sounded in Zach's head: prayers are often the last thing to go.

But as time went on, aspects of Babka set off red flags. Her drinking bothered him. The frequent lack of food in the house. The unannounced drop-ins (Charles, the jazz man, wasn't unique). Even small things, like her cloying air freshener. Most of all, he was irritated by her work—not her commitment to it or the time she spent doing it, but the work itself. If not incomprehensible, performance art struck him as ludicrous and self-indulgent. Why it was called "art" in the first place and how anyone could put it on a par with "the arts" was beyond him. Though some of her productions were cute and clever, to him they boiled down to schtick. Admittedly, he had a tendency to reject what he could not understand (see *Ulysses*, twelve-tone music, meditation)—and when exposed to the obscure, he sometimes became defensive—but the fact remained: Babka's "art" annoyed him, occasionally to the point of disdain.

One sunny Sunday morning, Brubeck on the stereo, they were in bed under the skylight—Zach working on a crossword puzzle, Babka, swathed in her yellow silk robe, jotting notes for a new piece—when she suddenly unscrewed the finial off one of the lamps and plopped its shade on her head. He knew this was how she worked, making notes, and trying out props as she diagrammed a new script. A few weeks ago, when he discovered her wearing a kitchen colander on her head, its aluminum dome stuck with wildflowers, he had made the mistake of guffawing. She accused him of being too "obtuse" to see the juxtaposition of the colander (symbolizing the housewife's domestic prison) and the wildflowers (thwarted freedom trying to push through), and she'd given him the deep freeze for a couple of hours afterward.

This time, determined to behave, Zach set aside his crossword puzzle and tried to convey a humble interest in the lampshade.

"You're allowed to laugh," she said. "This is *supposed* to be funny." The Barnard Alumni Association had enlisted Babka to perform at her class reunion and she was planning a piece on gender and comedy that would explore the question, "Why are male comedians allowed to be both funny *and* sexy while female comedians are seen as desexed?" Zach chuckled when she tied the lampshade to her head with the sash from her robe and waddled toward him, Charlie Chaplin-style. "How sexy is this?" she asked.

"A man toddling in a lampshade wouldn't be sexy either," Zach said. "Where does the sexism come in?"

"When a woman does it, she's *making* men laugh. She's in control, which disturbs the conventional power balance."

"I get that. It makes sense. And it's provocative."

"Thanks. I'm also going to weave into my feminist critique an homage to five great women comedians."

"Let me guess: Sophie Tucker, Fanny Brice, Gertrude Berg—who am I missing?"

"Joan Rivers and Gilda Radner," Babka replied. "You see! You couldn't even *think* of five women. Comedy is dominated by men."

"Jews too, right? All five of your women comedians are Jewish. I bet you're going to have fun with this one."

Babka smiled. "I hope so. But the spoof's in the pudding."

That's when—consciously or not—he stepped in it. "This comedy and gender thing could be very complex and deep. Maybe it would be better if you wrote an article about it."

"Better than what?" her smile vanished.

"Acting it out. Seems a shame to bury big ideas in performance art." He noticed the expression on her face. "Sorry. I guess I really don't get it."

"Performance artists deal with big ideas all the time," she seethed. "We use our words, bodies, and props to express the truth of the human condition."

He nodded but pushed it. "I guess I've always felt that if art has to be explained, it's not working."

Babka shuffled across the studio in her daffy plush slippers—Ronald Reagan's face on one foot, Nancy Reagan's on the other—and opened the louvered doors of the kitchen alcove. The wide caftan sleeves of her yellow robe obstructed Zach's view but he could distinguish the sound of the freezer door and the syrupy trickle of frozen vodka from the sound of the refrigerator door and the louder splash of Tropicana. Ten in the morning and she was making herself a screwdriver.

"Are you actually drinking already?"

"My house, my habits," she said and turned her back on him.

She was right, of course. Yet, Zach couldn't get past her sensibility any more than he could get past Cleo's religion. He wanted to love someone without reservation.

"I didn't mean to upset you," he said. "I just want to understand your profession."

"My *profession*?" Now she faced him, fiercely. "You make me sound like an accountant. I don't think you've understood a word I've said."

If he wanted to get past this, Zach knew what he would have to say next. "I *do* understand, Babka. My sense of humor jumped the track, that's all. I love your stuff; it's brilliant."

Her expression softened. "I need to find some ankle-strap shoes for my Sophie Tucker," she said as she returned to the closet.

Zach picked up his crossword puzzle but couldn't concentrate. If he was able to tolerate Cleo's racist memorabilia, why not Babka's performance art? Cleo had pickaninies, Babka had ostrich feathers. Cleo skewered history, Babka skewered art. Yet here, too, there was a difference that made all the difference: Cleo's collection was a blip in an otherwise even personality. Babka the performer appeared to be synonymous with Babka the person, and Zach wasn't sure he could take the double dose.

A few months later, he went to a little theater in Brooklyn to watch her perform a piece she called "Jewry Duty," which began with a fusillade of joke lines:

"What's a Jewish dilemma?"

"Free ham."

"How does a Jew know when his wife's dead?"

"The sex stays the same but the dishes pile up in the sink."

"What's the difference between circumcision and crucifixion?"

"In a crucifixion, they throw out the whole Jew."

"How do you fit six million Jews in one car?"

"Two in front, three in back, the rest in the ashtray."

Zach couldn't take any more. He got up without waiting for intermission and, along with about a dozen other people, left the theater. Her performance was inexcusable. Nothing could justify it—not artistic freedom, not satire, not parody, not anything.

"I saw you leave," Babka said when she let herself into the studio an hour later.

"Half the audience left, in case you didn't notice." Zach was packing, shoving his underwear in the duffel.

"Half stayed."

"What you did on that stage was sick. Sick and sickening."

"I'm glad you're upset," she replied, coolly. "The piece was *supposed* to be disturbing."

"Well, by that standard, you've got yourself a hit."

Babka grabbed her cleansing cream and started wiping off her makeup. "You felt threatened, so you shut down. You missed the point of the piece."

"Oh yeah, what was the point?"

"That people tolerate hate speech as long as it's couched in humor. Their bar for shock gets so high that everything slips under it. They don't even notice when a joke goes too far. Denigration turns to dehumanization but they're still laughing." She seemed to ignore Zach's packed bag. "Remember the experiment where researchers discovered that if you toss a live frog in a pot of boiling water, it will keep trying to jump out, but if you start it off in cold water and gradually turn up the heat, it will die without a fight?" She threw the soiled tissues in her wastebasket and swiveled to face him. "Well, the audience was my frog, I started them off on ordinary borsht belt humor then gradually turned up the heat. The ashtray line should have horrified them, but what happened? A few people, including you, walked out. None of you protested, you just turned away and took no responsibility. The rest *stayed*. My jokes got more and more detestable but they didn't yell at me; they stayed and they *laughed*."

"That's because they were shell shocked."

"I'm telling you they laughed. No one shouted me down. No one threw a program at me."

"You could have prepared us for what was coming. Producers usually warn us when a play is going to include strobe lights or gunshots so we don't freak out. At least you could have announced that there'd be a talk-back session after the performance. You could have put a note in the Playbill, some kind of apology."

"In case you haven't noticed, I don't do apology."

ZACH DIDN'T LEAVE her that night. Something kept him in the gypsy tent with the huge skylight and the willful, wacky Babka Tanenbaum—his skepticism no match for her enchantments and his rationalizations. They weren't the first couple to have differences. So what if performance art was Greek to him? Habeas corpus was Latin to her. Mustn't nitpick the relationship to death. Excellence is the enemy of the good. Nobody's perfect. Babka unsettled him but she also captivated him. Maybe because, for all her mishegas, she was fiery, adoring, and never boring. Maybe because she was sexy. Maybe because she knew the long version of the kiddush by heart.

CHAPTER 16

THE EVIL TONGUE

ON THE BUS FROM PORT AUTHORITY TO THE NEW JERSEY Jewish Community Center where Babka would be performing, Zach opened the *Times* to a full-page ad that took his breath away: Cleo's face, life size, promoting the Harlem Chamber of Commerce, with the headline: "Experience the Vibrant Rebirth of 125th Street. Let the New Harlem Surprise You!" He tore out the page, folded it, and put it in his breast pocket.

At the New Jersey bus depot, he was met by Babka's host, the director of the JCC's Arts and Culture Committee, a voluble octogenarian who grilled him all the way to the venue.

"It must be a kick, living with such a talent. Where does Babka get her ideas?" The woman took her veined hands off the steering wheel as she gestured, making Zach tense. "Does she rehearse or improvise? I just *love* the title of tonight's show, don't you?"

Zach didn't remember the title until they drove into the JCC's parking lot and he saw it on the marquee:

BABKA TANENBAUM IN

"MOLLY GOLDBERG WAS A YENTA"

TONIGHT AT 8

Babka's popularity in Jewish settings perplexed him since most of her performance pieces focused on stock characters and caricatures ("Jewry Duty" being in a category of its own). Yet she was a favorite of synagogues and JCCs, and won raves from reviewers in Jewish publications. Almost every article cited her yeshiva training, as if it gave her license to abuse.

The JCC's auditorium was state of the art—plush seats, digital lighting board, a broad stage. The curtain rose on the facade and courtyard of a brick apartment house, a dead ringer for Zach's old building in the Bronx. Babka was leaning on a windowsill, her bosom padded to appear matronly, her hair pinned up in a bun. Channeling Molly Goldberg, the matriarch of the fifties television family, the performer called across the courtyard to an unseen neighbor:

"Yoo-hoo, Mrs. Mandelbroit! You home? Oh, hello there, darling. How come you weren't in shul last Shabbos? You missed a wonderful sermon about gossip."

"What?" Babka cupped her hand to her ear. "No, not Hollywood gossip—*normal* gossip, like when we talk behind each other's backs. It's a big Jewish crime, you know. Worse than murder." She leaned further out the window. "Why? Because it don't just kill one person, it kills three: the one who says it, the one who hears it, and the one they're talking about. It's called lashen hora. The evil tongue.

"The punishment for gossip? Oy, gevalt." Babka shook her head. "*Stoning*! Can you imagine? For a bissel chitchat, you could get killed with rocks." She flicked her wrist as if to shoo away the idea. "So I'm thinking maybe we should stop." Craning her neck toward her invisible neighbor, she replied, "I know we don't mean any harm, but it's better we stop for a while . . ."

Suddenly, from the kitchen behind her came the amplified sound of bubbling liquid. "Oh, no!" Babka glanced over her shoulder. "My cholent's boiling over! Stay where you are, Mrs. Mandelbroit. I'll be right back." She ducked inside the building. Twenty seconds passed. Zach heard quizzical murmurings from the audience: "Was that the end?" "Should we clap or what?" "You think maybe something happened to her?"

Suddenly, Babka was back at the window. "My cholent's okay but my stove, oy vey, such a balagan! So, did you hear the news? Arlene and Larry Futterman are adopting a baby from China. My cleaning lady, who's friends with their cleaning lady's sister-in-law, says Larry had a vasectomy during his first marriage on account of his first wife not wanting any kids, but . . ."

Blackout.

Babka did four more short sketches that night, each received enthusiastically. After taking her bows and signing a few programs, she and Zach were driven back to the bus depot. She snuggled against his chest and fell asleep at once, her cheek a millimeter from the folded-up page in his breast pocket. When they arrived at Port Authority, Zach stopped in the men's room and threw away Cleo's picture without looking at it.

Her Molly Goldberg piece newly endeared Babka to Zach. It made up for her Tibetan bowls and the Tamil kolams by reassuring him that his girlfriend came from the same world he did. Not that his mother ever gossiped—how could she when she barely spoke to anyone? Still, the monologue evoked the chatter he'd overheard in the old neighborhood, the birdcalls of the Bronx. And because Babka knew that world, Zach felt he knew Babka.

Except when he didn't. Like the time he found a roll of institutional toilet paper under the bathroom sink and she confessed to stealing paper products from public restrooms—something she called "a little caper." And the night at the movies when she scavenged an empty popcorn bucket from the trash and presented it at the concession stand to claim the "free refill for every jumbo bucket purchased." Though in denial about her ethical lapses, it once crossed Zach's mind that relieving him of his hundred-dollar bill might have been one of her little capers.

On a freakishly frosty evening in October, as they were climbing under the bedcover to get warm, he caught a glimpse of her tattoo.

"I heard they have a new way of removing those things with lasers."

Babka sighed. "What's your problem, Zach?"

"It bothers me."

"What doesn't bother you?" Babka sat up.

"I'm just saying—"

"You have to stop obsessing over my frigging tattoo." She pulled up her Barnard sweatshirt baring her naked chest. "This is what I look like, Zach. You want me, I come defaced. I come with vices." Yanking open the drawer of the bedside table, she pulled out what looked like her cosmetic case and dumped its contents on the fur spread. "I have a pack-a-day habit. Take it or leave it."

At the sight of the Marlboros, the Bic lighter, and the lid from a jar of Hellmann's mayonnaise that clearly had done service as an ashtray, Zach's first thought was an inane, "Wait a minute! Didn't my ad specify a nonsmoker?"

Babka lit up and took a deep drag. She said she'd started smoking years ago when her husband was hit by a car and the cop at the accident scene gave her a cigarette to calm her down. She'd quit before she met Zach and stayed off until she hit a wall on the gender and comedy piece. The next day, when Charles happened to come by for his shower, she'd mooched a couple of cigarettes from him and got hooked again.

"I'm definitely going to quit." She stamped out the butt in the Hellmann's lid. "It's the second item on my to-do list."

"What's the first?"

"Finding a job." She packed up her smoking supplies and put the cosmetic case in the drawer. "I'm broke. That's why I don't buy groceries. I owe two months rent. The phone company's threatening to cut off service." She collapsed against Zach's chest.

No wonder there was no heat in the studio. He put an

arm around her but couldn't let the subject go. "You know you can't be buried in a Jewish cemetery with a tattoo."

"Oh my God, will you ever quit trying to reform me? News flash: I'm going to be cremated."

Rabbi Goldfarb's voice thundered in Zach's head. "Asur! If you burn the body, you shock the soul. You incinerate the luz, the bone of resurrection. When the Messiah comes, he needs that bone to rebuild your body for eternal life in the world to come." Rabbi had demonstrated the location of the luz on himself, reaching behind his head to the knob where the base of his neck met his spinal column. Zach remembered asking him how the Messiah would rebuild the bodies of those who were incinerated in the Nazi ovens. "Don't worry, their place in heaven is guaranteed," Goldfarb said. "They didn't *choose* to burn."

The next day, Zach moved back to Spring Street. Babka dropped off a fresh-baked babka with a note. He returned to her studio but only to pack up his things. She was wearing her yellow robe, five screwdrivers to the wind and counting.

"You're leaving because I smoke?" she asked.

He shook his head.

"The stupid tattoo?"

"No."

"Because my work is weird?"

"It's not any one thing," Zach said. "We're just a bad match. We're not happy."

Abruptly, she switched gears and went on the attack, told him what an easy mark he'd been, how gullible and naive. The missing hundred? She'd snitched it. Wall Street?

She'd once worked as a temp in the back office at Merrill Lynch. Charles the sax player? He was also her sometime lover.

When Zach was halfway down the stairs, he heard her yell, "I never wanted kids anyway!"

"Babka was a mule passin' for a pony," M. J. declared later.

"And I was a horse's ass," Zach said from the red velvet couch.

M. J. snickered. "In Dallas, we got a name for a man who's both stupid and an asshole."

Zach replied, "Heterosexual?"

CHAPTER 17
TO THE PLAYGROUND

ON JULY 12, 1990, A THURSDAY MORNING, THE PHONE rang on Zach's desk.

"Hi, it's me." As though that voice could have belonged to anyone but Cleo. "I know I shouldn't be calling but Terrell's been asking for his daddy." (Long pause) "Incessantly." Zach gripped the receiver, his heart jumping around in his rib cage. "Before I tell him anything definitive, I thought I'd give you a chance to meet him." (Short pause) "Or at least see him."

She'd had a boy. Zach wasn't supposed to have been told the baby's name or gender, not by the obstetrician or the lawyers, and certainly not by its mother. That was their deal. She had signed it. "Scott's issue" was the legal term for the child she had carried to term despite his wishes; he'd been supporting "Scott's issue" financially, as promised, and she'd kept her word for three years. Why go back on it now? Too late; she'd said it. Scott's issue was a person. A boy. *Terrell.* Terrell? What the hell kind of name is that for a son of the tribe of Levi?

"His little friends are always talking about their fathers and some of the dads pick them up at day care, so naturally Terrell wants to know where *his* daddy is. I can usually distract him with a book or toy but he's whip smart for a three-year-old and he won't let go of the idea that he must have a daddy somewhere, and frankly, I haven't had the guts to tell him the truth, but I can't postpone it forever so before I say something neither of us can take back, I thought you might want to weigh in."

"Weigh in?" Zach couldn't keep pace with the onrushing torrent of her words.

"Reconsider. Whether you might want to be . . . " She stopped. "I know it's a long shot. You're probably sitting there fuming and—"

"Cleo—"

"If you want to stick to our deal, this is the last you'll hear from me. But if you're willing to listen for a minute, I have a proposition." Her usually fluid sentences tumbled over one another as if to preempt his hanging up. She wasn't breaking their contract, she said, just being a mother, and this wasn't about the two of *them*, she wanted to make that clear; she was doing fine, didn't need Zach for anything. "But a boy needs a father, so before I tell him his daddy died . . . "

Absurdly, Zach heard himself ask, "Died how?"

"I don't know *how*! Mountain climbing, skydiving, spelunking. I'll make you sound like a spectacular hero, for his sake. Terrell's a spectacular kid and he deserves to have a great father, dead or alive. The point is I've got to tell him *something*. Soon."

Cleo was a proud woman, Zach knew better than anyone how difficult it must have been for her to make this call. “One second,” he said, “let me close my door.”

His office door was already closed but he put her on hold, buying time to think. Few responses rose to the level of a speakable sentence. The sensible reply, “Thanks, but no thanks,” would have ended their conversation, a course clearly dictated by the fact that what got them into this bind in the first place, their original dilemma, had not changed. The lawyerly answer, “A deal’s a deal,” would have been similarly dispositive. The Jewish answer, one that meets a question with a question and leaves an opening a mile wide, was the one that rose in his throat. The phone’s flashing red light reminded him of emergencies, heart monitors, fire alarms, exit signs. He released the hold button.

“What did you have in mind, Cleo?” An opening a mile wide.

She said next Tuesday at noon, she would bring Terrell to Adventure Playground in Central Park, the one up the hill across from Tavern on the Green. Zach could meet them there—or not. If he didn’t show up, she would understand that he wanted their deal to stay in force. If he was curious about what his genes had produced, he could come, have a look at the boy, and leave. But if he was open to revisiting his decision, he could, without identifying himself to Terrell, and with no obligation to her, spend the afternoon with the boy—watch him play, talk to him, give him an IQ test, check his reflexes, do whatever he needed to do to get a sense of whether he wanted his son in his life. After that, Cleo would give him three days to think it over and tell her his decision.

When Zach didn't immediately respond, she assumed she had not made herself clear. "In other words," she said, "it's an eight-day proposition. Between now and Tuesday, you'll consider whether or not to come to the playground. If you show up, you'll have that whole afternoon to observe him. Three days after that, by midnight Friday at the latest, you'll let me know if you want him. But if you do, you'll have to swear to be fully present in his life—not mine, *his*. Terrell needs a real father, an involved father, or none at all. I won't let you get away with being a drop-in dad."

Breaking a contract *and* making demands! He had to admire her chutzpah!

"Here's the addendum," she said firmly. "If you don't show up at the playground, or if you come and later decide you don't want him, then you're toast. Once I tell Terrell you're dead, you have to *stay* dead. Don't imagine you can turn up someday to claim him. You can *never* change your mind."

Listening was Zach's first mistake. Yet as far as he could tell, her proposal gave him an out every step of the way—come, don't come; stay, don't stay; say yes, say no. It was an offer he could not refuse. Gazing out of his office window at the square patch of blue stitched between the tall gray rooftops, he said in a level voice, "Fair enough." But when he hung up the phone and rushed to Herb's office to report the conversation, he was trembling.

"You're right, it's a no-lose proposition," his friend said.

"But nothing's changed. I'm still Jewish, Cleo's still not. I'm still carrying my mother around with me."

"An afternoon with the kid might be all it takes to make up your mind—and maybe end your obsession with Cleo. Then again, it might pull you back and change your life." Herb squeezed Zach's arm. "If I were you, pal, I'd go to that playground."

For the next five days, trial transcripts swam before Zach's eyes. He couldn't read or reason. His colleagues seemed to be talking gibberish. Old movies and sitcoms filled his nights. Mornings, he was too sleep deprived to go to the gym. Part of his torment was not related to potential fatherhood but to the fathering he'd already botched. Cleo gave him too much credit for his relationship with Anabelle—which, though idyllic when he broke up with Cleo three and a half years ago, had greatly deteriorated since.

A pure delight as a child, his daughter had morphed into an angry adolescent, their connection no longer strained merely by geographical distance but by a deeper, wider gulf. During her most recent visitation, Zach had felt defeated by her hostility and diffidence. She'd been sullen, critical, absent for hours at a time, refusing to say where. One night she was two hours late for their usual lighting of the Hanukkah candles and Zach would have called the police had M. J. not persuaded him to give her an extra hour to come home. Another night, she'd stumbled through the door past eleven o'clock, clearly stoned. Her calls to her friends in Melbourne had jacked up his phone bill to the point where the grand total could have bought her an airline ticket home. Five days into her stay, he was ready to send her back.

She'd been with him for nearly a week when he talked her into going to the movies. She chose *Steel Magnolias*. Afterward, he asked if she enjoyed it.

"It was okay," she said. Back at the loft, she threw herself on the couch and turned on the Rangers vs. Islanders game. She'd always been a Rangers fan. The score was tied 0–0 at the end of the first period.

Zach ventured, "You think they have a chance at the Stanley Cup this year?"

"Who cares?" she snorted and stalked toward her room.

"What should we do tomorrow?" Zach called after her.

"Whatever."

The next morning, he padded into the kitchen in his pajamas. "I just had to step over your dirty laundry to get to the sink," he said. Anabelle didn't look up. "Your wet towel and dirty underwear? You left them in a heap in the middle of the bathroom floor. Please go and pick them up."

Acting as if he were invisible, she served herself Raisin Bran, milk, blueberries, hunkered down over the bowl, and read the back of the cereal box while she ate.

Zach raised his voice. "Would you please pick up your laundry and put it in the basket?"

No response. She finished her cereal, plunked the bowl in the sink, and opened the coffee canister. That irked him, too. At fifteen, she had no business drinking coffee.

"*Now*!" he shouted. "I want you to get your crap off the floor this minute!"

Anabelle slammed the canister on the countertop. “And I want you to stop being such a fucking dictator!”

Her brazen impertinence clearly demanded a response, but what? She didn’t care about clothes or anything else, so what could he deprive her of? Besides, penalizing her would only give her another reason to resent him. The last thing he wanted was for her to return to Australia with a sour taste in her mouth. He wondered if other fathers worried so much about being liked by their kids. Maybe leaving stuff on the floor wasn’t such a terrible infraction. Teenagers were famous for being slovenly. Yet wasn’t it his responsibility, as much as Bonnie’s, to set standards? And didn’t he have the right to demand respect from his daughter? The right, yes. But, he realized in that frozen moment, not the power.

He walked around the counter and took her by the shoulders. “First, *you* have to stop being rude,” he said. “Then you have to pick up your things.”

She didn’t twist away, just looked him in the eye and spit out, “What if I don’t?”

The gauntlet thrown, their faces inches apart, Zach replied in a voice as hard as the granite counter, “If you don’t, I will gather up your laundry and throw it in the hamper. But I will be deeply disappointed in you. We will share this space for the rest of the month, and you will continue to be mean and moody and I will keep trying to make you happy.” He took a breath. “I will wish to God that I knew what was making you so angry and why you’ve been so hell-bent on hurting me, and I will be indescribably sad.”

His bare feet rooted to the floor, he released his daughter's shoulders but kept her gaze until she looked away. She returned the coffee canister to the cabinet, rinsed out her cereal bowl, and, with a stiff spine, walked over to the bathroom and closed the door. Zach made a couple of scrambled eggs for himself. He sat at the counter and read the morning paper. He did not turn around when he heard the bathroom door open, Anabelle's footsteps, the closing of her bedroom door. Ten minutes later, she came out wearing a turtleneck, jeans, and her winter jacket.

"I'm going for a bike ride," she said, coolly.

Zach helped her maneuver her bicycle into the elevator. "I'll be at the office if you need me," he said, equally cool. As always, he had stored up vacation and personal days so he'd have more time to spend with her, but if she was going off on her own again, he may as well go to work. "Let's meet back here at six and have dinner at seven." She nodded before the elevator door slid shut. When Zach went to the bathroom to take his shower, there was nothing on the floor.

At six, he came home to find her watching the news and eating cold leftover pizza. Without saying a word, but within her hearing, he canceled the restaurant reservation and made himself another plate of scrambled eggs.

For the rest of the month, they tiptoed around each other, she morose but not belligerent, he formal but not aloof. Zach left it up to her to program each day as she wished—she was old enough to find the movie listings, the museum calendars, the sports team schedules—but beyond a trip to the bowling alley, she initiated nothing.

Zach made simple suppers and she ate hers facing the TV or else took her plate to her room.

On Christmas Day, he suggested they have dinner at an Indian or Chinese restaurant, the only places open. "Thank God for the Hindus and Confucians," he joked lamely, "or we Jews would starve on December 25."

Anabelle chose Indian.

Poori or naan, tandoori or curry, that was the extent of their conversation until she suddenly leaned across the table with a determined look on her face.

"I have a serious question, Dad."

"Shoot." He said. No matter what was coming, it had to be better than silence.

"What's your problem with women?"

Zach almost laughed. "Relationships are complicated," he replied, finessing it.

"You keep letting women go: Mom and me. Cleo. Babka. I'm not sure I want to wait for the other shoe to drop."

"What other shoe?"

"Me," she said. "I don't see why I should travel halfway around the world to spend time with a father who didn't care enough to fight for me when I was little. I'm sure it's only a matter of time until you drop me a second time."

Zach felt as if he'd been punched. "That is *not* true, Annie! I was . . . "

"Stop! It took a lot for me to work up the nerve to say this. I need you to just *listen.*" She chose a crisp of papadum from the breadbasket only to crack it into a dozen pieces.

"Okay," he nodded. "Sorry."

Anabelle twirled a lock of her hair, the way her mother used to. "I think I should stop coming to New York. And you should stop going to Melbourne. It's too much of a hassle. Upsets everyone's routines. And it's way too expensive. We shouldn't do it anymore. We should just quit."

Zach suddenly panicked. "NO WAY." He swept aside the papadum crumbs and grabbed both her hands. "I love you more than anything. I miss you from the moment you leave until the moment I lay eyes on you again. I count the days between our visits. I plan our time together because I want you to have fun and be happy here. You mean everything to me. You *must* know that."

"I don't know that. All I know is, you let Mom and Gil take me really far away."

"No! Wait! I don't want to speak against your mother but . . . " But he did, because he had to; it was the only way he could make his daughter understand how they ended up ten thousand miles apart. He had to tell her about that scene in the bathroom on Thanksgiving night, the paralyzing shock of Bonnie's revelation, her insistence on following Gil to Australia, the harrowing, nonnegotiable finality of her decision. And though it would surely weaken him in her eyes, he told her the truth about his breakdown, the shattering despair, the sense of absolute desolation and helplessness. "I was crazy about your mom. I couldn't believe our marriage was over, that we couldn't even talk about it. She wouldn't listen. Her mind was made up. Not only did she love someone else, she was moving away and taking you with her, and I couldn't do anything to stop her because you were a baby and a baby belongs with her mother. I wanted to fight, I swear it. But I was devastated. Numb. Hollowed out. It's no excuse, but I had nothing left."

Their food came then, four platters, each under a brass dome—vegetable pakoras, chicken tandoori, lamb vindaloo, basmati rice—all at the same time. Two waiters raised the four domes simultaneously.

Anabelle stared at her lamb. "I can't eat right now."

"Me neither," Zach said. "Let's just sit here until we're hungry, okay?"

She nodded.

He asked the waiters to put the brass covers back on. "You want a Kingfisher?"

Anabelle looked at him as if he'd lost his mind. "Dad, they won't serve me."

"I'll order the large bottle. We'll share it."

The beer loosened her tongue even more. She was also pissed at Zach for leaving Cleo. "We weren't just a threesome, you know. Cleo and I had our own thing. We were chums. Then suddenly she's gone and you never explained why."

Zach was quiet for a long moment, his finger circling the rim of the beer glass until it whined. Then he explained why he had to break up with Cleo. For the first time, he told her about his promise.

He left out the part about Terrell.

After their Indian dinner, Anabelle didn't turn back into an angelic child but the chip on her shoulder softened. The next day, when she agreed to go ice-skating with him at Wollman Rink in Central Park and they had hot chocolate at the Boathouse, there was no further talk of canceling his trip to Melbourne in July or hers to New York the following December.

On New Year's Eve, Zach took her to see the Broadway production of *Six Degrees of Separation*. Anabelle said she wasn't surprised by the white couple's gullibility; people believe what they want to believe, especially when the made-up story is so much better than the truth. The next morning, her mother came by in a taxi to take her to the airport. Anabelle kissed him goodbye.

WHILE ZACH WAS deciding whether to show up at the playground, he thought about his tough times with Anabelle and wondered if, on top of the complications of shared custody and religious difference, he might one day have to face a similar rebellion from Terrell—and be inadequate all over again. Other fears took hold: If he did decide to meet Terrell, some primal fatherly instinct hardwired in his genes might make him say yes before absorbing the enormity of the commitment. Or he might say yes out of some macho urgency to prove he could handle his responsibilities. Or simply to give himself an excuse to cross paths with Cleo on a regular basis.

Worse yet, what if, after spending hours with the boy in the playground, his paternal instinct didn't kick in? An absence of feeling could make him say yes out of shame or denial, which would not bode well. It was bad enough to abandon "Scott's issue" before he was born. To reject him in the flesh would be callous and so antithetical to Zach's sense of himself as a moral being that he could imagine himself saying yes just to avoid the self-loathing. Then, he would have to pretend to love a child who would have to pretend to not know he was faking it.

Other possibilities shook him up: What if Zach proved to be the unlovable one? Suppose he said yes to Terrell and Terrell said no to him? What if he never found his bashert and never had more children? Terrell might be Zach's last chance to ensure that a Levy from his father's line survived in the world. The past being predictive, he would probably keep falling for the "wrong" women, by which he did not mean Cleo. The failure of his other romantic endeavors suggested the folly of privileging Jewish credentials above all the elements that make for a meaningful connection between two people. If his bashert did finally show up, what would she think of a man who let his daughter be taken across the globe, and then rejected his own son? If he didn't tell his future wife and children about his secret son, and Terrell one day showed up on their doorstep, then what?

AT ELEVEN O'CLOCK on Tuesday, Zach locked his office door, stripped to his boxers, and changed into the outfit he'd deemed appropriate for an afternoon in the playground—Springsteen T-shirt, cutoff jeans, flip-flops, and Mets cap. Shivering beneath the air vents, he yanked the zipper to close his gym bag and knocked over his coffee cup. Brown rivulets trickled under his phone and puddled on the yellow legal pad, transforming his case notes into a muddy watercolor. Every day for the last five, he'd made some blunder that broke his quotidian rhythms. If he wasn't dripping soup on his tie or leaving his credit card behind at the dry cleaners, he was slicing his lip while shaving or screwing up the photocopy machine—small indignities but discomforting to a man who, already depressed at having turned forty, was about to face a decision that, one way or the other, would alter the rest of his life.

Catching sight of himself in a store window in his baseball cap and flip-flops, he thought he looked like an overgrown kid who'd shot up too fast and scissored the legs of his favorite jeans rather than donate them to Goodwill. Compounding his youthfulness was the hairstyle Bonnie used to call "Dennis the Menace meets Lord Byron," the shaggy cut his mother had devised to mask his flaws. Though a teen growth spurt had long since recast his skull in proper proportion to his stick-out ears and the scar on his eyebrow, which once seemed to disfigure his face but now lent it gravitas, Zach had instructed all subsequent barbers to follow Rivka's template. Today, he counted on his Dennis doppelganger to ease his way into the playground.

He entered the park at the West Sixty-Seventh Street entrance. As he veered left toward Adventure Playground, a striking tableau in front of the Tavern on the Green stopped him in his tracks: newlyweds posing for pictures in a horse-drawn carriage. Once upon a time, on a June day just as soft and sunny, he and Bonnie had struck the same pose and moldering in a box somewhere was a photo to prove it. Also a ketubah, the Jewish marriage contract, handwritten by a Hebrew scribe and signed in the presence of witnesses. If she hadn't left him, he and Bonnie would would have been married seventeen years now.

Turning from the sylvan scene, Zach continued up the path, perspiration encircling his neck like a wet rag, his pulse quickening with each step, not from the incline but in anticipation. At the crest of the hill, the vibrant life of the playground pulsated within its iron fence. He unlatched the gate and stopped midstep, intoxicated by the hubbub—boys in whisk broom crew cuts, girls in summer sunsuits, the whir and squeal, the pastels and primary colors, the jumble of tyke bikes and sand toys.

"Shut the gate, Mister!" barked a woman in a hot pink halter. "We don't want one of these kids toddling off to Times Square!"

Mothers and nannies swiveled toward the new arrival, their eyes narrowing as they detected no toddler in the man's wake to justify his presence. (Should have strapped a Snugli to his chest and stuck a doll in it, Zach thought belatedly.) He latched the gate and shambled to an empty bench as if it had his name on it. The seat felt as hard as the women's stares. He checked his watch: he was twenty minutes early. And he was the only man in the playground. All the adults—pushing swings, handing out snacks, giving bottles, changing diapers—were women. Helping toddlers up steps and down slides, admiring lopsided sand castles, wiping runny noses, and rocking babies—all women, many of them scrutinizing *him*, some surreptitiously, others openly suspicious, as if at any moment he might unzip his fly. Whatever gave him the idea that a shaggy haircut and cutoff jeans were all it took to make him look like he belonged here? And where were all the other dads?

Eleven fifty-four. Six more minutes in the riflescope of the Playground Surveillance Squad before Cleo and Terrell would arrive and legitimate his presence.

Five minutes past twelve. Still no sign of them. He leaned his head back and shut his eyes—no doubt to the relief of the monitoring moms (What predator would nod off?)—and considered how honorably Cleo had fulfilled her end of the bargain, not contacting him until last week, and then only to give him the option of reconsidering. She would be surprised to know how often he'd had to restrain himself from sneaking up to catch a glimpse of her and their child. Now, minutes away from seeing them, he wondered how a forty-year-old makes conversation with a three-year-old. Especially if the forty-year-old can't get a fifteen-year-old to give him the time of day. And how Anabelle would feel if, on her next visit, he presented her with a half brother.

The wooden slats dug into his spine. His neck was in an awkward position; feigning sleep wasn't easy. He snuck a peek at his watch. Twelve seventeen. Punctuality had never been Cleo's strong suit. He swung his legs up on the bench and stretched out under the trees, sunlight dappling his body like camouflage, his thoughts adrift on the white noise of children at play.

CHAPTER 18
A CHURCH IN THE SANDBOX

"SORRY I'M LATE."

Zach opened his eyes to Cleo Scott in a dress of cornflower blue, a string of coral beads around her neck. She wore dark glasses so he couldn't see her expression. She was holding a book. He bolted to his feet. They shook hands; he wished he could have held on a few seconds longer. Her skin was still luminous but for the fine lines, like parentheses, at the corners of her mouth that appeared to have been etched there by laughter, and her air of calm self-assurance made Zach wonder if, over the last three and a half years, she had suffered less than he.

"You look great, Cleo."

She didn't comment on how he looked, just pointed across the playground. "Terrell went straight to the sandbox. He's wearing the red plaid overalls. Feel free to talk to him. I haven't taught him about stranger danger yet. He's used to friendly guys."

Her familiar lilac fragrance weakened Zach. What guys? Pierced by jealousy, he wondered, How friendly?

She gracefully lowered herself to the bench and did that thing she always did when she wore a skirt—flared it, then tucked the ends under her thighs.

"He's had his morning nap and his lunch. We usually hang out here until four, so take your time."

The book on her lap was *Hands Clasped No More: Black-Jewish Relations and the American Dream* by Jack Fingerhut, the professor whose carping had poisoned the Black-Jewish Coalition from the start. Back in 86, Cleo had blamed the group's dissolution on Fingerhut for his having dismissed other people's suggestions out of hand, and accused the blacks in the group of duplicity and intransigence.

"How come you're reading *that*?" Zach asked.

"He's coming on the show Sunday."

"But you hate Fingerhut."

"I don't have to like the man to interview him. He's provocative, he'll get people calling in."

"I can't believe that schmuck has written anything worth reading," Zach said.

Cleo raised a hand to shade her eyes from the sun. "I'm confused. Did you come here for a book discussion?"

He had been stalling; they both knew it. Only yards away from his child and he was dragging his feet, afraid of what he might feel. Now, he turned toward the sandbox and, at the distance of a first down, located the boy in red plaid overalls. The muscles in Zach's legs tightened as he drew closer. Terrell's face was in profile, inclined toward his labors in the sand and offering only the soft curve of a butterscotch-brown cheek, an uptilted nose, a neck as slender as a stalk. His hair was fuller, rounder, and springier than Cleo's tightly coiled cap. His knobby ankles stuck out between his Mickey Mouse sneakers and the cuffs of his pants. Long limbed for a three-year-old, Zach thought. He'll be tall, like his father.

"Hi, Terrell."

No response. The boy was busy patting, pinching, and molding the sand forms he had already created—a tower attached to a boxy structure and off to one side, four or five blobs of sand plunked here and there.

"You're Terrell Scott, aren't you?"

"Uh-huh." He smoothed the surface of the tower with his diminutive palms.

"I'm Zach. Did your mommy mention I might stop by?"

"Uh-huh." Terrell remained laser focused on his construction project.

"She say anything else?"

"She said you might play with me." Terrell scooped up some of the wet sand in an attempt to shape the head and legs of some animal.

"I'd be glad to play with you," Zach said, though the only game he could think of at the moment was hide-and-seek and he wasn't about to hide from the child he had just found.

Terrell finally looked up. He had Cleo's pale blue-gray eyes and gorgeous lips, Zach's ears (and Yitzhak's before him), Rivka's cleft chin, Nathan's broad forehead, the high cheekbones that distinguished Ifs Scott in Cleo's family photographs, and Althea's dimples. But the sum of his features was more beautiful than its parts.

Terrell cocked his head. "Whatcha staring at?"

"Nothing," Zach lied. "I'm just waiting for you to decide what we should play."

"Okay, but first, I need to finish my church."

"Your church?" Zach swallowed hard.

"No, my grandpa's church. I mean it *used* to be my grandpa's church only he died when Mommy was little. My grandma took me there. It's in Memphis."

Zach curled his toes in the sand. "What are those things?"

Terrell followed his gaze to the sand blobs. "Goats. Grandma also took me to a farm. Could you make a pregnant goat and put her next to mine?"

"A what goat?" Zach was sure he'd misheard.

"Preg-nant. One of the lady goats was having a kid." The boy fixed on his face as if expecting another stupid question. "That's what you call a baby goat: a kid. Same as people babies."

Zach picked up a fistful of wet sand. "You know what a baby lion is called?" He told himself he wasn't testing the boy, just making conversation.

"Cub."

"Baby sheep?"

"Lamb."

"Baby swan?" Zach wasn't sure of the term himself.

"Sig-net," Terrell replied, matter of factly. "Now stop asking questions, I have to concentrate." He found an old

Popsicle stick in the sand and carved a Gothic-shaped outline onto the side of his boxy sand structure then filled it in with squiggles and crosshatches.

"That's a stained glass window," Zach said, hoping to sound less dense. He molded a goat-shaped blob with a big stomach and added it to the others in the meadow.

"I have to make two more windows," Terrell said. "As soon as I'm done, I'll go get Malcolm and we can play house."

"Who's Malcolm?"

"My doll. He's in Mommy's knapsack."

Terrell had a boy doll. "You finish the windows, I'll get Malcolm," Zach offered, glad for any excuse to return to Cleo's bench.

"Okay, I'll meet you at the pyramid." Terrell pointed to a wooden climbing structure with graduated steps that narrowed to its peak.

When Zach explained his mission to Cleo, she smiled. "He's a piece of work, isn't he?" She reached under the bench for her knapsack.

"He seems really smart." Zach shuffled his feet, waiting for her to throw him a bone of intimacy, a hint of her feelings. She just looked as if she was waiting for him to say something wrong.

"He also seems kind of obsessed with your dad's church."

"Really? That's what you took from your time playing with him?" She sighed as if tolerating a very tedious person. "Terrell gets obsessed with lots of things. Three months ago it was dinosaurs. Before that, Big Bird."

"He said your mom took him to church."

"Why shouldn't she? My father preached there for years."

"I was wondering if he's been going to Sunday school."

"Are you crazy? You've just met him and you're already worried that he's been indoctrinated?"

Zach couldn't suppress a grin. "Point taken. May I have Malcolm?"

Cleo retrieved a dark-skinned baby doll from her backpack.

"Last name X, I presume," Zach teased.

"Terrell named him after we read a children's book about Malcolm X; I argued for Mahatma." She pulled a small yellow baby blanket from her satchel. "I'd better show you how to swaddle him or Terrell will make you keep redoing it." She placed the naked doll on the blanket.

Zach couldn't help noticing Malcolm's tiny tubular penis. "Not too well endowed, is he?"

"He's anatomically correct for his age. A boy needs a doll that looks like him."

The doll wasn't circumcised. Did she mean the boy wasn't either? Zach came at the issue obliquely. "His skin's a lot darker than Terrell's. Does that matter?"

"What matters is Malcolm's black and so is Terrell."

"Terrell's half-white," Zach said, maybe a bit too emphatically. He paused. "And half-Jewish."

Cleo sent him a sharp look. "He's had no reason to know that yet, has he?" She handed Zach the swaddled doll. "Have fun."

Zach carried it over to the wooden pyramid. "Hi, Malcolm!" Terrell smiled and snuggled his baby close. "You certainly look nice and cozy."

"What do we do now?" Zach asked. Anabelle was never into dolls. "I don't know how to play house."

Terrell patted him on the shoulder as if comforting a deprived child. "Don't worry, I'll show you." Under the boy's assured direction, they acted out several scenarios—bedtime, breakfast, naptime, lunch, and so on—giving Zach both a sense of the boy's personality and an idea of Cleo's routine. Terrell had empathy. He was nurturing and affectionate with the doll and patient with Zach, who was quick to register his son's intelligence and sweetness. Zach, less patient, was relieved when Terrell became distracted from playing house by a noise that sounded like a snare drum. It turned out to be pebbles skittering down the sliding pond. Without so much as a by-your-leave, Terrell ran toward the owner of the pebbles, abandoning Malcolm, who, moments before, had been promised a lullaby at bedtime.

Like father, like son, thought Zach. Desertion runs in the family.

As the afternoon sun made its slow downward arc in the sky, car horns and an occasional police siren wafted up from Central Park West, the only reminders of life outside the playground. Inside, a different life continued to hum. Women monitored children who ran, fell, climbed, cried, snacked, and fell asleep in their carriages. Cleo sat on her bench in her cornflower-blue dress reading, or pretending to. Zach watched Terrell play with the pebbles, then glide down the aluminum slide fifteen or twenty times, chase other kids around the paths, scamper up and down the pyramid, and play pretend with his friends in the tree house, which was variously recast as a ship then a locomotive then a fire station.

Terrell suddenly came running toward him. "I have to pee!"

"Okay, relax! I'll take you to the men's room."

CHAPTER 19
IMAGINE

CLEO FELT LIGHT HEADED, HER TONGUE FURRY, AND realized she must be dehydrated. The small glass of cranberry juice she'd downed at dawn had been her last liquid. Though her bag was crammed with enough snacks for a week in the wild, she'd forgotten to pack a bottle of water and Terrell had finished the can of apricot nectar that she'd sent over with Zach when he came asking for the doll. There was a water fountain across the playground but the idea of drinking from it turned Cleo's stomach. She had once seen a man coax his German shepherd up on its hind legs to slurp from the spigot and homeless people were known to use the park's fountains as washbasins. Nonetheless, her wooziness left her no choice but to rehydrate at the public trough.

She didn't get very far before she was stopped by Sookja Lee, the mother of a four-year-old who wore leg braces and thick eyeglasses and spent his days in a pint-size wheelchair. Sookja sat on the same bench every day and never missed a trick. She pointed to Zach.

"That your new beau, Cleo?"

"Nope. Just a friend."

"Cute!" Sookja winked. "You sure?"

"I'm sure. When I find a beau, I'll let you know. You do the same, okay?"

"Me? Don't hold your breath." Sookja wiped her son's lips and pushed his chair farther into the shade. "I bring a guy home, he takes one look at my boy, and he's gone."

"Men!" Cleo said, an exclamation that, among women, needed no further elaboration. "I'm dying of thirst, Sookja. Excuse me."

Finally at the fountain, Cleo gripped the concrete bowl and drank copious amounts of cold water, careful to keep her lips from touching the spigot. The sorority of the playground never ceased to amaze her. Women who might never socialize outside the park shared the most intimate details of their lives once inside its fence. What else did they have to do? If you're responsibly monitoring your kid, you can't read or do sudoku. You have to stay alert—this was New York City, after all. But you could talk to one another and you could listen, hour by hour, day after day, which was how Cleo knew that Sookja's ex-husband had been having an affair with his secretary, and Alison over there had breast cancer, and Sherry's kid was starting therapy for her OCD.

Walking back to her bench, Cleo stopped to say hello to Sookja's little boy who couldn't speak, walk, or feed himself. Ifs Scott used to say, "Love the lame and count your blessings." Cleo berated herself for being insufficiently grateful that her son had been born with a working body, his cells and synapses intact, his molecules and atoms in proper alignment. She had endured morning sickness, depression, and insomnia—the pregnancy from hell—and in her eighth month was such a mess that her mother had to take a leave from the Bergmans' employ to come up north and care for her. But her labor was brief, delivery without incident, and Terrell was—*is*—flawless. Father or no father. She ought to be counting her blessings instead of praying for her ex-boyfriend to come back.

If by some miracle he said yes, she was going to demand a lot of him. He would help Terrell with his homework, serve as class parent, and attend teacher conferences, which was more than he had to do for Anabelle, who was never here during the academic year.

Admittedly, Terrell could be a handful—stubborn, temperamental, sometimes irrationally fearful. To parent him well, you had to know how to get him to go back to sleep after a nightmare (lie beside him and sing "Love Walked In"), nudge his dawdling on the way to day care, quiet his tantrums when he was overtired. You had to indulge his "why" marathons, (Why is the sky blue? Sugar sweet? Mommy sad?).

Being the December dad of a fun-loving Aussie may not have prepared Zach to father this particular three-year-old. What if he said yes and couldn't hack it?

Back on her bench, revived by the water, Cleo continued turning the pages of her book while stealing furtive glances across the playground. When she saw Zach's body incline toward Terrell, seemingly listening to him, she felt confident that her son's adorable charm and precocious vocabulary would make him irresistible. Then, she reproached herself: no child should have to audition for a parent's love. Yet she couldn't help rooting for Terrell to pass muster, especially after the *Times* recently reported that six out of ten black children in America grow up without a male parent. And fatherless children are much more likely than other kids to quit school and get into trouble, while those with fathers in the home—even inadequate, inept fathers—fared far better. On her Father's Day show this Sunday night, she would open the phone lines for listeners to talk about the report and the inevitable would happen as it did every year: a few callers would extol their loving dads, but most would have sad stories of having been abandoned by their fathers and raised by overwhelmed and underappreciated single mothers.

A father's absence was a presence, like an erasure forever visible on a clean sheet of paper. The feminist in Cleo was loath to pursue her ex-boyfriend but the mother in her felt a father was worth fighting for. Which was why she was sitting here, pretending to read, while she spied, prayed, worried, waited, and wondered what it would take to make Zach Levy say yes.

"THE MEN'S ROOM'S too far away. I can't hold it in!" Terrell moaned, clutching his crotch.

"Well, you can't pee *here*!" Zach said.

"Yes I can. All the boys pee through the fence. But I need you to unsnap me."

Zach released the snaps along the inseam of the red plaid overalls and Terrell went clamming for his penis in his tiny Jockey shorts. Zach bent over to get a closer look and smiled to himself. The circumcision was probably performed by a doctor in a hospital a few days after Terrell was born. Cleo must have ordered it to inoculate her baby boy against sexually transmitted diseases. Zach didn't care what her reason was. He didn't care that it had not been done by a mohel as part of a ceremonial bris with covenantal blessings and a family celebration. The point is it had been done. And done well.

FROM HER SON'S telltale stance—chin down, hips forward, back swayed—Cleo recognized that he was urinating. And from the man's posture—arched over the boy like a huge comma—that Zach had a clear view of what, undoubtedly, he was looking for. A few minutes later, the two of them came bounding toward her.

"I'm hungry, Mommy!"

"Carrot sticks coming right up." She reached for her bag.

"Not carrots! Ice cream! He'll buy me a vanilla pop if you say it's okay."

Cleo licked her thumb and rubbed a sand smudge off the boy's cheek. "It's not okay, sweetie. You had two Oreos after lunch. That's enough sugar for today."

"Oreos" was what Cleo used to call African Americans who denied their heritage—"Black on the outside, white on the inside," Zach thought.

"Ice cream is made from milk," Terrell added, flashing his adult playmate a conspiratorial grin. "So it's healthy."

Zach shrugged in mock innocence. "We were comparing notes on our favorite treats and I said some sweets had no nutritional value, like licorice, for instance, but some are made from dairy products, like ice cream which contains protein so . . ."

"All right! You can get him a pop," Cleo said. She would pick her battles when it mattered.

Zach invited her to accompany them down the hill to the vendor's cart, where he bought Terrell a chocolate-covered vanilla Popsicle, Cleo a bottle of water, and himself a giant pretzel. From there, they continued to the Sheep Meadow and plunked themselves down on the lawn to watch the Ultimate Frisbee game in progress among hard-driving players. Cleo noted Zach's particular interest in the women athletes and wondered whether he had found his Jewish soul mate by now or was still searching. Either way, she suddenly realized, if Zach took the boy, his wife would become Terrell's *stepmother*. Jesus. Talk about unintended consequences: Cleo wanted her son to have a daddy, not two mommies.

Should the miracle come to pass and Zach became part of her son's life, he would also, of necessity, be part of hers. Like other parents with shared custody, she would have to coordinate her schedule with him—and his now or future wife—arrange pickups and handoffs, playdates and vacations; consult, negotiate, and compromise. Holidays could get thorny given the demands of two households. Terrell might have to spend alternate Thanksgivings with "them" or else make an appearance at each parent's table and eat turkey twice in the same day. Christmas would, by right, be Cleo's holiday since it meant nothing to Zach—unless the first night of Hanukkah happened to fall on Christmas. That would present a problem. Passover, too. Suppose the seder fell on Easter Sunday and Cleo wanted Terrell with *her*? Perspiration beaded on her forehead. Once Terrell knew he had a daddy, he'd want *both* parents to see him in his school plays, music recitals, and ball games. A gallery of images flashed by: Terrell's graduations, sitting side by side with Zach, the wedding—she and Zach accompanying Terrell down the aisle. Sharing grandchildren.

"I need to take a walk. Okay with you if I stretch my legs for a little while?" she asked, rising from the grass.

Without looking up from the Frisbee game, Terrell replied, "Sure, Mom."

She turned to Zach. "Unless you're planning to leave now . . ."

"No, no, go right ahead. Meet you back at the playground."

Cleo headed up West Drive to Strawberry Fields, where she always retreated when she needed to chill out. The sunburst of terrazzo tiles with the word "Imagine" at its center was hallowed ground to Beatles fans. Tourists approached the circle with a hushed reverence, depositing their tokens of esteem—a photo, an origami bird, a bunch of flowers—as they knelt before the word. Some sang.

Some wept. That it could be so freighted with feeling, that it could simultaneously inspire hope and grief, rebellion and pacifism, dreams and disillusion, made Cleo marvel at the power of a single word.

Imagine. Her son, a Jew.

She couldn't.

Imagine. Her son, fatherless for the rest of his life.

She couldn't.

Back at the playground, she located Terrell, wearing only his Jockey shorts. He was running back and forth through the rainbowed spray of the sprinkler and squealing with glee, while Zach, smiling from the sidelines, held his shirt and overalls.

"Time to go," she called. Cleo pulled a towel out of her bag. Terrell ran to her and she wrapped him up like a bundle. With a glance at Zach, she added, "I'll hear from you by Friday."

It was a declarative statement with just the hint of a question mark. "You will," he said. He handed her the boy's clothes and she dressed him.

"Thanks for playing with me, Mister," Terrell called out.

As they turned to go, Zach saw Cleo surreptitiously wipe away a tear, then watched her take the boy by the hand and lead him through the gate and down the hill.

CHAPTER 20
ADVICE AND COUNSEL

TODAY WAS THE TOMORROW HE'D WORRIED ABOUT YESterday and now there were three more tomorrows ahead before he would decide his and Terrell's future. When he got home, M. J.'s door was wide open.

"Well, am I an uncle or not?" A beaker of iced gin, a bowl of olives, and two martini glasses materialized on a silver tray. "Take a load off and tell me everything! What's he like? How'd you feel?"

"He's terrific. You would love him." Zach plopped down on the velvet couch. "He's got an incredible vocabulary for a three-year-old. Amazing imagination. Fearless. Cute as hell. And you should hear him sing."

"I didn't ask if he was a promising candidate for Yale. I asked how you *felt* about him."

"Good. Great." Zach popped an olive. "A little overwhelmed by *how* great, frankly. I kept wanting to touch him. I couldn't believe he was actually there . . ."

"And? But?"

"I still can't imagine being his father."

"You *are* his father."

"So far, I'm just his sperm donor. If I become his father, I'm afraid I'll betray my—"

"Halt! If this is gonna be one of your Holocaust monologues, I'd rather go sit in an outhouse breeze. I've had a hard day's night—drama queen on the prep line, bread ran out before the second seating. Can we talk about the future of the Jewish people tomorrow?"

"Sorry."

"Just tell me what's going on in your head."

"I'm scared."

"Of what?" M. J. emptied the martini shaker into the two glasses. "Walk me through it: exactly what's involved if you take him? What's the worst?"

"Shared custody could be a hassle."

"Manageable."

"Cleo would have to be flexible on weekdays. My caseload is unpredictable, I can't always be home at a certain time—"

"And *you'll* have to be dependable on Sundays so she can get to the studio on time," M. J. countered. "You might have to cut short those bachelor bacchanals in Westport or East Hampton or wherever randy straights go for fun. Your social life might flame out for a while."

"What social life?"

"Those sexy at-home seductions. With a toddler around, you can't have women in sheer nightgowns turning up at the breakfast table."

"Okay, you got a giggle out of me." Zach kicked his loafers under the coffee table.

"I'm just saying—you already keep your sex life under control when Annie's here. If you take Terrell, the other eleven months would be G-rated too. Is that a problem?"

"Not really."

"So what's left to worry about?"

"Do I have to spell it out?"

"The J-E-W-S?" M. J. rocked his head back in mock fatigue. "The last time you asked Cleo if she would convert, she was pregnant. Maybe she's changed her mind."

"Not likely."

"So he'll be half-Jewish," M. J. said, lightly. "Half is better than none, right?"

Zach knew some interfaith couples had made it work but he couldn't see how. Would Terrell say the Sh'ma at his place, the Lord's Prayer at hers? Would he consecrate the wafer *and* bless the matzah? Could his Jewish half believe the world is still waiting for the Messiah if his Christian half believed the Messiah already came, died, and got resurrected?

"Half gets complicated," Zach said, finishing his drink. "Suppose he's not thrilled with a menorah and some dreidls and potato latkes. If he says he wants me to have a Christmas tree like his mom, I'd have to say no. Some fun dad."

M. J. cocked his head. "What if you called it a Hanukkah bush and stuck a Jewish Star on top?"

The chef advanced them from martinis to T-bone steaks, linguine in garlic and oil, a good bottle of Barolo, and brownies with homemade hazelnut ice cream. It was eleven o'clock when they finished eating.

Zach helped with the dishes. "I'm wasted, M. J. If I don't go home now I'll fall asleep standing up. Thanks for putting up with me, for listening, for feeding me so well—for *everything*." He dragged himself across the hall and climbed into bed but didn't conk out. He flipped his pillow to the cool side and kicked off the sheets. Still awake twenty minutes later, he got up and warmed some milk in the microwave, his father's go-to treatment for insomnia. The playground scene kept rewinding in his head, Terrell's voice alternating with Cleo's and Rivka's—a three-part fugue that kept him from sinking into oblivion. No use fighting it. He spent the rest of the night in the rocking chair in Anabelle's room, watching a pillar of moonlight roll across the floor until it merged with the pink creep of dawn. When the sun edged over the roof of the building across the street, Zach reviewed his case notes, staggered to the shower, and got dressed for court.

Caffeine and adrenaline carried him through his opening statement. The Slater case was a twin of the one he'd argued years ago on behalf of the cop with dreadlocks, except for the added component of military law. Shlomo (formerly Stuart) Slater, an army chaplain who'd been ordained in Conservative Judaism, had recently come under the influence of a Hasidic master and now considered himself a baal teshuva, the Jewish equivalent of a born-again Christian. In keeping with his new religious rigor, Slater had grown a long beard and ear curls, which he insisted neither interfered with the performance of his pastoral duties nor his capacity to minister to soldiers of all faiths and denominations. The Army disagreed and charged the chaplain with violating military regulations, which require a "neat and conservative appearance," a standard decided on a case-by-case basis. After being found guilty in a military court, Slater had asked the ACLU to appeal the judgment in federal court and Zach Levy had been assigned to the case.

Zach began his argument with an exegesis on the power of hair to signify something larger than itself:

"Like a religious Sikh, Muslim, or any other observant male, the chaplain wears his hair in a manner consistent with the tenets of his faith. As clearly as his uniform proclaims his service to the United States Army and his insignia proclaims his rank, Shlomo Slater's beard and payess proclaim that he is an Orthodox Jew, thereby conveying to the world what he stands for. No one has to guess.

"Were he your neighbor, you would not offer him a lobster roll or ask him to drive you to the mall on Saturday. If he declined to shake your mother's hand, you would know it was nothing personal. Were you his private-sector employer, you would not be permitted to discriminate against him because of his beliefs or demand that he violate his conscience to keep his job. We Americans pride ourselves on our respect for the religious practices of our fellow citizens. We grant each other the dignity of difference.

"My client is not petitioning for the right to be trendy. He is asking for the right to express his religious beliefs. If a political activist can wear a campaign button to signal his partisanship and a union member can carry a picket sign to show her affiliation, a member of the clergy should be free to wear the symbols that bespeak his fidelity to his faith. For Shlomo Slater, hair *is* speech. The American Civil Liberties Union contends that the Army has deprived him of his First Amendment rights and must affirm and reinstate his religious freedom."

Zach wished he could define his own Jewish identity as succinctly as he'd defined his client's. Hair was speech for Slater because he knew what he wanted to say.

When the trial broke at noon, Zach invited the chaplain to lunch at his favorite Vietnamese restaurant.

Slater waved a paper bag under Zach's nose. "I brought my own. I keep kosher."

"Of course. Sorry." Zach blushed. What was he thinking? "I'll get an egg salad sandwich at the deli and meet you over there." He pointed to the small park that straddled Chinatown and the courthouse district. "It's a great spot for people watching."

Slater nodded and started toward the little park. When Zach joined him on a bench, the chaplain unfurled his bag, took out a soft roll, said a blessing over it, and gave half the roll to Zach. They ate the bread watching the lunchtime parade of lawyers, judges, jurors, court clerks, and stenographers mingling with the local Asian waiters, fishmongers, and office workers.

"Our boys are always falling for them," Slater muttered, tearing open the wax-paper wrapping on half of a roast chicken. "It's a shonde."

"Falling for whom?" Zach knew shonde meant disgrace.

"Asian girls." The chaplain wrenched off the drumstick and jabbed it in the direction of a woman in a high-necked, Mao-style jacket. "A Jewish soldier meets one of them, she's smart, beautiful, comes from a close-knit family so he thinks she's like us; he falls in love and marries her." Slater gnawed on the chicken leg. "But they're *not* us. They're as goyish as that black woman you got involved with."

Zach squirmed. He regretted confiding his dilemma to Slater. Bad move.

"You should never have been with her in the first place," the chaplain scolded.

Zach unwrapped his egg salad sandwich.

"You knew it was against Jewish law to go with a gentile girl but you didn't know gentile girls could get pregnant? What did you think was going to happen?"

"I wasn't thinking. I just loved her."

"That's what they all say." The chaplain shook his head. "Okay, you did it, so what now? First, you have to pray for forgiveness. Tell the Almighty you made a terrible mistake and you'll never do it again. Then, you have to call that woman and tell her you're not taking her boy. You can't take him. He's not yours."

"He's definitely mine," Zach said, balancing his sandwich on his lap.

"Genetically, maybe, but not halachically. If you take him, he'll be a bad influence on your other children. I'm not saying he's a bad boy. I'm saying when your Jewish children see their father loves a Christian child the same as he loves them, they'll think it's not so important to be a Jew."

"You're telling me I should walk away from my own flesh and blood? How can *that* be right?"

"Because according to Jewish law, he's not yours. If he's a gentile, he's not Jewish and if he's not Jewish, he can't be yours." Slater ate the last of his chicken. "Remember that the Fifth Commandment doesn't say, 'Honor your child,' it says, 'Honor your father and mother.' May they rest in peace. You made your mother a vow. Don't think you can fulfill it with a mamzer grandchild."

The word meant bastard. Zach's thigh muscles went into spasm, sending his sandwich off his lap and onto the filthy ground. He threw it in the trash basket. He'd made a colossal mistake. A lawyer is supposed to *give* advice, not solicit it.

"Forget I asked," he said.

"Forget is what *you* should do," the chaplain retorted. "Forget you ever saw the boy." He dumped his chicken bones into the brown paper bag and dropped it in the trash on top of Zach's dirty sandwich. Reaching in the breast pocket of his uniform, he opened a small, worn booklet entitled *Birchat HaMazon* (Grace After Meals) and gestured toward a page as if he expected his lawyer to say the prayer with him.

Zach grunted, "No, thanks," and stood up, eager to escape. "I have to get back to court. See you inside." That afternoon, sitting beside his client at counsel's table, he had to keep reminding himself that he wasn't just representing Shlomo Slater, he was representing the Bill of Rights.

CHAPTER 21
RUNNING OUT

ON HIS WAY HOME FROM COURT, ZACH STOPPED AT THE video store and rented *Kramer vs. Kramer*—because he'd heard it was a stark portrait of single fatherhood—but before playing it, he decided to go to the gym to make up for the workout he'd missed that morning. However, the effort it took to change his clothes and put on sneakers triggered a fatigue so incapacitating that he could barely rise off the couch to insert the cassette. Surrendering to passivity, he watched the movie until Dustin Hoffman's character found it impossible to balance his responsibilities to his five-year-old son and still keep his job. Zach switched to the Mets vs. Braves game, where a less agitating scenario was in progress—New York ahead 6–0, Atlanta at bat, two outs, nobody on. After an uneventful inning, he picked up the phone and ordered Vietnamese takeout, the dishes he would have had if he hadn't opted to eat on the bench with Slater.

Even after stuffing the remains of the meal in his garbage pail, the food left a strong funky after odor in the loft. He gathered up the cardboard cartons and brought them down to the basement to dispose of them in the incinerator. The building super was flaked out beside the furnace, sound asleep in his ratty, old desk chair, snoring. What a sad way to spend a summer night, Zach thought, then realized his own situation was not much better. He hadn't felt this alone in the universe since Bonnie and Anabelle moved out. No one was waiting for him, missing him, needing him. M. J. was cooking at Lovage. Herb was romancing some new flame. And none of Zach's other friends knew about his dilemma so before he could confide his misery, he would have to update them, which would take way too much time and energy. In truth, he could throw himself into the incinerator this minute and no one would know or care until the super woke up and smelled something odd.

The thought of going back upstairs to his empty loft made him feel sick. He tightened his sneaker laces and went out for a run—west on Spring Street to catch the breeze off the Hudson, then south to Battery Park, which was where he got it into his head to repeat on foot the route that he and Cleo had taken on their bikes soon after they met. A Central Park loyalist, she had never explored Manhattan's smaller parks so he'd mapped out a bike route that took them past the verdant neighborhood squares, hidden gardens, and jewellike green triangles that defied the city's geometric street grid. They'd begun the tour right here in Battery Park, biked to Washington Square Park, then to Union Square, where they'd stopped at the

Greenmarket and bought warm apple cider, a wedge of New York State cheddar, and fresh cinnamon donuts, and then with sugary lips shared a kiss beneath the statue of Abraham Lincoln.

After covering that same route, Zach jogged up to Gramercy Park, then to Paley Park on Fifty-Third between Madison and Fifth, where they had leaned their bicycles against a locust tree and kissed at the waterfall cascading down the sidewall of the office building. Now, he noticed a tented sidewalk sign in front of the pub across the street—TAP BEER 50 CENTS—and rooting in the pockets of his running shorts, came up with two quarters and three dimes, enough for a beer and a 60 percent tip. The place was nearly deserted. The bartender let him nurse his Heineken through the end of the game—final score, Mets 6, Braves 1—as well as the entire half hour of the eleven o'clock news. About to make a pit stop before continuing on to Clinton Park, which had been next on his bike tour with Cleo, Zach changed his mind when four hulks in motorcycle jackets pushed through the front door of the bar and went charging to the men's room. He left with a full bladder. The sound of the waterfall across the street was nearly his undoing. All the East Side restaurants were closed and the closest bathroom he could think of was at Herb's place farther uptown so he pushed through his exhaustion and sprinted up Fifth Avenue and finally staggered into Herb's lobby.

The doorman greeted him with a cold stare. It was past midnight and Zach was dripping sweat on the Oriental rug. "Is Mr. Black expecting you?"

"He's not—but please call upstairs and tell him I'm here: Zach Levy."

The gold fringe on the man's shoulder epaulets shimmied as he stepped over to a marble ledge and picked up the house phone. Mercifully, Herb was home. "You may proceed," the man said as if waving Zach in to see the wizard.

When the elevator opened on his floor, Herb was standing in the hall in a silk robe that matched his pajamas. "You look demented, man. What happened?"

"Hell's Angels." Zach made a beeline for the bathroom, stammering, "Didn't want to take my dick out." He peed for what seemed like two solid minutes.

"You're not making sense," Herb said.

"Been running on no sleep and bad Vietnamese food. Okay if I crash in your guest room?"

"All yours," Herb said, leading the way. "There's fresh towels, toothbrush, razor, whatever you need. I have an early meeting tomorrow but I'll leave you a change of clothes so you can go straight to court."

Zach sat on the made-up guest bed and took off his sneakers. "Slater's been carried over until Monday. I'll have plenty of time to go home in the morning and change for the office, but I do need some cash." Turning the pockets of his running shorts inside out triggered a split-second recall of the missing C-note. His life had not improved since Babka. Everything was more complicated, not less.

"I'll leave you a twenty on the hall table," Herb said. "Help yourself to breakfast. I think there's an egg. And some olives." Herb closed the door behind him; had he been M. J. Randolph, he would have turned down the covers, brewed a pot of chamomile tea, and refused to let Zach go to bed until he had unburdened himself. Tonight, though, it was good that Herb was Herb; he offered something that, at this moment, Zach wanted more than succor: blessed silence. A man needs both kinds of friends.

He passed a wet washcloth over his face, stripped off his grungy running clothes, and slid between the sheets. The guest room, though likely intended by the original architect to be a nursery, was decorated like a deluxe double at the Waldorf—quilted window cornice, sharply pleated draperies, tailored tuxedo chair, matching desk accessories. To Zach's bloodshot eyes, these details suddenly seemed pitiful. For the first time since they'd met, Zach felt sorry for Herb. The man had a classy apartment but no family to fill it. When the digital clock read 3:00 a.m., Zach started counting the hours and minutes to Cleo's deadline and fell asleep double-checking his arithmetic.

The clock read 7:57 when he was awakened by the old dream—the castle, the stampeding baby carriage, his child self running after it as fast as he could. This time, however, when the stroller toppled into the river, he dove in and rescued the baby. After all these years, the dream's new ending was a great relief to Zach. Except the baby's face kept changing. First it was Yitzhak's, then Terrell's, then the face of a child Zach didn't recognize. A child yet to be born.

CHAPTER 22
ADVANCED RESEARCH

AT TEN O'CLOCK ON THURSDAY MORNING, THIRTY-EIGHT hours before Cleo's deadline, Zach arrived at the office, wearing Herb's clothes, to put in some face time at work, a charade of busyness punctuated by several trips to the coffee machine, water cooler, and other people's desks. At twelve-thirty, he and Herb went out to lunch.

Zach ordered a burger; his friend, after studying the menu intently, chose the soy croquettes.

"Since when are you into bean cuisine?" Zach asked.

"My girl's vegan. I've got to learn to like this stuff."

"Since when do you have a girl?"

"Six days ago."

Zach leaned across the table. "Great! How come you never told me?"

"You never asked."

Zach nodded and looked away.

"It's okay, man." Herb mock punched Zach's shoulder. "You've got issues. How'd you sleep? Guest room comfortable?"

"Perfect. Thanks for taking me in. What's her name, the girlfriend?"

"Nancy Gordon."

"I thought you were saving yourself for Cybill Shepard."

"Cybill was my fantasy. Nancy's real. I'm in love I think."

"Fantastic! How'd you meet her?"

"She called to recruit me, white-shoe law firm, she's a headhunter—"

"You can't leave the ACLU, Herbie! We promised we'd be lifers together."

Herb grinned. "I'm not going anywhere. I nixed the job offer but I've seen Nancy five nights out of the last six."

"Wow! For you that's serious."

Herb chewed his croquette as if his teeth could unlock its flavor. "I'm telling you, man, I think she's it."

Zach slid his chair sideways to escape a shaft of sunlight. His burger had come with a logjam of fries and a dollop of ketchup in a pleated paper cup. He stared at his plate. He salted the meat without tasting it first. Lately everything needed salt. The two men slipped into the effortless silence of close friends.

"Is she Jewish?" Zach finally asked.

"Christ, man! Give it a rest! Do you care about anything else?"

"Unlike some people, I don't have the luxury of *not* caring."

"That supposed to be an insult? I just told you I'm crazy about this woman and all you can do is ask her religion? No wonder you're alone."

"I'm sorry the one promise I made to my mom who barely sur—well, actually, didn't survive the Holocaust strikes you as petty," Zach said. "But you're right. I'm alone and you're not and I'm glad you have someone. I can't wait to meet her." On the restaurant's sound system, Tony Bennett crooned his regret at having left his heart in San Francisco.

Again silence, until Herb chuckled. "Nancy told me a great joke last night, wanna hear it?"

"Absolutely. I'd much rather laugh than eat."

"Two Polish Jews are lined up before a firing squad. One refuses the blindfold. The other says, 'Hershel! Don't make trouble.'"

Zach managed to smile and sigh at the same time. "That's funny," he said. "And it tells me your girl must be Jewish. Who else would tell an ironic joke about a guy named Hershel?"

Herb nodded, almost sheepishly. "Nancy's grandfather came from Russia. Her last name, Gordon, used to be Grodno; the immigration people changed it at Ellis Island." He pushed his croquette around on his plate. "Talk about ironic: you're obsessed with Judaism, I end up with the Jew."

Zach pulled a paper napkin from the dispenser and wiped his mouth. "I'm ready for the firing squad myself, Herbie. Would you mind if I split? You can have my burger. I'm going home." Zach took a couple of twenties from his wallet. "This one's from last night and this one's for lunch. My treat."

Herb asked, "What should I tell the office?"

"Tell them I choked on a soy croquette."

ZACH DIDN'T GO home. He walked downtown, stopped to listen to a folksinger in Washington Square Park, then trudged over to Hebrew Union College on West Fourth and Broadway, a building he'd passed a thousand times but, until now, never had reason to enter. Its bright, spacious library bore no resemblance to a rabbi's study or the musty book room in his childhood synagogue. About a dozen young people were working at wooden tables, hunched over texts, taking notes. Zach approached the librarian and in his best library whisper told her that he wanted materials on the legal status of a person with a Jewish father and a Christian mother, adding—in case she'd assumed he was that person—that he was an attorney.

The librarian had a round face, limp blond hair, a shiny forehead, and an accent that reminded him of his father's lontzmen. Based on her voice and Slavic looks, he guessed her to be a Soviet émigré. She said, "Our rabbis just make new rule about this—here, you heard about it?" She handed him a laminated sheet headed "Responsa: Reform Judaism and Patrilineal Descent."

Zach's eye skipped down to the underlined sentence: "Henceforth, any person with a Jewish father may be counted as a Jew if he or she performs appropriate and timely public and formal acts of identification with the Jewish faith and people."

"Any idea what they mean by 'formal acts of identification?'" he asked.

"To have Jewish papa not enough. Must *do* Jewish things. Wait, I bring you books."

While she was in the stacks, one of the students announced, "Mincha," and almost everyone in the library headed out the door for the afternoon prayer service—which Zach knew to be one of those "timely public and formal acts of identification with the Jewish faith and people." He also knew he'd be welcome to join them, might even be recruited to "make a minyan," the quorum of ten Jews required for public prayer. Moreover, he would count for a minyan, not just at the liberal HUC but in any Orthodox prayer group in the world. He knew this because walking through Williamsburg one day he was buttonholed by a couple of black hats who needed a tenth man to make a minyan and they didn't ask if he was lapsed or ate shrimp as long as he satisfied two criteria—had a Y chromosome and a Jewish mother. He was "Jewish enough" to marry the daughter of a rabbi or even a kohen, the elite priestly class, simply on the basis of Rivka's membership card.

The librarian returned wheeling a cart loaded with books. "These are syllabus for Judaism 101," she said with a toothy smile. Zach couldn't help but bristle. When he was thirteen years old, he could have *taught* Judaism 101. He was able to read the Torah without vowels, lead youth services (shacharit, mincha, or maariv), and recite Maimonides's Thirteen Principles of Faith from memory. He used to be Rabbi Goldfarb's star pupil but over the last twenty-seven years, he'd forgotten everything and now he was stumped by the most rudimentary question of all: Who is a Jew?

According to the first book he thumbed through, "A Jew is someone whose mother and grandmother were Jewish or who converts according to Jewish law. If a gentile woman converts before giving birth, her child is Jewish; if not, the child must undergo conversion before he or she can legally be considered Jewish."

That sounded pretty airtight, yet there had to be a loophole or the Reform movement would not have found a way to issue their new rule that legitimated the children of Jewish fathers and gentile mothers. Zach tore through volume after volume, checking out every index entry that seemed germane, but the more he read, the deeper his confusion. Different experts contradicted each other left and right. Traditionalists called Reform's new edict about patrilineal descent "a travesty" and "a deathblow to the cohesion of the Jewish people." Given the far-flung diaspora and the high rate of intermarriage, these experts said, it was crucial to maintain a single answer to the question: Who is a Jew? Otherwise, Jews who care about Jewish survival would be unable to marry their offspring to each other with any confidence that they were perpetuating their own. There must be a single standard; matrilineal descent must continue to rule the day.

But authors with equally impressive credentials put forth compelling arguments to the contrary, namely, that the new law establishing the legitimacy of patrilineal descent was buttressed by classical texts and could actually *ameliorate* the crisis of intermarriage. Zach's mother had warned him about this "crisis" twenty-seven years ago, but she tended to be so hyperbolic about Jewish survival, he'd always dismissed her fears. Now it appeared that she was right. One book said that nearly two million American Jews had only one Jewish parent, and only two out of five children of Jewish-Christian intermarried couples identified as Jewish at all. But not because the children rejected Judaism. Mostly because *they* had been rejected by rabbis who wouldn't welcome them, synagogues that didn't allow them on the bimah, or because the Jewish family of the intermarried Jewish spouse had inflicted on the Christian spouse enough hurts and humiliations to send their children in the direction of other faiths or none at all.

As a lawyer, Zach was fascinated by the ideological divisions, but as a man facing a huge decision, he wanted a direct answer. He returned to the librarian's desk. "I know this is asking a lot, but do you think there's someone here I could talk to about all this? A rabbi or professor?"

"They're all on holiday. Is summer, you know."

"I know. But there must be *one* knowledgeable person left in the building." The tasseled cords on her embroidered blouse reminded Zach of tzitzis. He leaned forward and whispered, urgently, "I really need to talk to someone. Anyone."

Kindness shone from the librarian's eyes. "Maybe Professor Cantor still here. She came today to return books. I try her extension."

Five minutes later, Zach was standing in the office of Irina Cantor, a sixty-something woman with Granny Smith cheeks, straight white hair cut in bangs and cropped at the jawline, a smock dress, and Birkenstock sandals, who wore no makeup or jewelry and looked like an unreconstructed hippie. When he told her his full name, her eyebrows shot up and disappeared under her bangs.

"Ah, Mr. Levy," she said, "so you have a Jewish father and you want to know if you . . ."

"No, it's about my son," Zach interrupted, feeling the pressure of Cleo's deadline. "His mother's a Baptist, a preacher's daughter, a black woman. I just met the boy for the first time a couple of days ago. I don't know what to do about him."

"Please, sit down," said the professor as she turned off the electric kettle whistling on the table behind her desk. "I grow my own lemon verbena. It makes the most delicious herbal tea, much better than the bags. Want some?"

Zach nodded, relieved to be asked to stay.

Irina picked a handful of leaves off the plant, dropped them in a teapot, replaced its lid, and let the tea steep. "Verbena does well in this window but I always take the plant home for the summer. Do me a favor and put it by the door. My husband will kill me if I forget it."

Zach carried the pot to the place she designated and set it down. Anyone coming in would knock it over but that was where she wanted it. While the tea was brewing, she put a strainer on one of the two HUC mugs. Meanwhile, Zach surveyed the framed pictures on the wall. In one, she was marching with a group under the banner

"Historians Against the War." Another showed her and a stocky bearded man sailing a catamaran, she at the tiller, he on the mainsheet. There were other photographs of the couple (their hair grayer with the years), posing in the plaza before the Western Wall, surrounded by family, cutting a cake that said, "Happy 40th Anniversary." And a framed citation from the Association for Jewish Studies. The wall arrangement was neat, her desk a riot of books and paper.

"Excuse the mess," she said. "I'm about to leave for the summer and I have to pick up my grandson at day care this afternoon so if you don't mind, I'm going to continue working my way through these piles while we talk. Unlike Gerald Ford, I'm able to do two things at once. Now, tell me how I can help."

Zach recapped his life at warp speed—his promise to Rivka, the break with Cleo, her phone call, the playground, the emotional anarchy of the last few days, the chaplain's advice, the frustration of his library research. While he was speaking, Irina Cantor was in perpetual motion, spinning the wheel of her Rolodex, adding cards, subtracting cards, rifling through scholarly papers, glancing at their titles, tossing some in the trash, sticking orange Post-its on the keepers, scribbling "Read page__," or "Clip page ___," or "See Index," before shoving them in the Channel Thirteen tote bag that lay open at her feet.

"So what do you think?" Zach asked at the end of his recitation.

At that, Irina stopped moving, sat back, and folded her hands across her middle. "I'm a history professor, not a rabbi. I'm affiliated with a Reform institution, not a beit din—that's an Orthodox court that decides Jewish law—"

"I *know* what a beit din is," Zach said, perhaps a bit too impatiently.

"When his students were confused, the Rambam—Maimonides, who was a twelfth-century sage—"

"I *know* who the Rambam is . . ."

". . . wrote his students a letter in the form of a three-volume treatise called *The Guide for the Perplexed*. Jews have always been perplexed about big questions."

Zach returned the professor's soft smile. "I'm not asking for three volumes, just one well-considered opinion. What would *you* do?"

"Take him," she said, instantly.

It was the straight answer he wanted, but it didn't suffice. "I want to be sure I understand this. Are you telling me I should raise a Christian child?"

"I didn't say I'd tear the mezuzah off my doorpost and tack up a crucifix. I said I would take my son into my life and my heart." She poured Zach's tea, transferred the strainer to her mug, and poured hers.

"And then?" Zach asked.

"Then I'd tell him how sorry I was to have missed the first three years of his life, and how thrilled I am that we're finally part of each other's family, and how much I want to make up for lost time. I wouldn't say a word about religion until I sensed that he felt absolutely secure with me—which could take quite some time—but when a natural opening presented itself, I would talk tachlis with him."

This time, Irina, not wanting to insult Zach, had not offered a translation.

"Tachlis?" Zach asked.

"The heart of the matter. Practical details."

"So, practically speaking, what would you say?"

"Something like, 'I know your mommy takes you to church and puts up a Christmas tree, which is wonderful. But since half of you comes from me and my ancestors, I'd like you to know about the traditions I grew up with.' If he shows interest *and* his mother goes along with it, I would homeschool him in the Jewish basics. Maybe start by explaining the ritual objects around the house, your kiddush cup, the havdalah candle, your kipah and tallit. I would take him through the Jewish calendar." She gestured toward the photographs. "I've shared my passion for sailing with my kids. You can share your passion for Judaism with your son. If he balks, so be it. The most important thing is to make sure he grows up to be a kind, caring human being. In the end, isn't that what everyone wants for their kids?"

"Not everyone comes from a people who lost a million children in three or four years."

"The *world* lost a million children, Zach."

"To me, the Holocaust is *personal*. My brother was murdered in cold blood by people who professed to be good Christians. If my mother had been *your* mother and you'd given your word, would you still take a Christian child?"

"You just told me your mother became a pediatrician to German children."

"She had no choice."

"It's not so black and white. If she had the opportunity to spend an afternoon in the playground with your little boy, I have a feeling she would release you from your vow. If she were my mother, I'd explain to her that Reform Judaism traces the Jewish line through the father as well as the mother—please excuse me for saying so, but you strike me as a Reform Jew at most—and I would tell her, unequivocally, 'Your son is a Jew, therefore your grandson is a Jew—if he wants to be.'"

Irina blew on her tea to cool it. "If she were sitting in that chair, I'd point out that the law of matrilineal descent is *not* in the Torah; it only dates back to the rabbinic period. For thousands of years before that, Jews reckoned their children's bona fides through the father, not the mother."

The professor picked up a Bible and fanned its pages. "Remember all those boring genealogies—Abraham begat Isaac who begat Jacob who begat twelve sons? They're listed that way because inheritance rights, tribes, priesthood, blessings, God's instructions—all passed from father to son and, like your Terrell, many of the sons had non-Jewish mommies. Joseph and Moses married Egyptian women, biblical kings married foreigners, but regardless of their wives' provenance, their kids were considered Children of Israel. So, the idea of patrilineal descent isn't some radical innovation; it's original Judaism. Your son is a Jew because *you* begat him. That's what I would tell your mother!"

If only Rivka could hear this.

"Now, let's talk about Cleo," Professor Cantor said as

she resumed her clean-up operation, stacked books, threw out more papers and a couple of candy wrappers, tested ball points, and tossed the dry pens in the wastebasket. "How do you think Cleo would react at this point if you said you wanted to convert Terrell?"

"Negative. Impossible."

"Wait a minute. Wasn't *she* the one who called *you* last week? You said she's always known about your promise to your mom. Why would she have taken the initiative unless she was ready to be more flexible? If you explained to her that, under Jewish law, child conversions are provisional and reversible she might be willing to listen."

"How do you define 'provisional and reversible'?"

"When child converts come of age, they're asked if they want to renounce the conversion or embrace Judaism of their own free will. Almost all of them elect to stay Jewish. But there's a catch."

Zach said, "It wouldn't be a law if there weren't a catch."

"Orthodox rabbis won't convert the child in the first place unless the parents promise to do things like keep a kosher home, observe the Sabbath, and send the child to yeshiva." The professor yanked a tissue from her Kleenex box, folded it neatly, and tucked it in the zipper compartment of the tote bag.

Zach sighed. "In all honesty, even if Cleo agreed, which she won't, I couldn't make good on those commitments myself."

"Fortunately," the professor smiled, "on that score compassionate rabbis look the other way."

Zach's interest was piqued. "So what's involved in a child conversion?"

"You take him to a mikvah, he gets dunked, you recite a blessing, go before three Orthodox judges and declare in Hebrew, 'I want this child to be a Jew.' Poof, he's a Jew." Irina sipped her tea and looked at Zach over the rim of her mug. "Do you happen to know if he's circumcised?"

"He is."

"Lucky for him. But he'll still have to have a mini-bris called a hatafat dam brit—no big deal, just a symbolic scratch on the penis—but it has to draw blood to count as covenantal."

"Cleo would never permit that."

"I've learned not to predict what other people will or won't do. But let's assume you're right and conversion is off the table. How would you raise him?"

"I guess with two faiths," Zach replied, "which seems like a recipe for disaster, arguments, problems." The steam from his mug made his face sweat.

Professor Cantor nodded. "It just passes on to the child the problem the parents couldn't resolve themselves."

"I don't know what I'd do with Jesus."

"Exactly. Christianity and Judaism are simply *not* theologically reconcilable—either Christ was God's son or he wasn't, either he died for humanity's sins and was resurrected or he didn't. That's not something a kid should be asked to decide."

Zach stared out the window. "Any idea what happens to kids raised in two faiths?"

"Most of them end up belonging to neither. They're

afraid to choose one religion because to them it feels like choosing one parent over the other." When the professor finished her tea, she took a roll of paper towels from her bottom drawer, wiped out the mug, and set it on the side table beside the electric pot.

"So, you recommend . . . what exactly?" Zach tried not to appear pleading.

"Draw straws."

"Come on, Professor."

"I'm serious," Irina said. "I have a friend who's a brilliant child psychologist—and *very* Jewish—and she says parents who can't agree on one faith for their child should simply draw straws. She thinks it's better for the kid to be raised a Christian than become the rope in a religious tug-of-war."

Zach tore off a paper towel, gave his mug the same treatment, and put it on the table beside hers. The professor's desk was beginning to look orderly. "So what happens when people you respect give diametrically opposite advice?"

"What happens in US jurisprudence when there's a conflict among the circuit courts?" Irina asked.

"The case goes to the Supreme Court."

"There was once a Jewish Supreme Court—"

"The Sanhedrin," said Zach with confidence. "It disbanded in the year 358."

Her eyebrows flew up under her bangs. "I'm impressed. You went to a good Hebrew school."

"My rabbi was demanding. I miss him."

"That's nice," she said. "We all miss our best teachers.

Anyway, ever since the Sanhedrin went out of business, Jews have had to decide the big issues in the courtroom of our conscience. My Sanhedrin has ruled that Terrell should be welcomed into Judaism and not be defined out. Your mother's Sanhedrin—and the chaplain's too, I gather—would argue that the only way to preserve Judaism is to bar the door. I know it's confusing but at least we're all motivated by the same objective."

"Which is?"

"Jewish survival. Sounds highfalutin but that's what it boils down to."

"Do I have another option?"

"You can let the boy stay a Baptist and stop fighting for Judaism."

"It's not Judaism I'm fighting for, it's Jewishness."

Irina burst out laughing. "You remind me of my grandson. He's four. The other day, he asked me why Christians are Christian but Jews are only Jewish. It took me a minute to realize that he was hearing Jew-*ish* the way we say that something tastes 'sweetish' or looks 'pinkish.'"

Zach nodded. "He's right. 'Jewish' sounds like a gradation of the thing, not the thing itself."

"Which actually makes sense. Most Jews *do* practice gradations of Judaism. I know I think of some of us as more Jew-*ish* than others, don't you? A friend of mine is glatt kosher, stricter than heaven's caterer. Another keeps kosher at home but not in restaurants. Another won't eat meat in restaurants but will eat fish and dairy. Then there's me: I'll eat anything anywhere."

"Me too."

“So what you’re calling ‘Jewishness’ is really a spectrum of Judaisms. Before you tell Cleo how you’d like the boy raised, you have to locate yourself on that spectrum. You might start by making a list of your priorities.”

Zach wasn’t sure how to set priorities when everything seemed important. He would want to share the High Holy Days and Passover with Terrell the way he and Anabelle shared Hanukkah—but would he insist on celebrating all the Jewish holidays with Terrell or was that negotiable? He definitely wanted to instill Jewish values in his son—the pursuit of justice, an advocacy for the underdog, the poor and sick—but plenty of gentiles, including Cleo Scott, held themselves to the same moral and ethical standards that he did and he knew many Christians and Muslims who had the same commitment to justice as he had. So maybe he didn’t have to couch these values in religious terms. Maybe this, too, was negotiable.

“I’m still working on my priorities, Professor.”

“I can sense that, but don’t overintellectualize the process. Keep it simple.” Irina Cantor opened the bottom drawer of her desk and exchanged her Birkenstocks for a pair of running shoes with Velcro straps. “I always walk to the day care center, it’s my only exercise,” she said, then hauled her Channel Thirteen bag over one shoulder, picked up the verbena plant on their way out, locked her office, and led Zach to the lobby.

He held the door open for her. “Thank you for your time, Professor. Whatever happens, it’s been great learning from you.”

Out on the sidewalk, the professor repeated, "Just try to keep it simple. Show your son a joyful Judaism and maybe, at the end of the day, he'll want to join us. The magic word is 'maybe.' I just love that word. It keeps the door open. 'Maybe' can take a person to a whole new place. Now, I really must be going!" She turned east and called back over her shoulder, "Say hi to Terrell for me!"

CHAPTER 23
GHOSTS

THE DAY OF RECKONING DAWNED BRIGHT, CLEAR, AND innocent of its consequence. Sleep deprivation had left Zach Levy with no strength for the exercise machines, but he was first in the pool at the gym. This time, though, instead of swimming at full throttle, he swam for serenity, his eyes on the tiled floor where the lane lines were as sharply drawn as the choices he faced: Tradition or fatherhood. Guilt or desire. His promise to his mother or his responsibility to his son.

Pools were complicated places for Zach. His parents' attitudes toward swimming had aroused in him a sense of danger unrelated to drowning. During the polio epidemic, they wouldn't allow him near a public pool except for the schvitz, and even after he'd been inoculated with the newly invented Salk vaccine, they distrusted enclosed bodies of water and preferred going to Orchard Beach in the Bronx or one of the Queens or Brooklyn beaches. Rivka viewed the Atlantic Ocean as a moat of safety separating her from her former captors and would stare at the horizon to reassure herself that Europe had not moved any closer to the Rockaways or Coney Island.

Zach raised his head from his fifth lap to check the clock on the wall. Seventeen hours and twenty-three minutes till his deadline. He flipped over and started doing the backstroke. Snapshots of childhood summers came back to him, days when he and his parents, with all their gear, made the long schlep to the ocean beaches by subway, commandeered a patch of sand (always close to the lifeguard stand), and spread out their Army surplus blanket, his father setting up the aluminum beach chairs they'd bought on sale at Woolworths, his mother slathering Zach with Coppertone and covering the cooler with a towel to shield it from the sun. True to form, Nathan would squint at his book for five minutes then nod off, while Rivka dragged her chair into the shallows, the better to monitor Zach as he dive-bombed through the breakers like a crazed porpoise. Somehow, he had never questioned the illogic of this frail, timid woman assuming shore patrol, much less imagined her rescuing him. Just as he had never seen his mother play the piano, he had never seen her swim. Only when the temperature broke eighty degrees and the sea was as calm as a lake would she wade waist deep into the water and, with the skirt of her flowered bathing suit floating around her like the pad of a water lily, pull the bodice away from her chest, and let the water in.

"A mechayah," she would say, a pleasure. As far as Zach could recall, that was her only expression of bliss, ever, which made it cruelly ironic that she was in the midst of a mechayah moment when she discovered the lump.

His father's relationship to water was more robust but no less fraught. Though Nathan had a smooth racer's crawl and the underwater breath control of a deep-sea diver, his summer outings were complicated by his antipathy to public restrooms. He preferred to endure the subway trip home with chafed thighs, wearing a damp, sandy bathing suit under his trousers, rather than use a changing room.

"Sue me, I'm modest," he'd replied when Zach first questioned his habits.

"Modest?" Zach exclaimed in disbelief. "At the schvitz, you walk around naked."

"At the schvitz, I'm among friends."

Not until he saw a Catholic boy's intact foreskin did Zach realize that "friends" meant Jews. And not until his father confided in him did he understand that to pass as a Christian Pole while he was on the run, it was a matter of life and death to avoid public urinals and bathhouses. Even after twenty years in America, unless he was in a certifiably Jewish venue, Nathan would keep his private parts under wraps.

Zach hoisted himself out of the pool after completing thirty laps and headed for the locker room. A couple of naked teens were slapping each other with towels. "Quit that, you little faggots!" the attendant yelled, transforming their innocent horseplay into something else.

Watching them, Zach was flung back to his own childhood humiliation, the time Rabbi Goldfarb walked into the boys' bathroom at Hebrew school and caught him and Simon Persky red handed, as it were, trying to measure themselves with a six-inch ruler. Rather than tease or shame them, the rabbi had delivered an exegesis on the sanctity of the human body and the mitzvah of human reproduction.

"God doesn't care how big it is, only what you do with it. Someday, it will plant the seeds of the next generation of the Jewish people, whom God has elected to be a holy nation. Use it wisely and you'll create more children and more holiness. Now back to class."

No one but their esteemed rabbi could have made two frightened kids with a ruler suddenly feel like carriers of Jewish destiny and vessels of divine intent. Simon Persky had ultimately married the daughter of a diamond merchant and fathered four sons, fulfilling Goldfarb's vision. Zach's record, thus far, was weak. What, he wondered, as he squeezed the water out of his swimsuit and hung it on the hook in his locker, would the rabbi say about the choice he faced tonight?

The minute he got to the office, Zach found a current Bronx telephone directory and was relieved to find "Goldfarb, Eleazar (Rev.)" alive or at least listed at the same address. A boy answered the phone, a student, maybe a grandson. Zach gave his name and seconds later, the familiar baritone was rumbling through the receiver, slightly rough edged now but as warm as ever. Instead of asking why Zach was calling after so many years, the old man simply said how wonderful it was to hear from him on such an auspicious date—the day after the shortest night and longest day of the year.

"Come for Shabbos dinner, Mr. Levy! The sun sets

tonight at 8:13 p.m. We'll eat early and schmooze until candle lighting time. Do you think you can get here by six?"

"I'd be honored," Zach said, eager for his old teacher to tell him what to do, and certain that Rabbi Goldfarb would have an answer that would not have occurred to anyone else.

Zach left his office at four o'clock to give himself time to meander around the old neighborhood. It was his first time back since his father's funeral. His boyhood home-life having been so pinched and gray, he had little reason to romanticize it. Yet, at least in retrospect, because he'd been rescued by friends, school, and sports, his youth was bathed in a glow inseparable from his sense of place. He was curious about how the area had changed, and he was homesick, not for his hushed, gloomy apartment but for a sense of hope that could only be recaptured where it once took root.

Emerging from the subway at the corner of Kingsbridge Road and Jerome Avenue, he noticed that the block-long armory still loomed large. Its conical towers and crenellated turrets were still intact though the building appeared vacant, its walls cracked and pockmarked. In Zach's child mind, the armory had been the analogue to Wawel Castle. But once his father slammed the photo album on his head and ruled Kraków unmentionable, he'd never again had the chutzpah to ask about the castle where his mother stood smiling beside Yitzhak's carriage. Yet Wawel continued to represent an idyllic time, the last place on earth, according to photographic evidence, where his mother was happy. Now, the old armory seemed a symbol of the fading vitality of the borough and of the boy within Zach Levy. Seeing it in the soft glaze of a late June afternoon, he wondered if Wawel had survived the war better than the armory had survived the peace.

The ghosts of lost landmarks accompanied him the rest of the way: Gone were the fishmonger, tailor shop, and bagel bakery. Daitch Dairy was now a bodega. A KFC, blazing with fluorescent tubes, stood in place of the candy store where Zach and his friends twirled on the swiveling stools and drank egg creams. Sam Kranzberg's barbershop was still there, though its striped pole no longer turned and Eddie Fisher's autograph, "To Sam Kranzberg, A cut above," had faded on the singer's headshot in the window.

Spanish and Asian lilts had displaced the Yiddish, Polish, and Italian street talk he'd grown up with. Herman's butcher shop was gone, replaced by a Korean nail salon, and the doorstep where he and his father sat chilled to the bone twenty-seven years ago was now carpeted with plastic grass. The awning over the Jewish Home for the Aged, once the repository for Nathan's breakfast leftovers and eventually for Nathan himself, had acquired a subtitle: "Four-Star Assisted Living."

Nostalgia turned bittersweet as Zach approached their old apartment building on University Avenue. The twin marble lions guarding its entrance wore a coat of greenish grime and its once majestic lobby looked like a deserted bus station. Gone were the King John armchairs and palace-size rugs, the faux fireplaces, the statue of the knight in shining armor, the tapestries and torches. Gone, too, the switchboard operator who used to greet everyone with a nasal "How ayah?" or "Who ya heah t'see?" Zach wished he could knock on the door of his boyhood apartment and be invited in, but it wasn't the fifties anymore, it was the nineties, a different world. No one would open the door to a stranger. Thomas Wolfe had it right: you can't go home again.

Turning into Eames Place, Zach found the branch library looking much the same as it did when he used to check out four or five books a week. The synagogue, however, had been bisected by a painted white line that divided it in half from basement to roof. One side of the building still bore the textured facade and Moorish windows of the Eames Place shul, the other side had been stripped and plastered over, its windows and doors fitted with bars. The medallion on the lintel said "PS 307."

The uniformed guard at the school entrance noticed Zach staring at the facade. "May I help you?"

"I had my bar mitzvah here in 1963," Zach said. He must have been frowning because the security man seemed to feel he deserved an explanation.

"You can't blame them for selling off half the building. Most of the Jews in the neighborhood left for the suburbs years ago. The ones who stayed needed cash to keep it up, and Bronx kids needed another school. So maybe everything worked out for the best. Still, if this happened to my church, I'd be mad too. It looks awful, right?"

Zach nodded. "Mind if I nose around?"

"Be my guest."

The synagogue library had been split into two jerry-built classrooms, no more walnut paneling, leather-bound books, or brass chandeliers. The door to Rabbi Goldfarb's study was now stenciled, PRINCIPAL'S OFFICE. Trotting upstairs to the gym, Zach found basketball practice in session and he stayed to watch. All the players were black. The boy with the nylon stocking on his head, a neck-load of gold chains, and a pierced nose was especially good, also a little threatening. Zach thought, I wouldn't want to end up in a dark alley with that kid, until it dawned on him that someday, Terrell might look like that kid.

What was once the synagogue's banquet hall and redolent of gladioli and flanken, was now the school cafeteria and stank of overcooked vegetables and scorched pots. Its green walls, linoleum, and bolted-down picnic tables were a far cry from the flocked wallpaper, parquet floors, and gilded banquet chairs Zach remembered from the confirmations, Hebrew school graduations, testimonial dinners, Israel festivals, High Holy Day services, bar mitzvah parties, and weddings that he'd attended in his youth.

Enough. Seeing the depredation of an institution he thought would last forever made his heart hurt. He went outside and walked over to the entrance of the part of the building that still functioned as a synagogue. Thankfully, the main sanctuary, though scuffed and scarred, was basically unchanged. Upstairs, however, a senior citizen's center had replaced his Hebrew school, the small chairs had grown full-size, and the bulletin boards were plastered with notices about Medicare and free blood pressure tests, not children's drawings and posters of young kibbutzniks. Only one sign attested to the original student population—the words BOYS ROOM on the door to the lavatory. For old times' sake, Zach went in and took a leak, recalling with unseemly satisfaction that his had measured three-eighths of an inch longer than Simon Persky's.

At exactly six o'clock, he crossed the street to the Goldfarb's modest brick house and rang the bell. A skinny, pimply faced kid in a knitted skullcap opened the door and greeted Zach in a high, cracked voice. "Good Shabbos, Mr. Levy. I'm Avrum Katz, Rabbi's assistant."

Avrum led him down the hall to the book-lined study where, every Monday and Thursday afternoon, Zach, Simon Persky, Gary Elkind, and Jerry Grumbach, had studied Torah and Talmud and practiced their respective bar mitzvah readings over and over. Zach wondered where Goldfarb's wife was tonight. Rebbetzin Malka used to meet the rabbi's pupils at the front door. A half head taller than her husband, with flashing eyes and a contagious laugh, she treated each boy as if he were the next Maimonides, welcomed him by name, asked after his family, and always appended a compliment—how handsome he looked in his new shirt or how beautifully he had davened last Shabbos. As soon as she'd settled all four boys at the study table, the rebbetzin would roll in a cart bearing snacks—homemade cookies, strudel, or rugelach, a basket of fruit, a pitcher of milk or juice—and then, poof, like a genie, she'd be gone.

During every study session, one of the boys would be called on to chant his Torah portion and its accompanying excerpt from the writings of the Prophets, while the other three would listen. Which explained why Zach knew Simon Persky's, Gary Elkind's, and Jerry Grumbach's Torah readings as well as his own, and they knew his. People often commented that by the time Rabbi Goldfarb's students were thirteen years old, they had committed to memory more sacred texts than the average Jew reads in a lifetime.

The room's carpeting, whose floral design Zach had memorized while suffering through Jerry's off-key cantillation, was now thatched with bare spots. Otherwise, Goldfarb's study looked as it did nearly three decades ago, only smaller, like Goldfarb himself. The same long table formed a T with the rabbi's desk, the same heavy-oak chairs surrounded the table, the same gauzy, straw-colored curtains filtered the late afternoon light, and Rabbi was dressed in his usual white shirt, black vest, and black trousers though today, sadly, the cuffs were frayed and the vest looked two sizes too big. Sadder still were the old man's eyes, once a deep brandied brown, now gray as slush.

"I've got supper for two, Rabbi," young Avrum said, wheeling in the cart. He proceeded to name the food as he placed it on the table in plain sight. "Hummus, tabbouleh, poached salmon, potato salad, cucumber salad, pita."

"And what to drink?" asked Goldfarb, though a pitcher of iced tea stood before him. Zach understood then that his mentor was blind.

"Iced tea. But we also have lemonade. Or juice if you prefer."

"Tea is fine. And for dessert? At my age, anticipation is half the pleasure."

"Rugelach and halvah."

"Metzuyan! Mr. Katz. Excellent!"

The boy appeared to be eleven or twelve, but he had to be at least thirteen or Rabbi wouldn't be calling him by his surname. The moment when Zach became *Mr.* Levy was one of the high points of his life. He was on the bimah in his new blue suit, having just completed his Torah reading and his bar mitzvah speech. Rabbi was gripping both his shoulders and looking down on him—down because Zach was barely five feet tall at the time—before bestowing on him the traditional priestly blessing. In stentorian tones, Goldfarb had proclaimed, "Until today, you were Zach. Until today, your father and mother were responsible for your actions. But from this day forward, you are Mr. Levy and from this day forward, you are to be responsible for yourself. May you always bring nachas—great pride and pleasure—to your parents and your people. May the Lord bless you and keep you . . ." Rabbi had spread open his voluminous tallis, stretched it out over Zach's head, and invoked the blessing, and when he finished, as was the custom of the congregation, everyone had shouted "Mazel tov!" and pelted him with wrapped candies, symbols of the sweetness of the day. Zach's heart had raced with joy and relief, but he had not laughed, or lunged after the sweets, because he wasn't a boy anymore, he was a man, a son of the commandments. He was *Mr.* Zachariah Levy.

Young Avrum was backing out of the room when the rabbi said, "Mr. Katz, you may be interested to know that

Mr. Levy's parasha was Mishpatim. Do you happen to recall the subject of that Torah portion?"

"Civil and ritual legislation," squeaked the boy.

"Exactly. So, isn't it interesting that Mr. Levy grew up to be a lawyer?"

"Very interesting," murmured Avrum. "I'll be right outside, Rabbi," he added as he closed the door.

Zach marveled. The Torah is divided into fifty-four portions, Eleazar Goldfarb had tutored God knows how many hundreds of students, yet he remembered the portion Zach had chanted twenty-seven years ago and the fact that he had become a lawyer. Between the rabbi and his wife, who never forgot anyone's name, the Goldfarbs could start a memory course. Thinking fondly of the tall, smiling rebbetzin, Zach asked after her.

The old man shook his head. "Gone five years, my Malka, may she rest in peace."

"Oh! I'm so sorry," Zach said, though he was more than sorry, he was devastated.

The rabbi rubbed his eyes. "So tragic, so gratuitous. She cut her hand opening a can—wouldn't go to the doctor. You remember my Malka, never a complaint, never anything for herself—and the wound got infected. She died of septic shock. I wasn't blind then, Mr. Levy, but I was too busy, too distracted."

Zach mumbled his condolences. Conjuring the rebbetzin, he recalled her big laugh, the extra squeeze in her hug, the niggunim she hummed as she wheeled in her cart, her long strides across the patterned carpet. Above all, he recalled, with considerable discomfort, his boyhood fantasy about her, about which he'd always felt guilty, not because it was erotic, but because it was disloyal. He used to fantasize that Rebbetzin Malka was his mother.

"Enough with my tsuris, Mr. Levy," said the rabbi. "Clearly, you've got troubles of your own. Speak, please. I'm here to listen."

His eyes were blank, but his concentration was palpable. After Zach finished describing his dilemma, Goldfarb was silent for quite some time before he answered: "A great sage once asked his pupils to define dawn, that moment when we recognize that light has overcome darkness. One of his students immediately replied, 'Dawn is when you can see well enough to tell a goat from a donkey.' Another ventured, 'Dawn is when it is light enough to distinguish a palm tree from a fig tree.' A third said, 'When you can tell a cart from a carriage.'

"With each student's reply, the great sage shook his head until eventually, the class gave up. 'Dawn,' said their teacher, 'is when you can look into the face of another human being and see your brother. Until then, all is darkness.'"

Come again? What was Zach supposed to deduce from *that*? Did Rabbi mean brother as in brotherhood, or was Zach supposed to literally look into Terrell's face and see Yitzhak? Neither reading jived with the commandment that Goldfarb had drummed into his students' heads twice a week at this very table: "In their ways you shall not walk." In other words, Jews were supposed to be proudly particularist and Judaism shouldn't be seen as a universalist movement. Unless Zach was missing something, the parable about dawn counseled the opposite.

"May I serve you dinner, Rabbi?" was all he managed to say.

"If you please, Mr. Levy. A little of everything but heavy on the hummus."

Somehow, once the plate of food was set before him, the old man transported each forkful of tabbouleh to his mouth without dropping a single grain. One could almost forget he was blind, but because his eyes were opaque, Zach experienced a kind of reflective blindness. It was like trying to read sign language from behind a screen. "I'm sorry, Rabbi, but could you clarify the moral of the parable? Are you saying I should accept Terrell even if he's not Jewish and never will be?"

"Who said never?"

"His mother. When she first told me she was pregnant, I asked if the baby could be converted. She said never."

"Only God knows never, Mr. Levy."

Zach shook his head in frustration. "At this point, I really need concrete advice, Rabbi. Yesterday, I spent hours at the HUC library and was hard-pressed to find two sources that agreed on the matter. Listen to this." He pulled out his notepad and read from it, "One scholar writes, 'A Jewish parent who raises his or her child as a non-Jew is finishing Hitler's work.' The next scholar says, 'Jews give Hitler a posthumous victory every time we permit a belief system—any belief system, even if it's Judaism—to become more important than a human being.' So what's the *least* terrible thing I can do? Reject my son or raise a Christian?"

The rabbi frowned like an angry god. "I find it obscene that anyone would give Adolph Hitler a role in a Jew's decision-making. But now that the Nazis have been brought into our discussion, let's go back to the guard who killed your brother. For argument's sake, suppose he had given your mother a choice: to let Yitzhak be raised as a Christian or to keep him Jewish and let him be killed. Which do *you* think she would have chosen?"

Without Rabbi's eyes in play, Zach couldn't read his intent but the answer was obvious. "My mother would have done anything to save Yitzhak."

"B'vadai," said Goldfarb. "Of course." He stopped to finish his poached salmon. "Rather than agree to stop teaching Torah, the great sage, Akiva, chose to be tortured to death. But in general, God seems to prefer survival to martyrdom. There's a reason why the core commandment of Judaism is, 'Choose life.' Your brother is dead. Your son is alive. Big difference. Today your son belongs to them, tomorrow he could be ours. As it is said, 'Where there's life, there's hope.'"

The old man must be losing it, grief can do that to a person, but Zach hadn't come here for clichés and he wasn't interested in talking about death and martyrdom. If by "choose life," Goldfarb meant choose Terrell, why didn't he come right out and say it? Exasperated, Zach watched the rabbi feel around the surface of his desk for his fountain pen and guiding his right hand with his left to keep the words from running over each other, scribble something on one corner of his desk blotter. Zach was pretty good at reading English upside down, but Hebrew was hard to decipher even rightside up. Goldfarb tore off the corner of the blotter and slipped it under a paperweight.

"I'm not following you, Rabbi. Can you be more specific?"

"Certainly, Mr. Levy. Two thousand years ago, a dilemma not unlike yours was put to our sages. The wise men began their deliberations, as poskim do, with a mode of thought called l'chatchila. Literally, l'chatchila translates as 'in the first place,' but its applied meaning is, 'the proper way to do something.' For example, the proper way to stir a meat sauce is with a meat spoon, not a dairy spoon. This rule stems from God's commandment that we must not bathe a calf in its mother's milk, which has been interpreted as a prohibition against the mixing of meat and dairy, a basic tenet of kashrut."

As the old man rambled on, Zach sank deeper into despair. What did the Jewish dietary laws have to do with Terrell? Still, he listened respectfully as his teacher amplified the story. "One day, a poor housewife came to the wise men and told them she had used a dairy spoon to stir her meat sauce, maybe in error, maybe her meat spoon was broken or one of her children had misplaced it. Whatever the reason, the woman asked the sages if she might be permitted to serve her family the meat sauce even though it had been contaminated by the dairy spoon. She knew she was supposed to throw out the sauce and start over, but she had run out of meat and couldn't afford to buy more. The sages knew they were entrusted with enforcing the laws of kashrut, but they also knew the woman was poor and her children were hungry so they struggled mightily to save her dinner. You might say, they had the *will* to find a way to resolve her dilemma. Which they did. By shifting from l'chatchila to an alternate mode of thinking called b'diavad, which means 'after the fact.' They decided *after the fact* that, because the dairy spoon had not been used for *hot* dairy food within the last twenty-four hours, its contact with the meat did not render the sauce unkosher."

Zach's patience was nearly gone. "I'm afraid I don't see what a dairy spoon has to do with my son. With all due respect, Rabbi, my time is running out."

"For me, too. For all of us."

"Please! Just tell me what I should do."

"Excuse me, Mr. Levy, but *should* is not helpful. Should ignores the housewife's humiliation, her children's hunger, the shortage of meat and money. The sages didn't think 'should,' they asked 'how.' They understood the complexity of the human condition. They had rachmoness, pity, compassion."

"Rabbi, okay! So I'm asking, *how*? How can I keep my son and also keep my promise?"

Goldfarb closed his eyes and stroked his beard as old men often do when they're thinking, or when they're not sure whether to say what they really think. He opened his gray eyes and faced Zach. "What exactly *was* your promise to your mother?"

"I *told* you. To do my part for Jewish survival."

"Define Jewish survival."

"Raising Jewish children. Don't you want me to raise Jewish children?"

Rabbi touched the tips of his fingers together. "How Jewish?"

"Enough to carry our heritage forward."

"Tell me something, Mr. Levy, how many Jews do *you* know who are carrying our heritage forward? How many are equipped to teach our tradition to their children? I myself know a half dozen Friedmans and Cohens who might as well be Fords or Carnegies for all they care about our heritage. If you'll pardon my rudeness, you can trace your genes back to Moses and Aaron, but can *you* carry our heritage from here to the bus stop?"

Zach winced.

The rabbi pressed on. "One man in my congregation got a PhD in French but can't be bothered learning Hebrew; a woman reads *Foreign Affairs* but wouldn't deign to dip into the Talmud. I know Blumbergs and Steinbergs who make time in their busy lives to memorize wine vintages and perfect their golf swings or tennis serves but can't find an hour a week to study Torah. You might want to ask *those* people to carry our heritage before you lay it on one little boy."

Nothing convoluted about that message, Zach thought. "You're right, I'm in no position to ask anyone else to do what I don't do myself."

"Ahhh," it was more like a breath than a word. Suddenly, and for no apparent reason, Goldfarb asked Zach if he remembered the story about Rabbi Hillel and the man who wanted to learn the whole Torah while standing on one leg.

"Of course, every Jew knows that story. Hillel summarizes the Torah by saying, 'What is hateful to you, do not do unto others.' You gave a sermon on it at my bar mitzvah."

"Thank you for remembering that, but do you remember who Hillel was talking to and what was actually going on in that scene? Think about it. The man made a seemingly frivolous demand. He challenged the great sage to teach him the entirety of a complex legal and ethical system in the length of time that he, the man, could stand on one foot, which, unless you're a Yogi, most people can't do for very long. But did Hillel ridicule him?"

"No."

"Did he turn his back on him or send him away?"

"No."

"Wouldn't you think the great Hillel had better things to do at that moment? After all, he was the towering Judaic intellectual of his time, right? He must have had acolytes to advise, tasks to accomplish, texts awaiting his amplification. He must have been a busy man, yes?"

Zach couldn't imagine where Goldfarb was taking this. "Yes, very busy."

"Yet he not only took the man's request seriously, he formulated that pithy, epigrammatic summation of Judaism's essence with such exquisite clarity that we still quote him to this day. Why would he bother?"

Zach pondered the question but came up blank. "I don't know."

"Do you remember who the man was, Mr. Levy?"

"Sorry, no." Zach felt he was about to be flunked.

"He was a prospective convert, a gentile who doubted that our Torah had anything to offer him. He was essentially daring Hillel to prove to him that Judaism was worth joining. Our great sage took the time to distill the whole Torah into one pure principle so that the doubter would understand what we're about and what he was missing."

The sun had dropped below the windowsill, tinting the curtains ocher and gilding the walls. "That's a beautiful drash," Zach said. "I wish I could come up here every week and resume my studies with you, Rabbi, I really do, but right now I'm desperate. I have to give Cleo my answer by midnight."

"What's the question again?"

"What's the *question*?"

As if he'd seen Zach's eye roll, Goldfarb said, "I know it's aggravating, but I'd like to hear you restate the issue you've been wrestling with for the last five days."

Zach couldn't leave, couldn't eat and run, had to wait until the Sabbath prayers were over. "The question is . . ." He built his reply slowly, in layers. " . . . should I take Terrell, or not? Should I raise him, even if he never becomes a Jew? Is it okay for a Jewish father to raise a Christian child? Should I remember my promise or forget my history?"

"Remember! Forget!" The old man's face beamed with pleasure. "That reminds me of the wonderful Jorges Luis Borges story about the man who falls from his horse, lands on his head, and discovers, when he regains consciousness, that he now has a perfect memory. Everything that happened before—every grape he'd ever pressed into wine, every cloud in the sky on a particular morning, every detail of every dream, every word anyone ever said to him—he remembered to the last detail. And he continued to remember everything that happened from then on. At first, this seemed like a marvelous gift, but before long, the man had accumulated so many memories he became paralyzed with the weight of them, and for the rest of his life, he could never again leave his bed."

Rabbi scooped some hummus on a pita and ate it without messing up his beard, his plate, or the table. "Jews are good at remembering," he continued. "We're always harking back to Abraham, Isaac, and Jacob; to Sarah, Rebecca, Leah, and Rachel; and reminding ourselves that we were slaves in Egypt. Always recalling the bad with the good: Amalek and Haman, the destruction of the Temple, the Strasbourg Massacre, Kishinev, Auschwitz, Treblinka. For Jews, memory isn't just history, it's us.

"Everyone dreads dementia because without memory, and memories, we are severed from the past. We lose our dignity *and* our legacy. You know this all too well from watching your father's lively mind evaporate into thin air. But God doesn't want us to remember *everything*. Too many memories—all the slights, wounds, even vows—weigh a person down. That's why we've also been blessed with the ability to forget."

If only, Zach thought. Memory hadn't paralyzed him yet but he felt it pressing down on him every day of his life.

Goldfarb washed down his meal with his iced tea. "You asked me if you should take the boy. I don't think that's the real question. I think the real question is: What's more important to you, the happiness of your child or the continuity of your people?"

That's what I'm asking YOU! Zach wanted to shout. His watch said 8:01 p.m. Twelve more minutes until candle lighting, then he would leave. For the next twelve minutes, he would control himself, not lose his temper, not scream when his teacher went off on a tangent, or spoke in circles, or answered questions with questions. For twelve minutes, he would study the design in the Persian carpet and think about Rebbetzin Malka.

"Mr. Levy? Your hand, please?"

Glancing up, Zach was astonished to see the old man reaching for him. He took his teacher's hand and trembled at the sight of their interwoven fingers. Affection had always been the province of the rebbetzin; Rabbi never touched his students except to bless them.

"As you've been pondering your dilemma over the last few days, Mr. Levy, I'm sure your parents, may they rest in peace, have been in your thoughts. I'm thinking about them right now. I wasn't just their rabbi, you know. I was their friend and privy to their sorrow. I know how much they loved you—both of them, though your mama couldn't show it—and I'm sure they dreamed of a long line of grandchildren and great-grandchildren to come after them. But I also know that they would no sooner have you be haunted by their dreams than by their nightmares."

Goldfarb squeezed Zach's hand, let it go, and, tilting his face toward the window, his blank eyes seeming to discern the hour from the waning light, called out, "Time for Shabbos, Mr. Katz! Hurry, please!"

As if awaiting his teacher's summons, Avrum rolled in the rebbetzin's cart, which now held a pair of candlesticks, a kiddush cup, two other goblets, a bottle of kosher wine, and two braided loaves of challah, loosely covered with a white cloth. The boy opened the closet, took out the rabbi's suit jacket, and deftly guided the old man's arms into the sleeves.

Somehow, formally dressed, Eleazer Goldfarb seemed to sit taller in his chair. "Traditionally, as we all know, lighting the Shabbos candles is a woman's mitzvah. However, if no woman is present, a man must perform this holy task. After my Malka died, I took on the candle blessing until last year when I accidentally dropped the match and set fire to the tablecloth. Since then, Mr. Katz has done it, but tonight," the rabbi turned to Zach, "we hope you will perform the mitzvah for us."

Hypocrisy, not gender inappropriateness, made Zach hesitate. He was about to commit several violations of the Sabbath—ride the subway back to Manhattan, turn on his lights, watch CNN, use his electric toothbrush, program his coffee maker. With all that, how, in good conscience, could he say the blessing? "I'd be honored, Rabbi, but I'm not shomer Shabbos so I probably shouldn't do it."

"Please, Mr. Levy. Enough with the 'shoulds' and 'shouldn'ts.' Just light the candles."

CHAPTER 24

THE LONG WAY HOME

IT WAS A NIGHT OF FIRSTS. AT THE AGE OF FORTY, FOR the first time in his life, Zach Levy kindled the Sabbath candles. He was tempted to drape a schmatta or scarf over his hair the way Rivka did every Friday night until she wasted away, but he settled for one of the plain black yarmulkes Rebbetzin Malka always kept in a basket near the door. Also for the first time in his life, he recited the Blessing over Children.

"Unfortunately, we don't have any kids at our table tonight," Rabbi said by way of introduction, "but let's say this bracha for the children we hold dear in our hearts:

"Girls—May you be like Sarah, Rebecca, Rachel, and Leah."Boys—May you be like Ephraim and Menashe. Children—May God bless you and guard you. May God show you favor and be gracious unto you. May God show you kindness and grant you peace."

As if summoned by the blessing, Anabelle suddenly appeared to Zach standing on a distant hill in a dark place, Australia no doubt, since New York's longest day was Melbourne's shortest. (Unless the gloom was a symbol of their estrangement.) Her last visitation had ended badly, she sullen and remote, he bedeviled by his inability to reach her. Since then, her letters, sparse in the best of times, had stopped altogether and their weekly phone conversations were so terse and tense that he had come to dread them. He'd already decided that, during his next visit to Australia, they would spend a week together on the Great Barrier Reef. They would go scuba diving every day, and have intimate talks over dinner, and by the end of their vacation she would tell him what he had done to cause her distress and advise him on how to be a better father to her (and the other children he might have someday). A second figure popped up on the hill beside her, a small brown-skinned boy in red plaid overalls. Divine supplication didn't come naturally to Zach, but he added a silent blessing for his son.

After saying the kiddush, Rabbi Goldfarb passed the goblet to Zach, who took a sip—the Manischewitz wine tasted like grape juice, like childhood—who passed it to Avrum, as is the custom, l'dor va'dor, from generation to generation.

"Come," said the rabbi. "Let's wash."

Avrum helped the old man to the kitchen sink where Zach blanked on what he was supposed to do with the double-handled cup on the drainboard. Was the correct sequence to start with the cup in his right hand and pour the water over his left or vice versa? Say the blessing before, during, or after he poured? And how many times was he supposed to splash it on each hand? Fear of doing things The Wrong Way in the presence of those who were more observant had probably alienated more Jews than Moses could shake a rod at. Why subject one's religious ignorance to scrutiny when it's so much easier to opt out altogether? Who wants to botch a ritual that others consider sacred, or humiliate yourself in public if you don't have to?

Thankfully, Avrum was first at the sink. Zach watched him hold one handle of the cup in his left hand and pour the water over his right hand three times, switch hands, and do the same thing on the opposite side, after which, while drying his hands, he said the blessing. Zach then stepped to the sink and performed the ritual The Right Way. He even remembered not to speak between the ceremonial hand washing and the blessing over the challah, a rule Rabbi once taught his students to memorize with the help of a triple-H mnemonic: "Hands, Hush, *Hallah*." Someday, Zach hoped to teach it to his children.

After giving thanks to the Almighty for bringing forth bread from the earth, Goldfarb tore off hunks of the bread and arranged the challah on a platter. "Pardon my hands," he said, "but I nearly sliced off my finger a few weeks ago and, since Judaism forbids self-mutilation, I'm no longer allowed to use a knife." Like Proust's madeleine, the bread's soft density and eggy flavor sent Zach reeling back to his parents' Friday-night table, and when Rabbi and Avrum Katz started singing "Shalom Alechem," the Sabbath song of peace, Zach had to fight back tears.

"Shalom aleichem, malachay ha'shareit, malachay el-yon . . .

"Me melech, malachay ham'lachim, ha-kadosh baruch hu."

Synagogue buildings can be sliced in half and kosher butcher shops morph into Korean nail salons, clear eyes could turn milky and clear minds grow opaque, but Jewish rituals endure, Zach realized with a surge of renewed wonder, as long as there are Jews to say and sing them.

Avrum excused himself, leaving Zach and the rabbi to reminisce about the friends who had moved away: Izzy the furrier with his second wife and three kids to Long Island; Sol and Herman, both retired now, to Florida. Zach's classmate, Gary Elkind was a software engineer in Seattle and, like Simon Persky, the father of four. Jerry Grumbach, who went straight to LA after college, had a big job at Twentieth Century Fox.

"Jerry has no kids," said Goldfarb. "He's gay."

The word fell from the rabbi's lips without judgment, as if there were nothing unusual about a man being a homosexual except insofar as it might possibly explain his being childless. Somehow, the old man had changed with the times. Zach wished he could linger at his study table and learn from him—not just how to grow more tolerant with age, but how he had forgiven God for taking from him, a dedicated scholar and devoted husband, both his eyesight and his beloved wife.

But it was time to leave.

"Before you go, come close," the rabbi said, hauling

himself upright on unsteady legs. He placed his hands on Zach's head.

"*Y'vorechecha adonai v'yishmarecha . . .*"

The last time Zach had received the Priestly Blessing was the day he became a man. Now, standing beneath his teacher's broad palms, he felt like a child.

"Shabbat shalom, Rabbi. Thank you for dinner—and all your help."

Goldfarb squeezed Zach's shoulders. "Any time, Mr. Levy. Any time."

Zach was about to turn the corner onto University Avenue when Avrum Katz caught up with him. "Rabbi wanted you to have this," the boy panted, holding out a torn shred of heavy blue paper. "It's the piece he tore off his blotter."

Zach found the cramped Hebrew script unreadable. "How old are you, Mr. Katz?"

"Sixteen in August." Avrum caught his yarmulke before it slid off his hair and reattached it, lopsided, with a small, metal clip.

"You must have been Rabbi's star student."

"Not really." The boy blushed.

"Yes, really, or he wouldn't have you around. It's obvious he depends on you."

"I'm lucky he lets me assist him."

"What else do you do besides greet visitors and fix his meals?"

"Read to him. Type letters for him. Do research. He tells me what to look up. I know his books, where to find things."

Zach held out the scrap of blotter. "Can you decipher this? And please translate it. My Hebrew's pretty rusty."

Avrum squinted at the writing through his thick lenses, "It says, 'Rav Zvi Hirsch Kalischer believed that children born of Jewish fathers and gentile mothers were "zera kodesh," holy offspring, and we must do everything in our power to ease the entry of such children into our community. Kalischer said Jews should welcome the zera kodesh and not push them away, for there is always a chance that great leaders of Israel will spring from their midst as they have in times past.'"

"Never heard of Kalischer," Zach said.

"He was a Polish rabbi. Nineteenth century. A Zionist before there was Zionism. He wrote amazing rabbinic commentaries and never took any money for his services."

The quote wrapped itself around Zach like a cloak of comfort and gave him, b'diavad, after the fact, a way to move forward. Clearly, he was the one who'd been addled and unseeing, too thickheaded to understand what his teacher had been telling him until, finally, the man had to spell it out for him in writing. Stuffing the blue scrap in his pocket, Zach said good-night to Avrum and started toward the subway.

In that liminal postsunset interim when the line between dusk and darkness is as invisible as air, Zach Levy imagined what he would say if an ancient sage asked him to define dusk: "It's the moment when you can't necessarily discern the right path from the wrong path but you must choose one of them before it's too dark to see anything at all."

Tonight, in the wake of his teacher's bruised holiness, he decided that the wrong path was the stairway down to the subway, the right path, above ground and open to the sky. He had no idea where the rest of his life would take him, but he knew where he had to go right now and how to get there. He would walk to Manhattan; walking always helped him think. Nathan used to insist it was only six miles from their apartment to the northern boundary of Central Park. If that was so, Zach should be able to cover the distance in two hours without breaking a sweat. He checked his watch: 9:07 p.m.

His father's daily walk to work would be his course tonight. Nathan's voice rode the summer breeze reciting: "University, left on Kingsbridge, right on the Concourse, another right on 161st, past Yankee Stadium, across Macombs Dam Bridge, left on Seventh, then all the way down to Central Park."

When someone expressed awe at his stamina, Nathan always said, "Once you've crossed the Carpathians, walking from the Bronx to Manhattan is a piece of kugel."

The Grand Concourse of Zach's youth had been a stately boulevard lined with apartment buildings named for British manor houses—Rookwood Hall, Bedford Arms, Windsor Court—its sidewalks strolled by women in belted dresses and hats with netted veils, and by men in sharkskin suits and horn-rimmed glasses. Tonight, a different population was promenading—women wearing capri pants and cork-soled mules, and men in gold chains and backward baseball caps. Canvas awnings no longer stretched from door to curb. Barbed wire and boarded windows proclaimed the reality of crime and fear. The sign in a storefront office said, "LAWYER-ABOGADO—Tenant Rights, Welfare Rights, Quick Divorce." Loew's Paradise, the storied movie palace, looked as pathetic as a superstar fallen on hard times, and the hotel that, in Zach's youth, had famously hosted Babe Ruth and Harry Truman was now a homeless shelter. Wherever he looked, Zach saw his old neighborhood in distress.

Most astonishing were the synagogues. A Lion of Judah etched into its cornerstone or a Star of David on the pediment was the only lingering clue to the original identity of each edifice. The Seventh-day Adventists had taken over Adath Israel, the shul where Richard Tucker, the great operatic tenor, had started as a cantor and where four bar mitzvahs or two weddings took place simultaneously to accommodate members' life cycle celebrations. The Tremont Temple was now the First Union Baptist Church; the Grand Concourse Jewish Center, reincarnated as the Love Gospel Assembly. Christianity had colonized the landscape of his childhood. And why not? What some abandon, others claim. To resent them made about as much sense as blaming air for filling a vacuum. Emptied of Jewish life, the great temples of twentieth-century Jewry were only bricks and mortar after all. Tradition can survive without a physical place, but a structure without meaning and purpose is nothing but a container for memories.

It was easy for Zach to stay connected to Judaism in the fifties and sixties, when the neighborhood had jam-packed synagogues and the streets were teeming with Jews on their way to buy Jewish food and do Jewish things.

Assuming he and Cleo could somehow solve the religion thing—a colossal assumption to begin with—Terrell would have just one connection to Judaism: his father. But what if something happened to Zach? Who would see to it that the boy went to Hebrew school, studied for his bar mitzvah, fasted on Yom Kippur? Who would dip apples in honey with him on Rosh Hashana, grate onions for latkes on Hanukkah, make haroses on Passover, and explain what everything meant?

Friends would have to fill the gaps, Zach decided. He would revise his will and make Herb the executor of his estate and, in concert with Cleo, the legal guardian of Terrell. He would ask Rabbi Goldfarb to be the boy's foster grandfather and oversee Terrell's Jewish education (with Avrum Katz next in succession). M. J. would be Terrell's surrogate dad because, though not Jewish, he was a world-class nurturer and had two additional qualifications: oil money and no heirs.

While mentally providing for his son in the event of his death, Zach almost missed the turn onto 161st Street. Walking past the stadium—dark tonight because the Yanks were in Chicago—it occurred to him that Terrell could grow up to be a Mets fan. Zach had been imagining scenarios of father-son togetherness. Yet, given how Anabelle had veered off, it was obvious that children don't come with a lifetime guarantee of parental compatibility. Oy gevalt.

Ahead, Macomb's Dam Bridge spanned the Harlem River, the moon floating on its surface like a thin slice of lemon. Just then, as if it knew he needed an extra push out of the Bronx, a blustery wind kicked up behind Zach and didn't calm down until he made landfall on the Manhattan side of the span and turned left on Seventh Avenue—now called Adam Clayton Powell Jr. Boulevard. He hooked his blazer on one finger and flung it over his shoulder. Though dawn was still hours away, he searched the face of every person he passed on the sidewalk and, remembering Rabbi's parable, tried to see in each the face of his brother.

"Who you looking at?" A large man blocked his way. Apparently, not everyone appreciated his fraternal gaze. "You see something you don't like?"

"I'm so sorry," Zach replied. "I was just daydreaming." The man shook his head, walked to the curb and crossed to the other side of the street.

From then on, Zach was careful not to lock eyes with anyone else as he surveyed the gritty, busy beauty of a summer night in Harlem—men playing cards on an upturned milk crate, women fanning themselves on stoops, young people huddled under street lamps, singing and smoking. He tried to imagine which of the domino players would take home his winnings and give it to his wife to put in their bank account and which one would spend it at the OTB parlor, what burdens were troubling those who seemed stooped with sorrow, where that scruffy-looking woman would sleep tonight, why that teenager was crying, which of the men whistling down the block had just put his baby to bed and which man, like Zach, had walked out on his child.

It made no sense, this late in the game, to be freshly

terrified of making the wrong decision, but at 118th Street, he panicked, frightened by compromises he might regret. Demands he might not meet. Disappointing others. Being disappointed. Or was he just afraid of complexity? Somehow, his walk had acquired a novelistic arc, a picaresque sweep. A river had been crossed. One borough to another, one lifetime to another; then to now.

CENTRAL PARK'S NORTHERN rim is suddenly visible up ahead, its silhouette feathered by the serrated outline of tall dark trees against a deep purple sky. Zach folds his blazer over his arm and breaks into a trot. He turns right at 110th, left at the traffic circle where Frederick Douglass Boulevard changes its name to Central Park West. (Cleo always said it was because more whites lived below 110th Street and they didn't want a black hero for an address.) Jogging down the park side of CPW, he murmurs each street number as he passes its signpost: 109 . . . 108 . . . 107 . . . 106 . . . 105 . . .

At 104th Street, he starts counting his footsteps, then his heartbeats.

It is five minutes of eleven when he pushes into the lobby of her building. The doorman recognizes him and calls Cleo on the house phone to tell her he is on his way up. Zach pulls out his folded handkerchief, mops his face, and puts on his blazer. Straightening his spine, he enters the elevator, his fingers trembling as he presses the button for her floor. He watches the numbers ascend. When the elevator slides open, he steps out into the hall and feels like a parachutist stepping out of a plane.

The door to her apartment is about three-quarters ajar, framing her lithe figure. Bare feet, white shorts, white T-shirt. Tiny pearl earrings. She doesn't invite him in, just stands there, unsmiling.

"I want him, Cleo." He says it and it is true.

"But?" Her hand tightens on the doorknob. "Do I hear a but?"

"Same as always. You know."

Her knuckles soften on the knob. "Yeah, I do."

"Can we talk about it?"

She opens the door all the way. "Maybe."

"Maybe is good," he says, and walks across the threshold.

THE END

ACKNOWLEDGEMENTS

I'M DEEPLY GRATEFUL TO SO MANY PEOPLE FOR TOO many things, especially:

- My beloved husband, Bert (always my first reader), daughters, Abigail and Robin (both accomplished writers and gifted editors), and son, David (a trained chef and restaurant manager), for their close reading of this novel, their invaluable critiques, and their loving support—and for saving me from my excesses.

- At Kuhn Projects, the amazing Nicole Tourtelot, my indefatigable literary agent, for placing the book in its perfect publishing home, and David Kuhn, founder of the agency, for his continuing wisdom and loyalty.

- At the Feminist Press, its executive director and publisher, Jennifer Baumgardner, who, as my editor and advocate, has both midwifed and mothered the novel from start to finish, empathizing with its characters and challenging me to tell their stories with ever more clarity and depth; assistant editor, Julia Berner-Tobin, for her sensitivity, sharp eye, and consistent commitment to excellence; and art director, Drew Stevens, for creating the book's superb jacket and overall design, and for his genial openness to my input.

- Friend and lawyer, Herbert Teitelbaum, who, in one memorable conversation, vividly conjured the world of the schvitz, and in another, explained the difference between civilian and military law in terms of First Amendment rights.

- Old friends, Leonard Majzlin and Carol Hall for acquainting me with some of the marvelous Texas idioms and down-home expressions that they came to relish during their time in Buffalo Gap.

- My cousin, Priscilla Darvie Donohue, a Bronx girl, who, by sharing her childhood with this Queens girl left me with indelible images of life on the other side of the Whitestone Bridge.

- *Ms.* magazine—of which I'm a founding editor and where I happily worked for eighteen years—whose dedication to illuminating the intersection of gender, race, and class, continues to educate and inspire me. (www.MsMagazine.com)

- And finally, Janet Dewart Bell, Helen Fremont, Marcia Gillespie, Anne Roiphe, Thane Rosenbaum, Menachem Rosensaft, Dani Shapiro, and Ayelet Waldman, who so generously took time from their own work to read this novel in galleys and provide the sort of endorsements a writer can only dream of.

The Feminist Press is a nonprofit educational organization founded to amplify feminist voices. FP publishes classic and new writing from around the world, creates cutting-edge programs, and elevates silenced and marginalized voices in order to support personal transformation and social justice for all people.

See our complete list of books at
feministpress.org